Bénédicte Newland was born in Johannesburg and lives in London with her husband and four children. After university she qualified as a solicitor. She lived in Canada for five years and whilst there wrote a column for the *National Post* newspaper.

Pascale Smets, Bénédicte's sister, was born in Brussels and lives in London with her husband and four children. She went to St Martin's School of Art and worked as a fashion designer in Paris before setting up her own fashion label.

Together they wrote the *Disp@tches From the Home Front* column in the Saturday *Times* on which the idea for this book is based.

Visit www.AuthorTracker.co.uk for exclusive information on your favourite HarperCollins authors.

BÉNÉDICTE NEWLAND
AND PASCALE SMETS

And God Created the Au Pair

HARPER PERENNIAL
London, New York, Toronto and Sydney

Harper Perennial
An imprint of HarperCollins*Publishers*
77–85 Fulham Palace Road
Hammersmith
London W6 8JB

www.harperperennial.co.uk

Published by Harper Perennial 2005

9 8 7 6 5 4 3 2 1

A catalogue record for this book is available from the British Library

This novel is entirely a work of fiction. The names, characters and incidents
portrayed in it are the work of the authors' imagination. Any resemblance to
actual persons, living or dead, events or localities is entirely coincidental.

ISBN 0-00-776321-2

Set in Sabon by
Rowland Phototypesetting Ltd, Bury St Edmunds, Suffolk

Printed and bound in Great Britain by
Clays Ltd, St Ives plc

For Mum and Pa

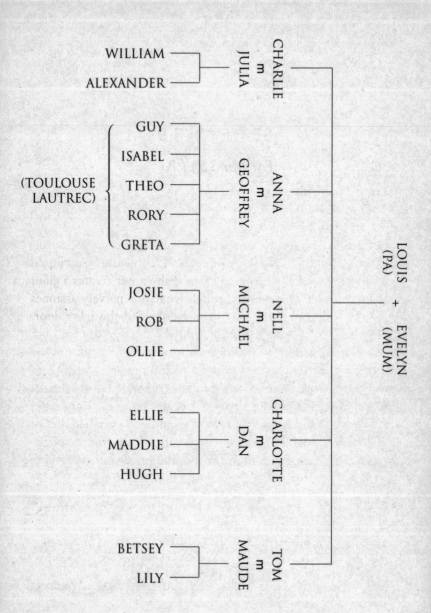

SEPTEMBER 99

From: Nell Fenton
To: Charlotte Bailey

Do not, repeat do not confuse dishwashing liquid with dishwasher liquid. Dishwashing liquid is in fact washing-up liquid in N America and when used in the dishwasher creates a giant foam monster that pours through what one naively assumes are the watertight seals on the edges of the dishwasher door. First tried to scoop the pouring tide of foam into kitchen sink but that immediately filled up with foam that would not die so then had to fill buckets with foam and run and throw them out on the deck. When Michael finally responded to my shrieks for assistance and wandered downstairs he (most unusually) had the good idea that we should sprinkle the small sachet of dishwasher powder that came free with the machine over the foam. Surprisingly it did in fact kill the beast. But everything very wet and foamy afterwards and him very smug.

From: Charlotte Bailey
To: Nell Fenton
Re: the beast

Didn't the size of the bottle alert you? Any sign of missing saucepans yet?

From: Nell Fenton
To: Charlotte Bailey

Bottle was huge. V easy mistake to make. Saucepans still mysteriously absent. Have unearthed one box of stuff so am now able to grate things or whisk things.

From: Charlotte Bailey
To: Nell Fenton

Have some ghastly problem with our drains at the moment, v stinky & wet at the bottom of the garden. Albert who is here to paint the kitchen full of gloomy predictions, have to say feel a bit gloomy myself but am resolutely trying to hide it as it only encourages him.

From: Nell Fenton
To: Charlotte Bailey

Sure it's nothing too serious. You know Albert would rather eat his own head than miss an opportunity to revel in a bit of doom and gloom. Have finally tracked down saucepans (in the basement under approx 1000 boxes of toys).

Went downtown today to buy lots of ugly expensive school uniform, for ugly, expensive (though apparently excellent) new school. Remarkably, Ollie though only doing mornings has to wear uniform on Fridays complete with blazer (absurd as he is not yet 3 and a midget to boot), so have had to go to all that expense so he can look like a small square waiter one morning a week. Felt really nervous about driving my big new car on big roads at first, but have discovered that a big road is in fact a good thing and you never need to mount the pavement to ease past an oncoming car like in London.

From: Charlotte Bailey
To: Nell Fenton

Don't know about that, find big roads really scary & am used to sweatily squeezing past other big cars in tiny roads though must admit despite much practice am still apt to misjudge spaces. My car is looking quite well used, though cheeringly not as bad as Amanda next door's. Not entirely her fault as I did reverse hard into her car twice while parking last week (Dan watching – made me nervous).

Fran is preparing for yet another driving test. Talks about it endlessly. Told her I'll reverse over her if she says 'I'm definitely going to crack it this time' once more.

Saw Helena in Tesco today, she trapped me by the bananas, her face a mask of tenderness as she enquired how I was coping now you've gone. Said I was just about bearing up (meant it as a joke but then noticed her eyes had alarmingly filled with tears), she did lots of nodding then said what a lovely neighbour you'd been and she'd always remember your unique approach to life. Said it like you'd died instead of just moved abroad. She paused a lot before she said 'unique approach' which made me suspect it was more a reference to the untidiness of your house than the uniqueness of your approach.

From: Charlotte Bailey
To: Nell Fenton

Hurrah. Have just spent £400 having video made of my drains in order to 'pinpoint problem area'. Unsurprisingly 'problem area' turns out to be where stinky wet patch is (drain cracked, lawn will have to be dug up). How to file video? alphabetically between Christmas & Easter? or between Dan's buttocks as sort of aide-memoire not to waste our money in the future (he insisted we have it done)? How are the children? When do they start school? Mine back this Thurs, Ellie v excited about going into year 1 and feel irrationally optimistic about Maddie starting in nursery.

From: Nell Fenton
To: Charlotte Bailey

Should definitely make Dan sit and watch the drain video (keeping the empty case between his buttocks while he watches). School started yesterday and they were all v cheerful when they came out which was a huge relief. School drop-off and pickup, the ultimate N American experience. No standing round in the playground chatting to other mothers. Everyone queues up in their huge cars and when you get to the school there's a 'drive-thru' and you hand your children out to a teacher, and at pickup lots of teachers striding around with walkie-talkies and when you reach the school there are your children waiting for you. They aren't quite handed out through a little window, but almost.

4

From: Charlotte Bailey
To: Nell Fenton

Very glad it went so well. Girls back yesterday too. Ellie thrilled about it, Maddie's start in nursery not so auspicious. In fact I could say ghastly. I had secretly harboured insane notion that world's weepiest child MIGHT go in without crying. Needless to say it turned out I had been wildly optimistic. Resolved to harden my heart against squirty & copious tears (so squirty & copious actually left a wet patch on my trousers), naturally failed miserably and had to bolt to the car.

From: Nell Fenton
To: Charlotte Bailey

Your problem is you're too good-humoured and your children grow attached to you. If you were a ratbag like me you'd find your children parted from you quite cheerfully.

Next-door-but-one came round today to introduce herself and brought her two daughters AND home-made cookies. Wish I could report she was wearing a pinny, but even without that, quite a pleasing piece of good ol'-fashioned neighbourliness. Younger daughter, Takara, is the same age as Josie (though approximately half her height) and they seemed to get along quite well. Older daughter was a pill, couldn't have made it clearer that she'd come round under duress, and slumped onto the sofa exuding adolescent surliness from every pore. Don't think from early indications Suzette and I are going to be soulmates. In the time it took to drink a cup of tea and eat a home-made cookie she managed to tell me 1) her husband is very brilliant and successful 2) her daughters are both very gifted and intelligent, also musical, 3) she has a troublesome time finding the right hairdresser as they all make such a fuss over her hair. Suggestion here was that her carroty mane is so very beautiful it's almost more of a curse than a blessing. She does a lot of languid flicking it back over her shoulders. She also very cleverly managed to weave her flat stomach into the conversation (her eyes definitely skittered across mine at this point). If I were more skilled at these things I could have raised the subject of bottoms, because I would estimate hers is at least 50% bigger than mine. She also brought me up to speed on her marital situation – current husband, Kane, is no. 2 and is half-Japanese which apparently makes their home 'very culturally rich'. Luckily she and husband no. 1 are still really good friends and Sophie (daughter of no. 1) adores Kane and just loves having two dads, so everything is wonderful. Altogether a very promising encounter, hope Josie and Takara do become friends as I shall very much enjoy hearing in what other ways Suzette is generally marvellous.

From: Charlotte Bailey
To: Nell Fenton

How fabulous, love the sound of her carroty mane. You do realise you equal each other out. Her shrunken daughter & oversized bottom equals your oversized daughter & shrunken bottom.

From: Nell Fenton
To: Charlotte Bailey

I've been going round this house trying to hang pictures etc and am discovering that though it looks very new and fancy it is in fact constructed of compressed cardboard. That, together with the fact that the downstairs is mostly open-plan, means the children can hear every hushed conversation we have even when they're in their bedrooms. Doorbell is v offensive too, plays an eight-note tune and sound comes through an intercom which is in every room so makes me jump out of my skin every time it rings. Also a ridiculous number of bathrooms and a sauna in the basement. Cannot envisage any circumstances under which I would want to use it.

From: Charlotte Bailey
To: Nell Fenton
Re: big vulgar house

Grant you everything sounds amazingly vulgar (speaking of which Dan suggested you could use sauna for 70s-style sex) but since everything is new, presumably it all works, also how fantastically liberating tastewise – no poncey agonising over whether it's better to buy genuine antique bog from salvage yard for 3x price of naffer but more practical reproduction one. In absence of your steadying influence did buy poncey antique loo for spare bathroom. Turns out you were right – impossible to clean as glaze v patchy. However, what you didn't know & I have triumphantly discovered is will only flush vv small poos.

From: Nell Fenton
To: Charlotte Bailey

You should put a discreet little picture up like a no-smoking sign but with a poo instead of a cigarette (wd also help with the cleaning problem).

From: Charlotte Bailey
To: Nell Fenton

'Drain patrol' came today to replace cracked piece of pipe. Rather mystifyingly, although you would think a trench the approximate depth & width of drain to be replaced would be adequate, it appears not. Excavations have now reached such magnitude, suspect they have become confused between the words 'pipe' & 'tube' & are actually building a tube station (tube theory further supported by the size of their quote). Hugh is overjoyed and desperate to get out there. V tricky to keep him in as workmen keep leaving door to garden open & he v darty & determined.

From: Nell Fenton
To: Charlotte Bailey

Probably will increase the value of your house though, being so close to a tube station. I've discovered intriguing feature of this house which is that floor throughout hall and kitchen which is granite? polished stony stuff anyway and which is speckled grey, black and white is perfect camouflage for anything at all, gratifying when this is dirt, but annoying when it's a small object you've inadvertently dropped. God forbid I drop a contact lens on it. Garage now completely full of empty boxes and packaging as we don't know what to do with it all so have been lobbing it in there. Suppose we will at some stage have to actually use it to put the cars in but will worry about that later.

From: Charlotte Bailey
To: Nell Fenton

Floor that hides the dirt, definitely worth the odd lost contact lens. I have dirt-accentuating floor and still lose stuff all the time.

Rained really heavily last night & in usual weekend fashion sent girls downstairs with Hugh to watch telly so we could have a lie-in. Lie-in cut short by sound of Hugh crying & Ellie calling me, v ominously citing Hugh & mud as the reason for waking us. Came down to find Hugh freezing & thickly coated in mud from what was once our garden but now closely resembles trenches of WW1. Ellie's explanation for letting him out was that 'he wanted to'. Whole episode entirely my own fault for being lazy and sluttish.

From: Nell Fenton
To: Charlotte Bailey

Count yourself lucky that it was only mud. Rob called me down proudly the other day because Ollie had done a poo on the potty and Rob had decided to wipe his bottom for him as a nice surprise for me. Had to completely strip both of them and clean quite a large surrounding area. Rob very pleased and expectant so I had to say 'well done for trying'.

From: Nell Fenton
To: Charlotte Bailey

Suzette and Kane invited us for a barbecue lunch today. Michael naturally grumpy, on the very limited exposure he's had to them says they are stupid and boring. I on the other hand thoroughly enjoy the little glimpses I get into their life and was therefore happy to go. Not disappointed in the least. Sophie, the older daughter, emerges sufficiently from her sullen silence when on her home turf to be obnoxiously rude to them both – wasn't hungry/didn't like any of the food served. Suzette eventually tensely excused her from the table and she slouched off inside. Once she'd relaxed after Sophie's departure, Suzette was in quirky mode, lots of tales of her madcap exploits, how she'd chased a racoon out of her bedroom in her undies (so a bit sexy too) at their cottage up north (everyone here has a cottage up north), how she'd driven to Montreal with the girls on a whim one night because she wanted them to absorb the French language (thought this bit sounded slightly bi-polar, it's about a five-hour drive . . .), how she'd charmed the Canadian border guards into not charging her tax after a shopping spree in the States (doubtless her glorious red hair played its part). Obviously her life is a chick flick and much more fun than mine. Very best bit was when we had ice cream. She was talking to Michael while holding up her spoon and slowly running her tongue along it. Not sure if she fancies him or if she's just one of those women who automatically flirts with all men. Michael, bless him, was looking at her with puzzled distaste which she no doubt read as scarcely controlled lust.

From: Charlotte Bailey
To: Nell Fenton

Michael probably just thought she had a tongue disorder.

Anna rang last night to get your address (again). Told me Rory and Theo had missed first one and a half days of school as

10

she'd got the date they went back wrong – thought they went back same day as Guy and Isabel so they missed the first day and then on morning of next day discovered Toulouse-Lautrec had badly chewed one of Rory's new school shoes and bitten the buckle off one of Theo's. So then instead of just sending them in trainers, decided to drop Greta at nursery and 'whizz' into Buckingham to buy boys shoes en route to school. Whizzed there but couldn't whizz on as she 'broke down'. This conversation conducted to the background of Geoffrey shouting 'You didn't break down – you ran out of bloody petrol again.' Anyway after fulminating for 20 mins about how this time she really was going to get rid of Toulouse-Lautrec, Anna came over quite sentimental, said she misses you and blood is thicker than water (about 9 times).

From: Nell Fenton
To: Charlotte Bailey

That dog will survive us all. Why would she get rid of him for something as trivial as eating school shoes when she failed to get rid of him after he ate Geoffrey's passport before he went to Dubai?

Went to a fundraising meeting at the school this afternoon (doing my bit). Also thought I might meet some other parents since you never meet anyone at the drive-thru. I took Ollie along since I always did in England to such things. Heart sank rather when I saw all the women v done up and manicured, meeting in a formal boardroom and NO children. Braved it anyhow and sat Ollie on my lap. They began with minutes from the last meeting – v bad sign. Ollie asking me questions in a loud voice from time to time but otherwise ok. It dragged on and on and Ollie was getting more and more pissed off.

Someone gave him some crayons and paper which kept him sitting quietly for a few minutes till I noticed he was chewing them and spitting them onto the table (not only embarrassing but also slightly worrying regressive behaviour). At this point the head of the school (a really giant arse) was addressing the meeting and all the other women were gazing at him with rapt admiration. Anyhow couldn't take it any more so shuffled out in disgrace. Shall not be going again.

From: Charlotte Bailey
To: Nell Fenton

Unclear about the headmaster's giant arse – does he have one or is he one?

From: Nell Fenton
To: Charlotte Bailey

Is one. Has a substantial arse but wd not be fair to describe it as giant.

From: Nell Fenton
To: Charlotte Bailey

Michael's new office held a party last night. Felt a bit of a twat as clearly everyone else had come straight from the office and was in work clothes and I was in party gear. Also we had to do a lot of standing around chatting and I wore my high boots which I always forget make me want to gnaw my feet off after 10 minutes. Still, met some people who are slightly more normal than the manicured soccer moms in their giant cars

12

from the school and one woman in particular, Nina, who Michael says is brilliant and lured over from Vancouver, is really delightful and has twin boys of Ollie's age, so that was promising.

From: Charlotte Bailey
To: Nell Fenton

Re overdressing – you should have explained to attentive circle of fellow guests (captivated by your English frankness) that this was just the kick-off to an evening of intense socialising and your real destination was a much bigger fancier party later on.

PS Fran v glum today. Had rather bad luck during driving test so didn't 'crack it' this go as she'd predicted.

From: Nell Fenton
To: Charlotte Bailey
Re: Wrinklies

Poor Fran, fear she'll try again though. Went to our posh mall first thing this morning. Disconcerted to see mall absolutely full of old people in snowy-white trainers and neatly pressed tracksuits. Apparently 'mall walking' is how old people get their exercise here, and obviously makes sense when v cold/ hot, but surprising when outside is gentle September sun. Perhaps winter strikes with terrifying suddenness here and you can't be too careful?

From: Rachel Lockwood
To: Nell Fenton

Dear Nell

I have again proved my shortcomings as a friend and failed to email you to see how all is going. Are you settling in? and how are the children finding school? Jonathan has started at the local school and seems almost insultingly unconcerned about leaving me in the morning. Probably punishment for the fact that I never made finger puppets or did Play-Doh with him. Also the food at school is better than the food at home because they get jelly. (Is there no limit to my inadequacy?) Send me your news, we are thinking of you all and are planning how we can scrape up the money to come and visit, if I can ever get Jack on a plane that is.

Fondest love to all
Rachel xx

From: Nell Fenton
To: Rachel Lockwood

Dear Rachel, all is well here though still lots of unpacking to do. The house is quite nice, v comfortable in a vulgar way and the children seem to like their school, so far. Not seeing much of Michael who's working really long hours but hopefully that will settle down. Toronto is fantastic for children, lots of lovely clean parks and the restaurants are cheap (as is everything, in fact) and very child-friendly. Would love you to come with or without Jack, we have lots of room, 3 spare bedrooms and about 84 bathrooms. Charlotte & co are

14

coming at Christmas I hope, but perhaps you could come for
Easter? Love Nell

From: Nell Fenton
To: Charlotte Bailey

The house is such a bomb site and I'm so desperate for some
help – Michael never around – have hired a very unpromising
cleaner called Cynthia. Got her through an agency and am
resolutely ignoring her obvious shortcomings, not least of
which is the fact that she seems a bit mad (mutters darkly all
the time) also I cannot understand a word she says though she
is Jamaican so I suppose English is her first language.

From: Charlotte Bailey
To: Nell Fenton

It's a time-honoured family tradition to have a dodgy cleaner
and at least you have one, Gina-the-cleaner is leaving me. Also
your house is finished so presumably things don't come off in
your hand all the time (Dan stuck in bathroom for 20 mins yesterday when door handle fell out on bedroom side), everything
a constant tip here AND I don't like new kitchen colour. Albert
keeps looking at me through narrowed eyes saying 'You don't
like it, do you?' so on top of hating it have to keep hotly denying
I hate it as Dan will definitely divorce me if I change the colour
again. Suspect Gina moving purely to get away from us and
the spectacular shambles and Dorset was just the first county
she came across into which debris from our house hadn't
spilled. Feel quite sad about it, even though she's dreadfully
unreliable (come rain or shine she might turn up) I'm really fond
of her. Think we're going to get an au pair next, instead. Fran

15

says the trick is to get a beautiful Swedish one as it's the ugly ones who go after your husband and the beautiful ones who think he's a sad old wanker.

From: Nell Fenton
To: Charlotte Bailey

I can't believe Gina lasted as long as she did, was totally unsuited to manual labour with that inner ear problem of hers.

From: Charlotte Bailey
To: Nell Fenton

Nonsense, she cleaned very well, only staggered a bit and hardly ever toppled right over.

I've been looking at au pair details from agency, incredibly depressing as makes me feel absolutely ancient. They all seem to have been born in the 1980s. Also they're all so WORTHY. When I was 18 I was getting drunk on the King's Rd & trying to get to grips with smoking without setting my dreadlocks on fire. Nowadays all 18-year-olds (Swedish ones at least) 'love to work with childrens'. Will have to choose a short one as shower in top bathroom has v low showerhead.

From: Nell Fenton
To: Charlotte Bailey

Think it's moderately unlikely that they would list drinking and smoking as hobbies on their application forms, however keenly they pursue those activities in their spare time.

From: Nell Fenton
To: Charlotte Bailey

I'm going to kill Michael. Went to another work party and this time checked with Michael how smart/casual it was going to be. He assured me it was casual. Should have known he would not pay attention to such details. Turned out to be a party for the people they really wanted to impress (unlike previous hoi polloi party) and as we arrived we were photographed for society pages (vv bad – was wearing fairly skanky cord jacket) and when we got in all the women were in full evening wear, and me in very ordinary navy trousers, Gap t-shirt and cardigan (silk admittedly, but much washed), also in my distress managed to get potato-sized blotch of red wine on my t-shirt in first 10 minutes. Chairman's wife came up and kissed Michael, who was mortified since he hadn't bothered to shave (party being so casual). Since he's half-man half-gorilla, it's not insignificant when he fails to shave. Serves him bloody well right.

From: Charlotte Bailey
To: Nell Fenton

How could you not know he'd get it wrong?? This is the man who says 'I like that dress' when you're wearing a skirt. Like any NORMAL man, will say any old crap that pops into his head just to shut you up, also much more likely to say it's casual wear as party clothes require much more input from husband – eg 'no your back doesn't look at all fat in that/knees don't look weird/the choker doesn't make your neck look short' . . . and if he were interested enough to correctly assess dress code he would be no good to you as he would not be married to you as he would almost certainly be gay.

17

From: Nell Fenton
To: Charlotte Bailey

It's true that clothes aren't his specialist subject, what with all those confusingly different names clothes can have. (Colours also v problematic for him, brown and grey – how can anyone tell the difference?)

From: Charlotte Bailey
To: Nell Fenton

Fucking hell. Central heating finally packed up last night, quite frankly can't believe the ancient & poisonous boiler has lasted this long. Albert came round today in a last-ditch attempt to try and revive it. After 45 mins of the boiler equivalent of heart massage announced 'it's a gonner', had urge to add 'still, it had a good innings' but felt it would be disrespectful. Should have replaced the whole lot before we moved in last year but since at that point we were operating on the 'only absolutely essential work to be done' principle and it was (just) working it seemed unnecessary. Now v necessary & timing worse as have just paid to have 'tube station' dug in our garden & I really want to come to visit at Christmas.

From: Nell Fenton
To: Charlotte Bailey

Deepest condolences on your loss but you still have to come at Christmas whatever happens.

Now Josie has made friends pesky child has been nagging for a birthday party. Had hoped that her birthday being over a

18

month ago and the move etc would have made her forget, but no, bless her retentive little brain. Also she wants to invite the whole class so am failing to benefit from huge advantage of an August birthday where one can invite the whole class with impunity since 60% are invariably away. Have arranged something called Mad Science for entertainers and having set stupid precedent of doing handmade invitations for the last 2 birthdays have had to come up with appropriately mad and sciency card. Was quite pleased with my idea of cutting out test-tube-shape cardboard, with big bubbles coming out the top. Only noticed when I had done about 20 that they are vv phallic when upended. Still, not bloody doing them again and anyway it might prompt gratifying August-type refusal rate.

From: Charlotte Bailey
To: Nell Fenton

Try not posting the invitations at all but instead storing them safely in a nappy-changing bag for at least 2 weeks then performing secret, frantic, last-minute phone round (on discovering them crumpled & dirty in bottom of said bag), should yield 30–40% refusal rate if past experience is anything to go by.

OCTOBER 99

From: Louise Corrigan
To: Charlotte Bailey

We're making plans to come to London. Walt needs to do some research in London for a piece he's doing for the NY Times and we have meetings about our book. Anyway we'd love to come visit if you can bear to have us. We'd be staying Nov 7 thru 15 if that's ok. If it's too much let us know & we'll go to a hotel. Speak soon x L

From: Charlotte Bailey
To: Louise Corrigan

FANTASTIC! We'd love you to come & stay, facilities a little basic at the moment though, central heating on the blink but should definitely have it sorted by the time you come, also roof absolutely watertight now. Dan can pick you up at the airport if you want, just let us know. Love C

From: Louise Corrigan
To: Charlotte Bailey

That's great. Don't worry about facilities, you know us, we'll crash anywhere. Re collection, don't sweat it, hon, we'll order a car to pick us up. Speak soon x L

From: Charlotte Bailey
To: Nell Fenton

oh god, oh god, oh god, never felt such a mix of emotions.

Lou & Walt coming to stay & house a total fucking bomb site. Mentioned in a masterstroke of understatement 'basic facilities' to Lou but she seemed to gloss over that, don't think my version of basic & hers quite the same eg she, non-goosedown duvet = basic, me sleeping on Lilo = basic. Lou said & I quote 'We'll crash anywhere.' Have you ever known a couple less likely to 'crash anywhere'? Last time they stayed (AND we were still living in Islington – the height of luxury compared to here), Walt spent his whole time gargling vinegar to 'cleanse his sinuses of dust mites'. God knows what he'll do here – have to send industrial vacuum cleaner up there. Also confidently predicted that central heating would be fixed by the time they visit. On the positive side obv they are excellent company & always full of fantastic stories about NY. Also Lou always gives me all her pristine-looking 'old' stuff. Ellie v excited to see Godmother as Godmother does lovely stuff like put handcream on her & read stories with expression unlike real mother who skips pages & never puts handcream on self let alone 5-year-old. Must now go & tackle spare room as although visit a month away will take at least that long to empty it – room actually not 'spare' at all but v much needed as giant junk cupboard.

From: Nell Fenton
To: Charlotte Bailey

You could have sent them to stay in a hotel, you barmy cow, and still have enjoyed their company. Living in a building site gives you a general dispensation from having people to stay. Went to a school-arranged social function this morning (trying to foster community spirit, lacking due to drive-by pickup). It was a breakfast at a fancy golf club which isn't exactly my thing but don't want to be a hermit so am making an effort. However, was entirely filled with same uptight gym-trained and manicured mothers from fundraising meeting, just many more of them. Have discovered irony is an unknown concept in this country so think they think I'm mad. Also never have manicures so am scruffy too.

From: Charlotte Bailey
To: Nell Fenton

Can't believe alarm bells didn't ring when you saw the words 'golf club'. Can't find anyone to fix central heating, though Albert, who is repainting kitchen at the moment, keeps dropping hints about doing it himself. Dan, who's usually so easygoing, is absolutely adamant that we must find someone else as Albert has plenty of other things to do & will take forever & if he does it will not have heating for the new millennium. Other danger is of course he'll get Smelly Gordon to help him. Dan doesn't care about that – but I do.

From: Nell Fenton
To: Charlotte Bailey

Well, at least if you don't fix your heating you'll have the money to come and visit us.

From: Charlotte Bailey
To: Nell Fenton
Re: not pregnant

Got my period last night had been slightly hopeful as it was 2 days late, though even considering past success in getting pregnant immediately realise it is probably unrealistic to expect it this time (am v old these days) still can't help feeling really disappointed. Dan quite sorry too as had got briefly excited about idea of swapping Volvo for an MPV.

From: Nell Fenton
To: Charlotte Bailey

At least you have a vague idea when yours is due. Since mine is a randomly occurring phenomenon am a bit hopeful every month and invariably persuade myself that my PMT symptoms are signs of early pregnancy. Anyhow I'm even more ancient and unlike you don't just need to brush against my husband when passing on the stairs in order to get knocked up so am sure you'll be there way ahead of me.

From: Charlotte Bailey
To: Nell Fenton

Short (and therefore suitable) au pair I interviewed by phone has turned us down as we don't have any animals and she loves animals. Am soooo pissed off, feel like ringing her back and saying don't need any bloody animals have 3 children with the table manners of baboons. Have wasted nearly 2 weeks buggering around & now have to start again & there is only one other on list who looks suitable, is short enough & has not expressed an undue interest in animals.

From: Nell Fenton
To: Charlotte Bailey

People who are that keen on animals are suspect anyhow and probably don't like children. No doubt she's a vegetarian too which would be really irritating. Speaking of irritating, Michael has decided we have to change our church AGAIN. Did it twice in England, now has again been listening to the sermons and thus finds things to object to and is insisting we find another church whose priest has views more in accordance with his own. Don't really care but why can't he just make shopping lists in his head during the sermon like a normal person?

From: Charlotte Bailey
To: Nell Fenton
Re: urgently needed au pair

Spoke to alternative au pair last night, sounds v nice, speaks slightly better English than me & laughed politely at all my jokes (good sign) then asked me if I believe in smacking (good sign? bad sign? can't decide). Refrained from saying I believe it exists (unlike fairies & Father Christmas) but thought this was too flippant a reply for such an earnest question & would probably confuse her, so simply said 'nooo?' in a hopeful way. Correct answer as she then admitted she'd turned down another family as they had said they DID smack. Can't believe what a bloody minefield interviewing au pairs is & how though we all pretend we're interviewing THEM, they are quite clearly interviewing US. Anyway felt really annoyed & whole episode has had the 'going-on-a-diet effect' (where knowledge of future abstinence makes you immediately hungry even though you just ate a pie). Though I think smacking is awful, wanted to quickly go up & smack them all.

From: Nell Fenton
To: Charlotte Bailey

Had Josie's belated mad science party yesterday. Have to say nothing struck me as especially mad or sciencey about it, except perhaps setting off quite a big rocket in the road outside. Still, they all seemed to enjoy it and were most impressed to have what one girl described as 'a proper tea', as apparently all they ever have here is delivery pizza and prefab cake.

From: Charlotte Bailey
To: Nell Fenton

Finally got sent some proper photos of new au pair – much better than the usual b&w headshots that make everyone look like they belong to the Baader-Meinhof. She is v pretty but looks about 14 though she is apparently 19. Children all v excited about her arrival (though not half as excited as me). Girls have been making her lots of welcome cards all week. Am considering making my own welcome banner inscribed with 'DELIGHTED TO HAVE YOU, NOW PLEASE DO SOME IRONING' as laundry situation now completely out of control – have actual TOWERS of clothes in laundry room which when they are knocked over (all the time) double as a 'soft play area' for Hugh.

From: Nell Fenton
To: Charlotte Bailey

I'm SO annoyed, I just came back from a haircut and saw Suzette as I was getting out of my car. I was quite pleased with it, it's much shorter and I think looks quite stylish. She came up to me looking slightly pained and said 'Oh, you cut your hair. Why?' I was so taken aback I was quite unable to think of a suitably clever rejoinder. The only small consolation I can find is she has swept her own fiery locks up into a loose bun today which only emphasises how weirdly tiny her head is. My hair will grow but her head won't.

From: Charlotte Bailey
To: Nell Fenton

Am sure your hair is v nice. You look much better with short hair. God is v kind & merciful as He has answered my prayers and finally found someone who appears competent (indeed passionate) re fascinating topic of our central heating. Keith – who is moonlighting from the gas board – did lots of sums about size of rooms & BTUs. Apparently we need a lot of pipework & 'rads' replaced (must always refer to them as 'rads' as it is quicker than saying radiators & Keith is very busy), also superly Keith says we need not 1 but 2 boilers for a house this size. Keith v concerned about 'radical heat loss' through the glass cupola on the top floor and suggested we get rid of it. No point explaining to a heat-loss Nazi that the cupola is pretty much the whole reason we bought this derelict wreck so just stood nodding with v thoughtful expression. Keith & Gerry are starting next w/e so may actually fulfil prediction to Walt and Lou of having heating, otherwise they'll have to go to a hotel as being without hot water absolutely appalling (even by my v low standards). I've bought one of those tin baths a la Steptoe & Son to bath children in kitchen as running up & down stairs with kettles and pans of water too nightmarish (Dan & I still maintaining our standards by resolutely having 4-inch baths in freezing bathroom), but children absolutely love huge excitement of bathing next to cooker, took some arty black & white photos of them having fun, unfortunately combination of tin bath, newspapers on floor to protect parquet & Hugh crying made them look like NSPCC advert rather than jolly family snaps.

From: Nell Fenton
To: Charlotte Bailey

God, how grim, recommend you drink a lot of sherry to help engender 'spirit of the Blitz' necessary to face such ordeals.

From: Charlotte Bailey
To: Nell Fenton

Have been using blow heaters to try & improve ambient temperature in house although it is unseasonably mild (thank the Lord). Oddly feels colder in the house than out in the garden but maybe it's just because we put coats on to go outside . . . absolutely refuse to wear a coat inside, though very much wish to. Used to be so resilient when I was young but am pathetic about the cold now. Ellie & Maddie are too, especially Ellie. Hugh immune to everything (sometimes wonder if the messaging to his brain is all there . . .). Modern blow heaters terribly irritating as they have inbuilt thermostats so they are constantly switching themselves off in case they do anything dangerous like actually warm the room up slightly. Ancient one I borrowed from Fran never turns itself off & gets the room toasty warm in no time – love it & would crouch in front of it all day if the girls weren't batting me out of the way to have their go.

From: Nell Fenton
To: Charlotte Bailey

Quite true about growing soft, can't bear the cold now (dreading the winter here) and never used to feel it when I was young. Remember having friends round who were not only frozen but starving too, because Mum always fed us so late. Sure it was character-building. Anna only used to let that ponger Driscoll sleep on her bed at night because he kept her warm.

From: Charlotte Bailey
To: Nell Fenton

Finished painting au pair Ana Frid's bedroom last night. Looks really lovely & by far the nicest bedroom in the house. All blue & white & Swedish-looking should make her feel quite at home or possibly homesick?? hope have not made tactless decorating faux pas. Anyway it has curtains that luxuriously close in the middle so she will be able to undress & dress in her own room unlike me. Also bought new duvet cover, did not run to new mattress though really should have since mattress absolutely ancient (got it off Mum who practically had it as a child). Quite sharp spring sticking out on both sides but have put that at foot end so hopefully will be ok.

From: Nell Fenton
To: Charlotte Bailey

Can't believe you still have any of Mum's evil old mattresses. You do realise not everyone was raised in the same haphazard way we were and is thus inured against beds with sharp protuberances or strange lumpy pillows. Good job she's short so hopefully won't impale herself immediately. Do think you should consider buying the poor girl a new mattress though.

From: Charlotte Bailey
To: Nell Fenton

Ana Frid arrived today. Dan picked her up from the airport & then drove her the 'scenic' route home pointing out London's teenage hot spots like Leicester Square & Oxford Circus. Photo she sent us quite inaccurate – she actually looks 12 not 14 & is tiny like a doll. Worried in case one of the laundry towers falls on her & she can't get out.

From: Nell Fenton
To: Charlotte Bailey

I'd be more worried about breaking the news to her that there's no heating or hot water if I were you.

From: Charlotte Bailey
To: Nell Fenton

Hurrah for au pair girl. Ana Frid completely fantastic. While laundry situation not yet fully under control at least now greater proportion of our clothes in drawers than on floor, Hugh's 'soft play area' all but gone, & Dan no longer wearing jumpers to office to hide unironed shirts. Girls completely in love with her & think she is v beautiful. Ellie says she loves her 'yellow hair & red cheeks' – doesn't sound so great when put like that.

From: Nell Fenton
To: Charlotte Bailey

Am v envious. Cynthia continues to exceed my expectations and I think may prove to be the worst cleaner I have ever had. She has told me that she's here in Canada on refugee status and although she wants to get more work it is very hard (possibly because she's so useless?). Means she is completely reliant on the money she earns from me and can't get welfare. Obviously this means if I sack her I will burn in hell.

From: Charlotte Bailey
To: Nell Fenton

Bloody hell, Keith and Gerry have worked all w/e and central heating still not fixed. Interestingly, while it is working v well in basement & on top floor, middle 2 floors are still freezing. Children have all caught nasty colds, no doubt caused by sharp climate change as you walk through the house. Although now v nippy out don't dare crank up existing heating any more as am fearful that downstairs warm front will meet middle-floor cold front precipitating rainfall in hallway. Have hot water in the basement but am not prepared to bath in kitchen. Also Albert very huffy about Keith the interloper and keeps lifting floorboards to inspect his work and then shaking his head disapprovingly. Unfortunately am quite certain it is only a matter of time before Albert shares his misgivings about Keith & Gerry's workmanship with me & I really don't think I can stand another conversation about pipework or 'rads' though at least Albert calls them radiators.

From: Nell Fenton
To: Charlotte Bailey

Any builder worth his salt thrives on delivering bad news. Probably wise to prepare yourself for the worst about the job they're doing. We've been preparing for Hallowe'en which is a lot of fun here, much bigger deal than in England. Shops have been full of pumpkins, hay bales and eight-foot bunches of corn on the cob stalks for ages (purpose is rustic decoration). I've bought all of the above in rush of excitement. Children are going to attend school in costume (racks of them in every supermarket so trouble-free). Ollie is going to be a Teletubby – Tinky Winky? the gay purple one at any rate, Rob is a dinosaur, and Josie is a witch.

From: Charlotte Bailey
To: Nell Fenton

Don't think Tinky Winky is v scary unless you are a homophobic anorexic, frightened of the colour purple. Hugh is accompanying the girls to a friend's Hallowe'en party. I've made him an excellent miniature dracula cape. He looks adorable in it & is v proud. E & M skeleton & witch respectively.

31

From: Nell Fenton
To: Charlotte Bailey

Different here, you can dress up in any costume, doesn't have to relate to Hallowe'en. Bit of a shame I think but have compensated by putting lots of spiders and bats on all the window sills round the house.

From: Charlotte Bailey
To: Nell Fenton

Albert & Keith have finally come face to face. Not good. I didn't really understand their conversation but I think Albert asked Keith some provocative questions about BTUs & stopcocks. Anyway Keith is really pissed off and asked me if 'that old geezer' will be around much. Was mendacious enough to say no as although Albert at the moment spends all day, every day here, Keith is working evenings & weekends so am reasonably confident I should be able to keep them apart.

From: Nell Fenton
To: Rachel Lockwood
Re: Happy Birthday

Dear Rachel, hope you are having a lovely day. You will no doubt be impressed that I am emailing you on the ACTUAL day of your birthday AND I have also sent your present (several days ago in fact) instead of my more usual practice of storing it in a drawer for 4 months. Hope you like it, would say you can change it if you don't, but that would be a lie. Love Nell

From: Rachel Lockwood
To: Nell Fenton

Dear Nell

It's true I am deeply impressed, and the beautiful sweater arrived today. I absolutely love it and only one day after my birthday, which is frighteningly competent of you (but we mustn't underestimate the pleasure of getting a birthday present at a totally random time of year – I say this in self-defence as I can never live up to the new you). I wish I could say Jack had put as much thought into his present, but actually he gave me some CDs and a coffee-table book on historic houses (yes, a coffee-table book though I am in fact his wife and not his hard-to-buy-for great-uncle). He'd clearly bought the presents on his way back from work the night before and quite frankly I'm so fed up with him generally, I don't think I'd even have bothered to feign delight if it hadn't been for Jonathan's eager little face watching me across the breakfast table. I think he felt a bit guilty because he promised to come home early and take me out for dinner but of course he phoned later and said he'd been held up, so that was that. Sorry for the long whine and thank you again for my lovely present.

Fondest love to all
Rachel xx

From: Charlotte Bailey
To: Nell Fenton

Hate people who talk about being stressed out, consider it to be poofy middle-class whingeing & v naff, so have come up with different expression to describe current state of mind. Think I will say am feeling very highly strung (good as this also implies v well bred & posh). Anyway am feeling v highly strung about central-heating situation as Walt & Lou arrive next week & last night after much hammering followed by silence followed by 'FUCK, FUCK, FUUUUUUUCK!' water started pouring through the living-room ceiling. Keith says ceiling will be fine as water 'rushed through' rather than trickled. Not quite sure why that's better but according to Keith it is. As Keith & Gerry are moonlighting all work takes place in the evenings or at weekends. Laying pipes etc necessitates great deal of hammering, fine during the day but tricky at night when you are trying to get offspring to go to bloody sleep. Can't exactly tell them to stop, as then they would stop. Floorboards up all over the house, a great hazard for someone as clumsy as me (narrowly missed putting my foot through spare-room ceiling). Furthermore, Hugh has discovered untold delight of lifting unsecured floorboards & placing girls' (& my) cherished possessions under them. When we realised he was doing this subsequent under-board hunt turned up several items including my diaphragm, rather embarrassingly found by Gerry who feigned not knowing what it was – thank God it was in its case so we could both pretend it was my dentures.

From: Nell Fenton
To: Charlotte Bailey

Dentures a very clever deception, after all would be terrible if Gerry suspected you sometimes have sex with your husband. Much less embarrassing to have lost all your teeth by your mid-thirties.

From: Charlotte Bailey
To: Nell Fenton
Re: Hugh's debut as Count Dracula

I allowed Ellie to be in charge of painting his face & slicking back his hair in Dracula-type mode. Unfortunately she was unsupervised when she did it so instead of using large pot of gel, prominently placed on basin for this exact purpose, she elected to scrabble through my bathroom cabinet until she found ancient pot of Vaseline which she used instead. Ana Frid has now washed Hugh's hair about 1000 times (so convenient in a tin bath) but to no avail as he still looks like a v short bouncer from Stringfellow's.

From: Nell Fenton
To: Charlotte Bailey

Our Hallowe'en was something of a partial success. There was trick or treating at our fancy local mall where bored and snooty shop owners stood in the doorways of their shops handing out candy, then we moved on to the houses in our neighbourhood. Called at Suzette's but couldn't linger as Rob traumatised by the crazed barking of her vile, jumpy, licky dogs. Suzette was in full costume, dressed as a serving wench and she told me with a trill of girlish laughter that she's 'crazy about Hallowe'en and the kids would be so mad at her if she didn't dress up' (surprising as Sophie had opened the door for us with her usual morose expression and wearing grungy jeans and a sweatshirt). This episode has proved that Suzette is much more young-at-heart than me (even my own treacherous children asked how come I didn't dress up like Suzette). Also she is a crafty dresser because wench costume perfect for some-one like her who has quite decent boobs but a really fat arse.

Anyhow we soon gave up, so many people out half the houses didn't answer and Rob wouldn't even approach the ones where there was barking. Will have to plan more carefully next year.

NOVEMBER 99

From: Charlotte Bailey
To: Nell Fenton

Albert has spotted staining on living-room ceiling and is very gloomy about it. He says 'given time' it will definitely fall down. Pointed out to him rather tersely, given time all ceilings eventually fall down & I am sure ceiling will be perfectly fine as water merely 'rushed through'.

Any snow yet? Thank God it's v mild here at the moment although house still feels bloody freezing in the middle.

From: Nell Fenton
To: Charlotte Bailey

No snow, better get some as I've spent a fortune on snow boots and snow pants for all of them.

The school has sent invitations to parent/teacher night. Extremely ominous, for Ollie and Josie they are printed and a 15-min time slot is allocated but Rob's has a handwritten note attached saying we've been given an extra 15 mins for him. Don't think it's because they have so many good things to say about him that 30 mins is required. Oh God.

From: Charlotte Bailey
To: Nell Fenton

Mustn't always jump to negative conclusions. Probably some perfectly innocuous explanation.

Central heating is FINALLY working. Can't believe living hell is over. Keith & Gerry here till past midnight in final push to finish (can't fault them for lack of hard work – through obviously the several gallons of water pouring through living-room ceiling last week presented something of a 'glitch'). I am so pathetically grateful to have fully functioning heating on ALL floors plus the unutterable luxury of hot water that has not come out of a kettle or saucepan. Dan & I quite unwashed (till this morning) as has just been too unpleasantly cold to barely get our but- tocks wet in an unheated bathroom. Not sure what Ana Frid has been doing but has managed to look relentlessly clean & wholesome. Feel like Scarlett O'Hara, swear I'll never go unwashed again (am sure I smelt a little bit last week – Dan certainly did). Now have to clean up house for Lou & Walt's visit though not quite sure how to address living-room smell (wet dog).

From: Nell Fenton
To: Charlotte Bailey

Why not get a dog and keep it fairly wet, then you'll have a perfect explanation for the smell?

From: Charlotte Bailey
To: Nell Fenton

Weather's turned bloody freezing, even fully functioning central heating is no match for the force 9 gale blowing off the heath & through the v gappy spare-room windows. Have had to buy & install window cling film, a sort of instant/disposable double glazing that you stick round your windows with v high-tech double-sided tape & then heat with a hairdryer till becomes taut and according to instructions 'invisible'. Never seen anything less invisible in my life – you can see it from the bloody street. Cling film stuff bulges alarmingly every time wind blows & am slightly concerned big gust of wind might cause it to burst from its moorings, fly onto the bed & suffocate Lou & Walt while they sleep.

From: Nell Fenton
To: Charlotte Bailey

Quite the reverse here, when you open a window you hear a sort of sucking sound like an airtight seal being broken. All double poss triple? glazed. Only air actually coming into the house has been preprocessed through huge machine in the boiler room where it is cooled/heated, cleaned and humidified. Feel like we are living in Brave New World.

From: Charlotte Bailey
To: Nell Fenton

Am worn to a ravelling (like vv tired person or Tailor of Gloucester). Preparing for Lou & Walt visit like preparing for state visit but without the fleet of servants to help. Ana Frid and I worked like maniacs all day doing marathon clean-up ready for their arrival tonight. House was in even more dire and muddy state than usual this morning due to fireworks party last night. Also had to rewash & iron all Lou & Walt's bedding as rather disastrously (& v heroically) removed poor, miserable coldy Hugh from our bed & took him into spare bed with me so Dan could get some sleep. Spare-room bed had been made up in anticipation of L & W's arrival. This morning, however, both me & the bed comprehensively smeared with dried-on yellow snot. So idiotic of me not to get bogey-free Dan to sleep there, tried to deal with it with baby wipes but to no avail. Dan helpfully suggested simply turning everything over but as Lou is always doing stuff like airing her bed don't dare risk it.

From: Nell Fenton
To: Charlotte Bailey

Though I consider baby wipes one of the finest creations of the human brain and have found more applications for them than I can count, don't think you can actually launder bedding with them. I'm tired all the time at the moment too as have been defeated in all my attempts to get Ollie to stay in his own bed. By simply screaming till he's sick he can get exactly what he wants, which is to sleep in our bed where he behaves like a washing machine on its final spin. Michael always crawls off to the spare room, but since he's quite frequently joined there by Rob, who, when scared, likes to sleep clamped against your body for security reasons and who, as soon as he's asleep, becomes a sort of kung-fu fighter, can't be too critical of this defection from the marital bed.

40

From: Charlotte Bailey
To: Nell Fenton

Walt & Lou arrived tonight night looking v glam & sunglassesy
(so wish I was the sort of person who could carry off sunglasses
in the winter, last time I tried Fran asked me if I had conjuncti-
vitis again). Lou has got v skinny since last time I saw her, says
she's addicted to bikram yoga and it's awesome for mind and
body. Walt not interested so he looks the same. Really lovely to
see them & both on v good form with lots of funny stories
about NY etc. Children asleep when they arrived so am looking
forward to the morning as know they will be overjoyed. Ellie has
already checked with me about 1000 times that Lou is actually
coming & actually bringing presents. Told her not to be so
grabby (v hypocritical as was secretly quite excited myself).

From: Charlotte Bailey
To: Nell Fenton

Lou & Walt visit going v well so far although slightly sticky start
this morning when Hugh hugged the back of Walt's legs before
I'd wiped his nose. Managed to get everything off with baby
wipes. Lou gave me a beautiful pair of chocolate calfskin gloves
& the children a lovely book each, which they received v
graciously (thank God as can be ghastly ungrateful little toerags about books & say things like 'Where's my real present?').
Obviously they didn't SAY anything but think L & W bit shocked
by state of the house in cold light of day. Think they imagined
if not finished at least we'd be at the decorating stage. Also
clearly cannot comprehend why anyone would choose to
move out of central London to a place without a Starbucks let
alone a tube station. Difficult to explain to someone without
children the utter tedium of constantly having to cart them to

41

local playground as tiny paved Islington garden a death trap. Anyway have to get off computer now to prepare delicious dairy-free dinner.

From: Nell Fenton
To: Charlotte Bailey

So is it no dairy now, as well as no red meat or wheat? Yum.

From: Rachel Lockwood
To: Nell Fenton

Dear Nell

How are you all? I've had so many compliments on the lovely sweater you sent me and today the man in the queue behind me at the supermarket started chatting to me and then asked me if I'd like to go out for a drink, which I attribute entirely to my new sweater. Admittedly he was no Adonis but it's such a very rare thing these days I was still a bit flattered.

Mum and Dad came to stay last weekend, they're both really well and send you their love. It was so nice to have them and Jack was very charming which was a relief since he complained endlessly about them coming before-hand. Mind you, he wasn't around much which was fine except we were all invited to our neighbours' for bonfire night and though he promised to be back in time he didn't turn up till halfway through the evening because he'd run into an old friend and obviously that was more important than keeping his commitments to us. I could see everyone, especially Dad, thought it was spectacularly rude but we all pretended it was the most normal thing in the world. I had to hide the fact that I wanted to jab him repeatedly with barbecue skewers because it would worry Mum and Dad (and be bad form at someone else's party). Anyhow I still had a nice weekend in spite of being married to bastard-head.

Fondest love to all
Rachel xx

From: Nell Fenton
To: Rachel Lockwood

Dear Rachel, perfectly natural to want to jab one's husband with a skewer sometimes and arriving late better than not coming at all. I'm so glad your parents are well, please send them my love when you speak to them next. All well here though Rob struggling a bit at school, doesn't really seem to notice it, told me yesterday he was the best reader in his class which sadly I think is the opposite of the truth but at least it shows there's no problem with his self-esteem. Love Nell

From: Charlotte Bailey
To: Nell Fenton

Lou & Walt had v bad night last night. Unfortunately it was extremely windy & they found it hard to sleep as stupid bloody cling film I put up at the window kept 'sucking in & then blowing out' making 'a loud whooshing sound' (which made Walt 'edgy'). Lou calmed him with a homeopathic remedy & then apparently they both managed to fall asleep BUT NOT FOR LONG because a particularly strong gust of wind caused a corner of fucking plastic sheeting on one of the windows to come loose & start flapping around so then sucking & rustling noise from other 2 windows was accompanied by whipping sound. Both tried to stick flapping corner back down but it kept bursting loose again and then a corner of the plastic whipped Walt's eye. Injury drawn to my attention by the fact that Walt came down with (v lovely) blue & black scarf tied diagonally across his head over hurt eye. Both he & Lou looked quite rough this morning. Have removed cling film from other 2 windows but the temperature in the room has plummeted & although heating is really cranked up & rest of the house v warm their room remains vv chilly also think Walt may have caught Hugh's cold, either that or has had v bad reaction to the Camembert he ate last night.

From: Nell Fenton
To: Charlotte Bailey

V sorry to hear about Walt's eye. Can be terribly dangerous tussling with cling film, also I believe that careful analysis of Camembert might reveal that it does in fact contain dairy products which I thought they didn't eat? Heard from Rachel yesterday, sounds like Jack still being a big wanker.

From: Charlotte Bailey
To: Nell Fenton

Actually bought the Camembert for us, didn't expect Lou or Walt to have any, but everyone a bit drunk & Walt decided in moment of recklessness to eat some. Anna rang this evening

44

& said they went to a Guy Fawkes party in the village where everybody was supposed to bring fireworks only they couldn't because Toulouse-Lautrec got to them & bit all the rockets & ate half the mega Catherine wheel she'd bought. Luckily he threw it up in the car on the way to the vet so they were able to go to the party after all, albeit empty-handed.

From: Nell Fenton
To: Charlotte Bailey

Shame it didn't blow him up.

From: Charlotte Bailey
To: Nell Fenton

Discovered today that a thermostat on a blow heater is in fact a GOOD THING as ancient one Fran lent me & I solicitously placed in Lou & Walt's bedroom to try & warm it a little caught fire this evening. Was downstairs with Ana Frid making the children's supper when I heard Lou shrieking from upstairs, ran up to find her ineffectually batting at the licking flames with a hand towel, grabbed hand towel off her so I could bat at it ineffectually myself. Fortunately Ana Frid took charge, sprinted back downstairs to get a saucepan lid, charged back in, unplugged heater at wall (which neither I nor Lou had thought to do) & placed saucepan lid over the flames which killed them. Then had to open all their bedroom windows to try & disperse the aroma of burnt electrical appliance – didn't work, really nasty acrid smell persisted to remind us all of my attempt to kill guests.

From: Nell Fenton
To: Charlotte Bailey

Reassuring to hear what a cool head you keep in a crisis. Suggest next time something bursts into flame you toss Ana Frid's passport into the fire so she has to stay with you forever.

Mind you, am not beyond reproach myself. In a crazed moment of guilt at uprooting the children, have bought them a kitten. Quite sweet if you like animals which my tenderest admirer could not accuse me of. Not an unqualified success since Rob was so scared of it he spent 2 days on the kitchen table, though it's no bigger than his foot. Anyhow on day 3 he suddenly announced he was going to try holding it after school. 'Holding it' turned out to be sitting on the sofa with a large cushion on his lap and having the kitten placed on the cushion for about 8 seconds by me. Still, I could see the effort it cost him and was v proud of him. This morning I came down in a nightdress with bare legs and the adorable creature scampered up my leg using my bare flesh as purchase for its little needlelike claws. Couldn't shriek and bat it away as I wanted to as I keep assuring Rob it can't hurt him, so gently removed it from my throbbing leg and hobbled upstairs to find some trousers to hide the trickles of blood. Reminded me of a couple of months ago when Michael was in the garden playing with the boys and his smile suddenly became quite fixed. Muttered to me that he had just been stung by a wasp, didn't want Rob to know (would never go outside again if he knew there was a chance he could be stung). Think by the time we have finished bringing Rob up we will both be like some sort of SAS commandos, or perhaps impassive martial arts masters, capable of withstanding terrible pain without reacting . . . Suppose everyone has to have at least one high-maintenance child. At least Josie besotted with the kitten and Ollie mildly diverted.

From: Charlotte Bailey
To: Nell Fenton

ARE YOU COMPLETELY MAD?? You hate animals. You hate them even more than I do & I hate them a lot. Ellie & Maddie constantly nagging for a dog, have explained to them it's never going to happen so instead they must train Hugh to do doglike things. He always eats like a dog anyway & has now become quite proficient at lapping water from a bowl. Will also spend up to 10 mins at a time 'sleeping' in his dog basket (large cardboard box). Had to set parameters when I found him growling, tied to the table leg with a skipping rope round his neck. Now when they take him for a walk they grumble that you don't see real dogs with leads round their middles. Don't like to point out that real dogs tend not to wear jeans & a sweatshirt & break off halfway through 'walkies' to watch Thomas the Tank Engine with juice & a biscuit.

From: Nell Fenton
To: Charlotte Bailey

Wish I'd thought of training one of my children as a dog before getting tiresome cat. Am inexplicably fond of all of them so would be happy to have any one of them as a pet.

From: Charlotte Bailey
To: Nell Fenton

Lou & Walt have made the acquaintance of weirdy neighbour Brian Turner. Saw them talking to him outside the front of the house. The 3 of them made an interesting sight – Lou wearing v high black Prada boots looked about 6' 2'', Walt next to her looked small & menacing in inky-black Gaultier suit with his 'eye scarf' – until you clocked his feet, Birkenstocks with thick pink socks, & then there was Brian, just medium normal-sized but with his outlandishly big woolly head & orange polo neck. Think Brian stopped to talk to them because of Walt's Birkenstocks (that & fact he's unbelievably nosy). What he doesn't realise is Walt is wearing them in an *ironic* way. Lou said Brian is v knowledgeable about historic walks through London & should I ever need any info on said topic he's my man. (Useful as this tip is cannot envisage seeking Brian's advice under any circumstances.)

From: Nell Fenton
To: Charlotte Bailey

Not clear – is it the wearing of Birkenstocks with a suit or wearing the Birkenstocks with thick pink socks that's ironic? Also how can you be sure that big woolly head and orange jumper aren't also intended to be ironic? Seems unlikely that anyone would have either of those things simply because they thought they were attractive. Mind you, saw Suzette this morning in an emerald-green angora sweater with one of those hideous cowl necks, which I suppose proves there's no accounting for taste.

From: Charlotte Bailey
To: Nell Fenton

I am now officially the perfect hostess. To make up for the blow-heater episode, asked Ana Frid, who irons beautifully, to do Lou's laundry for her. Anyway I really don't know how he did it, but somebody slipped my very beautiful new brown leather gloves & 3 stickle bricks into a white wash. Whole wash including a large quantity of Lou's white Hanro vests & knickers & a beautiful Yohji Yamamoto shirt have come out streaked with brown. Gloves obviously completely ruined (like tiny hard leather claws now) but stickle bricks absolutely fine, indeed better than fine, vv clean. Am so embarrassed, I know vests & the shirt particularly would have been really expensive. Even Lou, despite her impeccable manners, could not suppress small involuntary scream when I admitted about the shirt. Have had to spend a lot of time calming down poor Ana Frid who had the misfortune to be the person who put the wash on but as I don't believe she added the gloves & stickle bricks I really don't think she is to blame. We must do about 63 washes a day so why does Hugh pick the one sodding wash with Lou's stuff in it to sabotage?

From: Nell Fenton
To: Charlotte Bailey

I'm surprised with Hugh in the house you haven't trained Ana Frid to search the machine for foreign objects before putting on a wash. The other day I found a crumpled photo, some pebbles, an elastic band and a paper clip in Rob's pocket, all of which I naturally threw away. When he found out what I had done he was furious as apparently I had thrown away all the raw materials he needed to make himself a penknife. Who knew?

From: Charlotte Bailey
To: Nell Fenton

Lou & Walt have checked into a hotel for last 2 days of their visit to everybody's huge relief. It appears that Albert was right & Keith was wrong about the living-room ceiling. Having survived my attempts to kill them by hypothermia and fire I think it was the large clod of plaster that fell from the corner of the living-room ceiling narrowly missing Walt's head that finally did it. Thump of falling clod (& Lou shrieking 'GET OUT, GET OUT, GET OUT') alerted us all to the fact that part of the ceiling was about to come down so we all exited the room before being killed. I think I'm having a failure to cope. Hate this fucking house & want to check into the hotel with Lou & Walt (have become strangely accustomed to the now familiar sound of Lou screaming – but as she is now in a hotel & presumably nothing is catching fire or falling on her head I'm guessing the screaming has stopped). Although it's only the corner of the ceiling the mess is unbelievably terrible, EVERYTHING is thickly coated in gritty white dust even food in the fridge. Even Ana Frid looks depressed.

From: Nell Fenton
To: Charlotte Bailey

You should never have tried to have them to stay. The house is a bit grim now but it's a fantastic and beautiful house and you'll forget the pain like childbirth once you've finished it.

From: Charlotte Bailey
To: Nell Fenton

I suppose you're right. I know it will be finished someday, just don't anticipate it being in *my* lifetime. I think Albert sensed I'd HAD IT when he came in this morning because when he saw the living-room ceiling instead of saying 'I told you so' followed by 'obviously entire house now needs to be pulled down & rebuilt from scratch' he was unusually soothing & even patted my arm & then said it just needed partly cutting out & patching in & it wouldn't take long or cost much & this time he really would give me a quote before he started. Felt my mood lurch from complete despair to tearful relief & gratitude. Have had to replace Maddie's school shoes as we've lost one. So irritating, they were really nice ones I got in Bordeaux in the summer. Hugh acting innocent.

From: Nell Fenton
To: Charlotte Bailey

Lost school shoe nothing in this house. Unless clothes are stapled to Rob's body they're as good as lost. Only November and he's on his second winter coat.

From: Lou Corrigan
To: Charlotte Bailey

Thanks so much for having us to visit – we had a blast! The last two days in the hotel were really boring in comparison and the kids are great, we miss them already. I've mailed a little black shoe I found in my bag – I've no idea how it got in there – sorry! Speak soon x L

From: Charlotte Bailey
To: Nell Fenton

Was reading '7 Habits of Highly Effective People' & Stephen Covey (bald yet effective author) explaining evil of debt & how none of his 57 children have ever borrowed money – always saved to buy stuff, go on trips, etc, anyway got me thinking about how we are going to pay for our trip. Realise 1) there is no way our overdraft can take the strain of 5 transatlantic flights and 2) am not one of Stephen Covey's children, so am investigating possibility of obtaining new credit card (Sainsbury's) in order to finance trip. Will revert when decision re trip is made (by Sainsbury's, not me).

From: Nell Fenton
To: Charlotte Bailey

Delighted that Stephen Covey has at last said something that has actually proved useful though I thought you stopped reading that piece of rubbish after you dropped it in the bath. Needless to say Michael has changed his mind about his car and has decided he needs a giant SUV due to imminent arrival of the snow. Said to him, if only we'd known back in September that it was going to snow this winter we could have saved the bother and expense of changing cars. Was quite pleased with this piece of withering sarcasm, but he declined to answer.

From: Charlotte Bailey
To: Nell Fenton

Stephen Covey wrong about evil of credit card & purveyors of credit like Sainsbury's. Sainsbury's similar to 'Relate' as they will be reuniting a separated family this Christmas. Have provisionally booked flights arriving 17th leaving 29th. Dan will come later. Let me know if those dates don't suit. Actually don't bother as I don't think I can change them.

From: Nell Fenton
To: Charlotte Bailey

Excellent. We are very excited, though Rob and Ollie having some trouble with the concept that your arrival is not going to be today, or at worst tomorrow. Feel warmly affectionate towards Sainsbury's and hate people who don't have credit cards or, worse still, those people who have them and use them wisely.

From: Nell Fenton
To: Charlotte Bailey

Just back from parent night. I thought my heart could not sink any further, but was proved wrong by the appearance of school principal to join our meeting. Not, fortunately, the giant arse (head of whole school) but Mrs Doughty, v sensible if slightly scary woman (head of the lower school). The main concern is Rob's attention span (or rather complete absence thereof). They were very nice about him, Mrs Doughty spoke v affectionately of him, as indeed she should, he being a particularly endearing child. She said he is very complex—well, yar, had noticed that myself as it happens. Anyway the upshot is they want me to take him to an educational psychologist to see if they need to 'modify the school programme for him'. Came out of there feeling absolutely crushed. Struggled as usual to fill the allotted 15 mins re Josie as she, as ever, gives no cause for concern. Even more difficult with Ollie's teacher on account of the fact that greatest challenge he faces at school is not pooing himself (so far 100% success rate).

From: Charlotte Bailey
To: Nell Fenton

Makes you long for the days when your biggest worry was whether your boob tube would stay up at the Bourne Club disco. Try not to worry too much, he's such a lovely boy & clearly bright. (By the way, hats off to Ollie.)

From: Nell Fenton
To: Charlotte Bailey

Have been working v hard on turning the children into proper over-scheduled little Canadians. Josie and Rob do skating on Saturday mornings now. All Canadian children must know how to skate. It's the law (probably), anyhow don't want mine left out and they've been enjoying it even though it's a bit of a shag dragging ourselves out every Saturday morning and lugging all the skates and helmets etc along.

From: Charlotte Bailey
To: Nell Fenton

Sounds irritatingly wholesome to me.

Went shopping for Hugh's birthday yesterday, if only all present shopping this straightforward. Basically everything I bought if it was not a train was something to do with a train. Lots of wooden track from Early Worthy Centre, a couple of trains from there & then some Brio stuff to go with it. Brio invented by marketing genius who makes turntables, tunnels, etc, etc, unavailable elsewhere so obliged to buy the Brio version – genius lies in the pricing, chief executive at Brio factory plucks ludicrously high figure out of thin air, marketing director doubles it & then distributor's wife adds a nought. Net result being Brio engine shed costs about the same as the garden shed Albert is trying to persuade me I need. (Didn't buy it, just marvelled at the price.) Anyway Hugh now kitted out with basic train track a bridge & Brio Thomas the Tank Engine train & tunnel. V excited about giving it to him.

DECEMBER 99

From: Charlotte Bailey
To: Nell Fenton
Re: emergency situation developing

Haven't made/bought & therefore obviously sent out any Christmas cards yet & people keep sending the bloody things to me. Present buying also v much in arrears as was lulled into false sense of security by buying what I thought were loads of presents in October & then doing nothing till now. Checked present drawer yesterday – unfortunately loads turns out to be 3 & none of those particularly great. So now you must quickly tell me what you want & what your offspring passionately want that is also easily available, extremely cheap, light & easy to carry. Dan & I just going to give each other stockings this year – the felt sort filled with thoughtful little gifts not spanky stay-ups for pervy sex (although sure Dan would prefer to give me some of them rather than the waffle iron I am going to ask for – intend to become the sort of person who makes fresh waffles for breakfast). Re Xmas cards – have you received Selena's annual soft-focus photo of her children charading as a Christmas card yet? I haven't & am also eagerly anticipating Annabel's Christmas round robin describing in fascinating detail events of the past year – its highs, its lows, its ups, its downs, its ins, its outs, etc, etc . . . although actually there never are any lows, downs or outs. Last year, best she could manage was burning 50 home-made hot-cross buns intended for Easter fete tea. May have to ring you when it comes, to read it to you, as Dan doesn't derive the proper enjoyment from it. If only she knew how much pleasure her Christmas message brings.

From: Nell Fenton
To: Charlotte Bailey

Am naturally eager to share Annabel's holiday message with you. Christmas very much a time to spread happiness and am therefore delighted to be able to share similar (though email), from Suzette which came this morning. Am of course flattered, though somewhat taken aback to already be in the 'dear friends' category but one shouldn't look a gift horse in the mouth. Think it does add a little extra touch of class to share with her 100 closest friends the coy hints about her marvellously active sex life with Kane. Clearly if one is as attractive as she is, one's husband can't keep off rogering one senseless every 5 mins. Don't suppose this is so in Annabel's case, what with being married to a man of the cloth.

Dear friends

A very merry Christmas and a happy and prosperous New Year to you all. Another year has flown by and Kane and I and our beautiful girls are happy and well. As the years pass we find more and more joy in reflecting on our many blessings and as this year draws to its close we can certainly look back with peace and happiness in our hearts.

The girls are growing up so fast, Sophie is almost as tall as I am now, a real young woman, and they are both so funny and special and continue to do wonderfully well in their studies. We are very fortunate. Sophie is proving to be quite a gifted artist with many of her pictures displayed around her school and Takara is still a very keen gymnast and her coach tells me she shows great promise.

I have taken up horseback riding this year and started learning the saxophone as I am always looking for ways to expand my horizons. Music, of course, enriches the soul and riding is an amazing way to free your mind and refresh your spirit. My instructor is wonderful, though quite a tease. He calls me 'The Red Peril' – I can't think why!!

Kane and I took a fabulous vacation in California in the spring, the first we have had without the girls for some years. We had a great time, wonderful meals, walks along the beach, just spending time together and of course plenty of . . . romance! . . . it was like a second honeymoon and I packed lots of lacy lingerie and very little else, not that Kane needs encouraging in that direction at any time of the year!!

Our menagerie continues to grow since I can never resist an animal in distress, so we now have our two dogs, Buster and Bibi, both great characters. Three cats, Mittens, Lolly and Peetie – they consider themselves very superior to the dogs! We have also inherited a mynah bird called Min who makes us laugh with his tricks and a lizard called Spike who keeps escaping so this house is even crazier than before!

So, dear friends I send you all our warmest holiday wishes. May your tables be laden, your homes warm and welcoming and your dear ones be near you throughout this special season.

Suzette, Kane, Sophie and Takara

From: Charlotte Bailey
To: Nell Fenton
Re: All Things Christmassy

How can I get on her mailing list? Haven't so thoroughly enjoyed reading anything for ages. Glad to hear you're wrong about Sophie and she's not moody and unpleasant but is 'funny and special'. Took Fran to get her Christmas tree this morning (Joe away). She has another driving test next week and says by law of averages she will definitely, definitely pass this time, seemed churlish to mention don't think examiners take the law of averages into account when they decide whether or not you're roadworthy . . . anyway ended up buying a tree for us too. Even though we're coming to you, seemed miserable not to get one at all & the children all desperate for one. Spent the afternoon decorating it – tried not to be too blatantly controlling by immediately rearranging their decorations but instead will wait till they're safely in bed. Hugh's rather catastrophic method of embellishment was to just hold the decoration in the vicinity of the branch he wanted it to go on & then let go. Didn't work very well. So I spent the afternoon sweeping up decorations while he stood behind me going 'uh-oh'.

Got Selena's 'card' this morning, probably hasn't reached you yet so allow me to whet your appetite. This year it's a musical theme with Ariadne playing the lute (no, that is not a typo it really is a lute), Portia on a clarinet/oboe? can't tell really so bloody soft focus & dark (obviously whole scene candlelit) & as the piece de resistance Edwin playing a v manly harpsichord. Do they actually play any of these instruments? Can't decide whether it's worse to set the whole thing up as a gigantic pose or actually make your child learn the lute & harpsichord . . .

From: Nell Fenton
To: Charlotte Bailey

Yes, hard one to call, rather suspect they do actually learn them, after all have with my own eyes seen the girls wearing velvet cloaks with fur muffs. Am obviously now awaiting the card most eagerly. Mind you, not impossible that it came and I never saw it as I walked into the kitchen yesterday to find Michael opening a Christmas card, glancing at it then chucking it in the bin. As I have never yet seen him open anything that came in the post in our 87 years of marriage I was momentarily rendered speechless. When I did recover power of speech I gently enquired how many other cards he had thrown out. Unfortunately I was unable to elicit any useful information as he thought it might be a few but couldn't say who they were from, so now suspect there may be cards to which I have failed to retaliate.

From: Charlotte Bailey
To: Nell Fenton
Re: Christmas Bazaar (I shall be marvellous)

Dan says he is going to kill me as I have become involved in the fundraising committee at school and have volunteered to help run the Christmas bazaar. Am in charge of Christmas decorations stall so schlepped all the way to Old Street to specialist art shop to buy v thin sheet copper & tin with which to make charming leaf decorations (these will be sold on the stall), fingers now bloodied stumps & children & husband sick of me ignoring them while I make v tasteful oak-leaf garlands. Still have to make 100 mini felt stockings & Xmas trees (for children to decorate at the stall), have also promised foreign & therefore pleasingly educational Swedish Christmas bread for the cake stall which Ana Frid is going to show me how to make.

From: Nell Fenton
To: Charlotte Bailey

You are so bonkers, you're the only person on earth who'd go to that ridiculous amount of trouble for a school bazaar, and it's only so everyone will say oh-my-goodness-isn't-she-creative-and-original but secretly they will hate you.

From: Charlotte Bailey
To: Nell Fenton
Re: Hugh's naughtiest day

Bloody hell, Hugh a total nightmare at the moment. No doubt entirely my own fault as I am far too indulgent & practically always laugh at what he has done. Today he surpassed himself. Morning started fine, with a bit of quiet painting until he decided to go 'off-piste' as it were while I was upstairs putting away laundry. Ignored large quantity of sugar paper laid out in front of him & instead lavishly painted the kitchen walls. Paint claims to be washable, true you can wash it but it doesn't bloody well come off. That accomplished, he moved upstairs to busy himself in the living room by stripping the decorations off all the branches he could reach on our Christmas tree. All the while taking experimental bites with his small sharp teeth out of the fake gingerbread men decorations I made last year & mauling apples & satsumas I'd hung up on ribbons. He wisely decided against eating the gingerbread men as they are made from salt dough coloured with coffee (for authentic gingerbread appearance), instead spat bits out all over the living-room floor. His

61

next move – possibly a crude attempt to cleanse palate of vile salt dough/coffee taste? – was to eat most of the chocolates out of Ellie's Advent calendar. Finally (and v dramatically) got so cross about being stopped from eating chocolates he threw Ellie's favourite snow globe so hard he broke it. That done, he rested. What to do?

From: Nell Fenton
To: Charlotte Bailey

He can't help himself, it's the testosterone. V much hope that if I get pregnant again will be a girl as I richly deserve a rest from boys.

From: Charlotte Bailey
To: Nell Fenton
Re: a star is born

Have just returned in triumph from Maddie's nursery play. She was a star (in the literal sense – silver card head band with silver card star on front) & while she had no words to say & didn't appear to join in on any of the songs, morning a glorious success as she managed not to cry FOR ENTIRE DURATION OF PLAY. I, however, compensated by becoming v tearful at moving spectacle of world's weepiest child not actually crying.

From: Nell Fenton
To: Charlotte Bailey

We had a school concert at which there were no references to anything as controversial as the baby Jesus. What it lacked in religious content it made up for in length. Love school concerts. Hours of sitting on your bum listening to indifferent music badly performed. Josie's year only did 3 songs and Rob's only two and while onstage he only stopped fiddling with his willy in order to pick his nose. The bloody teachers have a choir and did 4 songs. Why do they imagine we want to hear them sing???

From: Charlotte Bailey
To: Nell Fenton
Re: Strengthening bread

Perhaps they have lovely voices which you would appreciate if you weren't so filled with bile. I on the other hand have spent a tranquil and fragrant afternoon making quantities of Swedish Christmas bread with Ana Frid & the children for Christmas bazaar tomorrow. While they look absolutely beautiful & delicious (lots of swirly shapes in saffron yellow with shiny egg glaze & raisins) they have the flavour of antiseptic bandages & the consistency & density of cement blocks. Ana Frid all upset & says we can't possibly sell them as they are disgusting. Pointed out to her that we have promised them & don't have time to remake them & also if we position them at back of table, buying public will have to point at them rather than pick them up so will be unaware of their fortifying density until after they have paid for them & by then it will be TOO LATE.

From: Nell Fenton
To: Charlotte Bailey

Food sold at bazaars is supposed to be disgusting, people expect it. Anyhow you could stick a little disclaimer on the bottom of each loaf saying 'Not fit for human consumption – may be used for dressing wounds.'

From: Charlotte Bailey
To: Nell Fenton
Re: Christmas Bazaar (I was not marvellous)

Christmas bazaar a mixed success. Disgusting Swedish bread sold out immediately (crafty placing at back of table ruse 100% successful) though had to avert my eyes whenever I saw any-body gamely trying to eat it (hotly denied any involvement but said marvellous Ana Frid & children entirely responsible). Unfortunately my v tasteful antiqued leaf decorations completely ignored by vulgar masses, so had to buy them all myself. Quite annoying as humiliating & expensive (particularly so as by the end had stopped Albert doing stuff to the house & redirected his energies to the more pressing matter of Xmas garlands), also my hands still covered in tiny cuts. Humiliation turned out to be something of a theme for whole bazaar as had made large colourful poster to advertise fun activity of miniature stocking & tree decorating with words 30p each or 3 for £1. Nobody had actually noticed this v easy to make mistake until Dan turned up he then went round laughing rudely, telling everybody and then actually BROUGHT THE HEADMISTRESS OVER TO SEE THE POSTER. Bastard. (Won't be seeing me naked for quite some time.)

From: Nell Fenton
To: Charlotte Bailey

Well, I volunteered to help at the Christmas party at our church. Turned out to be a sort of (slightly) festive boot camp run by a group of unmarried women, stalwarts of the church, who clearly dislike children. Each child was issued eight tickets, one for each of the stalls. I was on the lollipop tree (a very exciting game of chance in which you stand to win a plastic toy worth almost $1, and at worst you get a lollipop). They had to play the games in a certain order and were only allowed one turn each. This was ferociously enforced. As each game took about two minutes that accounted for about 16 minutes and then there was a lot of wandering around boredly while they waited for our parish priest (who has very ill-fitting false teeth) to come and delight us with Christmas carols badly played on the guitar.

From: Charlotte Bailey
To: Nell Fenton

Hugh Sr, Penelope & Toby came for a pre-Christmas lunch today. For some mad reason (and Dan didn't stop me) decided it was a good idea to have a big dinner party night before (last night). Dinner party inevitably became quite drunken (Fran & Joe involved). Fran even fell over in the road on the way to their car which was v funny, then Joe announced he was also v drunk so they had to walk home with her falling over every 20 steps, cabs impossible to get at this time of year. Dan & I both had fucking awful hangovers this morning – as children in a state of huge excitement in anticipation of visit from gift-bearing grandparents & exciting Uncle Toby, they all woke up extra, extra early. Hangover so bad actually still felt a bit drunk this morning and v dizzy whenever I had to bend over which unfortunately was all the time as we barely cleared up last night & had to load dishwasher, mop floor, etc, before embarking on lunch preparations. Toby on usual form, he's leaving his job in tele-sales (this job lasted a record-breaking 5 months) to travel round the world & write an epic novel. I made hideous mistake of asking why he couldn't keep his job in telesales & write his epic novel from his bedroom in their house in Eastling. I was then subjected to nearly 15 minutes of Toby standing right over me explaining with great passion how you had to FEEL the wind, TASTE the air, SMELL the heat. Toby so v eloquent about living life it seemed rude to interrupt him by doing lowly lunch-related activities such as turning roast potatoes so stood frozen next to the cooker sporting a pair of oven gloves listening to him until Dan came in and said 'Shut up, Toby', and he could SMELL the burning from upstairs. Given that Toby entirely dominated the conversation with his maps and itinerary, lunch v pleasant. Penelope who would be gold medallist if present-buying ever became an Olympic sport had achieved usual v high standard of gift-buying. Children fainting with joy, girls completely Barbied up.

From: Nell Fenton
To: Charlotte Bailey

Can't wait to read epic novel, am sure it's going to be a page-turner. What happened to the kite shop he was going to open? That was a sure-fire winner, always such a demand for kites. Cannot bloody well believe it, Michael and I have to take a driving test, we are only allowed to drive for 2 months on UK licence, so are already driving illegally, bit puzzling if one is safe to drive for 2 months presumably one is safe to drive. Made-up rule by some jumped-up little bureaucrat. Am quite sure that as I have been driving for approx 67 years my bad habits will be so deeply entrenched it will need a rocket launcher to shift them. I am going to get a lesson to be on the safe side. Michael has pooh-poohed my suggestion of a lesson as he is very macho and it is beneath his dignity.

From: Charlotte Bailey
To: Nell Fenton

Lessons probably a good idea as according to Fran (who failed her driving test again) fascist examiners will fail you on the teeniest tiniest most inconsequential detail. Fran absolutely furious about failing & insisting to me that she is a perfectly competent driver. I suggested as next test will be her 4th perhaps she should try simplifying things for herself by taking an automatic test instead & then she can concentrate on not crashing rather than the gears. This amusing little bon mot v ill-timed by me as I think she had post-traumatic test disorder because she burst into tears. Only way I could comfort her was to prove my confidence in her by promising to take her out in my car so she could get a feel of an automatic car. So now have the grisly spectre of having to take Fran out hanging over me. Packing going very badly as Ana Frid has gone back to Sweden for Christmas, so not here to distract Hugh who is driving me mad by 'helping'. Keeps removing things from the case when my back is turned & has just carried off a pile of the girls' pants & put them in the bin. Can't totally blame him though, as he had watched me earlier retrieve a particularly holey pair of Maddie's tights from the case & do the same thing so I expect he just thinks every so often you take something out of the case & throw it away . . . shall have to keep a sharp eye on him. Girls keep bringing me bulky objects that they ABSOLUTELY MUST bring & every time I say no this precipitates much weeping (from Maddie anyway). Ellie handed me a large boxed weaving kit she was given last Christmas & has never even opened & is insisting on bringing it. Too weak to argue any more so have put it in the case just to shut her up – must remember to remove it & hide it when she is in bed. Anyway, any last-minute requests from old Blighty? Perhaps a jar of Marmite that can smash in my case & spread itself over presents & clothes?

From: Charlotte Bailey
To: Dan Bailey

Flight really good, children were fantastic. Amazingly, Hugh really good too, slept quite a lot (v hotly on top of me) & was generally quiet & happy as allowed to watch unlimited telly. Only upset on flight was when Ellie shut her tray with a full cup of orange juice on it & it poured sideways onto crotch of teenage boy next to her & then I had to resist automatic maternal reflex to mop him up. I have managed to forget the bloody buggering travel cot, think I left it in the dining room so you'll have to bring it when you come (DO, however, have Ellie's weaving set). Nell & I have had to fashion Hugh a rather uncomfortable bed out of open suitcase filled with towels & blankets. Hope he stays in it & doesn't mind ridgey bit in the middle too much. Ring me later – just make sure it's not 3 in the morning our time. xxx

From: Charlotte Bailey
To: Dan Bailey
Re: 1st day

Sorry I missed your call (we were out buying Xmas tree) which Nell (not being tree-decorating Nazi like me) is allowing children to decorate themselves under Josie's supervision. Weather not particularly cold & absolutely no sign of snow. Apparently so far it's the mildest winter for last 16 years. Obviously completely my fault for fully kitting out entire family with Arctic snow gear & promising children lots of marvellous snow-related activities. Try phoning later. xxx

From: Charlotte Bailey
To: Dan Bailey

Sorry about abrupt end to phone call last night – Hugh had escaped his suitcase in the basement bedroom, staggered up lethal polished wooden stairs towards kitchen in v slippy sleep suit & appeared in the kitchen. Have now had to erect barricade of boxes in front of his bedroom door to try to stop him escaping. Bed, a monster of our own invention, sure it's incredibly uncomfortable & 6-inch sides not adequate to contain peripatetic 2-yr-old. Children had v exciting communal bath in Nell's jacuzzi tonight, we added a tiny bit of bubble bath which when combined with high-pressure jets of water & many splashing children created giant foam tower that overflowed onto the shiny marble floor. Highly polished marble perfect choice of material for a bathroom floor, as soon as it is slightly wet entire surface becomes rink of death.

Ring me tomorrow. xxx

From: Charlotte Bailey
To: Dan Bailey

Can you bring my knitting & Ellie's hippo? Misses him dreadfully & weaving set no good to cuddle. Also brace yourself as will be ovulating day you arrive. xxx

From: Louise Corrigan
To: Charlotte Bailey
Re: Christmas cheer

Happy holidays! Hope you're having a great time and the

kids are well and not too jet-lagged. Must be wonderful to see Nell and family again. Rang to speak to you in London (forgot you had left already) and got Dan who sounded not like himself and said he was missing you all a lot and didn't know what to do in the evenings. We're really well. Our book is going well and we fired our agent and have a great new one who already has two, possibly three, publishers who are interested. Finally settled on a title, 'Sexetiquette – The Manners and Mores of Modern Mating'. Also, we have signed a deal to write the sex advice column in a new weekly paper called NY Village Views. Walt and I celebrated yesterday by both having a manicure & pedicure at Bliss Spa. It was really fun, sat next to each other on throne seats while it was done, you & Dan must do it next time you come to NY. Send my love to everybody. Speak soon x L

From: Charlotte Bailey
To: Louise Corrigan
Re: Congratulations

Well done, you so deserve it. (Does this make you sexperts?) Love the title of your book, can't wait to read it.

We're having a wonderful time, everything incredibly wholesome & well run & Canadians so polite & welcoming. Extraordinarily, absolutely no snow though, which we're a bit gutted about. Still, cousins v happy to see each other again. Have fallen in love with local mall which Nell has been quite cutting about & have spent about 60% of time in either Gap Kids or fantastic vintage hardware store. Nell's house FABULOUS. Obviously dreadfully naff but warm & comfortable, with climate control 24 hrs a day rather than stupid turn-off at night central heating (although Nell complaining that the glue on all her chairs has died & they are falling apart now they have been removed from damp London smog, also her piano has gone completely weird because of change in atmosphere). Kitchen floor is polished granite & therefore bit of a hazard as Hugh has tiresome tendency to surreptitiously struggle china dishes out of low cupboards when we're not looking and then drop them so they smash (adorable little scamp). You're right about Dan, he's fully aware there is no point to him when we're not around. Always euphoric for 1st day or so after we go off but novelty of WWII videos & Indian takeaways palls quite quickly, leaving him with tragic realisation that there isn't more to life than wiping bums & noses & that is in fact his raison d'etre. Re pedicure/manicure for Dan, unlikely as Dan considers changing his socks the height of good grooming. Have a lovely Christmas Day. I'll phone on your b'day. Love C

From: Charlotte Bailey
To: Louise Corrigan
Re: Happy Birthday

Hope you're having a nice day, tried calling earlier. Have tiny present that I will attempt to sensibly post from here rather than London (flying back tomorrow to host Millennium New Year's Eve party). How was your Christmas Day? Ours fine until the evening, I had spent whole afternoon preparing Christmas dinner with Nell while gradually feeling sicker & sicker, unable to eat it as felt so nauseous, instead sadly watched from sofa until others halfway through meal & then had to rush off to be sick. As Nell's house v open-plan & what doors & walls there are appear to be made of hollow card, vomiting could clearly be heard in dining room. Dan came to check on me & said everyone (apart from Hugh) had gone v quiet & stopped eating . . . hearing anybody throw up superb appetite suppressant.

71

Anyway am fine now & nobody else appears to have got it.
Much love C

From: Nell Fenton
To: Rachel Lockwood

Dear Rachel, how was Christmas? Ours was lovely. Was really
glad they all came out, would have felt v homesick otherwise.
The children were so excited about everything that by Christmas Eve was concerned they might actually burst. V sad to
say goodbye to them all when they left this morning. You'll
definitely have to come and visit at Easter, am eager to encourage the people I am fond of to come and stay, have been
receiving lots of threats of visits from all sorts of grim people.
Being a useless godmother have of course not yet sent Jonathan
a Christmas present. Are aeroplanes still his thing or has he
transferred his affections? Love Nell

From: Rachel Lockwood
To: Nell Fenton

Dear Nell

So glad you had such a nice Christmas. Ours was a bit of
a strain, we went to Jack's parents who are very well
meaning but so formal and uptight it's impossible to
relax. Jack is not himself at all when he's around them,
he adopts this false jollity which frankly makes me want
to kick him. Mind you, I want to kick him most of the
time these days, he's so bloody difficult. His mother also
has many, many little china ornaments dotted around
the place and I can feel the tension coming off her in

waves whenever Jonathan is anywhere near them though he's really good about not touching anything. Jack kept buggering off on walks by himself leaving me in tete-a-tete with his parents. I really don't know why he makes us go there, he doesn't enjoy it any more than me but we had Christmas with Mum and Dad last year so I couldn't say no. They're also terribly disapproving of the amount he drinks – not that it made any difference.

I'm still hoping to come for Easter, though Jack changes his mind about it every time I bring it up which is infuriating. I'm seriously considering coming without him, it would be cheaper and we have no money as usual. Jonathan is still crazy about aeroplanes. I'll let you know as soon as I manage to get my act together about this visit.

Fondest love to all
Rachel xx

From: Charlotte Bailey
To: Nell Fenton

Flight back fine though Ellie complaining of stomach ache & had an upset stomach, awkward as flight v full so had to keep barging to front of loo queues & mime 'child with diarrhoea' to other passengers as Ellie too embarrassed for me to say it. Weather really gloomy & damp here (except in living room where must have been v dry in our absence as my 'no needle drop' Christmas tree has become extremely parched & bald). Would just take it down but need some festive decoration of living room for millennium dinner.

Did you hear about Anna's Christmas? Mum said it was lovely, house v chaotic & untidy but beautifully decorated with handmade paper snowflakes & stars. Unfortunately, fucking Toulouse-Lautrec managed to drag the turkey onto the floor in the 5 secs Mum had her back turned. Hardly ate any as Mum & Anna immediately wrestled it off him. Luckily no one else saw it happen so they just washed it and stuck it in the Aga. Missing drumstick did excite some comment when it came to the table but Anna told everyone it was a disabled turkey & it was rude to comment.

Can't be arsed to think about millennium dinner which is alarming & unlike me. Feel v grumpy & premenstrual. Any snow yet?

From: Nell Fenton
To: Charlotte Bailey

Perhaps you're pregnant, take a test. Poor little Ellie. Next time I see you you must show me how you mime diarrhoea. It is a skill no one should be without. When I flew to South Africa for Charlie and Julia's wedding, Josie had the most awful diarrhoea and went through all the nappies I had brought in about the first three hours. When I asked the air stewardess if they had any spare nappies she smiled helpfully and brought me some newborn nappies which didn't even begin to cover Josie's v chunky two-and-a-half-yr-old bottom. Ironically, she had really bad constipation on the flight home and stood in the aisle crying and saying, 'it won't come down.' I think by the end everyone in the vicinity was rooting for us and felt tremendous relief and satisfaction when a vile smell filled the air.

Massive snowfall last night, by the way.

From: Charlotte Bailey
To: Nell Fenton

Our millennium dinner has become SE London epicentre for all strays & waifs. People keep phoning to ask if they can bring a friend who has nowhere else to go. 'Friend bringing' useful bargaining tool though, got Joe to locate & buy truffles for me, for the savoy cabbage & truffle soup I shall be serving. Truffles & recently divorced, depressive friend will be his & Fran's contribution to the evening. Have recovered my spirits menuwise & am planning v British food (apart from truffles & wine obviously). Terrified that Geraldine despite strict instructions to only bring British cheese will ruin theme by bringing Brie or something. Don't know why I'm going to all this trouble frankly. New Year's Eve so overrated. All that pressure to do something marvellously fun & even worse on the millennium.

JANUARY 00

From: Charlotte Bailey
To: Nell Fenton
Re: New Millennium

How was your New Year's Eve? Ours better than expected, quite jolly really, food a bit horrid though. Most of it ok but partridges v dry & tough although everybody politely denied it. Also v British apple crumble had distinct (and somewhat Continental) garlic flavour as Dan, 'helping', had used a garlicky knife to slice the apples. As predicted the absolute wanker Gil spent the evening trying to grope Fran who in turn spent the evening trying to fight him off without drawing attention to herself as it's so humiliating for Geraldine. He has grown a beard for some part he's doing so is even more unattractive than usual. Geraldine got quite drunk & told me they never have sex any more. Bearing in mind he'd spent the evening trying to mount poor Fran, he's clearly up for it. She told me she is financing a one-man show (he has written himself) at the Edinburgh Festival. Quentin & Marcia spent the night with Rosamund (7 weeks) and Giacomo (3). Found Hugh & Giacomo posting CDs down gaps in the floorboards this morning. Having stopped them doing that, was alerted to next misdemeanour by loud thudding sound and discovered them jumping off the back of the sofa. Have the constant feeling with Hugh that

I am pitting my wits against him to keep him alive. Given his dreadful behaviour at the moment not quite sure it's worth the effort.

From: Nell Fenton
To: Charlotte Bailey

Our New Year's Eve fantastically dull. Feel even more strongly on New Year's Eve than on other nights that I would rather stay in (and I feel it v strongly indeed on other nights as you well know). Anyhow thought it would be too sad and pathetic to do nothing so accepted a party invitation from some rather grand people. They are great patrons of the performing arts and a high percentage of the guests were actors, or theatre reviewers, or people otherwise passionately enamoured of the theatre. Entire evening of conversation therefore about plays I have not seen, would not wish to see, indeed would go to great lengths to avoid seeing. Theatre discussion occasionally interspersed with discussion of recent or forthcoming poetry readings. Why any poetry lover, which I consider myself, would want to go and listen to poems read by some ghastly thespian showing off by reading in that stupid actory way they all have, rather than quietly reading them at home is a total mystery to me. Anyhow drank too much to deaden the pain so have horrible hangover and feel my brain moving loosely around in my head. Broke my own resolution to never make New Year's resolutions and made a resolution not to smack Rob any more as it does no good, really don't believe in it and never smack the others. Anyhow came down this morning and was making breakfast when Rob came up behind me and stuck his finger in my bum. As I was wearing jersey pyjama bottoms he encountered no resistance. Jumped out of my skin and turned around and swatted him. So that's going well.

From: Charlotte Bailey
To: Nell Fenton
Re: fantastic missed opportunity

See, you missed the perfect opportunity when surrounded by so many experts to ask what is the actual point of the theatre as nobody actually REALLY enjoys it, they just like showing off about it afterwards – ever noticed how if someone has been to the theatre they always make a point of weaving it into the conversation, whereas unlikely to be informed if same person has spent a much more enjoyable evening watching Kindergarten Cop. Re New Year's resolutions – as everybody knows 1st 2 weeks don't count as this is an 'adjustment period' until resolution fully kicks in.

From: Charlotte Bailey
To: Nell Fenton

I'm so annoyed, Dan has lent Toby money for his round-the-world trip. He won't tell me how much which makes me think it must be quite a lot. I know Hugh & Penelope have lent him money already & Penelope says Hugh is getting quite fed up & wants him to settle down to something. Toby rang this evening to say goodbye, was v charming & sounded v chipper as one might before 4-month holiday paid for by others. Said he would miss us all terribly & see us in April when he'd completed his magnum opus. Said to Dan afterwards that while obviously I am no expert in these matters suspect sweeping epic novels take more than 4 months to write so he told me not to be a cow & Toby was just being enthusiastic.

From: Nell Fenton
To: Charlotte Bailey

Don't blame you for being pissed off about Toby but as Anna will be glad to tell you, blood is thicker than water and Dan probably worries about Toby and is as anxious as you are for him to reach adulthood. Do think on the balance of probabilities unlikely that he will complete epic novel in 4 months (or indeed at all), but not Dan's fault so don't take it out on him.

From: Charlotte Bailey
To: Nell Fenton
Re: mad neighbour

Forgot to tell you about weirdy neighbour Brian Turner's most recent bonkers preoccupation which has been millennium computer bugs. Came back to stack of barmy letters delivered to all neighbours while we were away. Brian's apocalyptic predictions included failure of all computers leading to pollution of the water system, no food deliveries to shops, no electricity, gas, etc, etc, this in turn would lead to lawlessness on streets as starving, thirsty people (less well prepared than Brian & his tanklike wife Hildegard) would be forced to roam London stealing canned goods from each other. Among list of many recommendations to prepare ourselves for nightmare new millennium were obvious things like buying lots of tinned food, bottled water, candles, etc, etc, but Brian also, more ominously, suggested keeping a baseball bat by the front door to protect supplies from marauding strangers. Anyway saw Brian in our road today – I THINK looking sheepish (though hard to tell through his big woolly beard), brave of him to come out as he looks a complete arse now. (Though must secretly admit do have quite a lot of water & beans stored in cellar.)

From: Nell Fenton
To: Charlotte Bailey

You should have scampered anxiously up to him and enquired if it was safe yet to dispense with the baseball bat you've been keeping by the front door. I did stock up a bit too, I must admit, though I see with much irritation that my plan to only buy stuff that we would eventually use up anyway has failed as I have inadvertently bought loads of tins of baked beans with sausages in instead of plain baked beans, which the children do eat. Am not about to feed them tinned sausages, God knows what horrendous mechanically recovered body parts go into them.

From: Charlotte Bailey
To: Nell Fenton
Re: FRAN HAS CRASHED MY FUCKING CAR

Well, not so much crashed it as driven it in slow motion (while I shrieked instructions at her) into some railings outside St Margaret's. My car is ok, bumper just a bit scraped, unfortunately my nerves & railings are not. Definite dent in railings which unlike my nerves can't be fixed with large stiff drink. Fran is possibly the world's worst driver. She drives incredibly slowly while giving the impression of being recklessly out of control. Can't believe she isn't grateful DVLC allow her to take the test let alone entertain deranged notion she might one day pass it. Fran v indignant about 'railings episode' (too much of an indictment to call it a crash). She says they 'came at her'. Pointed out to her that if you head towards a stationary object it does tend to 'come towards you'.

From: Nell Fenton
To: Charlotte Bailey

You must be mad to let her drive your car. The roads are, after all, full of people and objects that can 'come at you' quite suddenly when you drive towards them.

We've decided to go to Cuba in March when the children have 2 weeks off school. Really looking forward to it. Only a couple of hours flight from here and looks fab in the brochures. Am very much not enjoying the cold and the snow and there are months to go yet.

From: Charlotte Bailey
To: Nell Fenton

God, how fantastic, am vv jealous. Weather miserable & grey here, not even interesting & snowy.

From: Nell Fenton
To: Charlotte Bailey

Have spent the last 3 days ferrying Rob downtown to see the school's recommended educational psychologist. Her main finding, $1800 and many man hours later, seems to be that he is a lovely boy. Glad that's sorted. Actually am quite cheered up, she doesn't seem to think there's much wrong. Insofar as I can decipher the very vague recommendations she has made, I think she has told me I am too pushy with him, but all couched in such euphemisms that quite hard to tell. She is concerned about his fears which she thinks are a bit extreme so has referred us to someone else. Yippee.

From: Charlotte Bailey
To: Nell Fenton
Re: money well spent

Suppose better to spend $1800 being told your son is lovely rather than not, though I would have happily told you he was v nice for $1000. Are his fears really that extreme? I know he's quite anxious but he seemed fine at Christmas.

From: Rachel Lockwood
To: Nell Fenton

Dear Nell

How are you all? One of my (many) New Year's resolutions was to email you at least once a week, which as you can see I have already failed to do.

I redecorated our bedroom (another resolution) but discovered quite quickly that something as apparently straightforward as hanging wallpaper is entirely beyond my capabilities. It looks dreadful, all wonky and the top was very messy too but I hid that by sticking on a frieze. I wasted so much wallpaper it probably wouldn't have cost much more to get a proper decorator to do it. At least Jonathan has been full of praise and says it looks beautiful.

I'll email next week without fail.

Fondest love to all
Rachel xx

From: Charlotte Bailey
To: Nell Fenton
Re: imminent arrival of nephew/niece

Spoke to Tom & then Maude this evening. Maude sounding remarkably cheerful despite being enormous & having awful backache. Tom says M has become source of great hilarity on streets of Paris, as she does not look at all pregnant from behind but absolutely gigantic from side & front as though someone has stuffed v large beach ball up the jumper of a thin normal person. All Parisian women have weeny babies and therefore nothing so inelegant as a stretch mark. Maude's girth regarded with incredulity & ill-concealed horror by the pouty Frenchwomen at her antenatal class. Apparently these classes complete opposite of NCT ones she did in London before she had Betsey. Whereas in UK any pain relief during childbirth is seen as huge failure, in France you're seen as complete idiot if you don't have whatever's going plus un pichet de vin rouge during labour (may have made that bit up). M sends you her love & says email her as she is too fat to go out & therefore v bored.

From: Nell Fenton
To: Charlotte Bailey

Poor Maude. Once your due date is past, time defies all the laws of the universe and practically comes to a standstill.

Had to take a theory test on driving today to qualify to take my road test. So many years since I have taken any kind of test (other than a pregnancy test) was more nervous than for my law finals. Managed to pass though there were questions that were not in the stupid book you're supposed to learn

83

from. Didn't know the answer to what a blue flashing light signifies (snowplough apparently), also a section on hand signals that I got all wrong. Since this is no longer the 1940s who the bloody hell uses hand signals when they are driving? At least the sort that signify an imminent manoeuvre.

From: Charlotte Bailey
To: Nell Fenton

Bloody hell what a nightmare. Always considered one of the very few advantages of being aged was that since I took my driving test in the olden days, at least didn't have to sit ghastly theory test. (Hand signals in Canada particularly fine idea, isn't it always minus 27?)

From: Nell Fenton
To: Charlotte Bailey

More or less, am sick of being frozen and this week I went with Rob on a school ski trip. He started skiing last week and really didn't like it much and I can't blame him, too many in the class and it was so bitterly cold, freezing wind blowing all day, so this week I offered to go along for moral support. Stood all day in the unspeakable cold, anyhow by lunchtime he said he liked it a bit better so I thought it was all worth it, then at the end of the day he went up on the button lift and as he got off one of the lift seats hit him on the back of the head and knocked him over. He was so upset, and you know Rob, not one to dismiss an injury lightly so don't know how I'm ever going to persuade him to go back. Also honestly don't know if I'll ever get warm again.

From: Nell Fenton
To: Charlotte Bailey

Michael is in the world's worst mood. Been stamping blackly round the house for about 3 hours, smouldering silences broken occasionally by explosive indictments of all things Canadian. He took his driving test and failed on just about everything, including incorrect use of the brakes when parallel parking?? Haven't seen him so furious in ages.

From: Charlotte Bailey
To: Nell Fenton

Good grief, how dreadful for Michael, told Dan who was horrified, he will call Michael to say something blokeish and supportive. Failing driving test complete torture for a man, sure Dan would much prefer to have a public announcement that he secretly wears a bra and panties under his clothes than a suggestion that he is anything less than a brilliant driver.

From: Nell Fenton
To: Charlotte Bailey

I have bought Rob a hamster for his birthday to try and build up his confidence with animals and Josie was so longing for one I got her one too. Much more expensive than you'd think. The hamsters themselves are cheap but the cages and all the equipment are not and I don't think I need remind you that two hamsters cannot share a cage. Cat seems pretty determined to eat them, keep finding her sitting on top of the cages.

From: Charlotte Bailey
To: Nell Fenton
Re: forgiving & forgetting

I think I was probably 4 or 5 when I put your hamster in with
Anna's & as you well know I thought they were just 'playing'.
How was I to know it was a fight to the death? I think it is time
for you to LET GO & MOVE ON.

From: Nell Fenton
To: Charlotte Bailey

I had my pre-test driving lesson, v nice instructor, but as I
predicted there are lots of stupid rules and my bad habits are
v hard to break. Michael has cheered up a bit as 3 of the other
English imports in his office have also failed their tests and
one was told he wasn't going to be doing the highway part of
the test as his driving wasn't safe enough. This is a bloke whose
hobby is driving across continents. Michael much soothed by
suffering of his colleagues.

From: Nell Fenton
To: Charlotte Bailey

I SIMPLY CANNOT FUCKING BELIEVE IT. I have failed
my fucking driving test, and not only have I failed, but I failed
before I got out of the driving-test car park. This was because
there was a stop sign, and road was completely clear so I
slowed the car to a standstill but didn't actually stamp down
on the brake and give the instructor a whiplash injury with
my 'stopping'. To make it a worse torture I was 99.9% sure I
had managed to fail before getting onto the road, but a tiny

unquenchable flame of optimism continued to burn in my breast till the bitter end so it was still a blow when he told me. He was quite nice actually and sat quite patiently listening to the stream of expletives with which I greeted the news. I absolutely refuse to take that test again so shall now drive illegally. I am a far better driver than most Canadians, they have no concept of obeying the overtaking rules on the highway so it's the most alarming free-for-all and they have loads of awful accidents.

From: Charlotte Bailey
To: Nell Fenton

Fuck a stoat. Would definitely fail my driving test if I took it now. This morning reversed v publicly (& hard) into post outside Ellie & Maddie's school. Fran EXTREMELY sympathetic about you failing your test and says this proves the fact that perfectly good drivers (like herself) can fail.

From: Nell Fenton
To: Charlotte Bailey

Hamsters are possibly the worst pets in the world. Gave in to the children's desperate pleas to have the cages in their bedrooms though it seemed very unhygienic and disgusting to me. Not only are they utterly boring all day, being fast asleep, they are then highly active and noisy all night, running endlessly on their bloody hamster wheels, so they are now banished to the basement. They also nip you all the time so I have bought the children cotton gloves to handle them but so far no luck persuading Rob to pick his up. So my plan that he would gain confidence and learn to love his little furry companion has been remarkably unsuccessful and if he is ever going to even touch the vile little creature, I am going to have to tame it for him, and animal lover that I am I believe perhaps rodents are my very favourite.

What should I get Maddie for her b'day?

From: Charlotte Bailey
To: Nell Fenton
Re: Maddie's birthday

I'm having a little dressing table with fairy lights round the mirror made for her. Have been very crafty all week threading brightly coloured love beads onto florist wire, to make flowers to go round light. Looks lovely so far but have loads more to do & v time-consuming. You could get some accoutrement to go with the dressing table, anything as long as it's pink or glittery.

From: Charlotte Bailey
To: Nell Fenton
Re: birthday preparations out of control

I have abandoned all pretence of looking after children & doing housework in favour of getting ready for Maddie's birthday party this w/e. She is having a kings & queens party. Albert who dropped in to fix a leaking tap ended up making her a fabulous throne from a kitchen chair and some MDF. Meanwhile, in between making sodding wire flowers (why did I ever start?), I've been sewing 2 royal dresses and a prince's outfit for Hugh, also one very sumptuous red velvet cloak lined with purple satin trimmed with what would have been ermine if I hadn't got Dan to do the black dots on the white fur, not so much dots as great big walnut-sized splodges. Really annoying as now the cloak looks like it is trimmed with Dalmatian. Am now on the home run, making drawstring satin party bags while bewildered Ana Frid has been instructed to substitute ironing with cutting out golden crowns from cardboard for children to decorate with stick-on jewels when they arrive. Had to have jewels sent express as had ordered them too late to be on time for party, might as well have bought real emeralds, the amount they're costing.

From: Nell Fenton
To: Charlotte Bailey

Sounds fab, and glad to see you're maintaining your usual high levels of barminess.

From: Thomas de Witt
To: Charles de Witt; Anna Hobbes; Nell Fenton; Charlotte Bailey
Re: new niece . . .

Lily born this morning at 4.37am
4.55 kg
55 cm
face like a monkey
Maude fine
more later
love Tom

From: Charlotte Bailey
To: Nell Fenton

Spoke to Maude this morning, said she'd rung you back but as usual got your bloody answerphone. Anyway sounded v elated & thrilled with Lily who she says is gorgeous in a simian sort of way. Said labour was ok until she got to transition which was really awful & then she went a bit mental & bit Tom's hand, also had to have loads of stitches on account of Lily having a giant's head. Betsey is delighted to have a sister. Tom emailed me some photos which you must have too. Told Maude I thought Lily looks like Tattoo from 'Fantasy Island'.

From: Nell Fenton
To: Charlotte Bailey

If that's the midget who was also in James Bond and said 'de plane! de plane!' then I agree. Mind you, monkey-face or not I feel quite envious, really want another baby.

From: Charlotte Bailey
To: Nell Fenton
Re: time well spent

Maddie absolutely thrilled with her dressing table & kept saying 'It's not Ellie's, it's actually mine.' The flowers looked lovely, until we turned the fairy lights on, that is. Unfortunately as I am not a great inventor in ilk of James Dyson had not foreseen that when the lights are left on for more than a few minutes at a time the heat from the bulbs (which is v efficiently conducted via the central metal washers) melts all the glue holding the petals together. Maddie had left the lights on while they went upstairs to brush their teeth. Came back down to find Hugh with a cereal spoon poking at the mixture of hot melting glue, florist wire & love beads dropping off metal washers onto the dressing-table top. Removed Hugh & glue-covered spoon & turned off lights. Amazingly Maddie completely calm while I (suppressing strong urge to weep) did lots of 'never mind, darling, I'm sure we can fix it!' (absolutely no idea how).

From: Charlotte Bailey
To: Nell Fenton
Re: epic (Indian) novel still at garnering stage.

Got a letter from Toby today. He has fallen head over heels in love with India & has decided to stay there & set his sweeping epic novel in India & Pakistan. Said he hadn't done much writing yet but lots of 'thinking & garnering information'. Sent us some photos of himself looking v brown wearing jubbah & riding an elephant. Children terribly excited to see Uncle Toby on an elephant, in a dress.

From: Nell Fenton
To: Charlotte Bailey

Toby's novel reminds me of the novel Rob is planning to write. Came to me in great excitement having thought of v thrilling title: 'The Crystal Wave'. Had to help him make his book – 8 sheets of paper in a cardboard cover with v dramatic writing for the title and some boldly drawn waves, but so far no actual text.

FEBRUARY 00

From: Charlotte Bailey
To: Nell Fenton
Re: Kings & Queens

Maddie's party was today, it nearly killed me. Hugh's prince's outfit made him look like Liberace, think he sensed this as v annoyingly wore it for about a nanosecond before crying & trying to take the trousers off. Also hired a helium canister with the brilliant idea of filling the house with a kazillion balloons. Unfortunately decided to economise when it came to buying the balloons, thinking all balloons are the same (they're not), discovered that if you buy cheap balloons & fill them with helium, after about 5 mins they are just little shrivelled balloon corpses lying all over the floor. Quite staggered by how rude & badly brought up some of the children are. Think when you have been to the trouble & expense of a children's party, you should be allowed to give at least one child a damn good thrashing. I choose Hamish Hunt, ghastly little toerag AND Maddie doesn't even like him, I only invited him to be kind – won't bother next time. Dan said afterwards he wanted to lie down in a darkened room cradling a bottle of red wine.

From: Nell Fenton
To: Charlotte Bailey

Always at least one child at parties that would benefit enormously from a thrashing and on the subject of ghastly little toerags, I find the boys of Rob's age here are spectacularly ill-mannered – a well-behaved child is definitely the exception. They just go and open up your fridge and help themselves to what they fancy, or get up from the table during a meal and go and turn on the telly when they've had 3 mouthfuls, the concept of staying at the table until the meal is ended is completely alien, very worst is a new friend of Rob's called Brandon (v unattractive – big red lips and small pinched nose). He came round and was horrified that Rob doesn't have a PlayStation, clearly had lost any ability to just play and suddenly announced he was fed up and opened the front door and ran down the street. Completely ignored me when I called him back so I had to chase the evil little sod and half carry him back into the house (resisting a strong impulse to drag him by his hair). Called his parents and said I didn't think he was enjoying himself and mercifully they came and got him quite quickly.

From: Charlotte Bailey
To: Nell Fenton
Re: Dummy Fairy hopelessly unreliable

Maddie has given up her bedtime dummy. She got a letter from the dummy fairy last weekend explaining now she was turning 4 it was (horribly overdue) time to give it up. What you have to do is leave your dummy out for the dummy fairy to take away & then a week later the dummy fairy brings you a present. Maddie keeps saying 'It must be a week by now' & it has been but the dummy fairy is unable to remember to go & get her a present so have to keep saying things like 'ooh yes, nearly'.

From: Nell Fenton
To: Charlotte Bailey

The dummy fairy is probably out drinking with the tooth fairy who I find very sluttish and forgetful after a couple of glasses of wine and who on more than one occasion has failed to fulfil her fairy duty.

Bit worried about Rachel, I sent her two emails and I haven't heard back. I spoke to her on the phone a couple of weeks ago and thought she sounded really depressed, she insisted she was fine, though fighting a lot with Jack.

From: Charlotte Bailey
To: Nell Fenton

Don't worry so much, it's just that sort of marriage and she's so busy she probably hasn't even read your emails. Meanwhile, good news on the dummy fairy front. She finally sobered up enough to get Maddie small furry blue box which she's thrilled with.

Not pregnant as usual, can't whine about it to Fran as it encourages her to suggest alternative remedies.

From: Nell Fenton
To: Charlotte Bailey

Well, you can't whine about it to me either, I've been trying for longer than you. I know what you mean about Rachel but I think this sounds worse than usual.

The children have a long weekend coming up and we have booked into a ski resort. Since I last skied 20 years ago and Michael even longer, we will no doubt both prove to be a great embarrassment to them all. Josie told Takara we were going and I almost fainted with horror because Suzette then phoned to suggest it might be fun if we all went together. Quite apart from my personal feelings on the matter, though Michael is not a violent man there's no telling what he might do if he heard we were spending a weekend with Suzette and Kane. Had to pretend there was something burning on the stove so I could hang up and get my head together. Quickly phoned Michael but he said nothing useful, just did a lot of swearing. Finally called back and said while it sounded like a lovely idea we had promised the children that this was going to be a very special family time, we'd never gone skiing together before, so not this time but perhaps next time, etc, etc . . . Suzette's voice became very gentle and understanding at this and she said something beautiful about the importance of families sharing new experiences. Now if we ever want to go skiing again will have to do it in the utmost secrecy.

From: Charlotte Bailey
To: Nell Fenton

Pan burning ploy vv clever but 'special family time' absolutely inspired.

From: Nell Fenton
To: Charlotte Bailey

Have discovered Valentine's Day here is an occasion of the most spectacular vulgarity. The fuss is amazing and every child gives a valentine card to every other child in the class regardless of gender, but to avoid the expense of buying proper cards they produce themed valentine card boxes which contain about 30 very small, very cheap little cards and a slightly larger, though equally cheap and nasty card for the teacher on such romantic subjects as Scooby-Doo, Barbie, Hot Wheels, etc. You then have the tedium of having to write out the cards to every child, Josie did her own, Rob got fed up after about 4 and so I forged his, and obviously I had to do Ollie's. Between them they have brought home about 75 cards which I will have to sneak into the bin bit by bit.

From: Charlotte Bailey
To: Nell Fenton
Re: Ah! what is love

You are so nasty & cynical. I think it's wonderful that with a simple little gesture like a Scooby-Doo card you can send out a heartfelt valentine's message that we cherish & love one another. I used a subtler method of showing my love for Dan. By simply doing nothing at all I demonstrated that

Love is not love
Which alters when it no luxury Belgian chocolates finds,
Or bends with the remover to remove.
O, no! It is an ever-fixed mark,
That looks on cuddly toys holding love hearts and is never tempted, etc, etc . . .

So now he knows I really love him & I'm not going to besmirch our love with a card or tawdry gift.

From: Nell Fenton
To: Charlotte Bailey

Just got back from our long weekend up north. The skiing was absolutely brilliant fun and have to say I was quite good. Michael was much less controlled than me and this combined with his substantial size and weight made for a terrifying cocktail and if there was anything to spoil the weekend it was the vision of this large hurtling object mowing someone down and the ensuing lawsuit. At one point he shot across the slope so fast he skied off the piste and part-way up a tree. Fortunately he was unhurt, and brought much enjoyment to a number of observers. We also went snowshoeing in the woods, really lovely but not easy. At one point we were standing looking at a frozen waterfall and a stack of snow on the tree above Josie just slid off and landed on her head. Not your wimpy English amount of snow, this was like a wheelbarrow full of snow, and poor Josie got a real shock and I proved conclusively that I am a very bad mother because I laughed. Had to then spend 10 minutes being sympathetic, scooping snow off her and apologising. We also went dog sledding, very expensive and supposed to be a great treat. Dog sledding is one of those once-in-a-lifetime experiences insofar as if you have done it once you know better than to ever do it again. Why is it so awful? Let me count the ways. I had visions of us all sitting on a sled driven by some hoary old Canuck, being whisked across the crisp snow, our cheeks glowing, etc . . . in fact, after some very, very cursory instructions, totally inadequate for something that requires quite a lot of skill, you are given your own dog team to drive. The dogs are by no means tame domestic dogs, they live outside year-round and have lots of rivalries going on so constantly snarling and snapping at each other, so the boys were really scared of them. I had Ollie and Rob sitting in my sled and Michael had Josie in his. To drive it you stand on a thin little bar at the back and hold two handles, on any uphill slope you have to take your feet off and run behind (so exhausting too) but NEVER let go the handles. Felt the necessity of compliance with this part of the instructions very keenly, as apparently if you let go, the dogs will run off and frankly I didn't trust them not to eat my sons given the chance. One of the things they stress is that the teams must not draw alongside one another as the dogs start fighting, so if the team in front slows down you must slow down too. This was something I managed to master, unfortunately the absolute arse behind me (pale weedy little man with pale weedy little children) couldn't manage it so his dogs kept pulling alongside mine, and the minute they did they'd all start snarling and trying to bite one another. As the boys were sitting on the sled at dog level they were terrified. The very best part, however, was that because the dogs live outside in such extreme temperatures they eat enormous quantities so they just crap all the time. They do it as they are running so every couple of minutes a turd flies out. The beauty of it is you have all the crap from your own team and the teams ahead to run through and better still the dogs' scrabbling paws cause little blobs to fly up, so I looked down at one point and Ollie had a ball of dog shit on the front of his jacket. I think even someone less squeamish than me would have been horrified at that. At this point I drew upon previously unknown levels of skill and dexterity. While continuing to drive a fast-moving dog sled I managed to remove my glove, reach into my pocket, extract a wet wipe, lean forward and swipe the dog shit off him.

From: Charlotte Bailey
To: Nell Fenton

Whole w/e sounds fantastic & if you are going to get dog poo on you might as well do it in an exciting way instead of just walking through it on a London pavement. Josie's dramatic snow-dump episode has very much captured the girls' imaginations and they have both drawn her cards of condolence.

From: Nell Fenton
To: Charlotte Bailey

I am so, so sorry about Hugh, poor little thing and poor, poor you. Dan said you'd be back from the hospital later, so I'll give you a call then. He said you were very wobbly so I recommend you have a large brandy, had one when I got home from the hospital when Rob had his first seizure, and I hate spirits. Very steadying though.

From: Charlotte Bailey
To: Nell Fenton
Re: world's most inadequate mother

Sorry about abrupt end to phone call – just to add to general chaos Maddie shut her fingers in the loo door. Hugh much better now but had the worst night of my life, he's had a cold for a couple of days (nothing exceptional) but on the third day – yesterday – his breathing just seemed noisier & faster than usual. Had no idea what it was, just thought it was a noisy cold. Put him to bed as usual but when I went up myself he seemed so miserable brought him into bed with me. By this time the sound & speed of his breathing was alarming so rang the Dr to the usual background of Dan saying 'He's FINE.' (Would be interested to see what would constitute not being fine. Possibly severed head?) Anyway callout Dr arrived & was obviously furious with us (lazy neglectful parents), told us he was having a moderate to severe asthma attack (when she said this felt like someone had poured ice-cold water down my back). Was too cowed & upset to say if you have absolutely never seen asthma it's difficult to recognise. Told us we should move out of the house till the work was finished (so that'll be for the next 10 yrs) as it was very possibly the dust causing the asthma. Asked us if we smoked in same tone as you might ask someone if they were a child abuser. Although able to say no to smoking would have said yes to an accusation of child abuse for ignoring Hugh's symptoms all day. Anyway she nebulised him (an inhaled cocktail of drugs), he was better after that but not fantastic. Dr told us to watch him overnight & if he deteriorated take him to casualty or call her again. Spent the rest of the night lying next to him rigid with fear listening to him breathe. Dr rang at 4 am to check he was ok which I thought was impressive. Took him to the GP this morning who sent us on to casualty. Spent most of the day in casualty and thought we might have to stay the night as his blood oxygen was 91% but then just before the registrar came round his blood oxygen went up to 97% so they let us out. He is much better now & sleeping in our bed. Dan went out & bought all this special anti-dust-mite bedding, you zip everything into these stiff plasticky covers so every time he moves it sounds like he is rolling about on top of a giant packet of crisps (should be fun when we get in there with him). Everybody has been incredibly kind. Albert terribly upset when Ana Frid told him about Hugh and hoovered & mopped all the floors. He is v asthmatic himself (almost impossible to believe since he smokes). Only possibly good news is registrar said we should not assume it is asthma, at this age could just as easily be a bronchiole infection. Was supposed to be doing my godmotherly duty & arranged with Anna to have Isabel to stay this w/e. I'd promised to take her shopping with Ellie. Don't know what to do now as I can't leave Hugh with Dan, don't trust him to be as neurotic as me. Glad I'm not pregnant after all as I feel I'm failing to look after the children I already have, certainly don't need to add another one to the equation.

From: Nell Fenton
To: Charlotte Bailey

I wish I was around to help, I'm sure you're worn out. Try not to worry too much, if there's a next time you'll know what to expect and what to do. I was moderately calm about Rob's second seizure and he didn't even have to stay overnight at the hospital, whereas the first time I really thought he was dying. Re Isabel, I bet she'd like to come anyway but don't go out shopping, not because you can't trust Dan but because you'll be miserably anxious all day and it isn't worth it.

From: Charlotte Bailey
To: Nell Fenton

I wish you were around too. I've been fine for help though – everyone has been so nice. Fran has been brilliant, always excellent in a medical emergency as she owns a medical textbook called something like 'Which Disease?'. She has been really practical & soothing and hasn't suggested any stupid alternative remedies. Came round last night when Hugh was asleep to listen to his breathing because I was worried about it. Anyway she said it was fine & she knows about asthma as Nathan had it quite badly when he was little although he's now grown out of it. Haven't decided about Isabel, will ring Anna later.

From: Rachel Lockwood
To: Nell Fenton

Dear Nell

I'm so sorry for the long silence. Anyhow I've finally managed to make a decision (an increasingly rare event these days) and have booked to come and visit you. Jack says he has too much work so it'll just be Jonathan and me but it's probably a good idea for Jack and I to have a bit of a break from each other anyway. We'll be there from the 19th April to the 30th. We're looking forward to it so much.

Fondest love to all
Rachel xx

From: Nell Fenton
To: Rachel Lockwood

Dear Rachel, I'm so delighted you're coming, can't wait to see you. Sorry Jack can't come but it might have been a bit boring for him anyway, Michael will be working most of the time so perhaps it's for the best. Send me your flight details nearer the time so I have less opportunity to lose them and I'll pick you up at the airport. Love Nell

From: Charlotte Bailey
To: Nell Fenton
Re: plan to kidnap Isabel

I did have Isabel to stay this w/e, Hugh much, much better

and thought it would be too disappointing to cancel her visit. I decided against the shopping trip though. Instead we took them all to the Lansbury for lunch & then to the zoo. Unfortunately the Lansbury which is usually pretty dead on a Sat lunch apart from a couple of families was quite busy & quite a few people were smoking, so spent much of the time standing outside with Hugh to avoid the smoke while everyone else very slowly finished their lunch. Not too bad initially but then of course it started raining so I was cowering in the doorway with Hugh in my arms while lots of surprised-looking pubgoers pushed past me to get inside out of the rain. Isabel very sweet & appreciative, also amazingly helpful. I had just put the children in the bath when the phone rang. Asked Isabel to watch them while I quickly answered it. By the time I came back after a brief conversation she had washed all 3, got them out of the bath & was putting a nappy on Hugh. Quite extraordinary. Think it must be a result of being one of 5 & effectively bringing yourself up. Must ring Anna & ask if I can have her permanently.

From: Nell Fenton
To: Charlotte Bailey

They are all remarkably self-sufficient children, but then they need to be, Anna's so laid-back she's virtually horizontal. Mind you, there is much to be said for it, I'm so hideously controlling I do everything for the children and am slowly atrophying what little ability they have to do anything for themselves. Odd to think Anna and I both sprang from the same gene pool really. Finally heard from Rachel – she and Jonathan are coming at Easter without Jack. Pretended to be disappointed but am quite relieved really. Rachel loyally said he has too much work by which she meant he's being too much of a wanker at the moment.

From: Charlotte Bailey
To: Nell Fenton

Told you not to worry about her. Glad she's coming out, it'll probably do her good to get away from him for a bit.

I'm taking Ellie to Paris to visit Tom, Maude, Betsey & new baby Lily. Hoping a bit of time on her own with me will have miraculous effect on her vile behaviour. Like having stroppy premenstrual teenager in the house at the moment. Everything a major scene, am exhausted by trying to predict her next mood swing. Hugh on the other hand entirely predictable insofar as you can absolutely count on him to do the daft thing. Got hold of my sharpest scissors today & despite being quite uncoordinated has given the mophead quite a vicious haircut.

From: Nell Fenton
To: Charlotte Bailey

At least it was only the mophead. Rob came home the other day with a substantial chunk of hair missing from the side of his head. Apparently he got some Blu-Tack in his hair at school and Alexandria, one of the girls in his class, had come to his assistance and cut it out for him. Was really annoyed and not even as if Blu-Tack would have been that hard to get out. Give Tom and Maude my love.

From: Charlotte Bailey
To: Nell Fenton
Re: Paris trip

New baby Lily vv sweet & trip to Paris was a great success.

Arrived on Friday & had lunch at Tom & Maude's flat & afterwards went toy shopping in the Marais. On Sat we went to the Jardin des Tuileries & Ellie & Betsey went on the trampolines, then we had strengthening hot chocolate at Angelina's. Afterwards went on this giant Ferris wheel while Tom waited on the ground with Lily. Whole experience most quintessentially French part of w/e as Ferris wheel complete death trap. I don't think anyone could accuse me of being particularly fussy about safety but we were swinging in a v brisk wind about 150 ft above the ground in this tiny carriage with the most unbelievably flimsy door which I'm absolutely certain would have opened had anyone fallen against it. Ellie & Betsey, oblivious to possibility of imminent death, kept jumping around so we had to keep shrieking at them to sit down (naturally nothing sensible like seat belts provided). Took everybody out for lunch after, to a restaurant specialising in andouillettes that somebody from Tom's office had recommended. Not entirely successful, although the first courses were quite nice (being andouillette-free). The sausages themselves ranged from pretty horrible to absolutely disgusting. Tom was the outright winner as had ordered one called 'Le Fermier Giles' described on the menu as 'le plus rustique du tout'. Although Tom said afterwards nothing could have prepared him for the taste, its appearance & smell really should have, a smell that only got worse when he cut into it – then all this stinking barely chopped intestine flopped out onto the plate. Tom courageous enough to order it but not enough to eat more than a tiny bit of it, which in the event was fortunate as the raging diarrhoea he had all evening would no doubt have been considerably worse had he eaten more. Was v apologetic to Tom about consequences of lunch but as he pointed out restaurant had been his choice & at least the meal was memorable . . . Left on Sunday after gigantic breakfast in café near Tom & Maude's flat (Tom unable to attend).

From: Nell Fenton
To: Charlotte Bailey

Tom incapable of learning by experience. He always has to be so gastronomically daring, he'll kill himself one of these days. Only person I know who'd eat sheep's head by choice.

From: Charlotte Bailey
To: Nell Fenton

Got another letter from Toby today. He's been in Goa for the last month living right on the beach. Think he must still be garnering information as he made no mention of how the novel was going. Letter vv long and much of it incomprehensible as he had failed to use any punctuation and only occasionally a verb. From the one bit that made partial sense gathered he is feeling very inspired and has 'hooked up' with someone called Ramon/Ramone – couldn't quite make the name out as his writing was really wonky too. He sent more photos, one of Ramon/Ramone (who has a really big chin) up a palm tree, even with a photo still couldn't tell if he/she was male/female, other photo was of v big rubbish tip.

MARCH 00

From: Charlotte Bailey
To: Nell Fenton
Re: interesting family

Had Mum's birthday dinner last night after which I am able to pass on some very wise thoughts. Pasta with a lemon & Parmesan sauce tastes exactly as though somebody has been a little bit sick over a bowl of spaghettini (fortunately was just the pasta course of quite substantial Italian meal so were able to forgo it with no ill effect though Mum battled on bravely, murmuring that it was delicious, until I removed her plate & threw it away as a special birthday treat) AND we have all become the most frightful bores about our children. Lots of topping each other's anecdotes about how brilliant/stupid/large/small our children are & since there are a lot of us & many children to discuss this took v substantial part of the evening. Mum was really pleased with all her presents. I gave her some fancy sable paintbrushes but the best present was Anna's, she'd drawn the most exquisite pen & ink family tree with everybody's names on leaves. As she was doing it till the last minute before she & Geoffrey left & he was hooting in the drive for her, she just ran out & grabbed v elegant Tesco carrier bag in which she'd put her overnight stuff & dumped it on the back seat. Was only as they approached London & she leant back to get her make-up out she discovered she'd brought 2 loaves of bread & a packet of ham.

From: Nell Fenton
To: Charlotte Bailey
Re: Ollie definite front runner

On the small-child front I could certainly have trumped everyone, have just taken Ollie to the doctor as I'm a bit worried as to why he's such a midget. Started life on the 99th centile and is now barely on the 9th, for height at least, not weight, being so stocky. Michael says he will be a widey, one of those short men who spend their life at the gym building up huge muscles to compensate for lack of stature. Anyway doctor didn't dismiss me as mad neurotic mother and is referring him to a paediatrician as there is no obvious reason why he should be so pocket-sized. Seems ironic that Josie is a giantess.

From: Charlotte Bailey
To: Nell Fenton
Re: celebrity invitation

I'll take your word for it that Ollie is a dolly – though he doesn't seem particularly diminutive to me, probably the force of his personality distracting from any shortcomings heightwise (so to speak). Have had v exciting invitation from Henry & Katrina. They are hosting a big party in Suffolk to celebrate Henry's birthday & new tv series. As we're taking the children they have rented us a cottage by the beach – am really looking forward to it, hoping to rub shoulders with lots of minor celebrities & then sell my story to the Express. We're taking Ana Frid to babysit the night of the party.

From: Nell Fenton
To: Charlotte Bailey

Am v jealous, Suffolk is so lovely. Bet it will be really good fun.

From: Charlotte Bailey
To: Nell Fenton
Re: Fran's monthly trip to casualty

Shut up – you're going to Cuba. I had Barnaby and Nathan today because Fran's been at the hospital with Jacob who launched himself down their stairs in a space rocket last night. Since the space rocket was a wicker laundry basket it was unable to withstand the G-force so Jacob crashed at the bottom of the stairs & has broken his arm. Fran is absolutely furious with Nathan, who was 'mission control', for being so stupid (although clever enough not to man the flight himself) but also furious with herself for failing to prevent it. I think she's being a bit hard on herself as when it comes to being accident-prone those boys are in a class of their own and the first she knew of their dastardly plan was when she saw Jacob streaking past her in swimming goggles shouting '3–2–1 blast off' before he leapt into the laundry basket & shot down the stairs.

From: Nell Fenton
To: Charlotte Bailey
Re: I'm pregnant

Have tried calling about 14 times but you remain selfishly out on your own business instead of conveniently in to fully discuss my momentous news. I'm very delighted in a slightly stunned way. Michael kept laughing when I called him at work – not sure if that means he's happy or slightly hysterical. Mum was surprisingly pleased when I told her considering she already has 197 grandchildren.

From: Charlotte Bailey
To: Nell Fenton
Re: you're pregnant

Can't believe it, that's fantastic, can't tell you how excited I am. How are you feeling & what is your due date, must be around Christmas??? Even Dan a bit excited.

From: Nell Fenton
To: Charlotte Bailey

Think I'm probably due end of November but I'm always so overdue will probably be Christmas Day. Feel a bit strange about having a baby in Canada. I'm dying to tell Josie who is always nagging for a baby (must be a girl) but obviously won't for a while yet.

From: Charlotte Bailey
To: Nell Fenton

Probably best not. I, on the other hand, keep telling people who don't even know you. Fran is thrilled for you. She's going to send you info on herbal supplements in pregnancy – sorry.

Got another letter from Toby. He's in New Delhi now & he's no longer writing an epic sweeping novel, instead he has decided to chronicle his experiences in India photographically & is going to come back & publish moving book of India's many faces, contrasting her splendour & opulence against her poverty & suffering. Dan looked really depressed by the letter so I didn't say (as vv much wanted to) well, luckily no one's ever thought of doing THAT before, or hope publisher won't mind blurry photos. Instead tried cheering him up by pointing out in my kindest voice that at least this letter made sense unlike the ones we got from Goa.

PS Ramon a bloke, know this as Toby said 'HE' as in Ramon (not Toby) got arrested.

From: Rachel Lockwood
To: Nell Fenton

Dear Nell

I was so delighted to hear your news and very impressed, I'm sure I couldn't manage four. Send Michael our love and congratulations. Jonathan and I are so looking forward to coming out to see you, Jonathan has never been on a plane and is beside himself with excitement about it. He's also very anxious that Ollie has not overtaken him in age while they have been apart. Fortunately I am able to completely reassure him on that score. Look after yourself.

Fondest love to all
Rachel xx

PS Things between Jack and me much improved, he seems much happier and calmer, so all well again.

From: Charlotte Bailey
To: Nell Fenton
Re: gifted offspring

I have some important news, don't wish to blow my own trumpet but I think both Maddie & Hugh may be 'gifted'. Maddie got her 1st reading book today and she is so brainy she can read it without actually looking at the page. (Possibly as the only word in the book is 'look'?) Meanwhile Hugh has mastered an amazing trick whereby he very slowly crosses his fingers then holds them up to me saying 'More?' & then when I eagerly respond 'Oh yes please!' very slowly uncrosses them & does it again, it's probably just practice but he somehow manages to make it look so easy . . .

PS How are you feeling?

From: Nell Fenton
To: Charlotte Bailey

I am familiar with the 'look' book, a simple yet compelling piece of literature. Hugh is obviously exceptional. You should expect great things from him. Feel completely normal, don't even have any food cravings which I had with the others, long may it last.

I've started our packing today, part of a new efficiency drive as am fed up with always finishing the packing at midnight on the night before we go away anywhere. Children are so excited. Find it very hard to pack for hot weather when surrounded by snow and the icy wind never stops. Bought them all sandals and new swimsuits last week, seemed strange getting them out of their snow pants and snow boots to try on this stuff. Shops are full of it to cater to the huge market of Canadians desperate to escape their arctic winter. Can't wait to get into the sun, feel I have definitely 'done' the snow thing.

From: Charlotte Bailey
To: Nell Fenton

All damp & drizzly here, would love hot exotic Cuban holiday or failing that a bit of snow (didn't get any at Christmas, you see) but no, instead must spend our money on much more interesting projects, eg stairs which are bouncy. Even I with my v limited knowledge of structural engineering know that bounciness in stairs is not a good thing.

We're going to Henry's party in Suffolk this w/e & while I expect neither hot exotic weather nor indeed snow am nevertheless v much looking forward to it.

From: Charlotte Bailey
To: Nell Fenton
Re: Henry's Party

Got back from our w/e in Suffolk last night. Had a really nice time, taking the children a huge success not least because it excused us from the scavenger hunt Katrina had organised on Sat. Hate that kind of thing as am absolutely useless at it & have no desire to blag things off people & equally hopeless at following a trail of clues (all Mum's fault for refusing to allow us to be Brownies). Instead took the children to the beach & then had very civilised lunch in Southwold. Went to the party in the evening which was in a marquee joined onto the pub/hotel where everyone else was staying. Had not anticipated party being mainly held in v well-ventilated marquee & was dressed to rub shoulders with hot celebrities in crowded room therefore inadequately dressed for ambient temperature which felt like −15°C. We arrived quite a bit after most people as had had to get children to sleep before leaving. Amazing how many normally cautiously sensible people completely rat-arsed by the time we got there. They had an unbelievably loud live band which started playing at about 10. Whole party like a fake boob pageant & Dan overjoyed as 'falsies' his specialist subject so he was walking round the room like CIA agent muttering under his breath 'fake, fake, nice try but obviously fake'. One daytime tv hostess in particular was walking around with her bosoms propped up & displayed like a pair of water-filled balloons. According to Dan, the very worst ones (which actually make him shudder) are big implants on someone flat-chested as then it looks like the surgeon has poked 2 grapefruits up under the skin. He claims not to like them too pert, which is fortunate for me. Dan's v thorough inventory was cut short by a phone call from Ana Frid to tell us that Hugh had been sick in his travel cot. Got back to the cottage to find v cheerful Hugh sitting on Ana Frid's lap eating bread & butter. Could think of no explanation for his throwing up except possibly all the sand he had eaten at the beach earlier. Cleaned up travel cot & carpet with industrial quantities of baby wipes & went to bed. With hindsight think we probably left party at right time as later became vv drunken & since am prone to drunkenness myself would no doubt have succumbed & made an arse of myself. Also avoided killer hangover that everyone else seemed to be suffering from next day. Finished the w/e with lunch in a pub with a v delicate-looking Henry & Katrina while members of the public came up every 5 mins to ask Henry for his autograph. Extraordinary.

From: Nell Fenton
To: Charlotte Bailey

They always give the best parties. We got back ourselves yesterday afternoon. Had an absolutely wonderful time, the weather was perfect and the water really is clear turquoise and the sand fine white powder like the pictures. The hotel was fabulous, lots of dark wood colonial-style furniture and lovely big rooms in a series of villas set in tropical gardens.

The only bad things were the warmth and sea air made my hair go very odd and stand up in a woolly halo round my head, also I couldn't drink which as you know is one of my favourite hobbies. There were tons of hermit crabs around on the beach which the boys dedicated themselves to seeking out. This was great as it kept them occupied for hours but they couldn't quite take the sweet sorrow of parting in the evenings and they kept sneaking them back to their room. Was first alerted to this when I put my hand in a washbag and felt something move against my fingers. Subsequent search of their room turned up two in a bedside drawer, one in a trainer and two in Ollie's pocket. Had to get them both to promise faithfully they wouldn't bring any more back before I could get Josie to agree to continue sharing a room with them, a promise they had some difficulty keeping so Michael and I had to conduct frequent spot checks (especially of Ollie's pockets). I actually feel rested which is a concept I have long since stopped associating with holidays, not that I don't love our family holidays in France but it is an unavoidable fact that one is just multiplying the general chaos, confusion and workload of one's individual family by a factor of 4 or 5.

From: Charlotte Bailey
To: Nell Fenton

Yes, Dan occasionally suggests holidays with just our own children which I know would be more restful but much less fun. Cuba sounds fantastic, quite a novelty to come back from a holiday without the sensation of needing another . . . How are you feeling by the way, any fatter yet?

From: Nell Fenton
To: Charlotte Bailey

I'm not actually, am at that pleasing and all too brief stage when my boobs are looking a bit splendid (quite pert in my swimsuit, not their usual saggy defeated little selves) and my bum has not yet started madly storing fat.

From: Charlotte Bailey
To: Nell Fenton

Don't ever have that stage, my bum always springs into action as the sperm touches the egg. Was just watching an old Easter video of Ellie & Maddie the other day & thinking how exceptionally large my bum looked (bending over to help Maddie retrieve an egg, arse fully framed in the shot) then remembered, ah yes, was half an hour pregnant with Hugh then.

From: Nell Fenton
To: Charlotte Bailey

All the benefit of our trip to Cuba has already dissipated

(except my face is slightly less grey than before) and the winter seems to be dragging on interminably. I'm really missing the English spring, trees don't even come into bud here till late May.

I've been taking Rob to weekly sessions of 'play therapy' to help him overcome his (many and varied) fears though I have to say it's the biggest load of crap I have ever encountered and $140 for a 45-min session. VERY, VERY faint hope that perhaps I am completely wrong and it might actually help him keeps me from giving up on it. It consists of me and the (so-called) doctor sitting there for half an hour watching Rob who is allowed to do as he pleases with the toys and sandpit. I am not supposed to react so he has quickly discovered that he can get away with throwing the sand all over the carpet. We then spend 15 mins discussing the significance of the way he has played (many dark and deep things are revealed by the fact that he buries dinosaurs in the sand – nothing of course to do with his fascination with palaeontology). Apparently at the end of all this he will no longer be afraid of dogs/bugs etc. Might as well burn a bunch of feathers and dance round him in a circle. Much cheaper too.

APRIL 00

From: Charlotte Bailey
To: Nell Fenton

Marcia & Quentin have asked me to be Rosamund's god-mother. Although I have selfishly sorted out my outfit have not yet bought a present, now urgently need to think of one as christening is next w/e. Rosamund v sweet, masses of completely crazy black hair, so am considering a hairstyling kit as a useful if not strictly religious christening present. What do you think & how are you feeling by the way?

From: Nell Fenton
To: Charlotte Bailey

Hairstyling kit lacks the solemnity required but would have the advantage of not being expensive and also not being stuck in a drawer never to see the light of day again as with all other christening presents.

Feeling fine though slightly sick and brushing my teeth makes me want to throw up.

From: Charlotte Bailey
To: Nell Fenton

Rosamund's christening was lovely. The service was held at this absolutely beautiful church in the city with raised mahogany pews on hollow stage-like floor with individual doors at the end of each one. As godmother, had to sit near the front. V stressful as hollow floor under pews incredibly noisy & little door at the end source of great joy for Hugh who spent entire service fighting to get at it so he could open & shut it, also girls v whispery & fidgety & kept dropping the v substantial hymn books onto world's noisiest floor creating interesting sonic boom effect. The vicar gave a v strict shouty sermon which thrilled & exhilarated Dan as although completely godless he can't stand Church of England's wishy-washy liberalism. Unfortunately when I bought my pretty godmotherly outfit for the occasion I had thoughtlessly failed to purchase alternative footwear in anticipation of the pleasant springlike temperatures we had been enjoying unexpectedly plummeting to those of an arctic winter. So when I arrived at the service with my bare legs & pink leather flip-flops poking out from under my full-length winter coat I was not in fact making a bold fashion statement but just trying to ensure at least my upper body did not become hypothermic. My feet looked so alarming, all mottled & purpley pink like uncooked sausage, that one chap actually said 'Gosh, your feet look cold.' Despite searing pain from slowly unthawing toes (we were inside by then) managed brave 'Oh no, not really.' Saw quite a lot of old friends including Cecelia who I haven't seen for years & who now has 3 children exactly the same age & sex as my lot as well as a v highly paid job as a fund manager. Asked her if she was going to have any more children but before she could answer her husband, Jim, who was practically on the other side of the room (& must have v sharp ears) did extraordinary leapfrog-type manoeuvre, vaulting over a bevy of small

119

children, & shouted 'NO WE'RE NOT.' Was worried I had introduced a contentious topic but not at all, Cecelia absolutely adamant that that was IT. Geraldine was there with Gil who has finished the part that required the beard so is now sporting designer stubble. Saw him leaning against a wall having cornered this very pretty girl who must have been about 20, chatting her up. She was doing lots of laughing & flicking her hair so presumably he was having some success, think Geraldine must have noticed this too as she marched up & removed him. The girl who is actually a cousin of Marcia's told me afterwards she'd given him her phone no as she had thought he was single. She was obviously mystified as to why he was with Geraldine, who was looking particularly frumpy & thick-ankled. Feel so sorry for Geraldine, she seems even more tense than usual at the moment, she has some really important contract negotiation coming up & amazingly Gil has managed to land a part in a play in Surrey so the repellent little toad is going to be away a lot, most probably trying to shag other women in his spare time.

From: Nell Fenton
To: Charlotte Bailey

Obviously you can't say anything to Geraldine but you might mention to Gil in a friendly and concerned way that if she finds out he's trying to pick up girls again she'll twist his balls off. Don't think flip-flops and overcoat sounds like a bold fashion statement, think it makes you sound like a homeless person. You're lucky no one gave you 50p for a cup of tea. V annoying of Cecelia to have all those children AND a high-powered job, shouldn't really be allowed on the basis that it makes the rest of us feel inadequate.

From: Nell Fenton
To: Charlotte Bailey

Rob brought home the script of his class play (or Spring Festival as they grandly call it), and a note to say he has two parts and therefore needs not one but two costumes. The reason he has two parts is not that he is their star performer but because each part is so incredibly inconsequential one is not enough, so now I have the bother of making two bloody costumes in which he will appear for about 2 seconds. Rob tremendously excited and full of elaborate plans for the costumes for his upcoming roles as a bee and a rooster.

From: Charlotte Bailey
To: Nell Fenton

Terribly annoying I agree although at least it's only once a year whereas here every birthday party is themed & fancy dress (have to admit guilt here as Maddie had her kings & queens party but at least that's just a cardboard crown and a cloak). Ellie was recently invited to an 'under the sea party'. I spent 2 days making her the most fantastic lobster costume so everybody would think I was wonderful. Ellie, who was oblivious to my plan of appearing marvellous, streaked in the door of the party, ripped the costume off & started charging round in her vest, tights & red wellies. When I tried to get her to put it back on she complained it was itchy & was spoiling her fun. Unfortunately she said this in front of party mother so I couldn't make her wear it as even if one is fabulous enough to have gone to the huge shag of making an exquisite & anatomically correct lobster costume would definitely be a BAD MOTHER if I then forced her to wear the sodding thing.

From: Charlotte Bailey
To: Nell Fenton

I've finally given in to Ellie's nagging for a proper pet (Hugh just doesn't cut it any more) so we're going to get her a guinea pig for her birthday. Fran, who used to be a volunteer at a guinea pig hospital, says it's best to buy them from a farm rather than a pet shop as pet-shop ones less hardy & may need to live inside. I've found a petting farm in Kent that says it sells them & they have some babies. We're going at the w/e & afterwards will visit Dan's Uncle Will who's been quite ill & Dan has been worried about him.

From: Nell Fenton
To: Charlotte Bailey

Find it hard to believe there is such a thing as a guinea pig hospital, let alone people who actually volunteer to work in them. Was it the terrible shortage of needy humans that made Fran decide to give up her time to help poorly guinea pigs?

From: Charlotte Bailey
To: Nell Fenton
Re: teen guinea pigs & miracle of new life

Shut up, you poisonous cow. We went to Lockett's Farm yesterday & now have 2 guinea pigs called Catherine & Susan. Rather alarming, as when we arrived I asked to see the baby guinea pigs that were for sale & was told by a laconic spotty youth that they couldn't be separated from their mother for another few weeks. Said rather tensely I had spoken to someone called Mick during the week who'd said they had baby g-pigs for sale.

Youth turned out to be Mick himself & just said, 'Oh yeah, sorry about that.' Did NOT hit him but instead explained in a v slow, calm voice that it was my daughter's birthday & we had come from London to choose a guinea pig so what did he suggest we do? Ended up getting two 'teenage' g-pigs. Tried to do lots of professional looking at their bottoms/teeth/paws as g-pig book tells you to but quite frankly had absolutely no idea what I was supposed to be looking for so we just chose sweet-looking ones. Was v dismayed to discover on reading g-pig handbook that they can live up to 7 yrs, would have thought by now you could get genetically modified ones that only last 18 months. As they were doing lots of lambing at the farm we went to watch the miracle of new life being brought into the world. Instead of being delighted & amazed at sight of baby lambs being born the children were completely horrified & disgusted so had to leave sharpish before they were permanently traumatised. We didn't get to see Uncle Will as there is something wrong with the bloody petrol gauge on my car & we ran out of petrol on the way there so instead spent a delightful hour and a half on the hard shoulder of the motorway waiting for the AA to come & refill the tank.

From: Nell Fenton
To: Charlotte Bailey

You will definitely regret getting those rodents. I hate our stinky pointless hamsters and always have to bully the children to feed them and clean them out. I just spent $80 on fabric and approx 1000 man hours on creating a costume, part rooster, part bee. Unfortunately I failed to employ any common sense when it came to sizing and the bloody rooster part is absolutely skintight on him and requires a lot of wriggling into. Perfect for a quick costume change by v uncoordinated child.

From: Charlotte Bailey
To: Nell Fenton

If recent personal experience is anything to go by, measuring doesn't seem to make any difference. Finally got round to making the girls' bedroom curtains as Brian Turner cornered me to complain about the black towels hanging at the window being 'unsightly'. Wanted to say, well, so is your big woolly beard but I'm not asking you to get rid of that, instead meekly agreed to do something more aesthetically pleasing. Although I measured the window several times the curtains are very mysteriously at least 6" too short. Have no idea what I did, but they look really stupid, like v short trousers, & although this arrangement may be more aesthetically pleasing to the man on the street (ie Brian) they are not more aesthetically pleasing to the woman in the bedroom (me), as well as being a daily reminder I'm not v good at maths.

From: Nell Fenton
To: Charlotte Bailey

That's what comes of doing foolish things like making your own curtains.

From: Charlotte Bailey
To: Nell Fenton

Got an email from Lou to say she and Walt have just signed with a publisher. Didn't say what their advance was, but I think it must be v good as they say they're going to use it as a deposit to try and buy the house they've been renting in Cape Cod. If they get the house, which they think they will, they appear (for some extraordinary reason) v keen for us to visit. Won't be able to as can't afford the flights but this is probably a good thing as knowing my luck would probably accidentally blow up their house or something.

From: Nell Fenton
To: Charlotte Bailey

Brilliant. Must send them an email to congratulate them. I've now had notes from Josie's teacher requesting a sloth costume AND from Ollie's teacher asking for a piglet costume.

From: Charlotte Bailey
To: Nell Fenton

Can't you send back a note saying you've just remembered you're paying a fortune in school fees so why don't they get someone else do it?

From: Nell Fenton
To: Charlotte Bailey

Had a v nice email from Lou asking us if we'd like to come and stay with them in Cape Cod too. Sounds so lovely and not too far from here so think we might go for a long w/e after the children break up.

From: Charlotte Bailey
To: Nell Fenton

Lucky you, wish we could afford to go but don't think we can ignore our bouncing staircase for much longer.

Geraldine came round for supper as Gil is away rehearsing for his play. Felt completely drained by the end of the evening. She's so exhausting, kept going on & on about Gil & endlessly asking my opinion about him & their relationship & either brushing my replies aside if it wasn't what she wanted to hear or asking the same question 15 times until she got the answer she wanted. Dan says she's like a drunk & needy Jeremy Paxman – can see why she's such a successful lawyer, she's relentless. V tricky evening, particularly as what I really wanted to say was: your boyfriend is ghastly & is sponging off you. Says she's overwhelmed with work at the moment but determined to make it to the opening night in couple of weeks. Really wants me to go with her & I've agreed & now I want to kill myself.

From: Nell Fenton
To: Charlotte Bailey

Geraldine always has the worst boyfriends. Kind of you to have her round though, even in the pre-Gil days she was fairly dire. Much as I love Rachel, and not in any way to compare her with Geraldine, I was slightly dreading her visit when things were so bad with her and Jack, am so relieved they seem to have sorted themselves out, it's awful having to feel a bit guilty for being happily married. As it is, I know she'd like another baby but Jack won't hear of it and here I am greedily having a fourth.

From: Charlotte Bailey
To: Nell Fenton

Don't be stupid, Rachel knows how much you want this baby. Doesn't matter it's your fourth. Glad things are going better with her & Jack, he's lucky to have her. How are you? Anything remotely interesting to report?

From: Nell Fenton
To: Charlotte Bailey

Not unless fact I've gone off garlic is interesting.

Just got back from Rob's school play. Rob did fine though would have been hard pressed to mess up since he had about 8 words altogether. I arrived really early but am clearly a Spring Festival 'novice' as all the front rows were already taken and many parents were setting up v high-tech video equipment on tripods (excessive for a 25-minute play per-formed by 6-yr-olds). I just had my beaten-up old camera in my handbag.

From: Charlotte Bailey
To: Nell Fenton

Toby's coming back the day after tomorrow. He rang to find out if we're around this weekend as apparently he's longing to see us all. Feel slightly suspicious as before when he was living in Kent would happily go for months at a time without feeling any longing at all. Can't say this to Dan as it might seem MEAN. Very much looking forward to experiencing his 'visual voyage through India'. Much easier to justify 4 months away at your parents & brother's expense if you have a 'visual voyage' to show for it, rather than just lots & lots of holiday snaps.

From: Nell Fenton
To: Charlotte Bailey

Suspect there will be lots of pictures of children with dirty faces and also lots of pictures of ancient old people whose life experiences are etched deep on their toothless faces.

Rachel arrived last night. Really lovely to see her and she's very cheerful. Told me Jack still being very nice and really wants her to have a good time. Felt a positive rush of affection for him and made me remember how fond I used to be of him, have got in the habit of feeling hostile towards him for giving her such a hard time. Jonathan is terribly sweet and is looking absolutely beautiful, golden-skinned and green-eyed. He's very precise and sensible and asks a lot of earnest intelligent questions, makes me realise what a hopeless pair of loonies Rob and Ollie are (though Jonathan doesn't seem to notice and is tremendously admiring of Rob in particular).

From: Charlotte Bailey
To: Nell Fenton

Good. I know Jack is difficult but he does have redeeming features & can even remember quite fancying him in my distant youth and though they obviously have a very turbulent marriage you do feel they're sort of meant to be together.

From: Nell Fenton
To: Charlotte Bailey

I hope so. Suzette invited Rachel and me over for coffee, I imagine so she could inspect Rachel and show off to her. Couldn't go because we had all the children and Rob is terrified of her dogs, so told her to come over to our house. Not fair to keep her to myself anyhow. She came over with some peanut brittle she'd made. Why oh why, one might ask oneself. Apart from being disgusting it's terribly hard to eat. Took a tiny corner to be polite, but a great jagged slab of it sat reproachfully untouched on a plate between us while we drank our coffee. Suzette was on top form and having skimmed her eyes over Rachel in the first 3 seconds and thus established that Rachel's boobs are considerably smaller than her own she recounted to us her bra-buying trip of the previous day. This was to a ludicrously overpriced underwear shop downtown, but the only place she can get bras that fit her properly. She told us what a fortune she had spent and how delighted Kane was and how he got her to model all the underwear she'd bought before bed. This was good even by her standards, combining the fact that she has lots of money, she has fabulous boobs and a great sex life all under one 'umbrella'. She then told us how she has taken up yoga and is very supple, more supple than some of the girls of 18 in her yoga class and then she went on to demonstrate her great suppleness by showing us some of the more difficult yoga positions. Rachel was very pleased to have met her and have to say I was quite relieved that it went so well as I have boasted to Rachel quite a bit about Suzette and it would have been embarrassing if she had let me down.

From: Charlotte Bailey
To: Nell Fenton

Watch out if she's taken up yoga – being naturally sexy anyway, tantric sex will definitely be the next step. Saw Toby this weekend looking very brown & well & full of talk about his new career as a photographer. Said his trip was absolutely brilliant & he wants to go round Europe next. Photos unbelievably cliched & most of the Goan ones not even in focus. Still, tried to be enthusiastic as I don't want to be a bitch. He brought fantastic presents for everyone, Barbies in saris for the girls, Hugh got a wooden cobra which he is thrilled with & terrified by simultaneously. Dan got an incredibly smelly jubbah (he claims he is very sexy in it but I beg to differ) & he brought me some lovely silver bracelets. V thoughtful presents, was quite touched. He's coming to stay at the end of the month for a couple of days as he wants to take some photos of the tramps at King's Cross.

From: Nell Fenton
To: Charlotte Bailey

Can't think of anything more attractive than a man in a smelly jubbah, you are clearly repressed. Photographing tramps at King's Cross a very interesting idea. Toby obviously has great depths. Am sure they will be v thought-provoking. Found quite a decent maternity-wear shop and have bought some reasonably nice stuff.

From: Charlotte Bailey
To: Nell Fenton

I have managed to avoid Gil's opening night and instead I now have a very, very upset Geraldine who has split up from Gil staying with me. Amazingly & fantastically she was the one who dumped him. She turned up unexpectedly to watch the final rehearsal with a bottle of champagne to celebrate v successful & early conclusion to her contract negotiations & his new play. When she walked into his dressing room Gil was sitting, talking to balding, ponytailed director with some nubile giggly girl called Daisy wriggling about on his lap. Geraldine said when he saw her he leapt up (tipping wriggly, giggly Daisy onto the floor) & asked her in an incredibly unpleasant way why she was a day ahead of schedule. She said she just suddenly thought she didn't need to put up with this bollocks. So she handed him the champagne & said, 'This is for you, Gil, good luck with everything,' turned around & walked out. He obviously realised he'd gone too far as he came running out after her asking her where she was going so she told him she had something to deal with back in London that couldn't wait & she'd ring him later. So then he was all relieved & waved her off & as she pointed out, didn't make even the most desultory attempt to persuade her to stay. When she got home she called an emergency locksmith & got all the locks on her flat changed, put his stuff down in the hallway & rang and left a message for him to come & get his things. Then she threw her mobile in the Thames & checked herself into the Dorchester for the night. And now she's staying with me for a couple of days till her landline no is changed & she feels able to face her flat alone. She's really down. I feel so sorry for her, she's been with him for 2 yrs & she says he was just wasting her time & spending her money. Dan says he feels sorry for her too but it now feels as if she's been staying with us for 2 yrs (it's been 2 days) & if she doesn't go soon will have to throw either himself or her in the Thames after her phone.

From: Nell Fenton
To: Charlotte Bailey

Oh my God, how awful for Geraldine. I never even met Gil and I hated him. Mind you, you don't need to get much past the fact that his name was 'Gil' in order to hate him. Very heroic of you to have her to stay though, she does sap the life out of you. Told Michael about it and he became so fixated with horror on Dan's behalf I had to remind him that the point of the story was that poor Geraldine has been buggered around for two years by some self-obsessed luvvie. That did fire his indignation momentarily as he very much hates actors.

From: Charlotte Bailey
To: Nell Fenton
Re: Geraldine driving me completely crazy.

Fucking hell, do feel really, really sorry for Geraldine but my tolerance levels are being stretched to the limit. She is completely useless round the house, ANY sort of housework/clearing up v much a spectator sport. While I stagger across the kitchen with a boiling cauldron in my hands & mat gripped in my teeth kicking children out of the way she will be trotting behind me completely oblivious & still talking. Last night at dinner had to resort to poking Dan with a fork & loudly telling him to shut up in order to get his attention & help. Obviously completely unreasonable of me as he was only trying to be polite & it was Geraldine I really wanted to poke & shout at but it seemed like rude manners what with her being a guest in our house & everything.

From: Nell Fenton
To: Charlotte Bailey

Not at all unreasonable, sure it did him good.

From: Charlotte Bailey
To: Nell Fenton

Geraldine went back to her flat today, thank God. When she was leaving did lots of gripping Dan's arm, staring deeply into his eyes saying 'Thank you for your wonderful support, Dan, I couldn't have got through this last week without it' – nothing to me of course, being but a woman my constant attention & sympathy is expected. Feel really pissed off as I was the one listening to her drone on while he kept escaping upstairs 'to check on the children' & then lie on our bed secretly reading car mags while I was trapped downstairs analysing why Gil always undermined her – usual conclusion was he had had an unhappy childhood instead of the more accurate & I believe widely held view that he is a world-class tosser.

From: Nell Fenton
To: Charlotte Bailey

Very generous of her, you'd think post break-up she'd embrace the 'world-class tosser' theory but I expect she'll come round to it. We all went away for the Easter weekend and stayed on a farm, so Rachel could see a bit more than just Toronto. Weather has improved dramatically, snow has melted and it is finally showing signs that it might not always be winter. Feel like a Narnian that's heard whispers that Aslan might be returning. Really felt quite springlike out in the country. Very picturesque farmhouse, the only small contretemps was when the boys were in the olde worlde roll-top bath, the back legs suddenly snapped off and it crashed down on its bottom. The boys were quite unconcerned, Jonathan was even rather thrilled by it, but I got a bit of a shock. Meant the rest of the weekend we all had to bathe at a rakish angle which is not to be recommended, especially late at night after a few glasses of wine (also has quite a negative impact on how well the bath drains, bucket and cups needed). The owners, very sweet old German couple, completely mortified by this calamity and kept dropping by with German delicacies by way of compensation. There's a very large Amish community near where we were staying so you see them all the time going by in their pony traps and ploughing their fields with oxen. We went to a market and I bought Ellie an Amish Barbie outfit for her birthday, it's very demure and comes complete with apron and bonnet. I offered to buy one for Josie but she declined as she prefers her Barbies to be dressed as hookers.

From: Charlotte Bailey
To: Nell Fenton

Excellent, Ellie will be thrilled & Amish Barbie can go with sari Barbie & new SAS Barbie (SAS Barbie = normal Barbie but with v short haircut & green & black pen on her face as recently customised by Hugh). The bath incident sounds like my house, everything falling apart as usual, stairs still bouncing & at least 5 of the windows have totally had it. Albert removed the counterweights in the sash window in Hugh's bedroom, he's trying to fix it by replacing rotten bits with car body filler. Unfortunately he didn't tell me, so while I was trying to open it, it slammed back down trapping ALL MY FINGERS. Was fucking agony & I couldn't move, as despite speed & weight of shutting window

134

it did not sever the fingers which were still tiresomely attached to my hands which were stuck in the window. Was weakly calling for Dan who was downstairs watching telly with the children. After what seemed like about 5 hrs Hugh nonchalantly wandered into the room & I did lots of frantic 'get Daddy, get Daddy' & he wandered off again with very aimless air about him but something must have registered in that tiny little brain because Dan did then come bounding upstairs & free me. Fingers still look puffy & it happened yesterday.

Our Easter egg hunt very jolly, but extremely quick. No scampering across acres of lawn past banks of flowers like in France, instead 2 steps across scrubby grass (5 if you're Hugh) followed by a bit of scrabbling among the very few mangy-looking plants left in our flower beds so the eggs which took me & Ana Frid hours to dye & decorate took all of 10 mins to find & then destroy esp as Hugh kept throwing them & loads of them got broken & muddy. By the way, isn't 'German delicacy' an oxymoron?

From: Nell Fenton
To: Charlotte Bailey

Your poor fingers. Really a very good thing they weren't severed though. Obviously you wouldn't have been trapped at the window if they had been but in the long run would have proved hugely inconvenient. Old couple gave us some little spiced German biscuits that were v good actually.

From: Charlotte Bailey
To: Nell Fenton

Don't believe you about the German delicacies, you're just fat &

pregnant & indiscriminate. Guess whether Toby is just staying a few days as originally planned or whether it's going to be a bit longer eg 5–6 weeks. Toby so pleased & moved by his moving & pleasing King's Cross photos of tramps & prostitutes he's decided to do another series of photos, this time chronicling London's many faces. He has also got himself a part-time job at a camera shop in Holborn which is actually fairly amazing & is moving in properly this w/e. Feel quite weary about it all, have only just recovered from Geraldine's visit & now I've got Toby AND he's even messier than Dan if that's humanly possible.

From: Nell Fenton
To: Charlotte Bailey

Told you tramp photos would be thought-provoking, though must admit, hadn't guessed they'd provoke him to think of moving in with you.

Saw Rachel off early this morning. A great struggle for us both as we stayed up really late talking last night, though worse for her as I'm not drinking at the moment so she had to do it for us both. She said she's been quite depressed for the last few months, Jack has been so erratic and difficult, going out really often and coming home very late. Apparently he often phones about 11 or 12 and says he's too drunk/tired to come home and is going to sleep on someone's sofa. She said she really thought their marriage was breaking down but recently things seem to have improved. Don't think I'd put up with Michael behaving that way but I suppose you don't know till it happens and if you've got children it's not straightforward any more. I so hope he carries on being nice to her. If anyone deserves a nice husband it's her and she's been so uncomplaining and I know she never exaggerates.

136

MAY 00

From: Charlotte Bailey
To: Nell Fenton

How are you feeling? Please tell me you've put on weight & are looking tubby. I have managed to gain 4lb since Easter with only chocolate & no baby to blame. Fatness particularly badly timed as weather has suddenly got v warm, making summer seem worryingly imminent. Good weather v useful re Hugh though, means I can shove him out in the garden all day which he loves, spends his day 'gardening'. Garden is a mess so there's nothing there for him to kill. Think Ana Frid feels his days should be a bit more structured but anything that shuts him up & keeps him outside is fine by me.

From: Nell Fenton
To: Charlotte Bailey

Am starting to look dumpy and unattractively shapeless. Was complaining about it to Michael who says my face is still thin. Since it's the one part of me that would benefit from being fatter, quite small comfort.

Josie's school play was today. Sloth costume a triumph – mind you, this is a place where sewing a costume makes you Martha Stewart.

From: Charlotte Bailey
To: Nell Fenton

Wish it was like that here, everybody so bloody skilled & competitive it's really tiring trying to show off.

From: Nell Fenton
To: Charlotte Bailey

Saw the paediatrician today about Ollie being miniature. I felt very dismayed when I saw him, he can't be more than five foot two, has a very high-pitched laugh, and laughs frequently so looks and sounds about 11. It seemed terribly tactless to be fretting about Ollie being so short to such a very small man. He looked at the charts of projected height and said 'Well, he'll be taller than his paediatrician.' Could manage only a very watery smile in response to this reassurance. Anyway he is sending him to have the bones in his hand x-rayed which will tell us something or other about his bone maturity and we also have to come back in 6 months by which time he is supposed to have grown 5 cm. Shall now feed him extra and pull gently on his head each evening to stretch him upward. I haven't heard from Rachel which is odd. I don't want to phone in case it looks like I'm being reproachful that she hasn't thanked me for the visit.

From: Charlotte Bailey
To: Nell Fenton

Don't be silly, she won't think that – just phone her. Marcia rang this evening for a bit of general chit-chat and told me that Cecelia is pregnant again. She was pregnant but didn't know it at Rosamund's christening. Now Jim isn't speaking to her which seems a little unreasonable. Would have thought given their strongly held views on the matter they'd have been more careful. Came off the phone feeling depressed & also jealous which is a vile emotion. Don't feel jealous of you because I know how much you want this baby but can't help feeling sorry for myself about failure to get pregnant when everybody else seems to be. Also can't discuss it with anybody else apart from you as either they think I'm mad for wanting 4th child (eg the now pregnant Cecilia) or they think no doubt rightly it's unforgivably greedy to whine about failure to conceive as I have 3 already.

From: Nell Fenton
To: Charlotte Bailey

Fucking hell, I really think Michael has exceeded his own personal best for being a stupid arse. He told me on Monday that some American bloke he has recruited, who lives at the moment in Montreal, is coming to Toronto next week for some meetings. Apparently the poor love can't bear hotels so Michael magnanimously told him he could come and stay with us. This means I have the pleasure and privilege of cooking meals and being generally charming to some perfect stranger for 3 days. This in itself merits a punch in the face but is not his greatest crime. He told me quite clearly he was coming on Wednesday of next week. Being intimately acquainted with the vague grasp he has on the importance of such details, I made a point of checking it was definitely Wednesday of next week and not Wednesday of this week. Recklessly took his assurances at face value. Unfortunately yesterday I was in bed with a vile migraine, was so bad I had to get Michael to come home early to pick up the children. Was lying in bed at about 6, admittedly feeling slightly better, when a call came from the office to say Steve Bradshaw had arrived and should he come straight on to the house? Michael came sidling into the bedroom to confess to me that when he said Wednesday of next week he had in fact been mistaken and it was Wednesday of this week. Too fragile to give him the kick he deserved but managed to find the strength to hiss an order that he go back to the office, take the man out for dinner and make sure he didn't come back too early. Then had to drag myself out of bed trying not to move my head too much to do the children's supper, clear out the 'fort' that the boys had built in the spare room and make up the bed.

From: Charlotte Bailey
To: Nell Fenton

At least *your* guest has not set up a DARKROOM in your house & is only staying 3 days. Having Toby to stay was not, until yesterday, quite as annoying as I had expected. He's hardly been around but yesterday arrived back from work in a friend's car & started unloading lots of weird-looking photographic equipment & great plastic flagons of dodgy-looking chemicals onto the pavement outside our house. He saw me looking out a top-floor window & when I opened it to ask what all the stuff was, he shouted up that he was setting up a darkroom in our spare bathroom & sorry he hadn't told me before but he kept forgetting to mention it, but he knew I wouldn't mind. The thing about Toby is he says these things in such a charming & reasonable way that you find yourself unable to come up with one single solitary reason why a room full of no doubt poisonous & probably flammable chemicals in a house full of young children isn't an entirely marvellous idea, so you end up agreeing & only much later do the less fabulous aspects of the idea (eg the vile smell & fact room is now entirely covered in black fabric with shutters NAILED shut) occur to you & by then it's too late. So now we've got a bloody darkroom/Hugh death trap stinking out the 3rd floor of our house. Hurrah.

From: Nell Fenton
To: Charlotte Bailey

Obviously guest + darkroom trumps unexpected guest, though am still v annoyed with both him and Michael AND when I was getting exasperated with the boys (who kept appearing downstairs during dinner, after having been put to bed), he said his children never come down once they've been told to go to bed, which made me want to serve the food directly onto his head.

From: Nell Fenton
To: Charlotte Bailey

Our hotel-phobic American left today. Since he was driving back to Montreal, presumably eagerly awaited by his perfect family, had rather assumed he'd leave as soon as possible. Instead after a leisurely breakfast he settled down on the sofa to read the papers. Couldn't believe he was making himself comfortable here instead of GOING AWAY as I so desperately wanted him to. Anyhow he finally buggered off, without any acknowledgement to me of the very considerable bother it was to keep the children and the house vaguely civilised for 3 days, not to mention the cooking which was particularly onerous since his wife is a cookery writer and doubtless a fabulous cook. Have told Michael in a gentle and loving way that I will rip out his heart if he invites a stranger to stay again without first consulting me.

From: Charlotte Bailey
To: Nell Fenton
Re: Gil vv stupid & Geraldine vv clever

Indeed, should have ripped his heart out, casseroled it and served it to Steve Bradshaw (& then his wife could write about it). Geraldine rang to read me a letter she got from Gil about his monologue at the Edinburgh Festival. He hopes she is not going to let her current feelings prevent her from continuing to be 'a patron to the actors' craft', ie will she still pay for his show? The letter talked about this unique opportunity to showcase his talent and what a terrible setback to his career it would be if he had to give it up. First time I've heard her laugh in ages. Then she read me the letter she has written in reply, gist of it being if he ever contacts her again to ask for money she'll sue him for all the money she has lent him over the past 2 years. She says he's a bit thick so will probably believe she really can do it & it'll put the fear of God into him.

From: Nell Fenton
To: Charlotte Bailey

Excellent and imaginative. Hard to think how you can set back a career whose high point has been a crap part in a theatre in Surrey. Still haven't heard from Rachel though I've emailed and left phone messages. Don't normally care about how hopeless she is at keeping in touch, but annoying when I'm worried about her.

From: Charlotte Bailey
To: Nell Fenton

Got a phone call last night from Peter, Dan's really nice cousin, to say Uncle Will has gone back into hospital. I think he's really very ill. Dan's terribly upset about it. He saw him about a month ago & said he looked v old & frail. Fran is going to have the children on Sunday so we can go & visit him. Toby's coming too.

From: Charlotte Bailey
To: Nell Fenton

Peter rang this morning, Uncle Will died last night. Dan's so sad. Funeral will probably be Friday which is a bit problematic as Ana Frid is going back to Sweden for her mother's b'day this w/e so there's no one to mind Hugh if I go, which I want to & Dan really wants me to.

From: Nell Fenton
To: Charlotte Bailey

Tell Dan how sorry we are. I'll say a prayer for Uncle Will.

From: Charlotte Bailey
To: Louise Corrigan

Dear Lou, thanks so much for your kind message, Dan was really touched by it. He's v sad, was terribly fond of Uncle Will, & he & Toby used to stay on his farm a lot during the holidays and loved it there. Dan was allowed to drive an Austin Princess around it when he was about 9 and even the tractor when he was a bit bigger. Also, even more importantly, he told me the farm was the scene of his 1st conquest – managed to get a local girl tipsy enough on Uncle Will's cider to get her to kiss him. Says this was a huge achievement as although he was 16 he looked 11 & she was very busty. Dan sends love. C x

From: Charlotte Bailey
To: Nell Fenton

Went to Uncle Will's funeral today. Took Hugh with us in the end, though Fran v kindly offered to have him, Barnaby has chickenpox at the moment & it seemed a bit much to ask, also can't quite face the inevitable outbreak of plague at our house that would ensue if Hugh went over there. Funeral was quite small & terribly touching. Peter gave a really moving tribute to his father, my appreciation of which was cut short by the fact that Hugh had somehow managed to find some window cleaner at the back of the crematorium and was spraying the hymn books with it. Penelope was first to notice & when she went back to try & wrest the bottle off him, he took it v badly indeed & bit her sleeve, completely mortifying. I then had to carry him out while he struggled & shouted 'No, Mummy.' I think Dan feels a bit better now the funeral is over & was really glad to see Peter who he hasn't seen for years. I've only met Peter once before about 100 years ago, he's absolutely charming, not really handsome but with a really nice face & thought Hugh was really funny & said seeing him spraying the hymn books was a very welcome distraction. Felt a bit in love with Peter for glossing over the biting & looking at it like that rather than the more conventional view that Hugh is evil little sod who should be incarcerated. Dan really wants to see more of Peter, he's coming for lunch in a few weeks. Hugh Sr told us Uncle Will has left Toby & Dan some money. Both are v touched about it.

From: Nell Fenton
To: Charlotte Bailey

Glad Dan feels better. Hugh is a little bugger but I think I can say with confidence that mine are WORSE. V nice new restaurant has opened nearby and in a moment of crazed optimism we decided to go there with the children. Not the sort of place where they provide crayons and colouring-in sheets (usual in the kind of places we frequent). Children instead entertained themselves by dropping cutlery and knocking over glasses. Tried to distract them and was having some success when Ollie, arsing around in his chair, somehow managed to get his head stuck between the bars at the back. He alerted us (and the entire restaurant) to this fact by howling and thrashing around wedging his head more firmly as he did so. Unfortunately, while Michael and I tried to free his head and calm him, Rob bored by the lack of attention slid silently under the table. At this point a waiter came over to see if he could help and trod on Rob's head. Don't think it was very hard but Rob rolled around clutching his head and squealing while the waiter crouched over him in horror. Longed to bolt home at this point but had already ordered so we grimly soldiered on and at least Rob and Ollie both somewhat subdued by their respective head injuries.

From: Charlotte Bailey
To: Nell Fenton
Re: Chair-repelling children

Mad of you to try & take them to a proper restaurant. Pizza Express about as fancy as we get. As soon as we get to a restaurant it's as though the part of their brain that controls sitting on a chair shuts down and they behave as though they'd never seen one let alone parked their bums on one. Last time we went out with them for lunch would have thought they were trying to stay on bucking broncos the amount they fell off & Dan really lost it when all 3 ended up on the floor simultaneously. So now we have made a rule they have to 'earn' pudding by staying on for more than 10 mins at a time. We're going to the President's lunch at the Chelsea Flower Show tomorrow. I'm really looking forward to it & have lots of ambitious but rather vague plans for our scrubby garden which I am hoping will crystallise into a *masterplan* once I have been inspired. Dan v dubious, says I am the Grim Reaper of the plant world so anything we buy will be a waste of money. Am planning to look marvellously elegant but so far have only sorted out what shoes to wear (brown wedge sandals), unsure what to wear on rest of body as also want to give the impression that I am quite earthy & sexy & not afraid of a bit of manual labour like a proper keen gardener. Have to say my feet do v much indicate I'm not afraid of manual labour. In fact, look like I have been pulling a plough barefoot. Spent all this evening watching telly with feet in buckets of hot water & have just scrubbed & moisturised them. Have to say if anything they look a bit drier & much more purple. Shall now have to ring Lou for emergency advice.

From: Nell Fenton
To: Charlotte Bailey

At least your feet a nice shape once you get rid of the crusty old skin and they get a bit brown. No pedicure in the world can remedy hideous kipper shape of my feet. Also easy to kill plants, anyone can do that, my special skill is to keep them alive but small and stunted despite lavishing lots of care and attention on them. (Climbers that never actually climb anywhere are my speciality.)

From: Charlotte Bailey
To: Nell Fenton
Re: I am very elegant

Unfortunately plan to look sexy yet elegant etc remained as plan only. After I'd emailed you rang Lou about gruesome feet situation & she said it sounded like I needed *professional* help but explained I didn't have time, so then she suggested I smother my feet in foot balm and wrap them in plastic overnight. Felt slightly ridiculous as I sat on our bed copiously squirting my feet with moisturiser & wrapping them in cling film but decided to persevere in quest for pedicular excellence. Got to sleep by resolutely ignoring horrible sensation that I was slowly suffocating from the feet up, unfortunately about 1am Maddie yelled out & I leapt out of bed half asleep. Don't know if you've ever tried to run with very greasy feet wrapped in cling film but let me tell you it's fucking impossible. Dan awakened not by Maddie but by me scrabbling & grabbing at furniture. Lost my balance & fell quite hard against the tall chest of drawers in our bedroom & really bruised my hip & chin (yes, chin, not shin, have big gloomy-looking bruise on it that seems to throw off foundation). My feet look much less dry but still weirdly purple & couldn't wear wedge sandals anyway as they made my bruised hip hurt. Had to wear flip-flops from godmother outfit instead but that was ok too as when I got my elegant/sophisticated blue trouser suit out of its suit bag, discovered it actually had quite a decent sized patch of mould on the left shoulder (undealt with baby posset?), so ended up wearing godmother dress that goes with godmother flip-flops anyway (dress also quite grubby but as it had not been festering in a suit bag, no actual mould on it & therefore baby wipes up to the cleaning job). Also failed to crystallise my *masterplan* as majority of the gardens absolutely hideous. It seems nowadays plants are passe & what your garden absolutely must have is large sheet of glass with water pouring over it or failing that a series of tall rusty-looking spikes sticking out of the ground that you can impale yourself on when you have tripped over your giant Zen pebbles.

From: Nell Fenton
To: Charlotte Bailey

Agree bruised chin surprisingly hard to conceal. When Ollie was a tiny baby was nuzzling his face once and he latched onto my chin and sucked it with great gusto. Thought it was adorable till I noticed a dirty great bruise on it later and putting foundation on it just seemed to emphasise it. Also everyone looks suspiciously at your husband if you've got a bruise on your face. Should get Toby to photograph you and title it 'The Woman Whose Foot Treatment Went Wrong'.

From: Charlotte Bailey
To: Nell Fenton

Geraldine's v kindly offered me her cottage in Suffolk for half-term as she doesn't have a let this year. Feel slightly bad as she offered it to me & then I bullied her into letting Fran come too as Dan can't. Think she's a bit nervous about so many children (told her Fran's boys are very well behaved).

From: Rachel Lockwood
To: Nell Fenton

Dear Nell

Sorry about the long silence. Things have not been going at all well and Jack has moved out. He rented himself a flat while I was in Canada. There isn't anybody else but he says he can't live here any more. I don't know how to comfort Jonathan. I can't say he's coming back in case he doesn't. I really don't know what to feel, mostly I feel blank. I will phone you soon but not just yet. Rachel x

From: Nell Fenton
To: Rachel Lockwood

Dearest Rachel, I'm so terribly sorry, I wish I could think of something to say to help. Please phone as soon as you feel able. Love Nell xxx

From: Nell Fenton
To: Charlotte Bailey

I finally heard from Rachel. That selfish bastard Jack has moved out, can't believe it. If a lovely wife and a wonderful son aren't enough to make him happy, hard to imagine what will. I hate him so much.

JUNE 00

From: Charlotte Bailey
To: Nell Fenton
Re: Suffolk

Been having a v lovely time, Geraldine's cottage is really pretty in a low-ceilinged beamy sort of way. The weather's been fantastic so we've been to the beach every day. Also done loads of crabbing (though spend much more time unhooking crab lines from each other's clothes than actual crabs). Yesterday had the unparalleled excitement of seeing the coastguard doing what we thought was an air-sea rescue until we realised it was just a training exercise & nobody was about to drown which for some reason caused Nathan & Jacob to start punching each other.

From: Nell Fenton
To: Charlotte Bailey

All sounds lovely. I on the other hand am in the thick of end-of-term tedium, had to go to an art exhibition yesterday and today it's a piano recital by all students taught by Josie's teacher. I don't care what the other children can do and I'm intimately acquainted with all Josie's piano pieces so I'm bored in anticipation.

From: Charlotte Bailey
To: Nell Fenton
Re: Inevitable casualty trip with Fran

Today bit of a washout as we spent 4 hrs in casualty. After breakfast Jacob sidled up to Fran & said 'Muuum . . . I've lost Captain Scarlett's gun' so Fran in usual manner of exasperated mother asked him WHERE he had lost it, turned out he had 'lost it' up his nose. V ironic really as apparently he only put it there to keep it safe from Barnaby. Casualty completely packed & by the time we got to see a Dr & then consultant all the children were practically running up the walls they'd had so much Coke & choc-olate from the vending machines (Fran & I being v liberal with the 50ps). Had to see a consultant as stupid bloody gun so far up Jacob's nose they could only just see it & said it was going to require general anaesthetic to get it out. Fran understandably so pissed off said she really couldn't remember a holiday ever where they hadn't ended up in casualty. Anyway just as the consultant was leaving, Jacob did the most massive, disgusting sneeze (onto consultant's hand) & the gun came out.

From: Nell Fenton
To: Charlotte Bailey

One of the few horrors I've so far escaped though I know it's amazingly common. Didn't Betsey put about 10 daisies up her nose once?

From: Charlotte Bailey
To: Nell Fenton

It was 13 actually but half were in her ears. Got back home

from the cottage this afternoon. Later than originally planned as Fran & I spent a good hour fixing a large hole where Nathan's head had gone through children's bedroom ceiling (he was bouncing on the bed at the time). Fran furious about it but did most amazing camouflage job skewering & then easing flapping piece of plasterboard back into place & thickly painting over cracks with emulsion we found in the shed (even coloured paint with tiny bit of coffee so it wd look old). Afterwards impossible to tell anything had happened. Fran says she is past master at fixing stuff as she's had so much practice.

From: Nell Fenton
To: Charlotte Bailey

Love hearing about Fran's children. Always helps to remember things could be worse and you could have children like hers when your own are particularly out of control.

From: Charlotte Bailey
To: Nell Fenton
Re: want to kill husband/brother-in-law

Think the general consensus of opinion would be that Dan & I have a v harmonious marriage & while I think Toby entirely feckless, am genuinely fond of him. So my sudden realisation last night that I v much wish to bludgeon both men to death with Toby's enlarger (not as rude as it sounds – tiresome piece of photographic equipment) came as quite a surprise even to me. Think this has prob been brought on by stink from Toby's darkroom & fact Toby has decided to buy a car. Both Dan & Toby completely ecstatic at car idea & entirely undeterred by the fact that at least for the time being Toby has absolutely no money. Keep having to field calls from eager car salesmen to find out how the test drive went, am thinking of circulating photos & details of Toby & Dan to all local car dealerships with explanatory note that they are both delusional & will not actually be buying a car any time soon.

From: Nell Fenton
To: Charlotte Bailey

Would have thought Dan was already blacklisted, with the amount of time he spends lurking around car dealerships. See now there is an upside to Michael making all his car-buying decisions in under a minute (though we have had some truly crap cars over the years).

We had dinner last night with our friends Nina and Richard (woman from Michael's office and v nice doctor husband). They told us that the night before their twins' birthday a couple of weeks ago, they'd got home drunk from a party and decided it would be exciting for the boys to follow a trail of chocolates through the garden to their presents hidden under a bush. They were so pleased with their scheme they set it all out before going to bed. The boys ran out in excitement next morning to find only a few chewed wrappers, as the birthday racoons had got there first. Luckily the boys thought the chewed chocolatey wrappers were the clues, didn't seem to notice that they were now randomly scattered and found the presents anyway which since they contained no food had only been slightly scrabbled at.

From: Charlotte Bailey
To: Nell Fenton

Blimey, they must have been quite drunk to see no downside to leaving the presents out all night.

Was out with Hugh most of today. Came back to 3 messages from Geraldine each one sounding increasingly urgent. V worried she'd been to the cottage and spotted Fran's handiwork on her ceiling. Rang back & she said she was just phoning for a chat. Felt such a rush of relief re ceiling, ended up inviting her over & DID NOT say, So why the mounting hysteria, you loony?

From: Nell Fenton
To: Charlotte Bailey

Like having your own personal stalker really. On the bright side, when you die you'll probably shoot straight up to heaven.

From: Charlotte Bailey
To: Nell Fenton
Re: please stop talking

Geraldine spent entire evening telling me how over Gil she is & how ready she is to 'move on' (new theme). I know she's having a horrible time at the moment & I am sympathetic, but I was so bored I almost felt like crying or at least joining in the car conversation Dan & Toby were having at the other end of the table – Hugh Sr is advancing Toby some of his inheritance money & he is going to use it to actually buy a car. Then he is going to drive about Europe being a photographer. Didn't believe it was possible for Toby & Dan to talk about cars more than they already were, I now see I was mistaken – reality of buying a car rather than talking about buying a car has moved the obsession onto a whole new level. V much wanted to hide in a cupboard with Hugh's bobble hat pulled down over my ears so wouldn't need to hear anyone talking about 'Tiptronic gear change' or 'fresh starts' any more.

From: Nell Fenton
To: Charlotte Bailey

Well, at least if Toby does get a car he'll be driving round Europe, not stinking out your house with noxious chemicals. Why not put Geraldine in the car with him and that way she really can 'move on'?

From: Nell Fenton
To: Charlotte Bailey

Rachel finally called last night. She sounded pretty bad. Said she's finding it very hard to get over the shock of Jack leaving. She knew things had been very rocky for quite some time but had no idea he was that unhappy. She says she came back from Canada feeling really positive and determined to sort out their problems and had been so pleased and surprised at how much he wanted her to have a holiday. Now she realises he just wanted her away. He told her he feels suffocated by their marriage and the responsibilities of fatherhood and says his leaving is best for everybody and it's the right thing to do. She hasn't been able to face telling her parents yet because she knows how distressed they'll be. I told her she must tell them, she needs their support and they're going to find out anyway.

I can't decide if I despise him more for what he's done or for the way he's justifying it.

From: Charlotte Bailey
To: Nell Fenton

What a bastard. Situation just awful but have to say I think if he feels suffocated she's probably better off without him.

From: Nell Fenton
To: Charlotte Bailey

I had my first antenatal today (prenatal here). Doctor seemed nice but one of those people who gets that white flotsam in the corners of their mouth when they talk. Tried v hard not to look at it but my eyes kept straying towards it. Anyway he prodded me a bit and says everything seems fine though he was surprised (given my great age I suppose) that I was adamant about no screening for abnormalities. Think he thought I was crazy because he then suggested as a poor substitute at least having Michael and me come in so he could go through the risks of being both ancient and pregnant. Graciously declined that one too. Can't wait to tell the children.

From: Charlotte Bailey
To: Nell Fenton

Love 1st antenatal, always v reassuring to have someone agree you're pregnant & baby not merely figment of your imagination. I'd love to tell Ellie & Maddie about the baby, presumably ok if you're telling yours?

156

From: Nell Fenton
To: Charlotte Bailey

Of course. Josie over the moon, begged me to go baby-clothes shopping there and then and has written a list of suggested names (including 'Sabelia' which she admitted was made up). Rob quite excited in a daft way. Ollie most disgruntled and said he was going to put the baby out on the road which seemed a little severe.

From: Charlotte Bailey
To: Nell Fenton

Poor Ollie, he's been the almighty ruler of your family for a long time, so the news must be quite a shock. Maddie & Ellie very pleased about new cousin, though dismayed you won't have produced it by the next time they see you, also obviously v unsatisfactory for you to have a baby without me having one too so had to field a lot of questions about when we are going to have one. Finally managed to shut them up by saying, 'When God decides.' Speaking of decisions, v important decision re what car Toby is going to buy has been made & he, Dan & Hugh are driving to Essex tomorrow to look at a 10-yr-old red Alfa Romeo Spider. An absolutely brilliant choice as we all know how reliable Italian cars are in general esp sports cars with 80,000 miles on the clock. Luckily this one has only had 1 careful lady owner so should be fine.

From: Nell Fenton
To: Charlotte Bailey

V stylish car though, which one obviously needs if one is an international photographer.

Josie had a retainer fitted on her teeth today to try and rectify the damage done by prolonged dummy sucking followed by prolonged thumb sucking. Have told her this is positively THE END of thumb sucking – even if being 9 not sufficient incentive for her, the exorbitant cost of orthodontics in this country is a powerful incentive for me and I will chop off her thumb if necessary. Before adopting this radical measure we are trying the more 'softly-softly' approach of wrapping her thumb in plasters. Dentist is muttering about her having to have headgear which she'd have to wear 14 hrs a day, all this simply preliminary to full-blown braces. Am afraid we will be left bankrupt and destitute but at least Josie will have perfect N American teeth.

From: Charlotte Bailey
To: Nell Fenton

Shouldn't have told her you'd chop her thumb off, she'll never believe you. Should instead have threatened her with the 'thumb fairy' who comes with her tiny fairy hacksaw & saws your thumb off while you sleep if you're still sucking it over the age of 8. Last time I took mine to the dentist about 3 weeks ago had a bit of a 'breakthrough' with Maddie as although this was her 3rd visit to the dentist it was the 1st time I actually managed to get her to open her mouth & she even went so far as allowing the dentist to count her teeth. We were triumphant.

Peter came for lunch today & I am completely in love with him. He's very funny & charming, but not in a show-off way, told the children lots of stories about him & Dan & Toby when they were little, his apple farm & his pig Naomi. They absolutely loved him & he thought my cooking was utterly marvellous. So now I've told Dan that I shall be leaving him to live with Peter who is much nicer & more appreciative & laughs at all my jokes, Dan says that's fine as long as I take the children or at the very least Hugh.

From: Nell Fenton
To: Charlotte Bailey

He sounds lovely and living on an apple farm incredibly whole-some and appealing. I recommend you make the switch at once. Benny (bloody buggering hamster) keeps escaping. Have spent a fortune on all this plastic tunnel stuff to try and keep him amused but to no avail. Don't even know how he's getting out and the children and I have yet again just spent an hour and a half searching for the little bastard. I'm sure if I don't find him the cat will. Unfortunately as the basement is so big and so very untidy it presents a considerable challenge. The only clue we had to go on was the fact that the carpet by the boiler room has been badly chewed up, so conducted a finger-tip search (as they say in the Met) of the boiler room which involved moving about 100 suitcases but sadly proved to be a dead end. Anyway gave up finally, will try again tomorrow, in the meantime the best I can hope for is that if the cat does find him she eats him completely, don't want one of the children finding half a hamster or just some paws.

From: Charlotte Bailey
To: Nell Fenton
Re: Why not drive 8 hrs to buy a camera?

Hamster definitely won't be dead, much more likely to have found himself a mouse girlfriend, got married and had babies and your house will soon be overrun with 'mamsters'. Obviously now Toby has bought a car (got the Spider last Sat) he & Dan can't talk about what car to buy any more. Fortunately he is planning to buy a camera so car talk has been superseded by endless camera talk & although he works in a sodding camera shop getting a camera from there would be TOO STRAIGHT-FORWARD, so instead Dan & Toby are driving to Blackpool in the Spider this Sat combining the excitement of putting an ancient & unreliable car 'through her paces' with the thrill of buying a second-hand Leica from someone called Reginald Coulthard. Toby told me proudly Leica is 'completely basic & does bloody nothing' – surprising as it seems to be costing a billion pounds. Dan super-excited at prospect of child-free day, says he'll be back in time to help put children to bed but some-how doubt it.

From: Charlotte Bailey
To: Nell Fenton

Dan not back in time to put children to bed last night, in fact not back till lunchtime today. Spider engine overheated & they broke down just before they got to Blackpool. The AA towed it to a gar-age, Dan & Toby got a taxi to Reginald's house & then spent night in a B&B. They took the train back this morning. Car being towed back to London tomorrow as garage in Blackpool couldn't fix it.

From: Nell Fenton
To: Charlotte Bailey

School about to finish – weeks ahead of England. Have avoided the ghastly prospect of having to entertain the children and have enrolled Josie and Rob in summer camp (at vast expense) for a couple of weeks. Quite extraordinary climate here. Though it was winter the day before yesterday I actually had to put the air conditioning on today, it was so hot and humid. Sudden season change has caught me out with gruesome winter legs (leg hair growing peacefully out of sight inside my trousers, undisturbed since Cuba) so have made emergency appointment for essential deforestation (particularly essential as we've got our visit to Lou and Walt next w/e and don't want Lou to know I secretly walk around all winter with hairy legs).

From: Charlotte Bailey
To: Nell Fenton

Think before you go you should warn beautician about your legs as it may be necessary to book a double appt. Any sign of the mamsters yet?

From: Nell Fenton
To: Charlotte Bailey
Re: still a bachelor

No, but hamster found alive and well and living (alone) in the basement bathroom cupboard. Had made himself quite a comfortable bed from the chewed-up carpet and bits of lining paper he had skilfully stripped from the inside of the cupboard wall. Obviously realised it was a fair cop and came quietly. Thank you for your thoughtful suggestion re legs.

From: Charlotte Bailey
To: Nell Fenton

I spoke to Anna last night. She's in an absolute rage. Toulouse-

Lautrec ate Isabel's science project. Poor Isabel really upset. It was a model of a nuclear power station for an inter-school competition & apparently it took her ages. Anna is going to help her make it again, meanwhile TL has been banished to the garden but he keeps howling & biting the heads off Geoffrey's begonias. Says she doesn't care about the begonias – they're hideous anyway – but the howling is driving her mad & the neighbours keep complaining. She's at her wits' end & is investigating a dog-obedience class in Winslow. Suggested she just shoot him instead, easier, cheaper & absolutely guaranteed to shut him up. Said she would dearly love to, but suspects the children (even Isabel) would mind.

From: Nell Fenton
To: Charlotte Bailey

Really no end to the vileness of that dog. I'd shoot myself sooner than go to dog-obedience classes with him. Children are all on holiday now so until they go to camp have been taking them to extremely nice, clean, DOG-FREE park round the corner from our house. It has a big area with water jets shooting in the air so have spent last 2 days lying on the grass watching them scamper in and out of the spray. Keeps them cool and occupied. Had a little light bleeding this morning. Feel fine though so probably nothing. Never had it with the others though so gave me a bit of a fright.

From: Charlotte Bailey
To: Nell Fenton

I'm sure it's nothing to worry about, spotting is quite common, but you absolutely MUST rest & lie down. How is it now?

From: Nell Fenton
To: Charlotte Bailey

Still happening. We cancelled going to Lou and Walt just to
be on the safe side. Anyhow Michael is home so have been
lying down mostly today (not that I think it makes any difference, anyway am sure it's nothing).

From: Charlotte Bailey
To: Nell Fenton

Really think you should see somebody. I've checked my pregnancy book & lying down DOES make a difference – it
increases blood flow to the placenta & helps it to anchor more
firmly. How's the bleeding now?

From: Nell Fenton
To: Charlotte Bailey

Still there, quite light though. Still feel pregnant and called the
doctor who said lie down and go to the ER if it gets worse.

From: Louise Corrigan
To: Charlotte Bailey

Michael called & left a message that Nell isn't feeling too
good & he doesn't think they'll be able to make it this w/e.
Is everything OK?

From: Charlotte Bailey
To: Louise Corrigan

Not really. Nell has had some bleeding & it's not tailing off. We're all pretending it's nothing to worry about. I know lots of women have bleeding in pregnancy & everything turns out fine, but it's always alarming. Feel very worried about her actually, took her so long to get pregnant this time, but she still feels pregnant so that's encouraging. Love C x

From: Louise Corrigan
To: Charlotte Bailey

Keep me posted, don't want to bother Nell. Speak soon x L

From: Michael Fenton
To: Charlotte Bailey

Got your message. Nell asked me to email you. She went to the hospital this evening, bleeding was quite bad but otherwise she seems ok. She's having a scan tomorrow about 1 your time. Will let you know.

From: Michael Fenton
To: Charlotte Bailey

Scan showed there was no heartbeat. Nell is very upset. She's sleeping now but call her later.

From: Charlotte Bailey
To: Nell Fenton

How are you today? How are the children?

From: Nell Fenton
To: Charlotte Bailey

I'm ok, been too busy getting Josie and Rob's stuff ready for camp to think about anything. Josie's very sad but trying to hide it as she can see it upsets me which is just awful. Rob seems ok, hasn't really said much. Haven't told Ollie, he was cross about the whole thing anyway, so am hoping he'll just forget about it. Magdalena, our babysitter, has been really kind and helpful but if she tells me it was God's will one more time I'll kill her.

From: Nell Fenton
To: Charlotte Bailey

The children went off to camp this morning and I was down in the basement with Ollie sorting out toys when he found his old car seat. He said, 'This can be for the new baby.' Feebly tried to get out of telling him by saying, 'I thought you didn't want a new baby?' Said he'd decided he did want it so I had to tell him the baby wasn't coming any more. He was terribly upset and kept asking why. In the end I said God wanted the baby so it had gone up to heaven. He picked up a whistle and started blowing it angrily saying he was going to blow God away.

From: Charlotte Bailey
To: Nell Fenton

How absolutely awful for you. There's no easy way to explain these things.

From: Nell Fenton
To: Charlotte Bailey

No, there isn't but I'm alright. We're going to start trying again in a few months so perhaps I'll get pregnant again.

From: Charlotte Bailey
To: Nell Fenton

I'm sure you will, but let yourself get over this first. We're going to use some of the money from Uncle Will to fix our stairs. Albert keeps jumping up & down on them to demonstrate how bouncy they are & how urgently they need to be 'sorted' – sure they would be much less perilous if he could refrain from doing experimental jumps on them all the time. They scare the crap out of me. If it's not too horribly expensive to get them 'sorted'

166

may even be able to afford to go to Cape Cod to see Lou & Walt. We've got our end-of-term quiz night fundraiser tonight. I'm feeling quietly confident as have been studying Ellie's junior atlas & we have Joe on our team & Fran says he's absolutely brilliant at quizzes.

From: Charlotte Bailey
To: Nell Fenton
Re: we are the champions

Oh God. Don't think I can ever show my face at school again. We won at quiz night & while this might appear cause for celebration we only won because we cheated. Is ok to cheat if you are 1) vv drunk (covered that base), 2) if you do it very openly in front of the judges (did that too) and 3) if you are coming last by a really long way at half-time. NOT, however, ok if cheating is so successful you streak into the lead, win & are presented with silver cup & lovely case of wine meant for people who are actually brainy. Dan says he was too drunk to care & phoning the news desk to get the answers is also a form of brainpower. He, however, will not be in the playground this afternoon fielding the pointed remarks about what a miracle it was to come up from so far behind. So only 2 more weeks of total humiliation before the end of term.

From: Nell Fenton
To: Charlotte Bailey

Just drink some of the wine you won before school pickup. Will give you the courage to brazen it out.

Children's camp fantastic. They get picked up at our door in

167

the morning and then delivered back about 5pm completely exhausted having done lots of wholesome physical activity, so can let them flop in front of the telly with a completely clear conscience. Rob brought me an object he made in woodwork. Have no idea what it's meant to be and seemed rude to ask so just admired it very warmly and put it up on a shelf 'to keep it safe'.

From: Charlotte Bailey
To: Nell Fenton
Re: Toby's gone

Am familiar with the problem of not being able to identify what I've been given, though at the moment straightforward with Maddie as she mainly makes me ashtrays out of clay (puzzling as none of us smoke – must be Albert's influence). We waved Toby off in the Spider this morning, he looked great for about 100 yds then stalled on the corner just as Brian & Hildegard speedwalked past with Hermann their repulsive little pug. They were taking him for a 'walk' although this doesn't involve any actual walking on Hermann's part as he is so breathless has to be carried everywhere. Hermann v nervous & noisy revving required to get Spider going again made him scrabble like mad in the rucksack on Brian's back. Thought, bloody hell, Hermann's going to have a heart attack & we're going to be sued but then the engine turned over & Toby shot off – wish I could say romantically into the horizon but was actually about another 100 yds into nasty snarl up on the mini-roundabout so then had to stand around waving for another 20 mins (girls insisted) till he finally inched out of sight. He's going to ring when he gets to Spain, not quite sure why from Spain in particular but ours is not to reason why.

From: Nell Fenton
To: Charlotte Bailey

Want to be a bit careful about startling Hermann too much.
Apparently pugs so overbred not only can they not breathe
but their eyeballs pop out all the time.

From: Charlotte Bailey
To: Nell Fenton

I've decided it's high time to start potty-training Hugh as 1) we
have read 'I want my potty' many, many times, 2) had several talks
about the potty, 3) thoroughly familiarised ourselves with it by sitting on it every night after the bath for last week. Hugh has never
done anything on it so had a demonstratory wee done by Maddie
to clarify its purpose. Hugh terribly impressed & pleased with
'demo' (Maddie, paid in Smarties, also v glad). Am feeling v positive & well prepared about whole thing. START TOMORROW.

From: Nell Fenton
To: Charlotte Bailey

Good luck. Josie was easy but Rob and Ollie were both a
nightmare. Any progress?

From: Charlotte Bailey
To: Nell Fenton
Re: the money pit

Not yet, have had to delay as he's a bit under the weather.

We've had a structural engineer come to look at our bouncy stairs. Guess whether it's a minor problem or whether they need major work done on them as they are coming away from the wall. Also guess whether it will be straightforward or as it is a suspended staircase likely to be complicated & expensive. Guess.

From: Nell Fenton
To: Charlotte Bailey

I'm guessing from the slight tension I detect in your tone that perhaps it's going to be expensive, but on the upside it's a beautiful staircase, you have the money from Uncle Will, and doing the work will probably save one or more members of your family from an untimely death.

From: Charlotte Bailey
To: Nell Fenton

Toby has rung sooner than expected & from France. Poor bugger did mammoth drive from Calais to some exquisitely picturesque fishing village near Marseille, only stopping when Spider broke down or overheated (6 times). So thrilled to see the sea, just parked & ran in fully dressed. Unfortunately by the time he got back to the Spider everything had been nicked out of body of the car. Only good thing is had slammed boot hard earlier & the lock on it had jammed so thieves didn't get the Leica, also he thinks they may have tried to nick car itself but couldn't start it, so that's a relief. Has to take car to a garage now to get lock on the boot drilled out so he can get at his camera & camping gear.

Hugh better. START POTTY-TRAINING TOMORROW WITH-
OUT FAIL.

From: Charlotte Bailey
To: Nell Fenton
Re: mr wee-wee pants

I think there is something seriously wrong with Hugh. He is
either missing crucial messaging between bladder & brain or
has the bladder of a mouse, which quite frankly is only POSS-
IBLE explanation for nearly constant stream of pee pouring
out of him between 9.15am when we started potty-training &
10.45am when we decided to bail out (quite literally) & put a
nappy back on him, he had peed on the kitchen floor FIVE
times. Didn't realise it was humanly possible to wee that much.
Fran says I mustn't be put off & must get straight back on the
potty so to speak, apparently this is normal for boys & I have
been lulled into false sense of security re potty-training by having girls with actual bladders first.

From: Nell Fenton
To: Charlotte Bailey

Fran quite right. You have to learn with boys the basic rule
that just because they've just peed, doesn't mean they aren't
about to pee again. One health visitor who I consulted in
despair helpfully suggested I put a coloured ping-pong ball in
the loo so when we flushed the contents of the potty (together)
ping-pong ball would bob amusingly in the water. This would
apparently render my seemingly irreversibly incontinent child
perfectly clean and dry.

From: Charlotte Bailey
To: Nell Fenton

Am probably just clutching at straws but today maybe teeny bit better in so far as Ana Frid managed to 'catch' I wee in the potty. Although given the fact Hugh is constantly weeing & she or I are constantly brandishing a potty had to happen sooner or later.

From: Nell Fenton
To: Charlotte Bailey

Nina told me when she was potty-training her twins she bought about 72 buckets and just left them everywhere which worked eventually. Might be worth a try.

From: Charlotte Bailey
To: Nell Fenton

Suspect I shall shortly start smelling like a tramp as have given up changing every time I get soaked in wee & just let it dry off (Ana Frid still endlessly changing her clothes & doing laundry). Wish I could report pleasing progress but if there is any it's only because my reflexes have improved. Fran says I will have a 'breakthrough' soon & must persevere. Only good news is H v predictable on pooing front, though he insists on a nappy for that.

From: Nell Fenton
To: Charlotte Bailey

Well, Hugh may be hard work but he's a walk in the park compared to Rob. Latest thing we have started is occupational therapy to try and address his determination to reverse everything he writes. Don't think he's dyslexic because he's making good progress with his reading and spelling. Apart from constant reversals he also suddenly goes off into this bizarre mirror writing (perhaps brain is in back to front?). Occupational therapist is a v nice woman but uses a lot of occupational therapy jargon that I feel I should understand but don't, so nod wisely. Hopefully this will be actual practical help to him unlike the stupid bloody 'play therapy' that I now want to kick myself for.

From: Charlotte Bailey
To: Nell Fenton
Re: Hugh completely hopeless

Have abandoned potty-training as have now realised it involves more than simply removing child's nappy so it can wee all over the house, there must be tiny inkling in mind of 'trainee' as to what is required of them, and although poor Maddie has barely been allowed off the potty all week, Hugh still entirely mystified as to its function. Final straw was when he made it absolutely clear today he has no idea whatever what his bum is up to, as despite repeatedly & hotly denying he needed a 'yukky wee' (his expression for a poo) then immediately did one on the playroom sofa. Luckily 'yukky wee' stayed mainly stuck to his bum so clean-up not TOO bad. He is now back in nappies to everyone's immense relief.

From: Nell Fenton
To: Charlotte Bailey

Very wise, just gets too disgusting and dispiriting in the end.

Could try again in France, at least they're outside all day there and can run around with a bare bum.

From: Charlotte Bailey
To: Nell Fenton

Last day of term & sports day today. Both girls magnificently unsporty but Maddie definitely has the edge on Ellie when it comes to being hopeless. Although for the nursery races you practically had to be headless not to win some sort of ribbon, Maddie & about 2 others (despite all being in possession of heads) were sadly not in possession of a single winner/2nd/3rd/4th/5th/runner-up, etc, etc ribbon by the end of the morning. Crisis averted by the fact the school had been thoughtful enough to provide a 'I'm a good sport' ribbon for the absolute drongos & while 'I'm a good sport' clearly code for 'I'm completely crap at sport', Maddie absolutely thrilled as these 'drongo' ribbons much harder to obtain than a 2-a-penny 'runners-up' one.

From: Nell Fenton
To: Charlotte Bailey

Mercifully our sports day here was conducted without parents so avoided a) the boredom and b) the humiliation. Last sports day in England Rob begged me so hard to join in the mothers race I reluctantly agreed and then mortified him by coming last. Anyhow Rob and Ollie both came home with ribbons bearing the legend 'participant', which led me to suspect they had not covered themselves with sporting glory either.

From: Charlotte Bailey
To: Nell Fenton

Dan & I had quite an argument about Smelly Gordon last night. He has suggested getting him in to fix the stairs, I have said absolutely not. Couldn't stand it. D says I'm being ridiculous & he is an excellent carpenter & v reasonable. Pointed out he has to have something major going for him in order to put up with the appalling smell emanating from every pore of his sweaty Scottish body. Have reached a compromise & I've promised at least to get a quote from him & Dan knows someone at work who has a carpenter to recommend.

From: Nell Fenton
To: Charlotte Bailey

Well, I completely sympathise but then you know me, I can detect off-milk or a dirty nappy at 1000 paces but couldn't he do the stairs while you're in France?

From: Charlotte Bailey
To: Nell Fenton

Maybe, if he's available then, even so, worried his smell will permeate the walls & still linger even after he has gone.

Have to start looking for a new au pair as Ana Frid starts university after the summer so will be going back to Sweden when we leave for France. Very much wish I could persuade her to forgo the challenge of a degree in biochemistry for what I am sure will be the far greater challenge of attempting to potty-train Hugh again. Despite my suggestion of this exciting alternative she has decided to take up Gothenburg University's offer rather than mine. How selfish is that?

From: Nell Fenton
To: Charlotte Bailey

Possibly the cold baths and falling masonry that greeted her arrival influenced her decision as much as Hugh's bottom.

Suzette has invited Josie for a long weekend in the cottage they have on a lake up north. Should be lovely for her as she and Takara are good friends, and being a child, a weekend with Suzette won't necessarily make her want to drown herself. Invitation gave Suzette the perfect excuse to tell me about the wonderful tranquillity and beauty at their cottage, how when she's there she feels a 'deep connection' with nature, how the lonely cry of the loons across the lake at dusk helps her get life in perspective etc, droned on about this until I wanted to run and drink a cup of weed killer.

From: Charlotte Bailey
To: Nell Fenton
Re: Gordon smells

Are you sure there's not a loony bin across the lake & Suzette isn't hearing & feeling a deep connection with the lonely cries of the loonies? Would make more sense. Got some Swedish au pair details, can't decide whether or not to get Ana Frid to chat to them as part of 'vetting' process or whether this is a bad idea as she might tell potential candidate all about us & that might put them off.

Smelly Gordon came round to look at the stairs & windows today, I don't care what his quote is he's not getting the job. Albert kept him talking for ages, completely extraordinary on 2 counts, 1) he can bear the smell & 2) he can understand a word Gordon is saying.

From: Nell Fenton
To: Charlotte Bailey

Rob and Josie finished at camp today. Off to the west next week which should be fun.

From: Charlotte Bailey
To: Nell Fenton

Got Gordon's quote today, it's considerably lower than other 2 I've had – the difference between Cape Cod being a possibility or not, so looks like Gordon will be stinking out the house after all.

From: Nell Fenton
To: Charlotte Bailey

Oh dear, perhaps you can get everyone those little nose clips they have for synchronised swimming.

Josie came back from the cottage yesterday. She had a lovely time and looks really healthy and brown. Kane dragged them round the lake with his boat for hours in a giant rubber tyre, nice of him, though he's probably as desperate to get away from Suzette as everyone else. Not sure Suzette found her usual level of inner tranquillity because Josie said she was crabby with Kane and she and Sophie 'argued a real lot'. Off to the Rockies tomorrow – must go and scrabble a suitcase together.

From: Nell Fenton
To: Charlotte Bailey

Got back last night from our trip. Rockies spectacular and we stayed first three nights in a lovely hotel called Banff Springs. Then went for 4 days to stay on a ranch (v authentic – used as the set in lots of Westerns apparently). Children adored it and had lots of shoot-outs and Michael bought them all real cowboy hats. First morning there Josie and I went on a 2-hour ride. Only felt a bit sore after morning ride (though can't remember when I last sat on a horse) so agreed to ride again to a barbecue by a river gorge in the evening. During the course of 2nd ride, became so acutely saddle-sore was gasping with pain every time my bum was jolted and I began to think I might never walk (or sit down) again. Also quite alarming, lots of scrambling up really steep and thickly wooded paths on horseback. By the time we got there (about an hour's ride) was in extremis and could just barely hobble. After the barbecue had to ignominiously return to the ranch in the wagon with all the really little children. Michael, Josie and Rob also went white-water rafting while I stayed with Ollie. Fortunately they all survived though would never have agreed to the children doing it had I known that part of it involved jumping in the river in a wetsuit and life jacket and being swept along just holding onto a bit of rope. Managed to almost get killed myself on the last day, alarming at the time but quite exciting in retrospect. Was in the corral with about 20 horses milling about when one of the horses got its bridle caught on the water trough. The horse totally panicked and threw its head back.

Must have done it with the most phenomenal strength because it yanked out the whole water trough which flew into the air making all the horses suddenly rear up and stampede to the far side of the corral. Had the presence of mind to run the opposite way to the horses and climb out. The children saw it happen and were terrified and thrilled. Quite a few people in the corral at the time but amazingly only one was knocked down and she wasn't really hurt. Made me feel quite daring and Wild Westish.

From: Charlotte Bailey
To: Nell Fenton
Re: day of mixed emotions

Sounds absolutely amazing, am v jealous. Be dangerous if we went though, as Hugh would definitely explode with joy. Dan terribly impressed with how daring you've all become esp as his idea of an adventure holiday is travelling with only 1 credit card & no back-up cash. Au pair dilemma solved, Ana Frid has a friend who knows all about us through Ana Frid & amazingly still wants to come & be our au pair. Spoke to her last night, every time I mentioned Hugh she said 'Ahh, he sounds so cute!' Resisted impulse to say 'Bloody hell you're hired' but instead did very measured 'Well. I think we'll get along fine please start in September please, thank you, please.' Ana Frid says she's terribly nice & we'll really like her. Feel most relieved to have sorted it out. Have also booked our flights to Boston & Smelly Gordon to come & fix the stairs, so all in all a day of mixed emotions.

AUGUST 00

From: Rachel Lockwood
To: Nell Fenton

Dear Nell

I was so very sorry to hear your sad news, I wish you'd told me before. I know how much you wanted the baby, it must be awful, try not to be too upset. I'm sure you'll get pregnant again soon. Jonathan and I are ok, we've been staying with Mum and Dad for the last couple of weeks. They've been wonderful, especially Dad who has occupied Jonathan endlessly on various projects they've dreamed up together. I'd have loved to see you when you're over but we'll be staying up at Jane's. It'll be good for Jonathan, he loves being with his cousins and it stops him thinking about Jack so much. Everyone has been so incredibly kind but I'm going to have to go home and sort myself out soon, I need to get a job. Jack wants to take Jonathan for a week later in the month so I think I'll start looking then. I'm really dreading it, I feel unqualified for anything and distinctly unemployable. Send my love to Michael and the children and look after yourself.

Fondest love to all
Rachel xx

From: Charlotte Bailey
To: Louise Corrigan

Couldn't talk when you rang yesterday, was rushing out the door to Dr's appt. Re cot – don't worry about borrowing one, we'll bring our travel one. We'll be arriving Thurs 17th, prob around 11.30pm. Can't tell you how much we are looking forward to coming. Love C xxx

From: Louise Corrigan
To: Charlotte Bailey

Great – good to arrive on a Thursday, Cape a nightmare to get to at the weekend. Have lots of plans for your visit, Walt will mail you directions closer to the time. Hope you're all ok. Is one of the kids sick? Speak soon x L

From: Charlotte Bailey
To: Louise Corrigan

No one's sick. I had a gynaecologist appointment – nothing wrong just still failing to get pregnant, everything is normal with me so now over to Dan who is vv resistant re his 'test'. Quite frankly don't know if it's worth making him do it as apparently if there's nothing wrong with him either & I still can't get pregnant next step would be IVF which I'm not going to do. So what's the point? Haven't told Nell any of this, she is still quite down about her miscarriage & don't want to discuss anything to do with babies with her. Love C xx

From: Charlotte Bailey
To: Nell Fenton
Re: designer garden

Catherine & Susan doing their best to spoil our lawn (only half-decent thing about our garden). Unless I manage to re-member to move their run at least once & preferably twice a day they eat the grass right down to the roots so you can tell exactly where their run had been by the very bald & perfectly rectangular patch they leave behind, so it wasn't looking great, that was until Dan stepped in to take over. He decided to reseed & fertilise it, so liberally sprinkled everything with seed & lawn food, concentrating his effort on the bald rectangles. I think it's fair to say it was a combination of factors which re-sulted in the many hideous but perfectly rectangular scorched patches where once there was grass. 1) excessive use of fertil-iser by husband, 2) beating sun, 3) failure of husband to water fertiliser in, 4) having husband who can never be arsed to read instructions for bloody anything resulting in points 1 & 3. Instead of looking just patchy lawn looks irredeemably awful. Dan suggested we place a large contemporary sculpture in middle of lawn & then everyone will think yellow rectangles are intentional.

From: Nell Fenton
To: Charlotte Bailey

Told you you'd regret getting guinea pigs. Can't find anyone foolhardy enough to take our pointless hamsters while we're away so am paying a fortune to a pet sitter who'll come in each day to feed the cat and hamsters. She dropped by so she could 'meet the pets' and I could show her everything and told me most earnestly that she'll play with the animals at least half an hour each visit. Was seriously tempted to ask if I could pay less and just have her come and feed the stupid things but thought that would make me look like a bad person. As to your lawn, can't look worse than mine, some weird ants have colonised our garden and have built vast subterranean networks under our lawn so your foot suddenly vanishes as you walk across it. Asked the young man who mows it to get rid of them and he obviously used something so toxic that half the grass suddenly died, not to mention the minor point that he's probably poisoned my children too. Hate to remonstrate with him though as he has this sweet round face and slow gentle voice and always looks terribly caring when I speak to him. By the way, how's Toby getting on?

From: Charlotte Bailey
To: Nell Fenton
Re: Toby

Toby is in Spain, the Spider is in France, that's all you need to know.

From: Louise Corrigan
To: Charlotte Bailey
Re: your arrival

May be in Boston for a meeting day you arrive in which case we could meet you at the airport & you could follow us to the Cape, not sure yet if meeting is definitely happening, where are you going to be for next couple of weeks so we can get hold of you? Speak soon x L

From: Charlotte Bailey
To: Louise Corrigan
Re: your arrival

Nell & her children are arriving late tonight, they're spending a few days here before she & I go off to France on Friday. I'll be back for the 2 days before we leave to visit you but Dan will be here (in London) all the time till we leave, so prob easiest to call him if you need to let us know anything esp if it involves directions. Love C xx

From: Nell Fenton
To: Michael Fenton

Awful flight, absolutely packed as ever. Children v good but Rob and Ollie both decided they needed a poo as soon as the meals arrived so then had to stack everything perilously on poor Josie so we could scramble out of our seats, had to get rude unhelpful stewardess to back her stupid trolley up the aisle so we could get to the loo and I parked Ollie on one loo and Rob on another but no loo roll in Rob's so was running between them with loo roll. A man sitting nearby said, 'You look as if you've got your hands full.' I said, 'I think I've died and gone to hell.' Anyhow lovely to be in England again and see everyone, Mum and Pa coming over a bit later. xxxx

From: Charlotte Bailey
To: Dan Bailey

We've arrived, train journey a bloody nightmare, it started badly at Waterloo when I bent over to move a case & 2 (yes TWO) crucial buttons flew off my shirt making it completely indecent, so then I had to wear Nell's cardi over the top to stop myself getting arrested for soliciting. Train v warm & having to wear buttoned-up cardi while trying to control 6 extremely over-excited children didn't help. Did something unbelievably stupid, left 2 of the tickets on the train when we changed at Lille, only realised what I had done as we were going to get connecting train so had to rush off to buy new ones – v panicky & last minute. On 2nd train Frenchman trying to get his case down dropped a bag & then a metal pole on Nell's head & then got all annoyed with her for having her head in the way. Nell said it REALLY hurt. Hell of journey finally over & children so delighted to be here. Anna & entourage here already, she has brought v unlikely vv organised friend who has come with her 3 sons, a tent & the hairiest legs I've ever seen. Tom & Maude arriving tomorrow. Love C xx

From: Nell Fenton
To: Michael Fenton

Quite a stressful journey but wonderful to be here. Unfortunately Ollie was so whiny I allowed him more or less unlimited chocolate to shut him up and he then threw up in the car on the way from the station. He gave me a bit of warning so was able to empty the toys out of his little rucksack and catch it in there. Tried to persuade him to let me throw the whole bag away and buy him a new one. Guess whether that was acceptable or not. Some silly French arse dropped a bag on my head on the train and was quite apologetic but then almost immediately dropped a metal pole on me and for some reason then got annoyed. As least it amused the children. House already pretty full and chaotic so the children in heaven. Speak to you later xxxx

From: Charlotte Bailey
To: Dan Bailey

Tom, Maude & the girls arrived from Paris last night. Lily completely gorgeous, doesn't look like a monkey any more. Betsey has shot up & is taller than Hugh now. She & he are soulmates, ignored the acres of garden & spent the morning playing in Tom's car, which I thought was adorable till I noticed they had busied themselves with removing all the rubber trim from around his boot. Geoffrey is cooking supper tonight with the help of Isabel & Guy. Anna isn't allowed to help, so we have all been trying to eat extra lunch. He's been in the kitchen all afternoon & I just heard Isabel shout 'Fucking hell, Dad' & storm out. Guy is still in there but apparently he'll be allowed out for a swim shortly. Anna's friend Harriet completely fantastic, super-helpful & completely cancels out Anna's hopeless vagueness. She's like a drill sergeant with her boys. Youngest one is called Ben, he's terribly handsome & 5, Maddie v much in love with him. Miss you, love C xxxx

From: Nell Fenton
To: Michael Fenton

We're having a lovely time though Geoffrey made supper tonight. Not too bad considering, but quite an odd selection of dishes. First course a choice of 2 different soups (packet – so nothing too much to fear) though think he may have added his own seasoning as both extremely salty. Then there were prawns in garlic and/or grilled sardines, both quite pleasant but served rather strangely with a v small dish of watery and v under-seasoned (to compensate for soup?) mashed potato – apparently he'd been going to roast them but had forgotten about them and had allowed them to overboil so drastically

186

they'd mashed themselves and quite a lot had simply drained out through the colander. There were also some underdone boiled carrots. Pudding, thank God, was a ready-made raspberry tart served for those who wished with a sauce made by melting all the manky leftover chocolate from their car journey (surprisingly delicious actually).

From: Charlotte Bailey
To: Dan Bailey
Re: the usual stuff

Wendy house has become our own little Gaza Strip as total war has broken out between Rory & Theo (tidy & extremely house-proud) & Hugh, Betsey & Ollie who keep trashing it. Guy v embarrassed by Rory & Theo & keeps telling them they're too old to play there & accusing them of being 'gay'. Feelings are running v high & Tom caught Theo with Betsey (probably worst perpetrator) in a headlock, so now everybody has been banned & there is much recrimination. Even Hugh with his very rudimentary brain is outraged & keeps shouting 'my Wendy house'. He completely adores being in the pool, so I just let him bob around till he starts shivering, then fish him out, warm him up & pop him back in. Anna & Geoffrey completely hopeless about watching Greta who has an absolute death wish. She's now jumped in the pool three times although she can't yet swim. Both times although Geoffrey was supposedly watching he's always so absorbed in his paper it's been someone else who's jumped in to retrieve her. They do have some armbands for her but as one of them has a slow puncture she lists alarmingly. Suggested to Anna it might be nice to buy a pair that keep both sides of her head out of the water, not that she ever bloody well puts them on Greta. Had planned to start potty-training Hugh again tomorrow, not sure I can face it, think I'm going to leave it till September. Love Cxxx

From: Nell Fenton
To: Michael Fenton

Can't wait till you get here. Rob and Theo have been getting in some spectacular fights though they seem to make up quite quickly. Still very wearing and though Anna always willing to intervene she never actually notices that they're about to kill each other unless I point it out to her. Too busy doing bloody charcoal drawings of the children to give them any actual practical attention. God knows where Geoffrey hides all day, obviously having 5 children has made him an absolute master at making himself scarce. Children miss you and so do I. xxxx

From: Charlotte Bailey
To: Dan Bailey
Re: more of the usual stuff

Dr had to come today as poor Greta has an ear infection (poss caused by having one side of her head permanently in the water?). When he arrived there were so many children milling around he asked whether we were running a 'colonie de vacances'. Harriet & her 3 boys leaving today so we'll be down to just the 21 of us . . . Hugh, Ollie & Betsey allowed back in the Wendy house now but banned from the chicken runs. Apart from terrorising the chickens by checking the nesting boxes every 5 mins there has been a v high egg casualty rate. If Betsey finds one she tends to love it to death by holding it so tight she crushes it, Hugh too hopeless to get any of his own but sometimes if Betsey has found 2 she'll very magnanimously give him one which he invariably drops or drops & then stands on. So now Hugh (in between stints in the pool) stands sadly by the chicken runs peering in & muttering 'poor shickens'.

Hadn't noticed till now it is possible to see relief on a 'shicken's' face. Not looking forward to the train journey back, feel like we've hardly been here at all. Will try v hard to hang on to all tickets this time. Love C xxx

From: Nell Fenton
To: Charlotte Bailey

Hope your trip back was better than the one out. Even without your lot still too many children here. May have to do a cull. Michael arriving later, Tom kindly going to Bordeaux to pick him up as I can be relied on to get lost. Have a lovely time in Cape Cod and give my love to Lou and Walt.

From: Charlotte Bailey
To: Nell Fenton
Re: Cape Cod fab

It's unbelievably picturesque here, like a Stephen King movie without the creepy bits. All the houses are clapboard & there are no sabotaging council estates or nasty bungalows. Everybody seems to display American flag over their front door which looks utterly charming & patriotic (if you did that in England you'd get firebombed for belonging to the NF). Have had a brief holiday relationship with Dunkin' Donuts, sadly had to end it as I've noticed linen drawstring trs don't need much drawing in any more. We've been going to the beach etc etc during the day while Lou & Walt work & doing stuff with them evenings – 'Lobster Shack' tonight, crazy golf tomorrow.

From: Nell Fenton
To: Charlotte Bailey

Sounds lovely, must try and rearrange our visit. Weather still fantastic here and children were over the moon to see Michael. Some friends of Tom and Maude's came for the day today with their little boy. Theo, Rob and Rory were trying to push Max, the father, into the pool when he playfully grabbed Rob and tossed him into the deep end. I wasn't watching but thank God Guy saw it and dived in to retrieve him. What kind of an arse throws a child of that age in the pool without checking they can swim??? Now have new pool-watching rota and adult in charge not allowed to read during their shift.

From: Charlotte Bailey
To: Nell Fenton

V sensible idea with all those loony boys & Greta around. Have discovered lobster is the perfect restaurant meal for children of Ellie & Maddie's age as it keeps them entirely quiet & occupied. Ellie ate a whole lobster by herself, cracked the claws etc etc without any assistance, Maddie also v good, though less skilled than Ellie at retrieving lobster flesh. Hugh while very, very pleased to see plier-type implement, small hammer & skewers on table instead of boring old knife & fork was something of a liability & had to be closely supervised at all times (esp after he hammered Lou's hand to get her attention). There was a very sweet family at the next-door table with 3 very well-behaved children & a newborn baby. The mother made having 4 look most appealing & easy particularly as she was discreetly breastfeeding her baby under some napkin-type arrangement while eating lobster one-handed – most impressive.

From: Nell Fenton
To: Charlotte Bailey

Only problem with that scenario is that neither you nor I have 3 v well-behaved children. Still want a baby though. Michael totally traumatised today, he took Ollie, Rob, Betsey and Theo out in the boat and decided it would be exciting for them to go through the lock. He said he was right about them being excited, which Ollie and Betsey demonstrated by standing up in the boat and staggering around when the water was pouring in through the lock gate, so boat already rocking violently. He said he was completely certain that he was going to lose one or more of them, had even ripped off his shoes ready for his rescue dive but then managed to wrestle Ollie and Betsey to the relative safety of the bottom of the boat, only to glance up to see Rob with one foot on each of the lock gates as they were opening (Theo and Rob supposed to be in charge of opening the gate but while Theo doing a very competent job of turning the handle Rob daftly standing with a foot on each gate slowly doing the splits). Anyhow all unharmed and Michael now sitting with a large gin and tonic clutched tightly in his hand. Says white-water rafting is nothing compared to taking that lot out in a rowboat.

From: Charlotte Bailey
To: Nell Fenton

Pity Michael is missing that part of your brain that says 'stop – this is a bad idea' when you're about to do something that's a bad idea. Had BBQ with folk-singer friends of Lou & Walt last night. Am sure they thought we were completely awful. They brought their sons Rocky & Sachs with them (Maddie kept calling them Rocky & Sex) who were totally cool & v rock'n'roll with pierced ears (one each) even though they were only 9 & 11. Parents terribly nice but dreadfully soppy & folksy. V embarrassingly the mother (Kyria) overheard me shouting 'Come here, you little bastard' at Hugh who had run off halfway through a nappy change. This, however, was not the lowest point. That came when they were playing their guitars & singing some of their songs to us round the campfire, Ellie was being really awful & difficult & kept loudly talking during their songs & when Dan tried to shhh her she kicked him. Anyway just when guitar playing & lyrics – 'my child, my child, I love you to the sky, my child, my child, I'll love you till I die' – ceased for a spot of unaccompanied humming, Dan who practically had Ellie in a half-nelson could be clearly heard hissing in her ear 'Shut up or I'll kill you.'

From: Nell Fenton
To: Charlotte Bailey

People who sing loving songs accompanied on the guitar should be publicly flogged. Very unfair to their children too. Who can possibly grow up normal with parents that wet? V salutary for them to hear a proper parent/child interaction.

From: Charlotte Bailey
To: Nell Fenton
Re: neighbours madder than in London

Lou & Walt went to NY early yesterday for some meetings to do with Sexetiquette. They've left us in charge of the house which is terrifying, sure we'll do something dire to it before they get back. L & W have many very odd neighbours who keep popping in (make Brian & Hildegard look quite normal). Had to field Bonnie yesterday – drunk 70-yr-old from down the road with orange lipstick on her teeth. She came by to look at the 'cute English kids'. Cute English kids thought she was hilarious as she kept lurching around the lawn, meanwhile Bonnie who found their childish laughter enchanting was laughing too & the more she laughed the more she lurched, & the more she lurched the more they laughed & so on & so forth. Only people not laughing were Dan & me, we watched in grim fascination as she staggered about, convinced she was about to totter through the hedge into next door's pool. Whole thing seemed to go on for ever but prob only about 20 mins till her exasperated life partner (Bogey) came & retrieved her.

This morning's visit was from Weird Jon, who came by to borrow Walt's mower. Weird Jon completely sober & v keen on yoga but not hot bikram yoga like Lou, instead 'Jonyoga', his own special made-up brand of yoga based on an intimate knowledge of his own body & complex isometric calculations of his own devising. Weird Jon very taken with Dan & is coming back this afternoon with his girlfriend Erica & the ingredients to make us all a delicious soy milkshake. Hurrah. Lou & Walt back this evening thank God – Walt much more adept than us at fending off the nutters.

From: Nell Fenton
To: Charlotte Bailey

Think you're just meeting average Cape Cod folk. Walt told me once everyone who lives there year-round is ancient or alcoholic or a recovering alcoholic or very weird or some combination of the above.

From: Charlotte Bailey
To: Nell Fenton

L & W have brought their friend Marco back with them from NY.
Marco a gay god. Incredibly good-looking & buff & vv funny.
Dan says he has just taken greatest photo ever of children in
knickers running between Lou in full-length 70s beaded kaftan
& cork platforms, Walt in black 1920s all-in-one swimming costume & goggles & Marco in flowered sarong & yellow see-thru
sun visor. Leaving tomorrow. Boo hoo.

SEPTEMBER 00

From: Charlotte Bailey
To: Nell Fenton
Re: must now saw off Maddie's arms

Got back today, children very sorry to be home & somewhat jet-lagged but apart from that fine. Have to admit Gordon & Albert have done a fantastic job on the stairs. They're nearly finished & they look exactly the same but there are no cracks along the wall & they no longer bounce. Don't think Gordon was expecting us back because Maddie came bounding out of the living room waving a gigantic pair of men's underpants. Definitely not Albert's as although he has a bit of a paunch, has a relatively small bum which led me to suspect they belonged to the giant-bummed Gordon. Shrieked at her to put them back where she found them & then took her off to sterilise her arms. Too occupied & horrified to deal with them there & then, thought I'd leave it till the morning. When we finally emerged next day Gordon was there (smelling & whistling) but the underpants were gone. Mind boggles as to why they were there in the 1st place. Dan says I mustn't think about it, must just go to my happy place & no doubt Gordon only took them off for authenticity as he was going straight out from work to his Scottish dancing class wearing a kilt.

From: Nell Fenton
To: Charlotte Bailey

That's so disgusting. Not Maddie's fault but I'm not sure I'll
never feel the same about her again. Once when we took the
children swimming Rob (totally inadequately supervised by
Michael) emerged from the men's changing room looking very
bulky round the bottom and when I investigated found he'd
ignored his own little pants and instead put on a very large
pair of Y-fronts he'd found lying around. Tore them off him
and took him home and scrubbed him in the bath but still
worried about what horrible bottom germs he might have
picked up.

From: Charlotte Bailey
To: Nell Fenton

V embarrassing situation today when Ellie came dancing into
the hallway, pirouetted up to me, Gordon & Albert who were
having a discussion about the shocking state of our windows
& started loudly singing 'Two Fat Boys', a lovely ditty of her own
invention while simultaneously poking the air near the stomachs
of the 'two fat boys' in question. Was torn as to whether to tell
her to shut up thus drawing their attention to her (too busy
discussing counterweights at this point) or just ignore her &
hope she'd go away. Opted for latter, she didn't go away but if
they did notice they pretended not to.

From: Nell Fenton
To: Charlotte Bailey

That's nothing. Rob asked a plumber we had in once why he

had 'a monkey face' and before I managed to drag him away, conversationally told his mate that he had a very small head.

From: Charlotte Bailey
To: Nell Fenton
Re: Geraldine a bit less bonkers

Geraldine came for dinner last night. She went to Spain to stay with her brother & his wife in a villa they'd rented. Said it was quite nice but she didn't get enough sleep because their baby kept crying in the night & then they got up annoyingly early & were v noisy. Reading between the lines got the impression her sister-in-law wanted to kill her as Geraldine said she was very ratty with her. She said Gil phoned her at work & wants to meet her for dinner next week, ventured to suggest this was a bad idea but she said she really felt fine about him & was amazed by how neutral she felt when he rang her & so she has agreed. Still sat on her arse while I made, served & cleared away supper but seems much happier & less tense, wasn't talking about Gil all the time & looking quite brown & pretty & much more like her old self in the pre-Gil days. By the way, how's Rachel, have you heard anything recently? Send her my love next time you speak to her.

From: Nell Fenton
To: Charlotte Bailey

Spoke to her a few days ago. She sounded better. Says Jack is being quite weird on the rare occasions she speaks to him. Jonathan ok though she says he doesn't like school any more and doesn't want to go back, which is a real shame. She hasn't found a job yet, not much available apparently and what there is she's been told she's overqualified for.

From: Charlotte Bailey
To: Nell Fenton

Glad Rachel's sounding better. Thank God stairs finally finished & Gordon has gone, Albert is bereft, I am overjoyed such a treat to be able to breathe through my nose again. School starts Thursday, Maddie is going into reception & I have marked this momentous occasion by getting her a haircut that is so catastrophically awful Dan says she doesn't look entirely normal, a v crafty move on my part as will hopefully make teachers extra kind to her. New au pair arrives at w/e which will be a huge relief as I'm failing to derive my usual quiet satisfaction from doing laundry, also since Gordon & Albert did not shut a single door in entire house while doing the stairs am having to wash all bedding, toys, etc, as well as substantial holiday backlog. Tried to tackle huge laundry backlog by turning laundry into fun activity Dan & I could do together in the evening so mixed us some cocktails & put on a video we could watch while sorting stuff out. Only flaw in this otherwise foolproof plan was we both ended up quite drunk, v emotional (watched Chariots of Fire) and still holding same pair of socks we had started the evening with.

From: Nell Fenton
To: Charlotte Bailey

We start day after tomorrow. Ollie will be in junior kindergarten and will be doing full days, praise the Lord for private schools. In the state schools here they don't do full days till they are SIX. Just spent a thousand million dollars on shoes, they each need 2 pairs of trainers as well as their school shoes which makes 9 pairs of shoes and in about a month I'll have to get them all snow boots.

From: Charlotte Bailey
To: Nell Fenton

Geraldine rang this evening to tell me about her dinner with Gil. Says it was fantastic because she came away from it thinking what an unattractive twit he was. He told her he was seeing wriggly giggly Daisy from the play & she said she realised she didn't care, just thought they deserved each other which was extraordinarily liberating. Of course he's after something – some of the hideous multicoloured oil paintings they bought together (he chose, she paid), she says she's decided they're stupid & pretentious so he can have them. I'm so relieved & quite surprised, obviously we all knew he was a total arse just glad she can finally see it too.

From: Nell Fenton
To: Charlotte Bailey

Good for her. Hope she meets someone else soon who's not afraid of the more strident sort of woman.

From: Charlotte Bailey
To: Nell Fenton

Ellie & Maddie went back to school yesterday. Maddie was very proud of her uniform & having her 1st day of school photo taken by Dan (hoping to get someone in his graphics dept to digitally retouch mad haircut), she didn't cry too much & school rang mid-morning to say she was fine which was unbelievably nice of them.

Fran came round to show off her holiday tan & we both spent

some time marvelling at how just days after all that time in the sun I manage to return to normal pallid tones.

Dan spoke to Peter this evening, he's on very good form, he's been going to a local cafe every week for ages as there is a very nice attractive Polish girl working there called Marta who he really likes & wants to ask out. Took Bert from the farm there today to see her & Bert reckons she definitely likes him back. Peter says he feels quite emboldened by Bert's opinion & is going to stop prevaricating (been building up to it all summer) & just ask her out. Am pathetically excited, he so deserves a nice girlfriend.

From: Nell Fenton
To: Charlotte Bailey

Vicarious romance quite exciting particularly if one's own last romantic thrill was 100 yrs ago.

Mine all back at school too. Ollie seems fine with full days, still managing to be one of the smallest in the class even though there are several tiny Chinese girls. Have started all of them in karate. Supposed to be fabulous for coordination etc. Judging by the way Rob does jumping jacks he could use the help. Wouldn't have believed it possible to go so spectacularly wrong on something that simple. Ollie in 'kinder karate' adorable in his little white suit but just stands around craply, occasionally flailing out an arm or leg. Josie looks as though she might have some natural aptitude which would be nice as she couldn't be accused of being sporty.

From: Charlotte Bailey
To: Nell Fenton

Our new au pair Astrid arrived today, am hoping she was v tired or premenstrual (or both) as after she had been introduced to everybody she most disconcertingly burst into tears & said we were a 'very bootiful family'. Have to say Dan & I entirely useless, he backed out looking embarrassed while I feebly patted her back saying 'there, there'. It was Maddie (who understands these things) who came to the rescue, she wrapped her arms tightly round her & said 'Don't be sad, we love you' & although initially this increased the 'booty' of our family & the volume of her crying it then subsided & in between hiccups she told us she was 'very huppy not sad'. Feel slightly alarmed, hope we haven't got a nutter on our hands.

From: Nell Fenton
To: Charlotte Bailey

Don't worry, once you start shrieking and the children start squabbling she'll realise you're not so very bootiful. Went to a dinner party last night where I did excellent work. Subject of the relaunch of a magazine called The Week arose. Went on at some length about how boring it was to the very nice man next to me, quite undeterred by his efforts to contradict me. Had the sudden hideous realisation that he was the husband of the editor so performed a very clumsy U-turn and being slightly drunk went too far in praising it. Am sure he thought I was mad as well as being a bitch.

From: Charlotte Bailey
To: Nell Fenton

Probably not a bitch just a bit schizophrenic. My most recent triumph of tact was asking some mother in the playground when her baby was due. Silly cow wasn't pregnant & quite affronted by the question. Have to say although obv felt some embarrassment, it was tempered by annoyance as if you've got a great wobbling stomach, you shouldn't stand around in a loose floral frock with your hands in the small of your back – to my mind that's just asking for trouble. This is the 3rd time I've been caught out. Dan says I'm not allowed to ask anyone if they're pregnant ever again unless their legs are in stirrups & the baby's head is crowning. Astrid settling in v well, extremely nice girl though still dreadfully soppy about the children. I broached the subject of potty-training Hugh with her, she was terribly enthusiastic, indeed prospect made her eyes fill with tears & she said, 'Soon he will be a little man.' Thought (but obviously didn't say) not very soon at all if last attempt is anything to go by.

From: Nell Fenton
To: Charlotte Bailey

Au pair that's happy at the idea of potty-training incontinent child is a pearl beyond price. We went to a 'beginning of the new Sunday school year picnic' today. By some extraordinary means the Sunday school committee manage to suck all the fun out of any event they organise, even something as innocuous as a picnic on a pleasant sunny day. Michael wriggled out of it but I feel we should support the Sunday school particularly as Rob is doing his first communion this year, so we went along and had even bothered to make a dish of chicken and coriander myself rather than buy something at the supermarket and pretend I'd made it. Games organised for the children were so half-hearted and generally dreary even Rob and Ollie who will join in with anything couldn't be bothered. Anyhow all so paralysed with boredom we ate really quickly and sneaked away. Made Michael, who'd anticipated a nice child-free afternoon, take them all to the park and had a nice peaceful time myself instead.

From: Charlotte Bailey
To: Nell Fenton

Quite tricky to sneak away from a picnic unless it's in a forest & you can dodge behind the trees. Bet it was really obvious you were leaving. Astrid & I are going to start the potty-training tomorrow. Dan v much in favour of starting on a Monday. He's just coming to the end of a huge biography of Churchill that he started on holiday – he's obsessed with it & constantly reading bits of it out to me esp the speeches. Said to me last night re potty training Mr Poopy Pants 'We shall not flag or fail. We shall go on to the end.' More annoying than it sounds as actually he has bugger all to do with the 'training', Hugh always safely in a nappy by the time he gets home.

From: Nell Fenton
To: Charlotte Bailey

Suzette forced me to come over for coffee (couldn't hide for ever) so she could torture me about her holiday (was wearing her hair in an extraordinary bun on the side of her head for reasons I did not choose to investigate). This summer they 'did' Europe and she has discovered Europe is NOT just a clump of countries but a place of 'fascinating variations'. With her unerring instinct for the obvious she managed to talk at length about their trip while never even straying towards saying anything noteworthy. Only mild interest I derived was from reading between the lines. Obviously this isn't an exact science but judging by the number of references to Sophie wanting to 'spread her wings' and 'needing her own space' they couldn't bear to be in the same room together. Also Kane more of a 'homebody' than Suzette (so he got pissed off with the holiday too). Suzette, on the other hand, loves travel, has a great wanderlust and loves to feel the wind in her hair. (So why the tight side bun?) Anyhow she got her photos out at which point I realised decisive action was needed so jumped up said I'd love to see them some other time but had to make some important calls. Feebleness of my excuse a result of my mind blanking with panic at the sight of approaching photos. How's the potty-training?

PS Suzette is starting a creative writing course, apparently she feels she has an 'unexplored talent' for writing and 'life is a journey of self-discovery'.

From: Charlotte Bailey
To: Nell Fenton

She's an inspiration to us all. Potty-training still fairly bad but not as entirely hopeless as last time. I made Dan ring Peter tonight to find out how asking Marta out went. Went vv badly indeed, in fact could hardly have been worse as when he got there the cafe was all boarded up, having been gutted by fire earlier in the week. Nobody around & nobody seemed to know where the owner or Marta was although woman in the knitting shop over the road said she thought Marta had gone to London to look for a job there. Peter absolutely furious with himself, says he should have asked her out weeks ago. Says it's absolutely typical & at this rate will never meet anyone.

From: Nell Fenton
To: Charlotte Bailey

Quite spectacularly bad luck for all concerned really. Had a long chat with Anna this evening. Don't know if she's told you but she has started Toulouse-Lautrec in obedience classes because he was so appalling in the summer. Her friend Zoe (a great dog lover – until now at least) looked after him while she was in France and he traumatised her children really badly by constantly stealing their food. He was so dreadful they got to the stage of just flinging their food at him if he came in the room, to stop him jumping on them. So poor Zoe in addition to having great stinking Rhodesian ridgeback roaming round had three terrified children throwing sausages across the room in self-defence. She's only been to 2 classes so far but he's apparently already showing signs of being unteachable and is very disruptive to the other dogs. Anna says she bloody hates him and they should have got proper Rhodesian ridgeback with a ridge not a cheap one without a ridge as she's sure that's why he's so stupid.

From: Charlotte Bailey
To: Nell Fenton

She did actually try to give him away when he ate 2nd nuclear power station but no one wanted him.

From: Nell Fenton
To: Charlotte Bailey

Rachel phoned last night. Jack has given up his flat and moved in with another woman. She says it's obviously not a new relationship and she was just incredibly naive to have believed there was no one else. As if he hasn't done enough to prove what a complete bastard he is he says he wants to buy a house with her and wants Rachel to sell their house so he can have his share of the proceeds. He actually told her a flat would be easier for her to manage now she's on her own. So thoughtful. I'm worried about her, she says she's sleeping really badly and can't eat. On top of everything Jonathan has started refusing to go to school so she has a huge fight with him every morning. At least she's found a job but she says the pay is pitiful and it's just a stopgap.

From: Charlotte Bailey
To: Nell Fenton

He really is a world-class bastard. Can't believe I used to like him, it's so depressing.

Dan got rung by Toby yesterday, haven't heard from him for absolutely ages. He told Dan he's had quite a mixed time. He's in Italy at the moment photographing the Dolomites. Apparently they are spectacularly beautiful but now he's sick to death of them. Says when you've seen one stunning peak you've seen them all. Doing a loop to go to Milan then Venice then back home via Marseille where he's hoping to pick up the Spider. Should be back by mid-Oct. Can't believe I'm writing this but Hugh really does seem to have finally got the hang of potty-training. Obviously has regular accidents but seems to get the basic concept. Astrid has been completely fantastic, endlessly patient and tireless in her enthusiasm for every wee, fart or poo he has done on the potty. Have confiscated Dan's book on Churchill after he took her aside & told her never in the field of human potty-training was so much owed by so many to so few. Not remotely funny & made the poor girl look really alarmed.

OCTOBER 00

From: Charlotte Bailey
To: Nell Fenton

There's a new girl in Ellie's class called Macy who has taken a great shine to Ellie. Her mother (Melody) came up & introduced herself. She is a drama teacher & is training to be a bereavement counsellor & spoke to me in v soft voice as though I had recently suffered a tragic loss (weirdly soothing actually) then whispered a request to have Ellie for tea next week. I murmured a very gentle yes in reply (any opportunity to offload a child always gratefully received). During the course of our very, very quiet conversation, which must have been all of 5 mins, Macy's brother Hal (who is the same age as Maddie so should know better) head-butted her to get her attention & Macy ran up & whacked her on the back. Although I tried to adopt an indulgent 'kids!! aren't they little scamps!!' face think I must have looked a bit horrified as Melody quickly explained that Hal was 'very boisterous' & had 'attention issues' & Macy was 'always terribly excited by the end of school'.

From: Nell Fenton
To: Charlotte Bailey

They sound like enchanting children. New people have moved

in opposite us, a couple with a little girl, and the father came over with the child to introduce themselves. They are Russian and they brought a bunch of flowers and a bottle of wine with a ribbon around it which was most charming and acceptable. Unfortunately I was looking very rough and my hair was super-greasy. They seem very nice and little girl is about Ollie's age. I think Ollie liked her because he fell to his hands and knees and barked like a dog. Rob v cross with him after and asked him why he had to be so embarrassing, but personally I thought little Sonya looked quite impressed.

From: Charlotte Bailey
To: Nell Fenton

Dog impersonation fab idea, nothing like a little doggy to melt a girl's heart.

Macy & Ellie are now so in love with each other Macy wants to have school lunches with Ellie & they have been nagging to have the same haircut. This presents something of a problem on our side as while Macy could cut her waist-length hair to the same wonky little bob that Ellie has, however much Ellie nags me I can't quickly grow her hair to her waist (nor indeed would I want to). Melody has a long frizzy mane so suspect she belongs to the 'the longer the better' school of thought.

From: Nell Fenton
To: Charlotte Bailey

I decided to reciprocate the goodwill of the Russians and demonstrate I am also a good neighbour so went round to introduce myself to Russian Wife. Took cookies, obviously couldn't be arsed to actually bake any but bought very realistic bakery cookies which I rewrapped in attractive cellophane package with a ribbon. She seems a very nice woman with a refined, intelligent face. Very sweet about my children (though of course she hasn't been exposed to them yet) and said she'd love all or any to come over and play with Sonya any time. Surprisingly, she seemed to really mean it.

From: Charlotte Bailey
To: Nell Fenton

Can't believe going to a bakery & unwrapping & then rewrapping the cookies could be so much less trouble than making your own, you lazy slapper. Problem solved re Macy & Ellie having matching haircuts as Macy has done a very fine job of cutting her own hair. Had only got halfway round before Melody discovered her crouched in the airing cupboard with a pair of scissors but as it is no longer the 1980s & Macy is not a member of the Human League, Melody had to take her to the hairdresser to get it evened up. She looks bloody terrible (even worse than Maddie), see now why Melody grew her hair so v long – it helped distract from her big hamster cheeks.

From: Nell Fenton
To: Charlotte Bailey

Rob's been complaining so much of stomach ache the last couple of days I thought I better take him to the doctor. Never know with him, he makes such a fuss about everything but this did seem worse than his usual hysteria so thought I better be on the safe side. Usual vague result – just a virus/see how he goes/come back if, etc . . . anyhow as we were leaving the surgery we passed a woman bringing in a little girl of about 3 with hair tightly plaited in cornrows. Rob paused in the doorway just as she was edging past him and he vomited tidily and lumpily onto the top of her head. Was so horrified was unable to do anything other than grab Rob and flee shouting sorry over my shoulder. Rob feeling much better now, mind you.

From: Charlotte Bailey
To: Nell Fenton

Thought I'd experienced every possible disgusting permutation of cleaning up sick, but I see now I was wrong.

Ellie went to tea at Macy's house today, think Melody is even more disorganised than me as she kept ringing to delay pick-up time as she hadn't fed the children yet. Turned up at 7 which I thought was generously late but they still hadn't eaten which under normal circumstances would be slightly worrying as Ellie can go all listless & be really vile if she's hungry. Needn't have worried as when I arrived she bounded up to me looking very pleased with herself & shouted 'Hello, Smello Mummy.' Reason for burst of energy & great good humour despite apparent lack of supper soon became apparent. As Melody quietly explained, if you allow children as many cakes & sweets as they want they don't see sweets as a treat & grow up liking fresh vegetables as much as chocolate from which I deduced Ellie had spent the afternoon eating a shitload of sweets. Have to say if Melody's experiment was working it wasn't apparent to the naked eye as when supper finally did appear (7.30) they all ate practically nothing & certainly none of the sweetcorn or broccoli Melody had provided. Ellie's table manners not improved by the v great quantity of sugar she had consumed but since Hal & Macy's manners considerably worse & I had drunk a bucket of gin & tonic handed to me by Melody as I walked in the door found I didn't care so much. Macy & Hal nightmarish but Melody actually terribly nice & despite some barmy ideas also v sensible about other things eg notion of having large gin & tonic to get you through an evening with your ill-mannered children rather than foolishly waiting till they are in bed to have it.

From: Nell Fenton
To: Charlotte Bailey

Some merit in the early-evening gin and tonic I agree but think I prefer the 'drink as a reward' approach once I've finally got rid of them for the evening. The 'eating as many sweets as you like theory' reminds me of a 'never say no' theory I read about once. Basic thrust was to always be very positive, and allow your children to reach their own conclusions about what they should and shouldn't do. Find the very idea quite terrifying, am sure if I didn't shout 'stop doing that' at least 100 times a day none of mine would even be alive let alone learning important life lessons.

Rob better now but Michael rather tiresomely has caught the bug and though not his fault obviously, can't help being irritated with him for it. Have booked us a weekend away for Thanksgiving (in October here).

From: Charlotte Bailey
To: Nell Fenton

Sure he'll be better by then & even if he isn't presumably reasonably competent at throwing up into a bucket (rather than on strangers' heads) so can be taken along anyway.

We had dinner at Fran's house last night where I sat next to a friend of hers who is a mother from Barnaby's school. She practises reiki. Anyway I told her about how I am trying to get pregnant & failing miserably and she became very earnest and sympathetic. She suggested doing reiki on me & Dan. Had drunk enough to be v moved by this kind offer but not enough to actually accept it but she then did also suggest acupuncture which I do think is quite a good idea. She has a friend who does it so am going to book an appointment. Dan says it's all a load of bollocks but I don't, what do you think?

From: Nell Fenton
To: Charlotte Bailey

Well, I do rather think it's bollocks. Though Michael did have acupuncture years ago for glandular fever and it did seem to help slightly so possibly worth a try. V wise to turn down the reiki. Don't have the faintest idea what it is but sounds highly suspect.

From: Charlotte Bailey
To: Nell Fenton
Re: magic tooth

Ellie's first tooth came out at teatime yesterday. It had been hanging by a thread for days making her look demented. Ellie v pleased with herself & we embarked on a round of phone calls to everyone to let them know her good news. All very jolly until we turned off the light & Ellie checked the pot for the zillionth time before going to sleep only to discover tooth was no longer in little tooth-shaped wooden pot. You cannot believe the grief that ensued (briefly considered phoning Melody for a bit of guidance) & while Astrid & I crawled around on our hands & knees Dan went off pot in hand to grill Hugh. Search as hopeless as interrogation as every time Dan said the word tooth to Hugh he just clacked his teeth together & shouted 'CROCODILE!' Meanwhile Ellie was rolling around on her bed shrieking 'I'm going to die, I'm going to die' & between sobs told me 'Macy says if you lose the tooth the tooth fairy touches your head AND THEN YOU DIE.' Imagine the fond feelings towards mental Macy that flooded me at this piece of wisdom. Anyway just as the wailing started to crescendo again Dan came bounding in pot in hand shouting 'I've found it.' Tooth looked somewhat bigger to me & when Ellie went to pick it up Dan shouted 'NO . . . you'll spoil the magic.' Don't think she'd really have spoilt the magic but she might have squashed the tooth since it was made from a tiny bit of mashed potato left over from the children's supper.

From: Nell Fenton
To: Charlotte Bailey

Can't say I've ever resorted to mashed potato but had to leave an explanatory note under the pillow once when Josie gave me a tooth for safekeeping and I immediately lost it. Might comfort Ellie to know that the tooth fairy was perfectly satisfied with the note, left Josie the money and made absolutely no attempt to kill her.

From: Charlotte Bailey
To: Nell Fenton

Had my first visit to Alannah the acupuncturist today, not at all what I expected, she's young, slim & pretty with waist-length curly blonde hair that she kept swishing around like curtains on Easi-Trak, was wearing usual alternative health practitioner gear though, bad jeans, combat boots & a very coarsely woven tunic-type top. Asked me loads of questions about myself which was v gratifying (would be quite happy to pay her just so we can talk about me for 40 mins), although all the ones about my period a bit gross, then she felt my pulse which apparently was v 'thready' – have absolutely no idea what that means but probably NOT GOOD. Then told me she thought my liver was hot or cold, can't remember which ('hot' probably as I think it is still recovering from dinner at Fran's). Then I lay on the table/bed & she stuck loads of needles into me. Didn't hurt apart from the ones round my ankles.

From: Nell Fenton
To: Charlotte Bailey

Very disappointing that she is pretty. An alternative health therapist ought to be slightly hairy and urgently in need of a bit of make-up. Expect she smells of patchouli though.

Excellent weekend away and weather so unseasonably warm we all swam in the outdoor pool (quite aggressively heated admittedly) overlooking a hillside of brilliantly coloured maples. We went hiking in Algonquin Park which is a huge area of wilderness with different hikes marked out depending on how fit/intrepid or weedy you are. Michael kept looking wistfully at the mega-hikes but fortunately I had the excuse of

3 children in tow and we opted for the mini-hikes. We decided to go despite the large number of worrying notices posted around warning visitors about a 'Fearless Wolf At Large'. This wolf apparently was not doing the done thing and running away at the sight of humans. The posters instructed you not to approach the wolf if you should see it and to contact the park wardens, presumably if you had not yet been eaten. It made me feel quite nervous and I'm already quite cowardly about the idea of meeting a bear. Though we carry bear bells (little bell you attach to your belt and warns the bear you are coming and that you would prefer not to have a confrontation) Michael always carries a big hunting knife in his backpack which I somehow find more reassuring than a small tinkly bell.

PS v sorry to hear about thready pulse and hot liver.

From: Charlotte Bailey
To: Nell Fenton

Bloody hell, grant you hunting knife slightly more comforting than small bell but surely carrying an Uzi would provide the most reassurance?

I've decided to have a Hallowe'en party for Ellie, never got around to doing her a birthday party and she came back from Soraya's 'ball 'n' burger bash' grumbling about the fact she never had one.

From: Nell Fenton
To: Charlotte Bailey

I thought I was a bad mother not having arranged Josie's party yet, 10 weeks after the actual birthday. Must concede that having the party six months after the actual day makes you a much worse one.

From: Charlotte Bailey
To: Nell Fenton

Nonsense. Delaying it prolongs the pleasant anticipation. I had the brilliant idea of making 26 papier-mache skulls for the party, which will be filled with sweets as going-home presents. Astrid & I did the 1st layer last night, guess whether when I came down this morning they were a) completely dry & ready for next layer, b) not quite dry but looking promising, c) slightly wetter than when we did them last night. I've now had to hang them all on the laundry rack & put them in the downstairs loo & train a blow heater on them. Loo now entirely unusable since, as well as fighting your way past 26 wet gluey balls of newspaper, it's very, very hot & smelly in there.

From: Nell Fenton
To: Charlotte Bailey

Skulls will probably freak the children out and make them cry.

Spoke to Rachel yesterday, said she'd dropped Jonathan at Jack's for the weekend and he introduced her to his girlfriend, Philippa, who looks about 20, has huge boobs, auburn hair and freckles. The sort of girl 'men go for' apparently. Felt so sorry for her – why that tosser Jack has to make her meet his melon-breasted floozie escapes me.

From: Charlotte Bailey
To: Nell Fenton

God, poor Rachel, she must be at the worst point though, I'm sure things will only get better now.

On a much more trivial note I'm so fed up with stupid fucking papier-mache skulls. I've now had a blow heater trained on them for 3 DAYS. Meanwhile Astrid has been cutting out bats & skeletons & I've scooped out about 1,764,230,000 oranges to turn into mini-pumpkins filled with green jelly. May commit authentic Hallowe'en-style murder as Dan is really pissing me off. When I started grumbling about skulls asked me why can't I just be like everyone else & buy Hallowe'en party bags at Marks & Spencer's? Asked him if he had any idea how much that would cost??? to which he INFURIATINGLY replied unlike having blow heater going day & night for days which is, of course, free.

From: Nell Fenton
To: Charlotte Bailey

Do feel sympathetic to Dan, must be quite hard being married to a woman who is congenitally incapable of learning from past experience. In what universe did you think making 26 papier-mache skulls would be anything other than a nightmare? Our Hallowe'en far more successful than last year and will certainly take until next Hallowe'en to get through the unbelievable amount of candy they all collected. How did your party go?

From: Charlotte Bailey
To: Nell Fenton

Absolutely brilliantly although Ellie a bit disappointed that Mental Macy couldn't attend as she became so hysterical at sight of papier-mache skulls hanging in the windows as she walked down our path that Melody had to take her straight home.

NOVEMBER 00

From: Charlotte Bailey
To: Nell Fenton

Saw Alannah again today, told me she had been at RADA but gave it all up to become acupuncturist & went to China where she studied for 93 yrs. Think acupuncture must keep you v young-looking as she only looks about 20. She thinks my failure to get pregnant is to do with liver (hot, cold? still can't remember). I really quite enjoy going, as apart from moments when she is sticking needles in me, can have nice relaxing childfree snooze. Feel v positive about getting pregnant.

From: Nell Fenton
To: Charlotte Bailey

Have to say I think your chances of getting pregnant would be better if you were at home shagging your husband rather than having a comfy snooze with Alannah.

From: Charlotte Bailey
To: Nell Fenton
Re: Toby staying again

Toby got back at the w/e. He ended up staying 2 weeks longer than planned in Venice as he was so entranced by its 'magical beauty'. Says he would have stayed for ever if his money hadn't run out. His hair's got really long & he's started wearing it in little bunches at the back. Hugh VERY admiring & wants to do his hair the same (Dan on the other hand told him he looked like Heidi). Bit worried about how long he's going to stay, he's being very vague, but says he's got to develop 'a shitload of film', etc, etc, also 'catalogue his work' & 'revise his portfolio'. As I type this can hear crashing & swearing as he sets up his darkroom again & the familiar aroma of hardcore-developing chemicals is starting to waft round the house.

From: Nell Fenton
To: Charlotte Bailey

Surely he could stay with his parents. At least they're not likely to drink any of the chemicals.

I've got round to organising Josie's party at last. It's going to be 'cosmic glow-in-the-dark bowling' followed by a sleepover. Sleepover appears to be de rigueur for all parties now, they all stay up till 4am and then are toxic for 2 days after.

From: Charlotte Bailey
To: Nell Fenton

Toby v craftily has got his job back at camera shop, also no space for a darkroom at his parents so it has to be us.

Re acupuncture – I think my liver must be cold because at my appointment with Alannah this week she lit what appeared to be a giant joint & waved it over my body. Had to lie absolutely still as she was wafting it around only mm from where my cold liver is & it was glowing red & dropping hot ash onto me. Didn't want to complain about hot ash dropping onto me as no doubt that's the bit that's going to heat up my liver & get me pregnant. Hope it works soon as I'm really fed up with having sex all the time & even Dan occasionally failing to show his normal enthusiasm.

From: Nell Fenton
To: Charlotte Bailey

Maybe time to give up the acupuncture. Trying-to-get-pregnant sex is strangely boring, but the sex part is an absolute prerequisite to conception whereas big-joint waving is not.

I've made a marvellous discovery which is that Ollie has secretly learnt to read. I'm starting to suspect his giant head might actually house a giant brain. I've been struggling so much with Rob, reading with him every night and his reading is a lot better, so had been vaguely planning to move on to Ollie. Now I find without any effort on my part he can read quite well. A most gratifying situation.

From: Charlotte Bailey
To: Nell Fenton

Fantastic about Ollie, Ellie's reading not too bad despite the fact that we always conduct her reading practice in the hallway as she's putting on her shoes to go to school & then I have to tell all the hard words to speed up so I can fill in that she's read a decent amount of pages in her reading record.

From: Nell Fenton
To: Charlotte Bailey

I phoned Anna last night. She sounded very cheerful though she told me she did a home perm on her hair a few days ago (ridiculously expensive having it done at a salon) and she thinks she might have left it on too long because her hair has gone very wiry and crackly and bits keep breaking off. Geoffrey says she looks like she was struck by lightning and though apparently Theo told her she still looks beautiful he then asked her to wear a hat when she picks him up from school. (Turns out Toulouse-Lautrec IS unteachable and has been expelled from obedience classes, trainer said she's only expelled one other dog in the 30 yrs she's been doing it.)

From: Charlotte Bailey
To: Nell Fenton

Anna unteachable too, she never learns or keeps her promises. Swore blind to Isabel she'd go to proper hairdresser after she dyed sides of her face orange in hennaing incident just before parent night.

Astrid's boyfriend Sorën is coming to visit. Was peripherally aware of his existence as there have been phone calls & mentions of him, but since Toby's been back she's been much more circumspect about mentioning Sorën & very smiley & solicitous towards Toby (told me she finds his bunches 'so cute!'). Anyway Sorën arriving Thursday for a long w/e. Astrid says he is a very caring vegan feminist who goes on lots of marches to do with women's rights & vegetables. He is studying how to be a writer at university & his work is sometimes angry, sometimes political & often both. As well as all this he's terribly good-looking & sexy – bearing in mind she finds Toby's bunches 'so cute!' am having a problem taking her seriously. She has now been to the health-food shop several times to purchase such delicacies as soy yogurt, egg-free mayonnaise & dairy-free ice cream.

From: Nell Fenton
To: Charlotte Bailey

Hard to know what's more attractive – 27-yr-old man with bunches or radical Swedish vegan. No wonder Astrid is conflicted.

From: Charlotte Bailey
To: Nell Fenton

Body (& probably liver) much warmer this week. While Alannah was doing usual liver-warming mumbo-jumbo she had the misfortune to sneeze (room quite smoky due to procedure she was carrying out) so she momentarily lost control of the large bundle of smouldering herbs she was wafting over me & stabbed me in the thigh with them. Burn from herbs not too bad really, the thing that really hurt was, when she jabbed me it gave me a terrible fright (had been snoozing at the time) & I shot out the leg she'd burnt, banging it & spearing the ankle needle in really deep. Was fucking agony & anyone who says acupuncture needles are so fine they don't actually hurt has never had one rammed in their ankle while they were sleeping.

From: Nell Fenton
To: Charlotte Bailey

Well, if you're going for the alternative 'holistic' approach you have to listen to your body and I think this might be a message from your body to say please stop burning me and jabbing me with needles.

From: Charlotte Bailey
To: Nell Fenton

Sorën arrived this afternoon, have to say I'm quite surprised the airline staff allowed him on the plane unaccompanied as he looks unbelievably young, at least 4 years younger than Astrid & she's only 19. His face is entirely hairless apart from a miserable wispy little goatee to go with his miserable wispy little body shrouded in a baggy black t-shirt with a picture of a cow being stabbed on it. He looked very pallid & depressed & not remotely angry or political. Barely said hello to Dan & me before disappearing into Astrid's room. Neither of them have yet emerged although it's been several hours. Dan & I have a sweepstake going as to what time they'll come out.

From: Nell Fenton
To: Charlotte Bailey

Probably the burden of all the caring he does that's making him depressed.

Josie's party was yesterday but am not much the wiser as to what it is that makes glow-in-the-dark bowling 'cosmic'. Possibly it was the unpleasantly loud jarring music. Unfortunately my plan for them all to have pre-teen fun styling one another's hair fell a bit flat (literally). Bought lots of rollers from the dollar store and got lots of mousse and hairspray, but despite everyone's efforts and quite lethal amounts of chemicals the best anyone got was a slight kink and one girl got a roller so badly tangled in her hair took about 20 mins of me combing and her yowling to get it out.

From: Charlotte Bailey
To: Nell Fenton

Sweepstake is off as are no longer sure of Sorën & Astrid's movements. We went out for lunch so they may have emerged or even gone out while we were out. Dan had the idea of knocking on their bedroom door to clarify the situation, but if they are there wouldn't really know how to explain the intrusion as can't exactly say 'just checking to see if you're still in there shagging'.

From: Nell Fenton
To: Charlotte Bailey

Can't you send Hugh in? Mind you, he's not what you'd call a 'reliable witness'. We've just got back from an agricultural fair they have every winter in the exhibition centre downtown. Lots of farmy stuff on display and tons of livestock there for the competitions (don't think Sorën would approve as I expect they'll all be eaten later). I got quite carried away by the romantic notion of the farming life and giving up our city existence for a rural idyll with rolling acres and a herd of cows (v torn here – there were cows entirely black, entirely cream or entirely caramel, and couldn't decide which were the most beautiful for my herd). We also saw a dog show and seeing all the clever working dogs momentarily forgot I really hate dogs and actually considered buying one to fit my new lifestyle (lots of puppies for sale). Luckily didn't go that far but there were antiques for sale and did buy a new dining-room table to replace hideous oak jobby, but now I reflect on it think it might look like a wildebeest as legs are v thin compared to the body.

From: Charlotte Bailey
To: Nell Fenton

I sympathise, recently bought some metal 'planters', v reasonably priced, possibly because once out of the context of tasteful antique shop I got them from they transformed themselves back into big silly pair of unmatched dustbins they really were.

Re Sorën & Astrid – am now able to shed some light on the mystery. Apparently Sorën has been really unwell since he arrived on Thursday evening and far from the shagfest we'd been imagining she's been nursing him. She looked really depressed, though frankly would have thought she'd be grateful for any excuse not to have sex with him. Think I'm going to give up the acupuncture sessions. Don't believe it works & I'm sick of talking about myself every session, also it's quite expensive

& so far all I have to show for it is a punctured ankle & a burnt thigh. Have a free session next week to make up for burning/stabbing incident last week but after that will call it a day, though don't know what I'll say to Alannah as she is v nice & absolutely adamant that if I give it enough time I'll get pregnant.

PS On subject of your herd, surely a mix of cream, caramel & black wd be the most attractive?

From: Nell Fenton
To: Charlotte Bailey

Rob had a seizure at school today. I'm so upset, I really thought he'd outgrown it – it's been well over a year since the last one. I got a terrible shock when the school called, drove there so fast I arrived just after the ambulance. He was very floppy and weepy, it was pitiful. Michael says he's not worried but he was really pale when he arrived at the hospital. The doctor is referring us to a neurologist at the Hospital for Sick Children which is meant to be very good. At least the seizure was very brief and we didn't have to stay long at the hospital but I feel completely worn out.

From: Charlotte Bailey
To: Nell Fenton

I'm so, so sorry, poor Rob, how awful for you all. At least it was only a small one this time & they are very, very infrequent. Ring me to let me know how he is.

From: Nell Fenton
To: Charlotte Bailey

Don't know what's going to happen to Rob's attention span now. Stupid useless clinical psychologist who did the play therapy with him told me that children with seizures have attention problems because the seizures 'scatter' their minds. Though I realise it's a load of crap can't stop it preying on my mind.

From: Charlotte Bailey
To: Nell Fenton

What bollocks, just completely ignore it. When is Rob's appt to see the neurologist?

From: Nell Fenton
To: Charlotte Bailey

Appt was this morning. He had a comprehensive physical which was all normal but he's referring him for a sleep-deprived EEG, an MRI scan and he's having a blood test for a chromosome abnormality called fragile X. 3 ghastly new things to worry about, I feel constantly on the verge of tears.

From: Charlotte Bailey
To: Nell Fenton

You don't really believe he has a chromosomal abnormality, do you? He's so obviously such a completely normal little boy. You should really try not to worry about it. Give Rob a kiss from me.

From: Nell Fenton
To: Charlotte Bailey

Got the instructions for Rob's sleep-deprived EEG today. Apparently lack of sleep gives a clearer result for reasons I don't understand. Because he's quite little he doesn't have to stay awake all night, he can go to bed till midnight, then we have to get him up and keep him awake until he goes to the hospital at 8am. Strictly no Coke or anything stimulating so should be tremendous fun trying to keep him awake. Will buy some new videos and toys to produce when things get critical. He's very excited about the whole idea and the other two are bitterly jealous.

From: Charlotte Bailey
To: Nell Fenton

Feel so sorry for you. In absence of being able to actually help in any way I shall keep posting you things. To this end I went to the Lego shop & got him a mountain/ski model. Sent it this morning but I don't think you'll get it before his EEG.

From: Nell Fenton
To: Charlotte Bailey

I'm so exhausted. We had Rob's EEG yesterday. Put him to bed at the usual time and I went to bed v early and set the alarm for midnight, woke him up and then dragged our two groggy bodies downstairs. Made myself a huge pot of really strong coffee because I was terrified of nodding off in front of the tv and waking up to find him asleep too. We played games and watched videos till 4 then I got Michael up and went back

230

to bed for a bit till it was time to get up and take him to the hospital. Very hard to keep him awake in the car. Poor little bugger could hardly walk by the time we got there so Michael had to carry him to the room. Laid him down on a bed where he immediately fell asleep. The technician did lots of measuring on his head, then glued lots of different coloured electrodes to his scalp (tricky with Rob as his hair is so dense it's like a beaver's pelt). He was so exhausted he slept through the whole thing though the technician was flashing lights in his face and occasionally ringing a loud bell. I tried asking him if he could tell anything from the readings but got the usual 'you'll need to speak to the doctor' brush-off. We're seeing the neurologist in 10 days for the results. We all went out for breakfast after and Michael and I drank another bucket of coffee and continued drinking coffee all day to keep going. Fell into bed last night feeling so tired but just couldn't get to sleep. Told Michael I felt strangely nervous and he said he did too. Realised we'd both drunk about 78 cups of coffee over the last 18 hours so lay there exhausted and jittery for much of the night.

From: Charlotte Bailey
To: Nell Fenton

Sounds like Rob was fine about it which is good. Sure you'll sleep v well tonight. I had my free acupuncture session today. Not only was I too pathetic to tell Alannah I wasn't coming back, I even went as far as booking another session which she was really pleased about as I think she's noticed I'm becoming a bit disheartened. (Possibly real reason for failure to get pregnant is not cold liver but absence of spine?) So now I'll have to phone her to cancel it as I've definitely decided it's a waste of time & money. When you are without spine it's much easier to cancel a session by phone & then just not make another.

From: Nell Fenton
To: Charlotte Bailey

It is very spineless but have to say have done it myself. Had an appointment once with an osteopath when I had that trouble with my coccyx. He turned out to be a thoroughly ridiculous person. He'd asked me to bring along some x-rays I'd had done (on which the real doctor had found nothing wrong). Adopted a very brainy air when reading them and immediately found something wrong. He then said 4 or 5 times 'Yes, I spotted that, the doctor didn't but I did' etc, etc. At the end he told me I'd need weekly appointment for the next 34 years and I meekly allowed myself to be booked in for the following week (then cancelled) rather than adopting the more honourable course of saying 'I'm sorry, you are an absurd little man and I have no faith in you. I will not be returning.'

From: Charlotte Bailey
To: Nell Fenton

I'm completely furious with that ghastly little tosser Sorën. Astrid was in floods of tears this morning. He rang her last night to inform her he slept with some girl he met at a pro-feminism rally. Although it didn't mean anything he can't be sure he won't do it again & apparently he has too much 'respect' for her to lie to her though not enough to keep his horrid plastic belt buckled, his trousers up & his pecker down.

From: Nell Fenton
To: Charlotte Bailey

Never ceases to amaze me how hideous little men can find women willing to have sex with them.

From: Charlotte Bailey
To: Nell Fenton

Amazing, isn't it? Astrid still very wobbly & everything is making her cry (incl sight of leftover soy yogurt in fridge). Toby's been really nice to her but I don't want him to be too nice as it'll only encourage her & then she'll do something annoying like fall in love with him.

From: Nell Fenton
To: Charlotte Bailey

Suggest you throw away all vegan 'specialty' foods to avoid further heartache for Astrid.

From: Charlotte Bailey
To: Nell Fenton

Fucking hell – as usual I've got myself into an extremely embarrassing situation. Spent the whole week MEANING to ring Alannah to cancel today's acupuncture session but just somehow couldn't face it so in the end rang her this morning, lied outrageously, told her Hugh was ill. Being (unlike me) a very nice person Alannah was terribly sweet & sympathetic & said not to pay for session as this was an unforeseen circumstance. Did feel really bad but then recovered my spirits enough to make a trip to the butcher to buy some sausages. Very, very stupid move as just as I was paying Alannah walked in (obviously having a bit of free time to shop as someone had just cancelled their appt at the 11th hour). Wanted to shout 'What are you doing in here, you're an alternative health therapist who wears roughly woven tunics, surely you're a vegetarian?' but instead blushed furiously, muttered something highly implausible about Hugh being suddenly better & sloped out of the shop, sausages in hand.

From: Nell Fenton
To: Charlotte Bailey

Well done you. Now you'll have to book another appointment or move to a different part of London.

From: Charlotte Bailey
To: Nell Fenton

Toby has acquired a girlfriend. It was only a matter of time, I suppose, as women seem to find him v attractive. Astrid quite miffed & says she doesn't think Keran is very pretty at all & she is much too thin. Keran (new girlfriend) is actually extremely pretty, v tall & annoyingly slender. She's come round twice already this week & then stood around the kitchen silently, looking thin & cold, while Toby chats to Dan about stuff like 'active steering'. Tonight, in desperate bid to make small talk & put her at her ease, commented on how pretty her name was & asked her where it was from. She told me it wasn't from anywhere & her mum just couldn't spell Karen. Don't know why, but after that, however hard I tried, could absolutely not think of a single thing to say so we lapsed back into a deafening silence while Toby & Dan loudly discussed torque.

DECEMBER 00

From: Nell Fenton
To: Charlotte Bailey

There was a huge snowfall last night and we of course were the only people on our street who didn't put the cars away in the garage, so today we look like the foolish foreigners we are. Suzette walked past with her disgusting dogs, just as I was digging my car out and asked in a concerned way if I was alright. A reference I suppose to sweaty redness of my face brought on by the unfamiliar exertion. Undeterred by the abruptness of my manner she then sweetly asked if we hadn't heard the weather forecast last night. Would have run after her and hit the back of her head with my shovel if I hadn't been so exhausted.

From: Charlotte Bailey
To: Nell Fenton

You could have just stuck the shovel out to trip her up, not as tiring as running & hitting.

Pa is going to be Father Christmas for our School Christmas Bazaar. Bit tragic really as old geezer who usually does it &

looks forward to it all year can't this time as his wife is really ill. Anyway head of fundraising committee (new mother to the school called Vivienne who takes her title v seriously) has decided to ignore his obvious shortcomings (heavy French accent) as he can provide his own costume. Think Pa is quite looking forward to it actually. I shall be running snow-shaker stall & although Vivienne sees me all the time at school obviously feels the matter is too important & complicated for idle playground exchanges & instead will only communicate via formal emails.

From: Nell Fenton
To: Charlotte Bailey

Hope Pa brings a bit less of the 'Grim Reaper' to the role than he does when he does it for his own grandchildren.

From: Charlotte Bailey
To: Nell Fenton

Have had 4 emails from Vivienne this week, one of which was the fundraising committee's policy on unruly behaviour – this the most fantastic piece of gobbledegook as although I read it twice with fascination was still really none the wiser, though did gather she was definitely against smacking other people's children.

From: Nell Fenton
To: Charlotte Bailey

Our Sunday school is doing a Christmas pageant, Rob is a

shepherd and Josie is the innkeeper's wife. Ollie was so heart-broken not to be involved I asked the horrendous old battle-axe who runs it if he could perhaps be a lamb? As I have been an exemplary supporter of the Sunday school she couldn't say no (though clearly wanted to) and said as long as I provided the costume he could sit among the shepherds. Ollie is over the moon, just hope he doesn't do anything too daft on the day as I have given firm assurances that he will be good as gold.

From: Charlotte Bailey
To: Nell Fenton

Sure Ollie will be absolutely charming & v sheeplike. Got Selena's Xmas card today, you will not be disappointed. Girls dressed in embroidered Tyrolean shirts, dirndl skirts & hair plaited & coiled into Belgian bun-type affair over their ears while Edwin superb in v tight lederhosen & one of those funny little Austrian pork-pie hats. They are all standing in rather thin snow & Edwin has one foot on a pile of logs & an axe over his shoulder, Ariadne & Portia are flanking him each holding a sheaf of spruce (poss branches off the tree Edwin has just felled?). While obviously Edwin v manly on account of pose & axe, effect somewhat undermined by fact he is wearing small shorts & make-up. Don't forget to forward Suzette's Xmas mssg.

From: Nell Fenton
To: Charlotte Bailey

Fear I might be off Serena's mailing list, didn't get last year's card and didn't have the foresight to send her an early card this year.

From: Charlotte Bailey
To: Nell Fenton

We just had our Xmas bazaar. Wish Vivienne HAD advocated smacking to control unruly children as had Macy visit my stall. Although every other child made their snow shaker in v ruly manner, I think Macy found it very stressful as she kept letting out little screams as she was doing it & if any other child's hand happened to be in vicinity of glitter or plasticine when she was reaching for it she would smack it away. Couldn't say anything like 'stop it or I'll hold your head down in my big bucket of water, you weird little freak' as Melody was right there saying stuff like 'gently, puppy, gently'. When it came to screwing the lid on the water-filled jar Macy couldn't do it but instead of letting me or Melody do it for her just got more & more furious until eventually she slammed the jar down on the table so hard water shot all over the child next to her. I was momentarily rendered completely speechless (as was the v wet little boy until he started crying noisily). Melody on the other hand immediately bent down over Macy saying 'Oh, puppy, was it an accident?' to which Macy replied 'YEAHESS' & started crying even more loudly than the boy. Actually feel really sorry for Macy – repulsive as she is, she's so clearly bonkers.

From: Nell Fenton
To: Charlotte Bailey

I have no respect for you. You should definitely have dunked her head in your big bucket of water and then claimed it was an accident. How was Father Christmas? Did he manage to make any of the children think the hour of their death was upon them?

From: Charlotte Bailey
To: Nell Fenton

He was v good really. I think some children were surprised to discover Fr Christmas is a foreigner but quite frankly pourquoi pas? Told him not to stoop or put his hood up so avoided the harbinger-of-doom look. He couldn't walk anywhere though. It was my responsibility to provide him with wellies (his in France) & unfortunately managed to bring 1 of mine & 1 of Dan's so he sat with his left foot partially posted into my wellie.

From: Nell Fenton
To: Charlotte Bailey

People probably thought it was a statement about diversity, having foreign, mobility-challenged Santa. Steve (hotel-phobic American now living in Toronto) and his French-Canadian wife, Marguerite, had us to a Christmas drinks party last night. She's pregnant again though her three are still quite small. Don't think it was on purpose but they seem very pleased. Quite like her but she's irritatingly perfect. The children came down politely to say goodnight looking attractive and wholesome in Petit Bateau pyjamas and then disappeared upstairs without whining or squabbling. The canapes were delicious and elegant and everything was just as it should be AND she's intelligent and funny, only justified criticisms I can level at her are she's fairly smug and her children have really bad names, Storm (seems quite a placid child), Willow (let's hope she doesn't turn out short and dumpy) and a boy called Dusty. Still do think I'm clutching at straws and maybe I should just be openly jealous of her (though obviously grateful not to be married to Steve).

From: Charlotte Bailey
To: Nell Fenton

Hats off to Marguerite for making sure her children were in clean nightclothes. Last time Dan & I had a drinks party all the children came down (whiny & uninvited) & while I could be justified in feeling moderately smug at the good taste of their nightclothes, Ellie's had a good deal of dried egg down the front.

From: Nell Fenton
To: Charlotte Bailey

We got the results of Rob's EEG and chromosome test today. Chromosome test normal as I was sure it would be, though a small, deranged part of me did worry that it wouldn't be. EEG unsurprisingly not normal, some spike activity which explains the seizures and slightly slow background waves which they really didn't explain in a satisfactory way – having raised it as a mild concern then said it was likely to be nothing to worry about.

From: Charlotte Bailey
To: Nell Fenton

That's excellent news. You really mustn't worry if they tell you not to.

From: Nell Fenton
To: Charlotte Bailey

I know that's true but do feel constant non-specific worry about him.

Suzette dropped round this morning on the flimsy pretext of asking me if Takara could stay over with us on Friday and then hovered around till I invited her in. Once she got inside she wouldn't shut up. The reason she wants us to have Takara (though I didn't ask) is that she and Kane are going to a tremendously grand party in Ottawa given by fabulously rich and important people. She then told me about the dress she's bought, deceptively simple apparently, but very, very beautiful and very expensive too. Her hair will be quite simple as well, loosely swept up and held in place by some exquisite antique filigree butterflies, with just a few tendrils trailing softly round her temples and nape. She then asked me about my Christmas shopping and having tricked me into admitting my shallow materialistic intention to buy all sorts of unnecessary presents for my over-indulged and greedy children, she took on a very saintly air and said her girls had asked her and Kane if this year, instead of receiving gifts, could they donate all the money they would have spent on each other to the animal rescue centre downtown where they volunteer as a family once a month. She smiled very tenderly in recollection and admitted she doesn't know where the girls get their ideas sometimes.

From: Charlotte Bailey
To: Nell Fenton

Burning question is will deceptively simple dress disguise her exceptionally large arse?

From: Nell Fenton
To: Charlotte Bailey

That's beyond the skill of mere mortals, but am sure the flaming beauty of her hair will draw everyone's eyes upwards and away from 'problem area'.

From: Charlotte Bailey
To: Nell Fenton

As well as the ever-present Toby we now have Keran as a semi-permanent fixture in our house. She comes round most afternoons after work to wait for Toby & as she's a nursery school assistant, her day finishes considerably earlier than his which adds up to quite a lot of silent waiting (usually in the kitchen). She's actually a sweet girl but her delicate prettiness & minuscule appetite make me feel like a hairy mammoth/sweaty guzzling pig. Also, even more tiresomely, Astrid dreadfully moody when she's around & obv doesn't like her much, mainly I suspect because Toby & the children do.

From: Nell Fenton
To: Charlotte Bailey

Have you considered possibility that it's not her delicate prettiness but fact that you are indeed a sweaty, hairy mammoth that makes you feel like one? Mum and Pa arrive day after tomorrow which is bit of bad planning on their part as they'll be in time for the school concert which will be the usual 2-hour snorefest. Incidentally we had Takara over yesterday and I distinctly overheard her and Josie talking about what they were hoping to get for Christmas and she seemed quite as enthusiastic and expectant as Josie about getting a greedy amount of presents.

From: Charlotte Bailey
To: Nell Fenton

Poor girl, think you should warn Suzette that Takara is expecting lots of presents (though obviously in a sensitive, concerned way).

From: Nell Fenton
To: Charlotte Bailey

Am forwarding you Suzette's Christmas message. I think you will detect the influence of her creative writing course.

A Christmas Greeting to Dear Friends

Another year older and wiser my friends,
With many fond memories, this old year ends.
What does the future hold? None of us knows,
Keep hope in your hearts through the cold winter snows.
We've loved and we've laughed and occasionally wept
But into the future so boldly we've stepped.

The love of our daughters, our most precious treasure,
And our love for them is beyond any measure.
Their characters growing in courage and grace
Along with their beauty of figure and face.
Our lives are a journey of wonder and thrills
Its ups and its downs, its occasional spills!

And thanks should be given for our married life
How bonds ever strengthen 'tween husband and wife,
A love that's so special, enduring and true,
It binds us together and trust is the glue.

We should all pause a moment at this time of year
To reflect and consider what we hold the most dear
Our homes and our hearths where there's comfort and
   rest
Of life's many pleasures, these are the best,
And so friends, I wish you joy, warmth and good cheer
For this Christmas season and all through the year.

From: Charlotte Bailey
To: Nell Fenton

V beautiful & moving, I'm speechless with admiration, she really is a Renaissance woman. Such a shame she couldn't think of a last couplet for that pesky 3rd stanza. Astrid seems to have cheered up, thank God. Been tiresomely tearful lately about the vegan Lothario & jolly grumpy about Keran always being around. Latest contender for title of most unappealing or inappropriate person she can fancy is grimy-looking youth with a pierced chin who works in the video shop. She's been getting out lots of videos & has told me she thinks Robin is 'so cute!'. Video shop is mainly manned by Robin, a very fat girl with glasses & no neck, & weirdly tall beaky woman with whom I am embarrassingly well acquainted & on quite friendly terms. Astrid v keen to know if Robin has a girlfriend as she says they've been quite flirtatious with each other & please, please, please could I ask Carol (tall beaky woman).

From: Nell Fenton
To: Charlotte Bailey

Do think sorting out au pair's romance above and beyond the call of duty but better to have her happy.

Mum and Pa arrived this afternoon. Pa of course sensibly went off to bed but Mum a trooper as usual and stayed up till 10 so 3am your time. The children absolutely thrilled to see them and I let them stay up quite late as a treat so getting them up for school should be fun. Mum says Anna is having all Geoffrey's family for Christmas which is a terrifying thought on so many levels.

From: Charlotte Bailey
To: Nell Fenton

Yes, Anna told me she'd invited them all but presumably they didn't HAVE to accept & by now they must know what they're letting themselves in for. Been endlessly asking Dan what he wants for Xmas. He keeps saying you decide – so I have – I've bought the most fantastic HUGE Victorian bath for him from new favourite shop, Bygone Bathrooms. It really was an absolute unmissable bargain & will look marvellous. Think he's going to be really pleased.

Peter is coming for Christmas. He's taking the whole thing v seriously, keeps ringing from the shops for guidance re Xmas presents for the children. Said my answers of 'nothing' & then 'any old crap' were 'unhelpful'. Dan says he rang him from Allders for some suggestions for my present (don't wish to be grabby but if he is going to spend money on me wish it wasn't in Allders & certainly not under Dan's guidance).

From: Nell Fenton
To: Charlotte Bailey

You are horribly grabby but also a gift-giving genius, I mean what man wouldn't be thrilled to get a bath as a present? Can just picture his little face lighting up on Christmas morning.

From: Charlotte Bailey
To: Nell Fenton

I've really gone off Carol from the video shop, firstly & most unforgivably she recommended the film Atanarjuat: The Fast Runner (shittest film I've ever seen) & secondly she was really mean about Astrid. When I asked her if Robin had a girlfriend she said 'No, why?' in v suspicious way so then I explained about Astrid & she said 'Oh no, he doesn't fancy HER, he likes PRETTY girls' & then Miss Fat No-Neck chipped in 'And he prefers blondes' & reached up to touch her custard-yellow head (only her fat arms wouldn't quite reach) so then I said v defensively 'I think Astrid is very pretty' & Old Beaky just rolled her Marty Feldman eyes & said nothing. When I got back from the video shop Astrid all excited & shiny-eyed & eager to know outcome of conversation so I had to tell her unfortunately Robin doesn't fancy her as he is very, very gay. She's going home tomorrow so fortunately will not have to deal with fallout from this latest romantic disappointment.

Showed Albert Polaroid of my bath (still at Bygone Bathrooms), he's v gloomy about it & says judging by the size of it he reckons bathroom floor will need to be strengthened. He's such an exaggerator, don't know how he can tell as bath only about 1" × 2" in photo (so therefore by my reckoning should weigh half a pound tops).

From: Nell Fenton
To: Charlotte Bailey

Suppose it's just possible Albert realises picture isn't 'actual size'. (Also, surely Miss No-Neck should easily be able to reach up and touch her head, what with head being closer to her body than for people WITH necks?)

The Russians asked us round for drinks tonight, also invited Suzette & co which was a stroke of luck as Mum has been v keen to meet Suzette. Russians as usual entertained fabulously. Served all these different vodkas and delicious food, included tiny nests made of leek each with three pomegranate seeds in, and tiny rabbit kebabs. Suzette was being very brainy, asking Pa lots of questions about mining in Africa, head tipped fetchingly to one side, serious but still beautiful. She also spoke to Mum about 'art' and told her at length about Sophie's remarkable artistic gift, all the more remarkable apparently because though Suzette herself is very, very creative she did confess that she is 'hopeless' at drawing. Finally had to intervene as I could no longer stand idly by watching Mum's face becoming more and more hunted and desperate. Suzette's attention then fortunately turned to Kane who judging by his demeanour had thrown himself with open arms at the vodka and was talking with great intensity though little coherence to Russian Wife. Don't think Suzette was very pleased as she practically frogmarched him out barely saying goodbye to anyone. Doubt there will be much goodwill to mankind in their house tonight.

From: Charlotte Bailey
To: Nell Fenton

V jealous of Mum meeting Suzette, have only just got over my disappointment that she was away when we came to Canada.

Albert has been to 'visit' the bath at Bygone Bathrooms & has come home to tell me with much satisfaction that not only will bathroom floor not withstand the weight unless we replace all the joists (apparently bath is cast iron & weighs 64 tons), but once filled with water & me 193 tons or water & Dan 65 tons), but also he reckons bath is too heavy to carry upstairs as even though the staircase has been strengthened, the fact it's suspended means it's just not designed to take that kind of load. Albert has 'calculated' only safe way to get the bath into the house will be to remove one of the spare-room windows & bring it in by crane (this will also involve cutting a big bath-sized hole in wall between spare room & our bathroom so we can roll bastard bath through on trolley thing). Don't believe a word of it, he just makes it up as he goes along, sure he's just saying it to annoy me (won't tell Dan either when I give it to him as he always believes everything Albert says).

From: Nell Fenton
To: Charlotte Bailey

It's the gift that keeps on giving, isn't it?

From: Charlotte Bailey
To: Nell Fenton

Shut up, I'm really depressed. Bygone Bathrooms rang to say

I had to come & get the bath as they were getting a big delivery of old basins from some stupid bloody hotel. Paid a friend of Albert's who has a lorry nearly what I paid for the bath to dump it in our front garden till I can get someone to haul it up the stairs as Albert says he won't do it. Spoilt the lovely surprise of Dan's Xmas present as large bath in our front garden needed some explaining. In the end the girls & I draped the bath in a sheet, put a ribbon on it & presented it to Dan. He looked quite stunned actually & kept saying 'Wow, it's big.'

From: Nell Fenton
To: Charlotte Bailey

Expect his true delight will become apparent when you tell him about the crane, the masonry cutter and the new joists. At least it probably won't get nicked, what with needing a crane to lift it.

From: Charlotte Bailey
To: Nell Fenton

How was your Christmas Day? Ours excellent. Children had the most wonderful time, Hugh Sr & Penelope came with usual incredibly lavish presents & Hugh Jr v well behaved & did lots of fairly random kissing (& no biting whatsoever). Toby & Keran there too & Keran even helped a bit (though obv silently). Peter is the perfect guest, he played endlessly with the children, peeled potatoes, brought lovely presents, beautiful embroidered cotton nighties for the girls, a train encyclopedia for Hugh & a case of wine for Dan, think he was most pleased with my present – one of those great big presentation boxes of make-up filled with orange blusher & pearly rose lipstick. I am indeed a v fine actress as later that night when we were going to bed Dan said he was glad I'd liked it so much as Peter had been quite worried about it & he'd told Peter to get me photo frames but Peter had insisted he should get something for me not the house. Isabel rang about 17 times in the morning with questions about stuffing & sprouts. Think she was feeling the strain a bit (Anna upstairs putting finishing touches to home-made Christmas crackers) because she was sounding more & more harassed until Guy started ringing instead & just shouting my instructions across the kitchen to her while TL barked in the background & Geoffrey yelled at him to shut up. Very serene Anna rang in the evening saying what a lovely lunch Isabel & Auntie Iris had made, only hiccup was that they couldn't find the Christmas pudding anywhere though she'd DEFINITELY bought one. Didn't matter though as she (Anna) invented her own Christmas pudding by squashing up mince pies & mixing them with vanilla ice cream & brandy, said it didn't look v nice but tasted absolutely delicious, also everybody really liked their handmade crackers.

From: Nell Fenton
To: Charlotte Bailey

We had a lovely day too and perfect snowfall for once, not too much to interfere with driving but enough to make everything look clean and to go tobogganing after lunch. Quite tired as sat up terribly late with Mum finishing off the stockings as I had hatched ludicrously unrealistic plan to make them each a beautiful highly decorated new stocking as old ones ugly and boring and of course it took 5x longer than time allowed. Learnt a v important lesson today, which is that if the boys eat a great many M&Ms and Skittles before breakfast they are too hopped up to be able to sit through Mass. Rob constantly slithering under the pew in front, but Ollie was even worse, kept collapsing onto the floor and then doing commando-style belly crawling under people's feet. When Michael tried to drag him up he grabbed an old lady's ankles to anchor himself. Luckily Pa caught her before she fell over. Michael then removed them both by the scruff of the neck and took them to little entrance bit where they bounced off the walls till the end of the service. Both got a bit weepy as they came back down off their high but fortunately had all the presents under the tree to cheer them up again.

From: Charlotte Bailey
To: Nell Fenton

Appear to be hosting New Year's Eve again. Marcia rang to ask what she should bring & then Geraldine rang to ask if I was still expecting her. This triggered dim recollection of dinner at Quentin & Marcia's where I sat next to world's most boring man (Roger, a structural engineer with a passion for potholing, who finished every stunningly dull utterance with 'does that makes sense?'), got vv drunk to alleviate intense boredom. By end of dinner was so shit-faced nothing Roger said made sense any more & apparently I invited everyone (including Roger) to our house for New Year's Eve.

From: Charlotte Bailey
To: Nell Fenton

Marcia just rang to ask if Roger really was invited to New Year's Eve dinner as apparently he tentatively mentioned it to Quentin. Would have said 'no fear' except 1) I am a lady & therefore do not wish to draw Marcia's attention to the fact that her friend is really, really boring & b) she thinks he fancies Geraldine as he asked if she'll be there & am v keen to encourage any romantic liaisons, so instead said 'but of course' in v gracious manner. Now have to invite several others to water down the Geraldine/Roger effect.

From: Nell Fenton
To: Charlotte Bailey

Sounds like you did a good night's work though your dreadful drunkenness proves that 1) you are not such a lady and b) surely even Geraldine wouldn't settle for someone who goes potholing.

JANUARY 01

From: Charlotte Bailey
To; Nell Fenton

New Year's Eve quite enjoyable, sometimes it's good to have v low expectations. Initially felt quite warmly towards Roger as when he arrived he brought v lavish bouquet, also had neatly combed hair & as I had done the seating plan knew he was not sitting next to me. Got a bit excited when I saw him talking v animatedly to Geraldine down the other end of the table & was just feeling a little bit pleased with myself re my match-making skills when Geraldine came darting up to me & asked if I could move everyone around at pudding because if Roger said 'honeycomb of caves' or 'does that make sense?' one more time she couldn't guarantee she wouldn't stab him with her fork. Moving Roger v bad idea as he then ended up near Dan & started asking him why there was a giant bath in our front garden. When Dan told him, Roger went up to inspect where bath was supposed to be going & said lots of boring bollocks, gist of which is Albert entirely right re absolute necessity of massively strengthening floor & also probably crane best way to get it into the house (fuck fuck fuckity fuck).

From: Nell Fenton
To: Charlotte Bailey

One day you'll look back at all this and laugh. Assuming bath doesn't crash through the ceiling killing several members of your family, that is.

From: Charlotte Bailey
To: Nell Fenton

Got a birth-announcement card from Cecelia this morning with a photo of all the children & new baby Dominic who is exquisitely pretty. Felt quite tearful when I got the card but actually everything making me feel tearful at the moment & am feeling quite under the weather. (I think I'm getting Ellie's absolutely horrible cold – she's been quite poorly & had an ear infection too). Last night when Dan v gently suggested, given what Roger had said, perhaps we should just sell the bath as, while it was a most lovely Christmas present, cost of installing it would be astronomical, I burst into tears. Did lots of appalling emotional blackmail about how I just wanted a lovely bathroom & now we were having to sell the bath I really LOVED & it was a present & you should just keep presents & be grateful for them (which reminds me had v embarrassing episode in Allders with v hoity-toity sales assistant who wouldn't let me exchange nasty make-up kit just because Hugh had used it a little bit). Anyway Dan then said we could keep the bath but it may be in front garden for quite some time till we can afford to install it.

From: Nell Fenton
To: Charlotte Bailey

You're probably just tired. Why don't you try not doing any entertaining for a week or two? (Crazy idea, I know.) Have planned a little rest for myself, booked another week in Cuba for March, v excited.

I've just sent out invitations to Rob's birthday party which will be quite the event as we have 'Reptilia' doing the entertaining and they are (unsurprisingly) bringing reptiles, including a python. Rob very thrilled and inviting everyone he meets to come to his party. Have his MRI scan next week which I'm dreading.

From: Charlotte Bailey
To: Nell Fenton

I'm sure scan will be fine. Room full of snakes & children sounds like a fine idea for a birthday party, no wonder Rob is so excited. Ellie's been taking some particularly vile antibiotics for her ear infection. In order to get her to take them – they actually made her gag (wish I could just stick them up her bum like in France) – had to bribe her with promise of little treat if she took them all week without complaining. Sent Dan off with her on Sat, Ellie came back looking like the cat who got the cream – or more specifically the little girl who got the Furby. Couldn't bloody believe it – that's like a main birthday present. Dan all defensive saying it was the only thing in the shop she wanted & negotiating with her is like negotiating with the IRA. Pointed out that had he taken her into the sweet shop as per instructions, rather than the toy shop that she led him into, could probably have got away with 50p pack of Rolos rather than £30 electronic talking animal. Now I look like a sour old spoilsport cow for complaining, while he looks like marvellous present-giving daddy.

From: Louise Corrigan
To: Charlotte Bailey

Thanks for your message, had a great birthday. We've been really, really busy but I still find time for a daily yoga session. I actually have abs now. Our book is coming out Feb 7 and Barneys are doing a big Valentine's Day promotion on Feb 12. We have lots of press lined up and a trip to San Francisco. Am super-excited. Speak soon x L

From: Charlotte Bailey
To: Louise Corrigan

V. depressed to hear about your abs. Hate people who prove exercise works. Am fat & exhausted by the excesses of Christmas, obv. quite tiring dragging round all that extra flab. Late b'day present in the post plus deranged letter from Ellie.

Barneys sounds fantastic as does San Francisco. Could you pls now refrain from telling me about your life as you are only emphasising the fact that your life is considerably more interesting than mine. Your cooperation in this matter would be greatly appreciated. Love C xx

From: Charlotte Bailey
To: Nell Fenton

Furby is driving me fucking insane. It refuses to obey manufacturer's handbook. Have made myself v unpopular with other mothers at school for being parent of child who started the Furby craze. Lydia's nanny told me how L's parents missed beginning of some play because they couldn't get the Furby to 'go to sleep'. In the end had to shut it in the oven as darkness (eventually) makes them go quiet. Suggested that as Furby not real living animal in extremis simply removing batteries quite effective.

From: Charlotte Bailey
To: Louise Corrigan

Have discovered partial explanation for extreme fatness as I am pregnant. I'm really thrilled but can't quite believe it, had got to the stage of thinking it really was never going to happen. This of course does not explain large wobbling stomach as at this stage baby about the size of a raisin, does however explain body's tenacious grip on post-Xmas fat. Felt a bit worried telling Nell but she was really pleased. Dan is very happy indeed as it means we will need a bigger car. Love C xx

From: Charlotte Bailey
To: Nell Fenton

Told Fran I was pregnant, she got really excited & emotional & immediately came over so she could escort me to the health-food shop down the road & buy me fish oil & vitamin supplements. She's got another driving test in a couple of weeks, she's given up on formal lessons because they're so expensive & has been practising with Joe instead, only she says he's a rubbish teacher as he shouts all the time & even swears which he doesn't normally do & she finds very unnerving. Don't hold out much hope for her passing which is a great shame, don't know if I can bear to hear the words 'mirror, signal, manoeuvre' any more.

From: Rachel Lockwood
To: Nell Fenton

Dear Nell

Thanks for the lovely presents. Presents that come in the post are always extra exciting. We spent a few days over Christmas at Jane's house and Mum and Dad came for a bit too. I had been dreading it rather but was pleasantly surprised at how nice and relaxing it was. I think I've got so used to the constant fights and tension over the years I'd forgotten life can be peaceful and I'm also gradually realising I feel relieved since we split up. Jonathan as always was thrilled to be with his cousins and hardly mentioned Jack. He's spending a couple of days with Jack and his girlfriend now before school starts again. I absolutely hate letting him go there, it must be confusing for him to see them together, but the alternative is not letting him see Jack, which would be worse. I tried to suggest she shouldn't be there when Jonathan comes to stay but Jack got very aggressive, accusing me of being jealous and started to talk about custody, so I dropped it. He's putting a lot of pressure on me about the house as well so I need to sort something out.

Anyhow enough grumbling.

Fondest love to all
Rachel xx

From: Nell Fenton
To: Rachel Lockwood

Dear Rachel, I'm so glad your Christmas went well, you deserve some peace and quiet. Our Christmas was lovely and Mum and Pa have been staying but they're going back tomorrow. Don't worry too much about Jonathan seeing Jack with someone else. I don't think young children think about that sort of thing. The confusing bit is that Jack doesn't live at home any more and there's nothing you can do about that. Don't let Jack bully you about the house. Next time he accuses you of being jealous you could accuse him of being greedy. It's not as if it would be unreasonable for you to feel jealousy anyway but Jack should know better than anyone that you're the world's most honourable person and are not beset by the same shabby feelings as the rest of us. Have to say I'm struggling a bit at the moment with the most rotten feeling. Charlotte is pregnant and while I know I should be happy for her I'm very ashamed to say I feel a squirming jealousy inside. It's so horrible of me to be like this and has really taken me by surprise. Don't think Charlotte suspected it when she phoned to tell me, it would make it so much worse to think she guessed. Anyway I'll get over it, haven't even confessed it to Michael, obviously much better to burden you with my trivial problems. Love Nell

From: Rachel Lockwood
To: Nell Fenton

Dear Nell

It's perfectly understandable, as long as Charlotte doesn't realise it you have nothing to reproach yourself with and of course it'll pass. I'm sure you'll get pregnant again anyway, it's far too soon to give up hope.

By the way, while I very much like the title of world's most honourable person, I believe the fact that I have frequent and detailed fantasies about running Jack and his ghastly, grasping girlfriend over with my car disqualifies me.

Fondest love to all
Rachel xx

From: Nell Fenton
To: Charlotte Bailey

Rob had his MRI at the Hospital for Sick Children yesterday. They had to sedate him heavily so he wouldn't move. I stayed with him for that part which was awful, he's terrified of needles, but the remote chance that I might be pregnant meant I couldn't go with him for the scan itself so Michael went instead. It makes a deafening noise and he was rolled into this narrow tube. Obviously Rob wasn't aware of any of it and they'd put earmuffs on him anyway but Michael was so upset at the sight of him disappearing into the tube and I think also the fact of him needing a brain scan in the first place, he had tears running down his face the entire time. When they came out I went to the recovery room with Rob. He was all groggy and floppy, which broke my heart, though he did manage to wake up enough for me to feed him the ice pops they gave him. Michael having vanished briefly reappeared with a giant stuffed dog. Last thing we need is yet another huge cuddly toy and as it was bought in a hospital gift shop probably cost $1000, but in the circumstances let it pass without comment. Rob was so out of it he didn't even register it but it seemed to make Michael feel better. We get the results next month.

From: Charlotte Bailey
To: Nell Fenton

It sounds completely harrowing & poor Michael. I'm absolutely certain it will be fine though. Really don't worry.

I went to Geraldine's birthday dinner last night, one of the grimmest evenings I've spent in quite some time. There was me, Geraldine, Marcia & someone called Polly from G's office. We went to v overpriced poncey restaurant in the City that used to be a bank and had all the gaiety & atmosphere of a morgue. I couldn't drink & Marcia didn't want to because Rosamund is terrible at night at the moment & it makes her feel worse but Geraldine & Polly compensated for us both. Instead of getting jollier as she drank, G became more & more gloomy & morose. Polly, quite a bitch, made it clear she thought being at home with children was a pointless waste of time & then started telling us how fat & lazy her secretary Bridget had become since she'd had her baby 6 months ago. Though obv I have never met Bridget, waded in & made an impassioned speech in her defence until Geraldine interrupted me & said actually it was true, Bridget rang in sick all the time & had been spotted out shopping, without her baby, on more than one occasion when she was supposed to have been ill. Shut up after that & the evening limped on to its glum conclusion. PS Got a letter from the school today to say Furbies have been banned.

261

From: Nell Fenton
To: Charlotte Bailey

Think you might have anticipated a girls' night out arranged by Geraldine wouldn't be the best fun you ever had. Electronic animal toys are clearly the work of the devil. Did you ever see Josie's Tamagotchi? They were a huge craze when Josie was about 6. Wasn't even animal-shaped, just a little stopwatch-type thing with unconvincing moving image of a pet that needed feeding and cleaning etc or the bastard thing would die. Had to take it away from her at one point when I found her getting up in the night to attend to it. Was so overjoyed when Josie finally got sick of it and decided to let it starve to death.

How are you feeling apart from not hung-over?

From: Charlotte Bailey
To: Nell Fenton

Fine, completely normal although embarrassingly hungry, feel like Toulouse-Lautrec – want to eat everything in sight.

Geraldine rang this morning to say she had a bloody terrible hangover & to find out if I was ok as she thought I seemed v quiet, which was nice of her. She said she's really depressed at turning 36 with no boyfriend. Am thinking of trying to set her up with Peter, slightly unlikely combination but you never can tell.

From: Nell Fenton
To: Charlotte Bailey

Suppose it's worth a try but would have thought it was a very long shot.

Don't know why this should be, but as soon as you move abroad people who you hardly ever see when you live near them suddenly think it's ok to invite themselves to come and stay. Have had an endless succession of threats of people planning to come since we moved here but happily most never get further than that. Just got an email from Sarah and Nick (not sure I ever thanked you properly for passing on my new email address to Sarah). Anyway they're coming to Canada and apparently it would be lovely to come and see us for a few days when they're in Toronto. Lovely perhaps for them not having to pay for a hotel but cannot see any loveliness in the situation for myself. Don't know how I'm going to break it to Michael (obviously it will be entirely my fault since she's my cousin). Have to make sure the children aren't in earshot as I predict there will be quite a bit of swearing. Children loathed Desmond the one time they met him. Thanks to his parents' relentless hothousing the unfortunate child is being transformed from an ordinary (if unappealing) little boy into a creepy little geek. Sarah actually went to the trouble of telling me that Dezzy will be missing a week of school on either side of half-term but the educational value of the trip will more than compensate. Even if he weren't 5 does she really imagine I care?

From: Charlotte Bailey
To: Nell Fenton

You are such a cow. I know she's incredibly irritating but she's quite sweet & terribly well meaning. Nick, however, is an absolute twat, awash with allergies which you shouldn't hold against him but somehow you do (& he calls Sarah 'Mummy' even when Desmond's not around). You should warn her that time spent with your children will not benefit Desmond educationally & may even empty his brain of useful information to replace it with jokes about bogeys & farts. Just to keep you up to speed on Furby situation, 'Furbymania' has reached fever pitch & Ellie has talked me into giving a Furby tea party, for which she has made & handed out elaborate invitations, not quite sure why I agreed to it, suppose I am hoping this gesture of reconciliation will result in some sort of entente cordiale between me & other mothers. Should in any case have one ally after Easter as Katrina called this evening to tell me her girls have been offered places at our school. They're buying a house quite nearby & moving in sometime in April.

PS I'm sure you'll be glad to be reminded that Sarah, Nick & Dezzy all strict vegetarians.

From: Nell Fenton
To: Charlotte Bailey

No need for a reminder, not only did Sarah tell me on the phone that they are vegetarians and that Nick has lots of allergies but then followed it up with emailed list of all dietary restrictions, complete with lots of smiley faces and exclamation marks.

From: Nell Fenton
To: Charlotte Bailey

It was Rob's party today, went very well, the snakes were a huge hit and very impressive. Piece de resistance was a custard-yellow python called Sunshine that was absolutely enormous and could very easily have crushed a child to death at any given moment. Fortunately it didn't as would have had a lot of tiresome explaining to do.

From: Charlotte Bailey
To: Nell Fenton

Handing out of Furby party invitations has rather backfired as although I gave E v strict instructions to only ask those who already had Furbies at least 2 & possibly 3 girls invited don't & as my suggestion that 'they all just share' (for duration of tea party only obviously) has gone down like a cup of cold sick, the few remaining parents who up till now had managed to withstand the intense pressure to supply their child with annoying electronic toy have had their hands forced (by me). Maddie also v tearful about lack of personal Furby so have promised to buy her a pink one.

From: Nell Fenton
To: Charlotte Bailey

Not sure only inviting those who own Furbies as tactful as you imagine anyway. Surely it would only accentuate the gulf between the 'haves' and the 'have-nots' and cause even greater discontent. Looks like you're buggered either way.

From: Charlotte Bailey
To: Nell Fenton

Furby tea party yesterday v sweet actually, though nearly crashed the car coming home after morning drop-off as had a boot full of banned-from-school Furbies without their 'mothers' that woke up & screamed when I rounded a sharp corner – extremely disconcerting. I made everyone a little pink felt hood with earholes for their Furby (like a hood on a falcon), supposed to make them go quiet. Hope now to close this chapter & resume normal playground relations.

FEBRUARY 01

From: Charlotte Bailey
To: Nell Fenton

Guess whether or not I shall be hearing the words 'mirror, signal, manoeuvre' again or not. (CLUE: apparently Fran's examiner was a fat lesbian who took an instant dislike to her & was 'unduly harsh'.)

From: Nell Fenton
To: Charlotte Bailey

Poor Fran, do think it's time she accepted some things are simply not meant to be.

I went with Ollie's class this morning to the ice rink where they're doing skating this term. I go every week to help them lace their skates etc and to give Ollie moral support because he hates it and is hopeless at it. He wears a big black helmet and metal grille face mask (mandatory) which make him look extra small. Whenever he gets the chance he comes up to the glass partition where I stand and watch (under strict orders not to move away) and stares at me blinking his eyes really fast to stop himself crying. I went up to his instructor after this week's lesson and said I thought he'd find the lessons more enjoyable if he didn't spend so much time scrabbling ineffectually to get up when he'd fallen down and could she help him up occasionally. Snotty cow said he just needs to learn to get back up on his own. Wanted to kick her feet out from under her so she could see how it feels.

From: Charlotte Bailey
To: Nell Fenton

Shame, poor Ollie. Ice skating stupid anyway.

Dan got a vg royalties cheque from his Christmas book, enough even to allow me to entertain grand notions of having our bath in our house rather than in our front garden. Only thing that stops me being thrilled about it is that Brian Turner keeps complaining to various neighbours that our front garden looks like a salvage yard & is bringing down the tone of our neighbourhood. Now feel v conflicted, although would be wonderful to be able to actually use it in a bathroom as a bath, notion that is causing Brian pain every morning when he & stupid Hildegard do their arse-waggling speed walking past it gives me v great pleasure.

From: Nell Fenton
To: Charlotte Bailey

Obviously torturing ghastly neighbours v satisfying but I think that ultimately having a lovely bathroom will bring you greater contentment.

Sarah and Nick arrive tomorrow. Every time the subject has

268

arisen over the last few days Michael has said, 'I just can't fucking believe it.' Don't know why he finds it so hard to believe, only too grimly real to me. The children have a couple of days off school after they leave so I've booked to go skiing, a kind of light at the end of the tunnel. Am keeping my mouth shut about it though as there is a danger Suzette will revive her idea that a ski trip together would be fun.

From: Charlotte Bailey
To: Nell Fenton

Roger (boring one from New Year's Eve) has recommended a carpenter to come & strengthen our floors. What is it with me & workmen, why can't they ever just be normal? While Don looks perfectly normal & Roger says he's excellent, Don doesn't talk, he shouts. Everything he says is about 10 decibels louder than a normal person, even Albert who doesn't usually notice stuff (eg Gordon's smell) visibly flinched 1st time Don spoke to him. Anyway Don's starting on the floors next week & Albert is going to sort out a crane.

From: Charlotte Bailey
To: Nell Fenton

Don the shouting carpenter is doing a really good job on the bathroom floor. I know this because he keeps telling me so & then making me come up to look at his very good work. Floor will be finished by the w/e which will be a relief esp as Toby always encouraging his shouting by getting into conversations with him. Have given up hope of Toby ever leaving, he was supposed to be going to Rio to photograph the carnival this month but hasn't got the money & Hugh Sr & Dan not lending him any more. Am so sick of hearing him & Keran having sex when she stays over (often) & she always cries afterwards, get enough crying from the children, without having to listen to weeping of emotional, post-coital Keran.

From: Nell Fenton
To: Charlotte Bailey

Could be worse. You could have SARAH AND NICK STAYING. I think if possible Sarah is more annoying than I remembered. There seems to be very little that is not a source of wonder to her and she follows me round with sparkly-eyed eagerness being amazed and delighted by everything. Anyhow they are living proof that there is someone for everyone as Nick, unlike Michael and I who both want to throw a bucket of cold water over her to curb her enthusiasm, seems to find her enchanting and not to mind the fact that she calls him Noonie. I thought Michael might actually start sobbing at dinner last night when Nick explained to him at very considerable length why his video equipment was superior to more costly gear on the market. He's a man who is not afraid to repeat himself and I think he might have suggested you'd be mad to spend more, seventy or eighty times. Michael was very brave and managed to control himself till we were alone in our bedroom where he permitted himself some quite unkind remarks about them both.

From: Charlotte Bailey
To: Nell Fenton

Last time I saw them in the flesh was at Clara's wedding where I had the very great misfortune to be on their table. Nick wouldn't eat any of the food at the reception as everything had something in it he was allergic to (a fact he kept entire table fully informed about) & then when he had beaten us all into stunned submission he gave entire table a blow-by-blow account of how to build your own Welsh dresser while Sarah beamed up at him approvingly.

From: Nell Fenton
To: Charlotte Bailey

I'll have to be very careful not to mention Welsh dressers – my spirit is almost broken and Michael is a man on the edge. Desmond endears himself to me more every day. Has so far asked me what the population of Canada is, then corrected me when I got it wrong. Sarah was there or would have said 'Why did you ask me if you already knew the answer, you little twerp?' Also asked me the population of Toronto, but wasn't going to fall into that trap again. He asked me how come Rob and Ollie didn't know about the Gulf Stream, if I knew the names of all the provinces of Canada (no), and why Rob does such bad writing.

From: Charlotte Bailey
To: Nell Fenton

Can't blame Desmond, he's just a product of his horribly pushy parents. You should feel sorry for him really, particularly as he'll no doubt end his days in the maximum-security wing of Wormwood Scrubs on account of having hacked his parents to death with a meat cleaver in a drug-addled rage.

From: Nell Fenton
To: Charlotte Bailey

You're such a comfort to me.

From: Charlotte Bailey
To: Nell Fenton

Prospect of bringing the bath into the house has made Albert all officious & he has gone into an organisational frenzy. By pulling lots & lots of strings he has persuaded a mate of a mate of a mate to hire us a crane for HALF A DAY. Apparently this is a huge triumph as normally YOU HAVE TO HAVE THE CRANE FOR THE WHOLE DAY. It's costing so much, absolutely cannot believe we are not being charged for half a month's use. Albert says he's going to have to inform the police & council about the crane & entire surrounding area will have to be 'coned off as a no-go zone'. Albert is bringing in his son Ricky, Frank, John, Terence & of course Smelly Gordon on the day to help roll the bath through the hole in spare-room wall. Everybody is in a foul mood, Dan because of all the palaver & hideous expense, Astrid because Sorën-the-vegan was supposed to visit this w/e & I said he couldn't (wormed his way back into her knickers at Christmas), Albert because I'm not treating his role with sufficient gravitas & me because I'm just fed up & my arse is fat.

From: Nell Fenton
To: Charlotte Bailey

Have to say this whole bath saga gives you the distinction of being madder than Mad Will McMad, winner of last year's mad competition. Anyway I'm really fed up too, Sarah has been closely supervising the food I cook on account of Nick's many and varied allergies. Why she doesn't just do the bloody cooking herself and save us all a lot of bother defeats me, perhaps she is too busy giving me marital advice. She said to me that Michael 'seems to be under a lot of stress' by which we both knew she meant he's surly and monosyllabic. She told me that when Nick gets 'down in the dumps' she makes a point of including a little love note in his packed lunch (packed lunch necessary because of allergies). I'm so wearied by her that even if I wasn't, as ever, too lily-livered, don't think I could be bothered to say what ails Michael is at present beyond the help of a love note, but I anticipate a full recovery WHEN YOU GO AWAY.

From: Charlotte Bailey
To: Nell Fenton

Idea that Nick has a packed lunch because of his allergies makes me want to kick him to death & notion that Sarah puts love notes in it makes me want to kick her to death too. (My feelings running quite high at the moment.)

From: Nell Fenton
To: Charlotte Bailey

I see you've entered the 'serene' phase of your pregnancy.

From: Charlotte Bailey
To: Nell Fenton

We are quite the talk of the neighbourhood. Had an unbeliev-ably stressful morning where our entire family & several neighbours (including Brian & Hildegard) stood on the patch of heath outside our house gasping as we watched a sweating crane operator attempt to steer a 2-ton bath which was swinging briskly in the wind through the spare-room window without accidentally smashing down the front of our house. Took 3 attempts to get it in by which time Dan was crouched on the grass in the foetal position whispering 'Jesus Christ' to himself. Toby, meanwhile, was leaping around shouting 'Yess, yesss, yessss! Fantastickkk!' like deranged member of the paparazzi who has just spotted Gordon Brown & Tony Blair in naked sex romp. Even started photographing Dan in his agony till Dan told him to fuck off, then lay on his back in the grass to capture flying bath from underneath. Only got up & stopped being so bloody irritating when Keran told him one of his bunches was brushing against a dog turd. Have to say Albert who was in the house with Gordon et al looked pretty pale by the end of it all & I heard several 'fuuucks' issuing from spare-room window as bath swung near the window & they tried to guide it in with ropes. Anyway bath is now in place, we are destitute & Dan has an awful headache from all the whisky he & Albert drank afterwards.

From: Nell Fenton
To: Charlotte Bailey

Glad the bath landed safely.

V happy to report that Sarah and Nick left this morning. Michael said goodbye to them before going off to work and was positively effusive in his good humour. I think Sarah thought I'd taken her advice about the love note and that the credit was hers for his improved spirits because she gave me a hug before she left and whispered in my ear that a bit of loving attention goes a long way with these men. Anyway mustn't be small-minded, after all the credit WAS hers for his improved mood. Even Rob and Ollie who are incredibly indiscriminate in who they like came and asked if Desmond could not come and stay any more because he only talks about boring things and he pinches.

From: Charlotte Bailey
To: Nell Fenton

Anna is organising a 47th birthday party for Geoffrey. Not quite sure why being 47 merits special attention when 40 did not but who knows what goes on in the vague recesses of her mind. She rang to invite us all but said proper written invitations would take a while to come as she is planning to do hand-cut lino prints when she can get a moment. Love Anna for that – whenever Dan says I've gone barmy & I should stop bloody well making things & just buy them like a normal person can always cite Anna as someone madder than myself. She's hiring a disco & she & her friend Connie are going to do the catering & I have volunteered to do his birthday cake.

From: Nell Fenton
To: Charlotte Bailey

Not convinced Anna is madder than you – may I refer you back to giant airborne bath?

From: Louise Corrigan
To: Charlotte Bailey

How are you and how pregnant are you now? We're both great. We had our Barneys launch which was really fun.

We had a whole afternoon of book signing with tea and heart-shaped biscuits. I suppose it was inevitable really but Walt and I were handing out a lot of sex advice . . . One woman came to us crying and asked me why it was she couldn't have an orgasm. 'I mean, everything else in my life is perfect. I'm beautiful' (she so wasn't), 'I have three absolutely gorgeous children' (I doubt it), 'and a husband who will do anything for me' (except satisfy you sexually), 'but I just can't do it. What's my problem?' My answer? 'Listen, honey, you can't have everything.' Off to San Francisco next week and Chicago the week after. Speak soon x L

From: Charlotte Bailey
To: Louise Corrigan

Barneys sounds fantastic. Of course people are going to want your advice, you're sexperts now.

I'm coming up to 12 weeks. Have my 1st antenatal next week & a scan in 10 days which makes everything seem a bit more real. Am v well but appear to be storing embryos in my buttocks as well as my uterus – they have both become v large. Also, although pregnancy book says 'you may be starting to feel a slight tightness in waistband area', have in reality been unable to get anywhere near closing a waistband for several weeks now which is a little dispiriting. Good luck in San Francisco & Chicago. Love C xx

From: Louise Corrigan
To: Charlotte Bailey

Could it be twins? x L

From: Charlotte Bailey
To: Louise Corrigan

I suppose so, though that doesn't really explain my bum . . .
Love C xx

From: Nell Fenton
To: Charlotte Bailey

Got back from our ski trip this evening. Was lovely, good
snow and not too dreadfully cold but unfortunately it worked
out rather more expensive than it should have on account of
the fact that I married a man who considers packing luggage
into a car an exclusively male preserve and who does not
understand that the words 'the other green case' suggests there
is more than one green case to be loaded in. I didn't become
aware of his failure to grasp the nuances of this phrase until
we were getting the boys ready for bed on the first night (at
this point we had quite a lively exchange of views about the
meaning of the words 'the other'). The overlooked green case
(so easy to miss, hidden as it was on the middle of our bedroom
floor) contained all the children's clothes and all my clothes.
Michael's clothes had arrived safely having been packed in a
different case and we also had the case with the skiwear and
swimwear. Ollie (being a creature of rigid habits) was very
upset at my suggestion that he wear his swimming trunks and
a t-shirt of Michael's to bed. Next day instead of a bracing
morning's skiing we spent our time at Wal-Mart in a nearby
town, buying trousers, tops, underwear and socks. Also
bought the boys pyjamas. Ollie so in love with his new pyjamas
on account of garish cartoon dinosaurs, he brought them with
him in a carrier bag to dinner and to breakfast for the rest of
the trip.

From: Charlotte Bailey
To: Nell Fenton

At least it wasn't the skiwear which would be much more expensive to replace, would v much like to harshly criticise Michael but as I forgot bloody great travel cot when I came to you feel it would be slightly hypocritical.

From: Nell Fenton
To: Charlotte Bailey

We went to the hospital today for the results of the MRI. No cause for concern apparently though there are 'normal variants' in his brain. Would have thought a variant was by definition abnormal but neurologist sanguine about it so I will be too.

From: Charlotte Bailey
To: Nell Fenton

That's such good news, you must be so relieved.

I made Geoffrey's cake last night & I was quite proud of it as it looked most impressive (3 tiered layers with fondant chocolate icing) – that was until Hugh got to it. While Dan & I were trying to have a tiny little lie-in this morning, Ellie & Maddie took Hugh downstairs with them to have some cereal & watch a bit of telly. When I came down the girls were in the playroom watching cartoons & Hugh was standing furtively by the cellar door. When I went into the kitchen, SOMEBODY had dragged a chair over to the worktop next to the cake, so my eyes were immediately drawn to the big hunk that had been clawed out of its side. Caught Hugh as he was scuttling into the playroom shouting 'The o'pear girl didit' over his shoulder. Several factors led me to conclude Astrid was probably not the culprit, she was asleep at the time and there was a great deal of circumstantial evidence pointing to Hugh – his chocolate-smeared face, the Hugh-sized chocolate handprints all over the kitchen & his v great love of all things chocolatey.

From: Nell Fenton
To: Charlotte Bailey

Think you're terribly unfair to jump to conclusions. Did anyone actually see Astrid 'asleep'? Of course she'd try and frame Hugh, knowing he'd be the prime suspect. It's an absolutely classic tactic.

From: Charlotte Bailey
To: Nell Fenton

Geoffrey's party was really good fun & even Geoffrey seemed to relax & enjoy it after initial bout of going round saying all the candles were a fire hazard & blowing them out. Didn't hear him shout 'Where the hell is Anna?' once during entire proceedings, although apparently he was doing it all morning as Anna had gone off on a long cycle ride to gather interesting things to decorate the house with & then disappeared into her studio for absolutely ages while she made twigs etc into 'living sculptures' & sprayed them all silver & white. Their house looked absolutely beautiful with Anna's silvery twig sculptures & candles dotted all over & the lights turned off to hide the mess & best of all TL sent away for the evening. Not sure how well Connie knows Anna, as she obviously hadn't realised 'helping' Anna means entirely taking over when it comes to anything remotely practical like feeding 100 people. She was understandably v red-faced

279

& grumpy until Anna drifted in with a sheaf of red roses interspersed with silvery twigs & handed them to Connie with a big kiss telling her what a darling she was. Anna is terribly charming like that & Connie was then mollified enough to request my opinion (as the cook of the family) on the seasoning of her chilli con carne. Am really off spicy food at the moment & being pregnant my gag reflex is on a hair trigger so as it touched the back of my throat felt it spring into action. Would probably have gone unnoticed if Isabel, standing right next to me at the time, hadn't yelled out 'Oh my God, Charlotte's going to barf' as I scurried out of the room. Felt incredibly embarrassed & I could tell Connie was completely fucking furious. Luckily Dan then appeared (with v large glass of red wine for her) & did a much better job than me of persuading her chilli was outstandingly good & everything makes me gag at the moment.

From: Nell Fenton
To: Charlotte Bailey

Don't know how Anna manages to collect friends like Connie, wish I could find friends who'd step in and do stuff like feed 100 people. How was the cake by the way, did you manage to disguise telltale claw marks?

From: Charlotte Bailey
To: Nell Fenton

Was delicious & its rather odd lopsided shape (had to cut off the clawed-out bit & re-ice whole cake) was assumed to be intentional & interpreted as 'artistic' esp as Anna had clustered silvery twigs round the base. She also served a v nice Christmas pudding that she said she found under the back seat of her car.

MARCH 01

From: Charlotte Bailey
To: Nell Fenton

Had my first antenatal today. V unremarkable & Dr looked SO bored until I mentioned how enormous previous babies had been & then he rallied & started muttering about testing me for gestational diabetes. Think I managed to persuade him I really didn't need test as had done it with Hugh, so hopefully will avoid spending another 5 hrs of my life in a hospital corridor drinking syrup & having needles stabbed in me every 45 mins.

I've invited Geraldine & Peter to dinner tonight so they can meet each other. Dan says it's a terrible idea & asked me what colour the sky is in my world. He's so bloody negative & while I agree it's not an obvious love match you can never tell.

From: Nell Fenton
To: Charlotte Bailey

Nice of you to try it but quite embarrassing and pressured for them I would have thought.

Only 2 weeks till we go to Cuba, vv urgent that my body is exposed to some sun as the relentless cold has made my entire body go mottled (except my face – uniform grey).

From: Charlotte Bailey
To: Nell Fenton

Have to say Peter/Geraldine dinner not a huge success. Peter much too much of a gentleman to indicate he thought Geraldine was anything less than charming company but she was bloody dire. Didn't really matter (she told me afterwards he's not her type), except that the poor bastard spent an evening being interrogated, firstly about his business's market risks/profit margins (& other boring bollocks) & secondly about what plays/ballets he'd seen recently, by the end of which we were all able to conclude that Peter is not very interested in the performing arts & also no Rottweiler when it comes to business. Geraldine on the other hand is very clever & very cultured. Worst thing about it was Dan being smug & right afterwards.

PS you sound quite lovely at the moment & re mottled effect think the term you are looking for is 'mortadella body' (have this too but only on legs & feet).

From: Nell Fenton
To: Charlotte Bailey

Very trying when husband is right, mercifully rare though. Thanks for advice as to how to describe body. Am forwarding you thank-you email from Sarah by way of explanation for the fact that I am just off to start packing up the house. I shall not be leaving a forwarding address.

From: Sarah Dimmock
To: Nell Fenton

Hi Nell!!

How are you all?? How's Michael's job??? Not too stressful at the moment I hope!!

This is just a note to say thanks for putting up with us!! Your hospitality was amazing and we all felt so at home!! It was wonderful having a chance to catch up with you, it's so easy to lose touch with our busy, busy lives and Nick really enjoyed his chats with Michael – he just loves his dry humour!! It was wonderful for Dezzy to have other kids to play with too!

Anyway here we are back in our own little nest now, but with such wonderful memories!! The last part of the trip was absolutely magical!!! Lake Louise and Banff were just stunning, we were bowled over!! We have all fallen so head over heels in love with Canada we're already planning another trip, next time in the summer months!!!

Anyway when are you next planning to come over? You MUST get in touch so we can have you round!!!

Love and hugs

Sarah XOXOXO

From: Charlotte Bailey
To: Nell Fenton

Moving far too much trouble!!!!!!!! Why don't you just pretend you're all DEAD??????!!!!

From: Nell Fenton
To: Charlotte Bailey

Got myself a fabulous swimsuit today. Marvellous internal engineering in the form of v grippy fabric and powerful underwiring makes my figure look considerably better than it deserves, also managed to find sandals that make broad little feet look almost normal. A v good day all in all.

From: Charlotte Bailey
To: Nell Fenton

Powerfully grippy fabrics that rearrange internal organs to simulate waist commonplace these days, but sandals that make *your* feet look ok – that really is amazing. Urge you to go back to that shop & buy several more pairs.

Had my 1st scan today, Fran came along as my 'husband' as Dan suddenly had a lunch with the Editor which he felt was more important than witnessing his unborn child for the 1st time. Fran terribly excited & held my hand v tightly throughout, which made radiographer think we were a couple. She had obviously read a pamphlet on how to treat 'alternative' families & she was doing such valiant work referring to Fran as my 'partner' she looked quite deflated when I told her she was just my friend & there because my husband was too much of a bastard to come (may have substituted the word 'busy' for 'much of a bastard' when I explained to radiographer). V exciting to see little blob, Fran says it's a boy.

From: Nell Fenton
To: Charlotte Bailey

Am most impressed Fran can determine sex from a 12-week ultrasound.

I received a heavy blow today. Suzette brought round some of her 'signature brownies' (v much like normal brownies, only drier) and some gloomy news. They are moving to Italy at the beginning of July. I doubt I will ever in my life have such a fantastically ludicrous neighbour again, but clearly she hasn't taken my needs into account at all in making her plans. It's almost as if she doesn't realise how irreplaceable she is. Kane has been offered a job in Milan, naturally it's a brilliant, challenging, lucrative, etc, etc, opportunity. I asked if her girls minded leaving their friends but apparently and fortuitously they are so excited about the marvellously enriching cultural experience they are being offered, they don't. Suzette is now starting Italian classes and asked if I'd like to go along with her, 'we must all keep growing and learning or we stagnate'. I said that sadly it was too late for me, brain was already completely stagnant so pointless trying to learn Italian as it couldn't possibly penetrate. This made her shake her head in a pained way and tell me I was an intelligent woman and I shouldn't have such low self-esteem. Luckily she has a friend who runs assertiveness seminars and who has written a book on building self-esteem which Suzette is going to lend me. Will I ever meet her equal again?

285

From: Charlotte Bailey
To: Nell Fenton

Oh my God, how terrible & no you won't (& I never got to meet her). I'm so depressed.

From: Nell Fenton
To: Charlotte Bailey

Went to parent night tonight, all well as usual with Josie. Rob's teacher was nice about him and he's making progress. Ollie's teacher clearly loves him and says he's doing very well and she hoped he hadn't been upset by the fish going down the drain the day before. He hadn't mentioned it so said I didn't think so but asked if she could be more specific re fish. Apparently she'd let Ollie help clean out the fish tank as a reward for some particularly fine work he'd done but as they'd tipped the water into the sink one of the fish had gone with it and they'd been unable to catch it before it had slipped down the plughole. After initial panic she'd told him the fish would swim through the pipes until it reached Lake Ontario where it would be very happy indeed.

From: Charlotte Bailey
To: Nell Fenton

Can't imagine Ollie with his flinty little heart could mind too much about a fish.

From: Nell Fenton
To: Charlotte Bailey

Vv late and just finished packing. Off at dawn tomorrow,

286

will report in a week, by then hopefully more caramel than mortadella.

From: Nell Fenton
To: Charlotte Bailey

We had a fantastic week, weather not quite as perfect as last year but not far off. Were on a different part of the island but beach was just as beautiful. The children all look lovely and even Michael and I look slightly less grey and shagged out. Took a trip to Havana. Am absolutely in love with Havana, want to live in a foreign film, drifting moodily round Havana and living in a slightly peeling yet architecturally stunning apartment. Unfortunately had to satisfy myself with a day trip by coach.

From: Charlotte Bailey
To: Nell Fenton

So glad you had such a nice time. Don't wish to burst your bubble but people with 'mortadella' legs & 3 smelly children tend to populate BBC documentaries rather than arty foreign films.

From: Rachel Lockwood
To: Nell Fenton

Dear Nell

It was lovely to hear from you and I'm so glad you had such a wonderful time in Cuba.

Jonathan and I are fine, he's a bit more settled about going to school now but he still takes against it from time to time. He asked me the other day what would happen if I went away too. Of everything Jack has done, I think perhaps shaking Jonathan's faith in me is the thing I can least forgive him for. I have put the house on the market and we had a very mousy and depressed-looking couple round to view it on Saturday morning. I had (mistakenly, I now realise) explained to Jonathan why they were coming and he was so angry at the idea of someone taking our house he told the husband he was 'stinky' and 'a stupid head'. As I'm in no rush to part with the house (the flats I've seen so far are very dreary), I did a very half-hearted job of telling him off.

My job is turning out better than I expected. Ron, my boss, is nice and I'm being paid a bit more (salary no longer pitiful, now merely pathetic) and I'm more or less running the office. I have a horrible suspicion though that he might be working up his courage to ask me out and even if I were ready to start seeing other people (which I am not) I wouldn't choose him, he's very kind but I can't overlook the fact that he wears those boldly striped shirts with contrasting white collars and has a bad comb-over.

Send more news soon.

Fondest love to all
Rachel xx

From: Nell Fenton
To: Rachel Lockwood

Dear Rachel, so glad to hear job is better, don't worry about
your boss, easy to deflect unwanted overtures by citing your
recent separation, absolutely no need to refer to unforgivable
comb-over/dress sense. Love Nell

From: Nell Fenton
To: Charlotte Bailey

We took the children to Niagara Falls this weekend. Quite a
drive but at this time of year when it's still too cold to do
outdoor stuff and you've been to the Science Centre 76 times
and the Royal Ontario Museum 104 times, matters start to
get desperate. Niagara Falls always a crowd-pleaser as the
extreme tawdriness of the 'attractions' are v alluring to
unformed minds. Went to visit a nearby butterfly conservatory
where Josie distinguished herself by running screaming from
a not very big butterfly that was flying not very close to her.
Find butterflies a bit gross myself but still, a bit of an overreac-
tion. V surprised yet happy to find a plastic pith helmet in the
gift shop – Ollie is an explorer in this year's upcoming Spring
Festival, pith helmet alone made whole trip worthwhile.

From: Charlotte Bailey
To: Nell Fenton

Praise the Lord & hallelujah, Geraldine has met someone. He
sounds FANTASTIC & most importantly keen on her. She met
him at a party, he's an orthopaedic surgeon, she says he's
absolutely gorgeous, really handsome, really sexy & really

289

cultured. I'm over the moon, absolutely dying to meet him but Geraldine says it's a bit soon as they've only been out twice. Told Fran who immediately asked 1) if she'd shagged him yet & 2) didn't he mind her ankles? Said 1) I doubted it, Geraldine not the sort to give it up quick, 2) probably hadn't seen them yet as doubted 1) had taken place and G has taken to wearing trousers a lot recently. Geraldine says she's going out with him again on Saturday & will phone Sun to give me the lowdown.

From: Nell Fenton
To: Charlotte Bailey

V pleased for Geraldine. This proves my point that there is someone for everyone – Nick and Sarah found each other after all.

From: Charlotte Bailey
To: Nell Fenton

Geraldine's date with Julian sounds absolutely dreamy. They had dinner at some fantastic tiny Italian restaurant near the river & then went for a long romantic walk along the Thames while he pointed out landmarks & told her fascinating titbits of historic information. As well as being v knowledgeable about all food esp Italian (mother half-Italian) he is also an absolute wine buff & only needs to sniff it, like a true pro, to tell whether or not it has corked. Said to Dan, wished I was v sophisticated about wine & knew how to sniff it rather than tasting it & then bleating 'lovely' as am too ignorant to tell the difference. Sadly only thing I ever sniff to check & then have any credible opinions on are children's pants & socks. Dan v cutting & said he sounds really annoying & sniffing wine incredibly pretentious. Am not to be deflected, I think he sounds marvellous. Anyway Geraldine said he told her she was 'vibrant & lovely' & kissed her (for first time). Obviously reported this to Fran who concluded they hadn't shagged yet.

From: Nell Fenton
To: Charlotte Bailey

Am with Dan on this one, think he sounds boring and a show-off but quite frankly that makes it more likely not less that it will work out for Geraldine.

From: Charlotte Bailey
To: Nell Fenton

Peter invited us to lunch at the farm this weekend, it's absolutely lovely, surrounded (as one might expect) by orchards. He has a Gloucester Old Spot called Naomi (or 'Nomeo' as Hugh insisted on calling her) as well as chickens & ducks. The weather was beautiful & the children spent whole day outside playing on defunct tractor, feeding 'Nomeo' & the chickens & throwing stones in the stream. We had incredibly delicious sausages for lunch made from Nomeo's predecessor, I v bravely ate about 9 (for the baby's sake). Peter walked us over to his old cottage. Doesn't know what to do with it now he's in the main farmhouse as he thinks it's too shabby to let. Don't agree, I think it's charming & lots of people (me included) find it really stressful staying in fancy rental places as the children have permanently greasy, dirty hands that they like to wipe on other people's soft furnishings.

From: Nell Fenton
To: Charlotte Bailey

Can perfectly picture the farm and I definitely want to live there.

Ollie brought home a piece of schoolwork this afternoon. Gather it was a sort of sin-and-redemption exercise, as they had to write about a bad thing they did and how they felt after. Ollie's was a lovely illustrated piece with text as follows: 'onec I was goeing to put a pencel in my cats bum but my sister sed no then I was sory.' Questioned Josie about this who confirmed she'd caught Ollie once with pencil poised and cat with tail in the air and bottom temptingly displayed. Fortunately she'd stopped him before he'd put his dastardly plan into action.

From: Charlotte Bailey
To: Nell Fenton

Ollie is an evil genius with a sick & twisted mind. That said, who hasn't at one time or another wanted to stick a pencil up a cat's bum?

Geraldine came round for supper last night, she looked great. She's got rid of her Gestapo helmet bob & had layers & little streaks put in her hair, also wearing the most fantastic sandy-coloured Jil Sander trouser suit which she said Julian had talked her into buying (apparently new hairdo his idea too). Julian is taking her to the ballet at the w/e. The Arts are Julian's true passion & he has told her it's such a relief to meet a woman who was intelligent, beautiful AND cultured. At bedtime when I was standing in big bra & big pants looking down at my large, lardy body commented to Dan how very far I am from being beautiful at the moment & he kindly said 'Of course you're beautiful' but then ruined it by saying 'beautiful to me anyway.'

From: Nell Fenton
To: Charlotte Bailey

Michael always pretends he doesn't think I'm a hideous blob when I'm pregnant, best you can ask of them is that they pretend. Also remember a man's brain is not equipped to make the important distinction between 'beautiful' and 'beautiful to me'.

APRIL 01

From: Charlotte Bailey
To: Nell Fenton

Keran's been staying over so often she's practically living here. Toby keeps saying he won't be here much longer as they're planning to get a place together. They don't appear to be looking (unless it's v secretly) so don't know how they expect to find somewhere. Keran irritating as ever, even her hair (vv fluffy) gets on my nerves. She's a nice girl but so dazed, stands motionlessly in the kitchen usually in front of whatever appliance Astrid or I are trying to get to. Even Dan getting fed up with it all now.

From: Nell Fenton
To: Charlotte Bailey

She does sound annoying but think of it as good practice for the succession of droopy adolescent boyfriends/girlfriends you'll have trailing through your house in a few years' time.

Josie's trying out for the school softball team this afternoon. My heart always sinks when she tells me she's doing a try-out because she never gets picked and is always crushed for days after. Sorely tempted to tell her not to attempt it to spare her inevitable disappointment but obviously can't say to one's child 'you're a bit hopeless, aim low' so have to bite my tongue.

From: Nell Fenton
To: Charlotte Bailey

V bad luck. Miraculously Josie picked for the 'development team' (sounds better than reserves) and more miraculously is perfectly satisfied with this result. I, on the other hand, am not. Will now have to drag her along to practices (often start at 7.30am) and matches in which she isn't even bloody playing.

From: Charlotte Bailey
To: Nell Fenton

Dreadful situation to be in. Much better to have children like mine, completely devoid of any sporting talent so absolutely no chance they'd be picked for any team, not even 'development team'. (Maddie's running so crap & her head wobbles so alarmingly think it would come off it not firmly attached.)

Fran has got herself a job, she's really pleased about it. She's going to be a witch's assistant. Lucasta (the witch) has a Co. called Spell-U-Like & she makes up spell boxes with little pots of potions & parchment scrolls & bunches of dried herbs with names like devil's foot, which she sells over the internet. Fran is helping to assemble the different boxes, hundreds of them, as apparently there's a spell for EVERYTHING. She says the pay is a bit crap but it's right next to Barnaby's playgroup so v convenient for a couple of hours till she picks him up. Have asked her to ask Lucasta if there are any spells to dispel dark-room-type smells or encourage brothers-in-law with vacuous girlfriends to hurry up & find a place of their own or failing that one to dispel backache & swelling ankles.

From: Nell Fenton
To: Charlotte Bailey

Told Michael about Fran making spells and he said she should be careful that she's not abducted by aliens who experiment on her because she's just the sort it happens to.

From: Nell Fenton
To: Charlotte Bailey

V upsetting incident this afternoon, got back after taking the children to karate and Russian Wife came running over to tell me our cat had been hit by a car but had run off and though she and car's driver had searched for her they couldn't find her. Was thoroughly horrified, am extremely squeamish and hopeless about things like that and usually leave all that sort of gross stuff to Michael. Unfortunately in his absence was obliged to be stout-hearted so set off to look for her. Didn't have to go far, she'd dragged herself up onto the deck and was lying by the back door. She looked dreadful. Children all immediately started crying while I hovered indecisively for a bit then fetched the cat carrier, wrapped her in a towel and put her in. Then we all loaded back into the car and drove to the emergency vet which happily is very close but sadly costs double what the normal vet costs being open when normal vet is shut. Gave the children lots of foolhardy assurances about her being absolutely fine. Was finally summoned to a little room for a hushed consultation with the vet. Upshot was treatment will cost between $700 and $800 with no guarantee she'll be ok. The sensible thing at this point would have been to tell him to put her down but couldn't face telling the children so meekly agreed to everything.

From: Nell Fenton
To: Rachel Lockwood

Dear Rachel, how are you? Had a horrible dream about you last night, you were out at sea in a small boat and it was getting really dark. I was shouting at you to come in but you couldn't hear me. Thought I better email you to warn you to avoid small, unseaworthy craft at night for the next little while. How is the amorous boss? Love Nell

From: Rachel Lockwood
To: Nell Fenton

Dear Nell

Thank you for the warning, which I shall certainly heed – easy to do as I seldom (or never actually) go out in small boats at night.

If my boss were rich and handsome rather than paunchy and thinning on top then my life would be a Mills & Boon novel because he did ask me out. Mind you, if this were a Mills & Boon he would obviously have ordered me to go out with him or something equally manly, rather than asking in a shy and hesitant way, blushing slightly as he did so. I felt horrible about saying no, as he'd obviously really had to pluck up his courage but it would be worse to say yes and encourage him. Anyway I think I let him down as gently as was possible and told him I could never consider seeing anyone while I am still married. Now he thinks I am some sort of paragon of virtue. I think I'm going to have to look for another job which is a shame, I'm starting to like it here.

Fondest love to all
Rachel xx

From: Charlotte Bailey
To: Nell Fenton

Editor has invited Dan & me to fancy pants dinner. I am completely dreading it. Find those kind of things totally terrifying – loads of brainy journalists saying brainy things to each other about brainy topics like the Maastricht Treaty & dangers of the euro. Even if I did have any opinions apart from ones on stuff like jus (stupid, what's wrong with gravy?) or Mary Jane shoes (hideous unless you're under 7) would be too petrified to express them anyway. Esp love the bit when you sit down & bloke next to you asks what you DO & then have to admit to being housewife so spend most of day driving to buy/collect food/children, loading food/children into car, cooking (food), serving (to children) & then scraping it (food) uneaten into bin, should have just left everything at the supermarket (food & children) & in between that just general wiping. Meanwhile bloke is looking completely terrified as realises has absolutely nothing to say, as either 1) his wife is top political commentator & has lots of fascinating opinions to be discussed on things other than gravy & shoes or 2) does not have wife or indeed girlfriend due to tall weirdly shaped head containing massive brain & is terrified of anybody with bosoms (unless Margaret Thatcher & then ok). Dan slightly dreading it too which is at least something so we can be pathetic & moany together, also am at that stage of pregnancy where I just look hideously dumpy & my hair's gone really weird, all fluffy on top & stringy at the bottom.

From: Nell Fenton
To: Charlotte Bailey

V gruesome I agree, having to disguise one's stunted intellect. I find nodding slowly and wisely at these kinds of things quite a useful fallback, and on the bright side if you've got ugly stringy hair people much more likely to assume you're brainy than if you had pretty blonde curls.

Cat is still clinging tenaciously (and expensively) to life. Have transferred her now to the regular vet (emergency vet $720) where he predicts she'll need about a week in cat hospital (hundreds more $$$). Seems totally immoral to spend all that on preserving the life of a cat but I am caught between children's v heartfelt desire to have her back and the fact I'd be wasting the huge amount I've spent already. Whole topic is making me very grumpy, proving as it does that I have no moral fibre.

From: Charlotte Bailey
To: Nell Fenton

Sorry to say I do think it's a bit immoral. Good thing about guinea pigs is they're so small & pesky they just die if anything goes wrong so don't cost you anything.

PS Didn't you really offend Charlie by telling him he should have just got a new dog rather than spending vast sums at the vet when his yappy little Jack Russell got run over?

From: Nell Fenton
To: Charlotte Bailey

Being inconsistent only to be expected in someone without moral fibre.

From: Charlotte Bailey
To: Nell Fenton

Toby dropped the girls off at school for me on the last day of term & came back completely bowled over by the artwork in their classrooms. Particularly enraptured by the collages in Maddie's class which he described as 'awesome & amazing'. Made a special point of going in to look at them when I picked them up & although I consider myself reasonably artistic could see nothing to distinguish them from any other fairly average 5-yr-old collage incorporating pasta shells sprayed gold & paper flowers. Anyway ever since (well over a week now) he has been beavering away at some surprise project & in between stints at the camera shop & trips to Southall has been doing stuff like photographing boxes of M&S chicken tikka masala. Am actually slightly curious to see what he's up to but he says I have to wait & see.

From: Nell Fenton
To: Charlotte Bailey

Don't know how you can stand the suspense.

Suzette came round today, ostensibly to give me some of their old cartoon videos for my boys. I think her real motive in dropping round was to show herself off in her riding regalia (weather less inclement now so she has resumed riding). She obviously fancies herself v much in her shiny-booted riding gear but am guessing she hasn't seen herself from behind because the stretchy riding trousers do her arse absolutely no favours. She also wore a close-fitting little riding jacket and a low-cut shirt revealing several inches of flaccid cleavage. She said she couldn't stop (though I hadn't asked her to) because Pedro her riding instructor gets very sulky if she's late for her lessons, 'You know what these Latin men are like!' She took the time to tell me (despite the danger of provoking Pedro) that riding is her great passion and that she is determined to carry on with it in Italy. She then scampered off, highly stimulated no doubt at the prospect of the telling-off she was about to get from Pedro.

From: Charlotte Bailey
To: Nell Fenton

Can't stand it when people absolve their conscience by giving you all their crap. Recently had to GO ROUND to house of well-meaning but appallingly insistent woman I barely know called Jeanette. She had a baby a couple of months ago & was absolutely intent on offloading some of her well-worn maternity clothes onto me. I realised I was going to have to be far ruder than I was prepared to be in order to get out of Jeanette's evil

301

plan to clothe me so just meekly resigned myself to my fate. Jeanette's maternity gear freakishly ugly, several 'frocks' even had crocheted inserts. For once in my life was v grateful for having a larger body than someone else. While it is difficult to say 'I'm not having that, it's revolting & it smells' v easy to say 'You are so PETITE – I won't fit that!!!!!' so managed to leave with only half a bin bag of stuff.

From: Nell Fenton
To: Charlotte Bailey

Better lie low or she'll give you baby clothes next. I got a touching though rather crazy letter from Anna today enclosing a picture she'd done of me as a child. She found an old photo of me when I was about 7 and apparently my expression was 'so poignant' she decided to make a drawing from it. Letter was pretty much a stream of consciousness and though it started in biro finished in orange pencil crayon (she'd gone to answer the phone and lost the pen en route). Anyway from what I could gather all the children are still alive and they are spending Easter in Cornwall. She did say Geoffrey had tried again recently to show her how to use email because she'd said she missed me but they'd abandoned the attempt because 'he got very stressed'. It's actually a very nice picture and a good likeness and I'm very impressed that the letter was not only correctly addressed but also posted.

From: Charlotte Bailey
To: Nell Fenton

I think she misses you quite a lot, was very sad you weren't at Geoffrey's party. Am as amazed as you, you got the letter – she rang me 4 times to get the address. Got my hair cut today in a v stylish bob with short choppy fringe that makes me look exactly like a blowfish. Should have listened to Fran. When I showed her a picture of the haircut in Red magazine she made astute though somewhat unkind observation that while cut was indeed v stylish & striking, as I don't look remotely like Isabella Rossellini on whose exquisitely formed head haircut was, feared it would not actually suit ME (lovely as I am). Decided to ignore this piece of well-meant but clearly erroneous advice as have always longed to look like Isabella Rossellini. As hair is now considerably shorter & all highlights have been cut out, colour is really dark & dreary & unlike on Isabella dark hair makes me look like I've been recently exhumed. Can't even get highlights put back in as if you dye your hair when you're pregnant baby grows extra arm (useful but unattractive).

From: Nell Fenton
To: Charlotte Bailey

Surely you've had enough experience of discovering that gorgeous hairstyle/outfit looks very different on you to the way it looks on the fabulously beautiful woman in the magazine.

From: Charlotte Bailey
To: Nell Fenton

Washed my hair last night & have discovered another intriguing feature of this haircut which is if I do anything as reckless as allow hair to dry naturally, the short choppy fringe sticks straight up in the air adding general air of surprise to overall 'blowfish' look.

From: Nell Fenton
To: Charlotte Bailey

Perhaps you should wear some of Jeanette's crocheted maternity wear to distract people's eyes from hair disaster?

We spent the Easter weekend at a little resort Nina recommended to us. Had such a nice time, it was really charming in a slightly run-down way and on a beautiful little lake called Stoney Lake. Josie's mad about fishing so spent most of her time fishing off the dock and the boys collected frogs from a little pond. There were stables nearby and Rob did some riding which he's getting really keen on (should get him together with Suzette). I'm so pleased with how he is around horses, not at all nervous, think I might take him out of karate which he's hopeless at and get him riding lessons instead in the summer.

From: Charlotte Bailey
To: Nell Fenton

Sounds absolutely lovely. Sensible idea to give up karate, riding much better & probably safer too, all those flailing arms & legs v dangerous.

Our Easter Day was lovely too but the weather so vile & rainy had to conduct egg hunt indoors. Hugh & Penelope over & Toby (despite saying they were going to spend it at Keran's mum's) was there with Keran. She did the usual silent standing around, cradling a can of Diet Coke as though it was the last batch of antibiotics in known world & she was anticipating imminent anthrax attack, but she was very sweet to the children & crawled around the playroom with Hugh helping him find eggs.

304

Also, extremely cheeringly, in rare verbal moment she told me her nan who has a house in Bow wants Toby & her to move in as the house is too big now her granddad has passed on. Tried to get a gamut of emotions to play across my face – surprise (was surprised actually), regret & finally quiet encouragement. Dan saw my gamut of emotions & said I mainly looked very, very pleased and surprised (bloody fringe is sticking up again).

From: Nell Fenton
To: Charlotte Bailey

A great feat not to look downright overjoyed.

We went to dinner with Steve and Marguerite last night. You'll be pleased to hear she's still v slim, though obviously quite pregnant-looking and goes to the gym 4–5 times a week. Everything in v good taste as usual and standard of food v high. She did tell Steve off at the dinner table for swearing, so a little bit of marital tension there – even I, control freak that I am, manage to postpone any necessary reprimands to spouse until AFTER the guests are gone, though of course if I were to tell Michael off for swearing would never have time for anything else.

From: Charlotte Bailey
To: Nell Fenton

Don't tell me about Marguerite, can't stand it (unless of course she has had catastrophic haircut with fringe that won't lie down).

Katrina dropped round this morning to say hello, they moved

in to their new house 3 days ago & she's feeling a bit over-whelmed as her nanny has gone on perfectly timed Easter holiday & Henry is away filming & she is trying to unpack with girls in tow & video not working (dropped in transit). Felt pro-found rush of sympathy re tremendous challenge of trying to subdue lively 6 & 4-year-olds unaided by the Disney corpor-ation, so immediately offered to keep her girls for the day which she accepted with immense relief & then bolted home to try & sort out Henry's wardrobe. Ellie & Maddie spent about 20 mins just gawping at them before Maddie finally broke the silence by asking if Tara's embroidered patchwork suede skirt was knitted – having established between themselves it was, all embarked on elaborate tv makeover show game in which Ellie was the host, Maddie & Tara 'contestants' & Hepzibah a very irate director whose every 2nd word was 'CUT!' (Hugh superb as director's cat). Ellie so taken with Tara & Hepzibah & their fancy clothes & celebrity tv show games, magnanimously invited them back the next day.

From: Nell Fenton
To: Charlotte Bailey

Looking after children without the assistance of Walt Disney too horrible to contemplate. When Steve was staying with us last year, seeing my children sitting quietly in front of a Disney video (probably absorbing all sorts of beneficial subliminal messages), he said Disney was dreadful and his children weren't allowed to watch it. Not only was this very rude as my children were at that moment engaged in this very activity, was also smug, superior and unrealistic – children not allowed videos grow up weird.

From: Charlotte Bailey
To: Nell Fenton

Totally agree (obviously). Videos v useful tool in helping children to learn to concentrate & focus. I've bought myself a really nice dress to wear to the terrifying dinner, it's black & A-line with 3 diaphanous layers of chiffon. A bit shorter than I'd normally wear but I've also bought fantastic 40s-looking shoes from Jigsaw with bit of a platform & big chunky heel. They make my legs look really quite decent & do good job of disguising prematurely swelling ankles. Only problem now is how to tame mad unruly fringe.

From: Nell Fenton
To: Charlotte Bailey

Suggest you wet hair and wear a bike helmet all day before the dinner (don't forget to remove it before you set off though).

From: Charlotte Bailey
To: Nell Fenton

Had an antenatal today where midwife measured height of fundus 3× as couldn't believe how high/big it was, says I'm about 3–4 weeks too big for my dates but says will probably catch up with myself later. Showed her some v attractive purplish veins developing on backs of my legs (had been blissfully unaware of them till Maddie asked why I had pen on my legs), she says they are the beginnings of varicose veins & I must wear a tight rubber wetsuit at all times to prevent them developing or failing that some lovely orange elastic tights which apparently are flesh-coloured (but only if you come from planet Zorg).

From: Nell Fenton
To: Charlotte Bailey

That will be attractive and comfortable too in the coming summer months.

The cat is home now and I am $1,500 poorer. Quite a remarkable recovery really, she looks a bit wonky and her mouth is lopsided when she miaows but she's otherwise fine. I could have had her back sooner and spent a bit less if I had been prepared to feed her through truly disgusting tube going into the side of her neck. Children v happy but even they're a bit grossed out by her scrawny shaved neck.

From: Charlotte Bailey
To: Nell Fenton

Yuck, poor thing though, totally understand not wanting to tube-feed it esp if it has a stringy neck.

I had my 21½-week scan today. Everything looks ok, couldn't see whether it was a boy or girl & didn't want to know, Dan thought he saw a willy but could easily have been the cord. Could not, however, fail to notice size of baby's nose (ginormous), radiographer also said legs slightly shorter than average for baby at that stage of development, circumference of abdomen, however, larger than average. Dan says baby looks like you, don't know whether he was referring to the big nose, short legs or fat stomach, poss all 3?

From: Nell Fenton
To: Charlotte Bailey

Glad all well with baby (apart from being a bit ugly, that is). Surely with short legs and big nose looks more like you though?

From: Charlotte Bailey
To: Nell Fenton

Dan & I saw what Toby's been working on today. He's made a series of collages using photos from his vast 'many faces of India' collection, bits of chopped-up saris, paper flowers & crumpled Indian newspapers interspersed with photos of stuff like ready-made Indian food. He even used pictures of the sari Barbies he brought the girls. Collages all have titles like 'The Glittering Empire?' If you can get over the fact they bear an uncanny resemblance to a very lumpy school project on India & observe them from a distance (say 30 ft) they're actually really pretty as the colours are lovely & he's done some which are predominantly pink or yellow or turquoise, etc. Toby a bit worried about how lumpy & heavy they are (bits keep dropping off in authentically leprous manner), also says they took him bloody ages to make & he had to buy loads of onion bhajis & turmeric for the yellow ones so they cost a fortune to make. Dan suggested Toby photograph entire collages which would solve all problems, which made Toby say 'yeah' about 165 times in a row.

MAY 01

From: Charlotte Bailey
To: Nell Fenton

I have proven myself to be a great asset to any sophisticated gathering, indeed I am quietly confident my presence at Editor's dinner provided not only considerable pleasure to many but would even venture to say some might even have talked about me next day at the office. Very much regret the time & energy I wasted beforehand worrying about the impression I was going to make as had I known then what I know now could have bypassed all the fretting & cut straight to feeling of complete humiliation I am currently experiencing. The evening started quite well & even felt reasonably attractive, given current limitations of hair etc (had been to hairdresser to have nasty bob blow-dried into neat little helmet so fringe briefly but completely under control), dress doing sterling job of disguising unpleasant middle section of body, while arms & legs looking pretty decent. I was seated next to top leader writer who apparently is brainiest man alive & indeed he did have several v brainy & pertinent things to say on subject of whether guinea pigs or hamsters made better pets (our chosen topic). On my other side was the sports editor. As I know absolutely nothing about any sport of any kind had to satisfy ourselves by agreeing sport was generally a GOOD thing & to be encouraged (esp in children). Went off to the loo just before coffee which was bloody terrifying as we were all seated round one huge long oval table in a vast dark panelled room with v slippy marble floor & I was of course at the end furthest from doors to the loo so had to walk vv carefully (in high slippy shoes across the room). Made it to the loo, did 25-min wee & then commenced long trip back. I was just nearing the table (end where Editor was sitting) when I realised had left my sodding handbag in the loo so would have to go back to get it. Just as I'd turned around & set off again, the Editor stood up with much scraping of his chair to make long v important speech so all eyes skittered to him & no doubt across my retreating back. Froze (back turned) momentarily in order to make split-second decision whether or not to continue with quest to retrieve hand-bag or stay hovering near Editor's chair with features arranged into look of quiet respect. Decided against hovering with quiet respect & continued long slow walk (by now even more con-scious of clacky sound of heels on marble floor & poss of falling over) back to exit doors. Was just nearing the table on my return as the Editor's speech was drawing to a close when I noticed several smiling faces (almost laughing they looked so joyful) directed towards me & Dan rolling his eyes & doing some weird backwards pointing. I looked behind me but there was no one there so went & sat down. I was just thinking sports editor looked quite red in the face when very proper-looking woman (books editor) leaned over to me & whispered, 'My dear, your dress is tucked into your pants at the back.' Top layer of diaphanous chiffon layer dress had snagged in tights waist-band creating interesting bunched/bustle effect that framed my fully exposed tights-clad arse. Have to say words failed me so simply untucked chiffon panel from my waistband so it floated dreamily back down while I silently hatched a plan to kill everyone at table except me & Dan & poss Editor as he was the only person present (apart from myself of course) who had not seen me sashay across the room with my bum hanging out.

From: Nell Fenton
To: Charlotte Bailey

You're quite a smooth operator. Dan must be so proud and what makes you so sure Editor didn't see your bum hanging out too? Anyhow think it's extreme, not to say unfair, to kill everyone at the dinner, can't you just go and live abroad?

Re your bad haircut, don't know if it was subconsciously a sympathy thing or not but had these really annoying sticking-out bits of hair round my neck this morning and momentarily allowed optimism to overwhelm common sense, thinking 'how hard can it be?' so decided to trim them myself. Unfortunately as it was at the back of my head couldn't really see much in the mirror and what I could see was all puzzlingly reversed (hands and scissors v annoyingly do the opposite of what you think you're doing). You guess whether I did a beautiful job that I'm very pleased with or whether I'm going to the hair-dresser tomorrow morning.

From: Charlotte Bailey
To: Nell Fenton

I got a panic-stricken call from Melody yesterday as her father had been taken into hospital with suspected unstable angina & she needed someone to pick up Macy & Hal from school. Said of course & attempted to sound calm – a pillar of strength indeed – which was tricky given that the prospect of an after-noon & possibly an evening with Macy & Hal was giving ME

312

unstable angina. Macy was very anxious about the fact it wasn't Melody picking her up as expected & kept nervously asking where Mummy was so had to be very soothing which I wasn't feeling as Hal was repeatedly trying to head-butt me. Was in the middle of making their supper & just thinking that everything not going too badly when I heard v loud squeaking coming from the playroom. Ran in to find Hal & Hugh 'training' Susan. They had tied a length of wool round her middle & were attempting to drag her over some Lego 'jumps'. Told them both off & sent them out into the garden where Macy & Ellie were skipping round in fancy dress. When I went out half an hour later to call them in for supper I was so assaulted by the sight of Hal waving a paintbrush & tin of paint, & the giant pink words 'Hal + Hoo' freshly painted on the side of the garden shed, I did not immediately register the headlessness of my alliums. When I did finally pinpoint what the strange unfinished look about my borders was, I did not launch into a screaming tirade as to why my alliums had been decapitated & why there was graffiti on my shed, instead I conducted some very calm Melody-type questioning & not once did I use the word 'fuck' or any variant of it. Apparently the alliums were an essential ingredient in a potion & snapping them off felt very 'snappy' & Hal + Hoo had been part of a 'spelling' lesson given by Hal to Hoo. Ellie just as much to blame as Macy about the alliums but at least she had the good grace to be really sorry & upset when she saw how sorry & upset I was. Macy on the other hand clearly didn't give a fuck & said sorry with smirkey little face which brought her closer to death than I suspect she'll ever come again. When Melody picked them up obviously keen not to add to her troubles by telling her her children were the spawn of Satan so did lots of bright smiling between references to their high spirits.

From: Nell Fenton
To: Charlotte Bailey

You deserve some kind of extraordinary valour award.

From: Charlotte Bailey
To: Nell Fenton

Toby got his giant collage photos back today, he's very dejected as he sent them off to some cheap place to be printed & developed & he says the colours aren't true & the printing is all weird. Showed me one of them but I rather liked it though it did look oddly 70s, anyway he refuses to be comforted & says they'll need to be redone before he can show them to anyone (apart from me, as he kindly told me I don't count). Most fantastic news is he & Keran are moving out to her nan's this w/e who Toby says is 'an absolute hoot' for which Dan says read 'senile'.

From: Nell Fenton
To: Charlotte Bailey

I'm in big trouble with Michael. I made him come to the school's annual fundraising ball with me (tickets $300). Must say in my own defence that I was seriously misled myself having been told by more than one person that they are usually quite good fun. Unfortunately this year's theme was a tribute to giant arse of a headmaster who is retiring. 'Tribute' turned out to mean an ENTIRE evening of speeches about the stupid, self-important plonker. Obviously I wasn't listening but I imagine they must have gone back to his infancy in order to find enough material to fill so many monotonous hours with anecdotes and general butt-kissing. Quite extraordinary.

Everyone at our table looked completely stunned with boredom except one woman who smiled with quiet approval through all 174 speeches. This leads me to conclude she is either a) on a lot of Prozac or b) a woman of exceptional courage and stamina. Anyhow Michael has laid entire blame for the evening at my feet and in the absence of me suddenly developing a life-threatening illness, which makes him realise how much he truly values me, do not foresee an early end to his muttered reproaches.

From: Charlotte Bailey
To: Nell Fenton

Well, I'm in trouble with Dan. I've invited Henry & Katrina to dinner with Julian & Geraldine next week, Dan is fine about having H & K, but really grumbling about Julian & Geraldine. Says as Geraldine is an appalling ball-breaker if Julian is really going out with her (& she hasn't just imagined him), he must either be mad or dire. Said he is neither of those things & G new gentler woman now that she is going out with Julian.

From: Nell Fenton
To: Rachel Lockwood

Dear Rachel, how are you and how is the house-selling/flat-buying coming along? All well here, though I have the alarming prospect of school ending in less than a month. Josie has exams at the moment, though if she is stressed by them, hard to detect. Have resorted to offering her money depending on her results as satisfaction in academic achievement not enough of an incentive for her. Charlotte terribly disapproving (bet she'll end up doing it herself) but at least seems to have fired Josie up a bit. How's Jonathan getting on at school these days and how is your boss? Send update please. Love Nell

From: Rachel Lockwood
To: Nell Fenton

Dear Nell

Glad you're all well and a very good thing Josie is relaxed about exams. Something to be encouraged I'd have thought. I think we have a buyer for the house but I haven't found a flat yet. I've looked at lots and they're either tiny or horrible and mostly both. I think I'm probably going to have to move further away from Oxford. In any event I'm going to have to step up my efforts in looking for a flat and a job, as Ron keeps looking at me with slightly wounded longing and has made his feelings about me so obvious to everyone in the office it's embarrassing.

Jonathan isn't enjoying school much. I was called in to see the headmistress this week because he'd bitten another boy. He absolutely refused to talk about it at first but later, in the bath, he told me the boy had been teasing him because he doesn't have a dad. I think they handled it really insensitively and the whole episode made me realise I wouldn't be sorry if he were to move school.

Anyway the idea of starting somewhere new quite appeals to me. Write soon.

Fondest love to all
Rachel xx

From: Nell Fenton
To: Charlotte Bailey

I think I must be the only mother on the planet whose pre-teen daughter doesn't like horses. Could take this aberrant behaviour with more equanimity if I hadn't spent a large part of the weekend driving the abnormal child to and from stupid Girl Guide riding camp AFTER having taken her downtown to smelly riding shop and spent a fortune on a riding hat. Went to pick her up expecting her to be sparkly-eyed and horse mad, found her instead subdued and a bit miserable saying she doesn't like horses and is scared of them. Will definitely have to enrol Rob in riding now (and just force his slightly larger head into the riding hat) to justify the expense.

From: Charlotte Bailey
To: Nell Fenton

We had our Henry/Katrina, Geraldine/Julian dinner last night. I was completely amazed to discover that Toby's dodgy collage photos ARE NOT slightly crap but 'witty & ironic' & even 'genius'. Toby & Keran turned up at the end of dinner when everybody fairly tanked up & while Keran loitered by the dish-washer & resisted my attempts to get her to sit down, Toby parked himself next to Henry & embarked on long immensely dull account of his career to date as a photographer. May have just been crafty ruse to stop him talking or Henry being heroically polite but H actually asked to see some of Toby's photos & even though he'd drunk the sort of volume of red wine to give him black lips & blue teeth really think he genuinely meant what he said. His extreme home-makeover show has got an exotic theme coming up & Henry says he'd like to use some of Toby's 'weirdly coloured, weirdly focused, very art house' photos on it. Only dark spot on otherwise fab evening was tragically Julian couldn't come as he got stuck at the hospital doing some emergency op. He rang at the end of the evening to speak to Geraldine & then asked to speak to me, he has a really nice voice, quite deep a bit posh & sort of melodious, was terribly apologetic & charming & used my name a lot which I always like. Came off the phone quite fancying him. Geraldine SHINING with love & looking great. Henry was being v funny & telling us how he couldn't stand the woman he co-hosts his show with & how vile she was to the contestants off-camera. Anyway Toby was like Tigger this morning & talking grandly about holding photo exhibition etc as Henry's PA rang to ask him to bring his portfolio over to show a friend of Henry's who owns a gallery that showcases new talent, so now he's gone off to buy a display folder as I don't think an Asda carrier bag qualifies as a portfolio.

From: Nell Fenton
To: Charlotte Bailey

Think Asda carrier bag might be quite witty. Julian sounds too good to be true, have you checked with Geraldine he hasn't got something creepy like three extra fingers? (Or perhaps he just thinks he's God. Common trait in surgeons.)

From: Rachel Lockwood
To: Nell Fenton

Dear Nell

How are you? We're fine and as Charlotte may have told you she very kindly put me in touch with Dan's cousin,

Peter, who has a cottage on his farm that he's going to let to us for the half-term week. We shouldn't really be spending any money but it's incredibly reasonable and Charlotte says it's lovely although Peter kept warning me it's very shabby (he should see some of the nasty little flats I've been looking at). We're so looking forward to it, tractors are second only to fighter planes on Jonathan's list of most interesting objects in the world. A week away from Ron will be wonderful too, I can't bear the atmosphere any more.

Fondest love to all
Rachel xx

PS Charlotte says she's so vast she looks like she's expecting 24 babies. A slight exaggeration surely?

From: Nell Fenton
To: Rachel Lockwood

Dear Rachel, so glad to hear you're having a holiday. Charlotte's told me too that farm and cottage are both absolutely lovely. Not sure about Charlotte and the 24 babies, won't be seeing her till July so can't comment except to say she looked like she was having 18 babies last time and then only Hugh actually came out. Have a wonderful week. Love Nell xx

From: Charlotte Bailey
To: Nell Fenton

Had an antenatal today, guess whether I am catching up with myself sizewise or whether I am now 4–5 weeks too big for my dates? Varicose veins coming along nicely desp. constantly sporting toeless orange elastic socks, also have a pile (just the 1 but extra big) & a fringe that sticks up – may have mentioned that before. Would ask Fran to get me a spell to get rid of the pile (still working at Spell-U-Like) as getting rid of Toby & Keran worked so well – they moved out Sat – but feel oddly embarrassed so shall apply haemorrhoid cream instead. Felt the baby move today, very sweet, almost made the pile worth it – almost, but not quite.

From: Nell Fenton
To: Charlotte Bailey

Poor you. Am no expert on piles but probably one big one better than several small ones.

From: Charlotte Bailey
To: Nell Fenton

Keran brought her nan round to meet us yesterday. Felt a bit ashamed actually as her nan kept going on & on about what a nice family we are & how kind we've been to Keran & how we've welcomed Keran into the bosom of our family & how indeed I was even a mother figure to Keran which was lovely as her own mum (Keran's) hadn't been much of a mum to her as she'd been so young when she'd had her. Had slightly mixed feelings at 'mother figure' comment as though am sure Keran's mum was v young when she'd had her, doubt she was 11 like I'd have had to have been in order to be Keran's ACTUAL mum. Still, Keran's nan very nice old lady & the children quite taken with her too esp her teeth which were vv white & tiny. Maddie so admiring of them, even told Keran's nan she liked her teeth.

Dan all rude as usual & said she was mad & insisted on calling him Toby even when Toby was next to him. Anyway her name is Dora – which I love. Am seriously thinking about it for new baby if it's a girl. Dan says absolutely NO WAY & over his dead body etc etc blah blah blah & why not just call the child Enid or Old Lady & be done (quite like Enid too actually).

From: Nell Fenton
To: Charlotte Bailey

Not sure why Dan imagines he has a right to an opinion re child's name. You must have let your standards slip in my absence. Quite like Dora too but think Enid does sound a bit Old Lady.

From: Charlotte Bailey
To: Nell Fenton

Had exciting news today – the gallery owner Henry introduced Toby to absolutely loved Toby's photos. Toby says he described them as 'organically natural, unforced & totally fresh, totally original'. Apparently his favourites were the bath ones that Toby took from lying down on the grass, so bath looks like it's flying in the sky ('totally Daliesque'), & out-of-focus Goan ones ('because we've all been there' – I haven't, have you?) & the collage photos ('so iconic' – or maybe ironic, can't remember). Anyway Toby is going to be a late but brilliant entry into a show called 'Contemporary Scream' with various other artists. There is only one other photographer in it but Toby says his work is much more conventional (so prob boringly in focus). Spoke to Penelope about it today, v touching as she is SO pleased & proud – just hope it lasts.

From: Nell Fenton
To: Charlotte Bailey

Wd very much have thought Toby was aiming for iconoclastic, not iconic, also unforced or unfocused? still, sure Toby doesn't mind. V pleased for him (and as you very well know I've never been stoned in Goa).

From: Charlotte Bailey
To: Nell Fenton

I have become a thoroughly ridiculous person. Pregnancy has turned me into someone who cannot go to an editor's dinner or even a humble shoe sale without making complete arse of myself. Am also not speaking to Fran AS I BLAME HER FOR EVERYTHING. Went to a shoe sale in Fran's building (Spell-U-Like is in quite a groovy warehouse with lots of other little businesses) & down the corridor there are 2 v camp shoe designers called Hektor & Luis. Fran rang to say did I want to go to their sample sale. Was moderately excited at the idea of cheap designer shoes so I agreed to go along. Sale very busy when I got there & Fran was already there drinking a glass of wine & staggering around in pair of atrocious purple court shoes. Hissed to her had she gone completely fucking insane? She then did whizzy eye motion which I gathered to mean 'look around you'. Did same whizzy eye motion myself & saw all Hektor & Luis shoes excruciatingly awful, so said shall we just go? Fran said no must at least just try on a couple of pairs otherwise we'd look really rude & then handed me the most extraordinary pair of spike-heeled black patent boots with white patent spats attached. Managed to get one of my porky trotters in & was just about to put other on for authenticity when Hektor (assume it was him – v thick German accent) came running up

322

shouting 'NO, NO, dis iss not in semple sale dis iss for Wogue shoot on Vensday!!!! how did dis showe ged here???? please to take showe ov immediately!!' Unfortunately as I tried to take it off the fucking zip got stuck on the spat bit so my foot was half in & half out & rapidly swelling. Fran meanwhile was cowering behind the shoe rack trying not to wet herself, so no bloody use. Hektor jumped up & down shrieking 'Please to take showe ov NOW!!' while I sweatily bleated 'I'm trying, I'm trying!' Then Hektor screamed across the room 'LUIS!!! dis voman hes her fad foodt stuck in de Wogue boot undt IS BREAKING ID!' This made Luis come running over too so by now all eyes were on the woman with the 'fad foodt' whose foodt was considerably fadder than before it went into the fucking boot. Luis also started to shriek but thank God someone sensible called Angela came over & calmly & quietly undid hidden Velcro fastening for the spat bit at the back, allowing zip to open fully & me to remove my very puffy red foot complete with red weals where it had been pressing against the zip. Limped off briskly with Fran in tow.

JUNE 01

From: Nell Fenton
To: Charlotte Bailey

That clumsy cow Suzette has fallen off her horse and sprained her wrist (would have thought having that big bum as her centre of gravity would have stabilised her). She told me with much wincing, in case I was in any doubt as to the pain she was in, that her horse got spooked by a siren and threw her. Anyhow I said, as one does, careful to erase any trace of sincerity from my tone, 'Let me know if there's anything I can do to help.' Now she keeps bloody asking me to ferry her children around. Don't mind too much with Takara, who's quite endearing in a daft way, but have enough sullen ingratitude from my own children without needing any from the ever-charmless Sophie. Picked her up from an after-school play rehearsal today and as I pulled up saw her extricating herself from the clutches of some lumpy-faced youth. Made the cardinal error of asking her in a 'hey, I was young once too' voice if that was her boyfriend. She said no in such a rude, offended tone I was very tempted to say 'So why were you letting him grope you then, you little trollop?' but luckily remembered in time that I didn't care.

From: Charlotte Bailey
To: Nell Fenton
Re: SGP unwell

Nothing proves you're over the hill more conclusively than adopting embarrassing 'hey, I was young once too' voice.

Susan our guinea pig is poorly. She has bad cystitis & has been peeing blood since last Wednesday. I've been taking her to the vet every 2 days for antibiotic shots. She's got quite thin & I'm quite worried about her as inexplicably I'm fond of her. Fran (whom shall henceforth be known as the Guinea Pig Oracle or GPO) luckily knows this man called Adrian Carter (the Guinea Pig Guru or GPG) who has written loads of books about guinea pigs, so I rang him & he basically told me to do the opposite of what the vet said (only dry food). Anyway GPG said no, no, no, must have celery, parsley & cranberry juice, also proper ladies' cystitis medicine, all makes sense to me & now I hate the vet & want to tell him he's crap. So now in between normal household activities am wrapping Susan the Guinea Pig (SGP) in a towel & syringe feeding her cranberry juice (helps make wee less alka-line). If she doesn't start gaining weight am going to have to start syringe-feeding proper food too. Looking after SGP is obviously preparation for Sept & indeed when she is wrapped in a towel & cradled in my arms is not dissimilar to tiny & v hirsute baby (with 4 v long front teeth). Keep having to save disgusting things to show useless vet, latest being her new weird craps. Anyway enough for now – shall keep you abreast of any new developments.

From: Nell Fenton
To: Charlotte Bailey

Am assuming this is a different type of guinea pig to the type of guinea pigs that just conveniently DIE when anything goes wrong thus sparing their owner any bother or costly visits to the vet? As you say, good practice for Sept and however ugly the baby is (and God knows you've had some uggers) will definitely be better-looking than Susan.

From: Charlotte Bailey
To: Nell Fenton

Lou rang – she & Walt are coming to London to promote 'Sex-etiquette' (very wisely staying in a hotel). They've got lots of press events lined up & various book signings incl a party at Selfridges. Lou told me the PR wants lots of sexy beautiful people at the party so that rules me out.

Susan still no better & I'm her sole carer, Astrid despite loving animals is too disgusted to do any of the gross stuff, Ellie's too little (& bored) & Dan just refuses.

From: Charlotte Bailey
To: Louise Corrigan

How are you? Really looking forward to seeing you both & am eagerly anticipating your Selfridges launch party. Brace yourself for the sight of me, I am enormous – far bigger than with any previous pregnancy. People keep coming up to me with their head on one side saying 'Any day now then?' When I wearily explain I have 3 more months to go the automatic response is 'So it's twins then?' me (very brightly) 'No, just the one,' they (looking confused) 'Are you quite sure?' me (even brighter) 'Quite, quite sure.' Have the definite feeling if I stand for more than 10 mins at a time my ankles may explode. Fran has bought new shoes for Selfridges party which make her about a foot taller than me in my Nike trainers. They do, however, make her fall over all the time so don't be surprised if I appear not to know her.

From: Nell Fenton
To: Charlotte Bailey

Take back what I said about being sorry Suzette is leaving. She came drifting over to me when I was in our driveway today. She has taken to supporting her sprained wrist with a gaily patterned silk scarf – she's obviously decided to be very brave and told me with a careless gesture towards the scarf that in spite of her injury it's important to her to feel feminine and you must never let yourself go. As I was standing there, hose in hand, wearing some skanky shorts and a t-shirt of Michael's, felt this to be quite a pointed remark. I said quite snappishly that it didn't seem worth dressing up to scrub black goo out of the paddling pool but she just gave a dreamy smile and drifted off again.

From: Rachel Lockwood
To: Nell Fenton

Dear Nell

We've just got back from the loveliest week in Kent, the cottage and farm were so incredibly pretty and we had wonderful weather. We're both a bit brown and Jonathan was delighted to have all that space to run around in, he made friends with a very sweet brother and sister who live nearby and roamed around with them a lot. Peter is such a nice man, quite awkward and shy but very sweet once you get past that. Most importantly he has a wide-ranging knowledge of WWII planes and took the trouble to retrieve some old models and books from the attic for Jonathan, though he probably regretted it because Jonathan then followed him round at every opportunity questioning him closely on the subject.

He asked us over for supper one night which was very sweet of him and he'd obviously gone to quite a lot of trouble. I don't think he's very used to cooking because he'd made enough rice for about 14 people and chicken in a sauce that tasted as if its main ingredient was Branston pickle. He showed us round the farmhouse after and I saw the room he uses as an office which is very scary indeed. Some of the piles of paper look downright peril-ous. Anyhow we've come to an agreement that Jonathan and I can have the cottage for a month rent-free in the summer in exchange for me helping him get some sem-blance of order into his office. He looked so embarrassed when we were discussing this arrangement you'd have thought he was asking me to have sex with him on the desk (not that there was space with all the mess any-way). I'm actually quite looking forward to bringing some order to the chaos, such is the sad banality of my mind. Now it only remains for me to persuade Ron to let me have a month off. Unless of course I get a new job in the meantime. Hope you are all well.

Fondest love
Rachel xx

From: Charlotte Bailey
To: Nell Fenton

Caring for Susan is turning into an absolute nightmare, it's a full-time job (think I need a respite carer for her so I can go off for a little holiday). She has added a v sore bottom to her list of ailments so now, as well as administering antibiotics 1x day, cystitis medicine 3x day and constantly cleaning out her cage, I am also donning surgical gloves twice a day to apply special bum cream to her suppurating arse, the discomfort of which caused her to do FIVE poos in a row during & after application today.

From: Nell Fenton
To: Charlotte Bailey

Perhaps the time has come to let go and send poor Susan to a happier place where bottoms are never sore. Dropped Josie off at school at 7 this morning. Her grade is taking a 4-day end-of-year trip to Montreal. She was very excited but I'm really going to miss her, I'm not used to her going away for so long, so found expression for my feeling by packing a lot of sweets in her bag.

From: Charlotte Bailey
To: Nell Fenton

I really have found respite carer for SGP in form of Adrian (GPG). Useless vet said he thought she should have x-ray to see if she has kidney stones but may not survive sedative, so then rang GPG who said sedative during x-ray COMPLETELY UNNECESSARY so rang vet back to say STOP. Emotion of it all a bit too much & cried on phone to GPG when I rang back to tell him I'D CANCELLED THE X-RAY (sorry about caps but whole day v traumatic). Anyway Adrian (GPG) says he'll take Susan & stupid old Catherine too so Susan doesn't pine for her or vice versa (can't imagine Catherine pining she's a v heartless cold little guinea pig compared to Susan) and he will try & sort her out. Am SO relieved. Driving them both round to Adrian's tomorrow so gave Susan special organic celery tonight & an extra helping of cranberry juice. Have ended the day with same wrung-out feeling I have after particularly gruelling episode of ER.

From: Nell Fenton
To: Charlotte Bailey

Do not wish to be unkind as you are obviously in a highly emotional (not to say bonkers) state but I think you have somewhat lost perspective on this. You need to focus on the fact that SUSAN IS NOT ONE OF YOUR CHILDREN and in the sad event that she does not survive this illness I feel sure any grief you feel will be quite short-lived. I am quietly confident that Dan shares my views on this.

From: Charlotte Bailey
To: Nell Fenton

Had another antenatal today. I am now 6 weeks too big for my dates. Feel teeny bit panicked, wondering if I'm just going to carry on getting bigger & bigger until I give birth by firing baby out as I have exploded. Midwife didn't seem concerned, said 'baby has lots of room' which means 'you have a flabby uterus'. How is 'oooh look at my tiny bump' Marguerite doing?

330

From: Nell Fenton
To: Charlotte Bailey

Saw Marguerite just this morning coincidentally. She has suddenly ballooned out to about 18 stone and has developed a strange warty rash all over her big fat face. Also think she is too fat to wash any more as she definitely smelt.

From: Charlotte Bailey
To: Nell Fenton

Adrian rang tonight to let me know how everybody was doing. The good news is Catherine who was initially a bit down in the dumps & missing me has perked up a lot. Adrian said (re Catherine) 'She's quite a little character, isn't she?' She bloody isn't, she's really boring, she just sits there & she's really squeaky when you try & move her, but he's quite concerned about Susan, says he thinks she has a fungal thingy on her skin which will require regular baths, & if she gets any thinner, syringe-feeding too, her bum is improving but very slowly & there is always the guinea pig hospital in Cambridge or Oxford or somewhere if things get worse.

From: Nell Fenton
To: Charlotte Bailey

Such a relief to hear Catherine has perked up. Are you going to continue consorting with crazy people when you (hopefully) get your marbles back? Speaking of crazy people, Suzette has decided to try and SELL me her vile mynah bird. Not even trying to give it to me. She doesn't want to take it to Italy, the journey would be too stressful for it, blah-blah, though she's taking all her other disgusting animals. I was so taken aback that she could think I would actually pay to become the owner of that horrible bird, I didn't immediately shriek 'No, Never, Not Ever, No, No, No.' She took this as a sign that I was considering the matter and went into hard-sell, it's a wonderful pet, highly intelligent, affectionate (pecks absolutely everyone, once pecked Josie v painfully on the nose) and has a vocabulary of over 70 words. Only thing I've ever heard it say was something that sounded suspiciously like 'dickhead'. Had a hard time getting her to shut up and even then couldn't get her to accept the answer was NO, so apparently I am now going to 'think about it and discuss it with Michael'.

From: Charlotte Bailey
To: Nell Fenton

She's as mad as a snake, Adrian isn't though, he just happens to think guinea pigs are more important than people.

We went to Lou & Walt's book launch at Selfridges last night, really good fun & v glitzy. Cocktails, fab canapes & of course endless sex talk. Weather beforehand was v gloomy & overcast which was great for me as I wanted to wear my olive suede boots with a groovy 70s kaftan Lou had brought me & needed to hide elastic stockings. Unfortunately when I came to put boots on (haven't worn them for months) I COULD NOT ZIP THEM UP AS MY CALVES WERE TOO FAT. I fully accept when you are pregnant you get a fat stomach & a fat arse, I had also resigned myself to fat arms, fat face, fat ankles but FAT CALVES are a fat too far. Dan said I made the most pathetic sight sitting on the edge of the bed whimpering & tugging ineffectually at boot zipper. He had a go too & when it became clear there was no way zipper would shut suggested

I just brazen it out as orange crenellated toeless elastic stockings so unbelievably hideous, everybody would assume they were Vivienne Westwood. He also pointed out with cool (almost feminine) logic that stocking colour 'accented' blobs of orange in kaftan. Felt quite tearful (not about fat arse, fat calves & fat head) but about what a nice husband I have. Did not go along with his suggestion, instead wore boots half done up with bits of elastic tied round the top to stop them flapping as kaftan covered top part of boots anyway. Lou & Walt looked incredible, Lou v stacked up & wearing full-length v tight vintage Pucci dress, huge silver hoops & her hair all piled up. With shoes & hair was about 6' 3" – looked FAB. Walt at least a head shorter looked like a Mafia boss from the waist up (white shirt, black jkt, dark glasses, etc . . .) but when he stood up from behind desk where he'd been signing books couldn't help noticing he was wearing a kilt with thick black tights. Everybody wearing the most extraordinary clothes incl one young gentleman who had minty-green scrunched-up ladies' pants on his head. Fran (in snakeskin platforms she got from Hektor & Luis) asked Knicker Boy why he had pants on his head & he told her he was studying millinery at London College of Fashion & pants were actually a 'sexy hat' he'd made specially for 'Sexetiquette' launch (dipped them in glue & stiffened them to give them a 'sculptural quality'). Anyway book signing v successful – Lou & Walt had 150 copies of the book at the launch & they sold them all. We're taking the children to L & W's fancy hotel for brunch on Sunday before they leave.

PS Bet Marguerite can do up her boots.

From: Nell Fenton
To: Charlotte Bailey

V much doubt it, her calves looked like a pair of enormous rugby balls and she was wearing carrier bags on her feet when I saw her last. Book signing sounds fantastic, wish I could have come. Pity you didn't wear your orange tights after all, you'd have been quite the thing.

From: Charlotte Bailey
To: Nell Fenton

Have had the most ghastly piece of news. Astrid came to me to tell me her mother fell off a ladder yesterday while white-washing the outside of their stupid fucking house & she has broken her leg in 2 places & will have to have an operation to pin it together. Think I must have looked really, really horrified & also I kept saying 'BUT IS SHE OK???' in slightly hysterical way which led a very touched Astrid to believe my profound concern was for her mother rather than MYSELF. Upshot is Astrid is leaving at the w/e as her mother is going to be immobile for weeks so Astrid has to go home to look after Anders & Benny as mother was thoughtless enough to carry on producing children after Astrid with no thought as to how she would care for them if she ever broke her leg. Astrid is very tearful & sorry about leaving abruptly but not nearly as tearful & sorry as me. Have no idea what I'm going to do.

From: Nell Fenton
To: Charlotte Bailey

That really is terrible. Can't you get someone to help temporarily? If it's any comfort I spoke to Marguerite this morning and Steve has left her and taken all their money so she's living on welfare with the 3 children now.

From: Nell Fenton
To: Charlotte Bailey

I am mainly just sitting quietly today in order to recover from yesterday, which has the distinction of having been the worst day of my life so far. Michael has been in Ottawa for 3 days so I was alone in bed when I woke to the sound of the garbage truck down the road. We managed to miss it last week so there was 2 weeks' worth of bags that have been sweating stinkily in the garage. You can't put them out the night before because the racoons tear them to pieces so Michael usually gets up early on garbage day and puts them out. V important that I didn't miss this collection as the pong from the bags was getting serious so fell out of bed and ran down to the garage. Started picking up bags and as I picked up one v smelly one about 1,000,000,000 really fat maggots fell onto the garage floor. As they hit the floor they started crawling away and under anything they could find. Despite the temptation to stop what I was doing and start screaming loudly, I carried on dragging the bags out, garbage truck v close by then, hopping over wriggling maggots as I went, then ran inside and got a spray cleaner from the kitchen and sprayed everything I could find. Loads of junk and boxes in the garage and everything I picked up had maggots under it. Spray cleaner had no effect on them, they even seemed to quite like it, so rushed back inside and managed to find some ant spray and tried again with that. Still no effect and by then I really had to abandon it because I was supposed to be taking them all to the dentist so decided to address the maggot problem on my return. Late for the dentist thanks to maggots and was so preoccupied with what awaited me when I got home didn't see a man who was crossing the road and had to jump on the brakes and swerve. Nearly gave us both a heart attack and was entirely my fault which he seemed to feel quite strongly, judging by his expression and gestures. Fortunately had an inspiration re indestructible maggots and found that pouring a lot of salt on them certainly made them a bit miserable even if it didn't cause instant death. Much lifting of garage junk, salt scattering and sweeping later had a large pile of half-heartedly wriggling maggots in the middle of the garage floor. We then had a couple of hours of normality until we went to the mall where I had a few things to do, including collecting a suit for Michael. Was carrying it over my arm, in a suit carrier with the hanger dangling down, with Ollie walking next to me. Ollie suddenly started screaming and I looked down and the hook of the hanger had somehow got caught UNDER his eyelid. Dropped the 37 bags I was carrying and tried to unhook it but in the end just had to yank it. Rob also screaming by now and a crowd of hovering onlookers had gathered. Ollie's tears were streaked with blood and I was so terrified of what I might have done to his eye I was half crying myself by then. Drove straight to the doctor's surgery, Ollie hysterical and saying he wanted Daddy, obviously felt I was an unsafe parent. Was trying to soothe Ollie saying 'Daddy will be back tonight' and we were already providing an interesting spectacle to all the other people in the waiting room when he started shouting 'Daddy's not coming back, he's in prison.' Have absolutely no idea where he got this from, don't even think he really knows what prison is, but had a hideous ring of truth to it and Rob didn't help with my public humiliation by starting to cry again and saying he didn't want Daddy to go to prison. Anyhow, his eye is fine, just a scratch on his eyelid. I on the other hand am a wreck.

JULY 01

From: Charlotte Bailey
To: Nell Fenton

Astrid left yesterday. Ashamed to say I cried a bit, she cried loads, girls, esp Maddie, cried, while Hugh wandered off to do a bit of digging. Anyway she has gone & I officially have no help & want to kill myself. Rang au pair agency & they have sent me quite a big list but majority of them aren't available until Sept, or they specify max 3 children (wimps) or they look like Beverley Allitt. Everybody keeps saying 'Ooooh you're going to need help when that baby comes' but actually will be ok then as I won't feel like someone has strapped a Fiat Panda to my front, it's now I need help. Fran says she's going to Step Into The Breach & come round to help clean which is v kind but she's rubbish at it & gets distracted by mail-order catalogues. Dan says we must start doing our supermarket shops on the internet & we can all just wear wrinkly clothes from now on as house/clothes don't matter, I just need to concentrate on keeping Hugh alive till he (Dan) gets back in the evening then he can take over (keeping Hugh alive).

From: Nell Fenton
To: Charlotte Bailey

Hardly know what to say except this too will pass. At least with a Fiat Panda on your front you can't get into the stinky maternity wear. Dan quite right, wrinkly clothes and ready-made meals are the way forward. And it's not like you haven't had practice at living in chaos.

From: Charlotte Bailey
To: Nell Fenton

Lou & Walt went back to NY today, had our brunch with them at their hotel yesterday. Hotel vv fancy & modern with gigantic empty white lobby with huge reception displaying enormous, phallic floral arrangement & staffed by receptionist with hair so tightly scraped back looked like she was in a wind tunnel. Good thing about gigantic empty lobby is it gives tiny-headed receptionist plenty of time to assess you as you approach the desk. If her expression of profound distaste was anything to go by I think she found us wanting (Hugh kept skidding on his knees like in Strictly Ballroom). Went up to Lou & Walt's room which had the most fantastic views & was so modern (flat-screen tv, minibar flush with wall, etc, etc) hard to tell what was what. Hugh of course needed the loo & suddenly became terribly embarrassed in front of Lou & Walt at idea of me or Dan being present. Wasn't really aware of what was going on as L, W, me & the girls were on their balcony looking at the river so was only much later during brunch Dan whispered to me Hugh had become v confused by stupid Philippe Starck bathroom fixtures & done (luckily) small pebbly poo in the bidet which he'd had to deal with. Brunch quite stressful as was keen for children to be well behaved in the world's least child-friendly environment. They were completely fantastic – I was the one letting the side down. Managed to drop a great deal of food down my front. I am super-clumsy at the moment and my gargantuan bump is a magnet to everything in sight, even other people's scraps. Finished brunch with enough spare food resting on my 'ledge' to feed the teeny model at next door table.

From: Nell Fenton
To: Charlotte Bailey

Think it sounds like a horrible hotel. Perfectly understandable mistake for Hugh to make.

I might have exaggerated a tiny bit re Marguerite's appearance and situation, but was only in the interests of making you feel less like a huge (jealous) whale. We went out with them for the day, took the children for a picnic to an island in the lake here. Marguerite, I'm sorry to report, still reasonably svelte in spite of being ready to go any day now. Not only have her bottom and ankles not ballooned out as you might wish, but she's also together enough to 1) produce a simple but delicious picnic, 2) remember to bring suncream to put on the children (had to borrow hers to apply to my scarlet-faced children), 3) obtain her children's attentive compliance without shouting and/or repeating herself eleven times (a skill that eludes me even at my least pregnant and most energetic). We had a v nice day but could not help thinking of you, and how if you'd been there instead of the still nimble Marguerite we'd probably have had to rig up some sort of trolley to drag you along.

From: Charlotte Bailey
To: Nell Fenton

Wish I could say am not THAT bad, but I am. Dan dropped us off at church on Sunday, idea being I could manage the 7-min walk back. Got as far as the phone box by the station, so 1½ mins, & then had to ring him to come & get me (mobile AWOL).

On brighter note, Geraldine has invited us to dinner at her flat to meet Julian, am super-excited, even Dan mildly interested.

From: Nell Fenton
To: Charlotte Bailey

We had Suzette and family round for supper last night, v heroic of me but feel a bit sorry for them, their house is nearly empty now. Also Josie is quite sad to say goodbye to Takara (they leave day after tomorrow). Doubt Michael could have been more horrified if I'd told him I'd started taking male hormones and should henceforth be called Neil. You'll be relieved to hear Suzette has regained some limited movement in her wrist though it's still very uncomfortable at night and painful if her arm is unsupported for any length of time. Kane' glassy-eyed stare and Sophie's expression of hostile boredom during this recount made me suspect Suzette has been keeping her loved ones fully informed of every detail regarding the progress of her injury. Evening was rather subdued, Suzette not at all on form though she did tell us of one crazy caper, obviously it happened a few weeks back, 'before the accident' (as she said this she cradled her wrist most tenderly). She was running very late one morning and it was time to drive the girls to school and she was still in her nightie, very short and flimsy apparently (she gave a flirty little glance towards Michael as she shared this information, but if the 'Lord, please take me now' expression on his face was anything to go by he failed to be titillated by the image). Being the madcap she is she simply dragged Kane's leather biker jacket on over her nightie and jumped in the car. (Should say for the record here Kane doesn't have a motorbike.) Needless to say on the way back from school the car got a 'flat' and she had to call the CAA. CAA man very kind and helpful though he did ask her if this was a new fashion!! Kane was really mad at her and has forbidden her from going out like that again. Cannot imagine Kane forbidding anything, but who knows what strength lurks behind that meek demeanour.

PS Mynah now with a new family with 'a great kid who has wanted one, like, forever' and being so clever it has already learnt his name (find this hard to believe unless of course his name happens to be Dick Head).

From: Charlotte Bailey
To: Nell Fenton

Don't be too hard on her, she's just clinging to her youth a bit harder than a normal person. Fantastic news, had an antenatal today and am now only FIVE weeks too big for my dates – poss body's had enough & has now decided to slowly reabsorb baby instead??

From: Nell Fenton
To: Charlotte Bailey

Doesn't really matter though, does it? As long as the baby isn't some weird giant.

*

By the way, Marguerite had her baby, a little boy, a bit of a tiddler, 6 lb 2 oz. They're calling him Burke (and there was I stupidly thinking Dusty was the worst possible name for a boy).

From: Nell Fenton
To: Rachel Lockwood

Dear Rachel, how are you? Any progress on the flat/job hunting? It's so boiling here, I've sent the children off to camp for the week – it was that or kill them, which I know I would immediately regret. We're off to France next week, really looking forward to seeing everyone. Have you sorted out when you're going to the farm? Let me know how everything's going. Love Nell

From: Rachel Lockwood
To: Nell Fenton

Dear Nell

Things aren't brilliant, I still haven't found anywhere to live and the people buying the house are getting really fed up with me dragging my feet over completion. Jack's enchanting lady friend seems to have got him by the balls because he's been bullying me endlessly about the house and I can understand that he might not care about kicking me out but it's also his son's home. I wouldn't have believed it of him, but there you are. I hope she makes him really miserable. Anyhow Dan's cousin Peter phoned me to ask what date we wanted the cottage and got me at a bad moment, I'd just come off the phone from a very acrimonious conversation with Jack (I think I might have frightened him, I thought it was Jack phoning back and answered the phone very ferociously). I probably told him more than I should have about my dreary personal circumstances but he was so sympathetic and sensible I just blurted it all out. I'm sure he thinks I'm a hysterical female now but he was very kind. He said if we're stuck we can use the cottage for the whole summer (apparently he's done nothing about letting it out and I have to say I believe him from what I've seen of his organisational skills). I don't know to what extent this offer was prompted by his terror at the prospect of me starting to sob on the phone, I think I sounded quite wobbly and he strikes me as the sort of man that would be panic-stricken by a weeping woman, but I'm going to phone him back in a couple of days and attempt to sound rational and see if he really means it. At least it would give me a breathing space till school starts again in September, I really don't want to land on Jane or Mum and Dad for weeks on end though they've both offered. I can look for a temporary job or we can manage with some of the money from the sale of the house for a bit.

Anyway, it'll all work out in the end.

Fondest love
Rachel xx

From: Charlotte Bailey
To: Nell Fenton

We were supposed to have had our Julian/Geraldine dinner last night but unfortunately about 40 mins after we had arrived at Geraldine's flat she got a phone call from Julian to say he was at A&E at Chelsea & Westminster, had done something to his Achilles tendon while playing tennis & was in a lot of pain. Geraldine was quite flustered & Dan offered to drive her over there but she said she was fine to drive herself so then we all had to leave (Marcia & Quentin there too). Marcia & I terribly disappointed not to meet him as we're both dying to. Geraldine showed us a photo of him, he's very good-looking, olive-skinned with very dark slicked-back hair. Her flat looks completely different. It's lost its I-went-to-John-Lewis-and-bought-everything-all-in-one-go look. She's had the vile beige carpet pulled up & the very nice wooden floors underneath stained & polished. Living room has been repainted this fantastic olivey-grey & all those alarming multicoloured oils that Gil chose are gone. She's also got rid of her horrible terracotta sofa & replaced it with terrifying putty suede one. Geraldine said it was all Julian's idea, suggested to her should he ever decide to abandon his career as a surgeon sure he'd do v well as interior designer. Dan says Julian's failure to show up again now makes him officially a figment of Geraldine's imagination & next thing that will happen is he'll suddenly die abroad.

From: Nell Fenton
To: Charlotte Bailey

Nonsense, sure he exists but, as I've said before, has some terrible flaw like extra fingers or two bottoms.

Packing not going according to my excellent and organised plan. Had to go for a top-level meeting with my beautician and the proximity of the shops lured me in to buy sandals (ones bought for Cuba vv uncomfortable) and thinking of Cuba brought back the sharp sting of Michael's comment regarding my swimming costume. Had considered swimming costume to be discreetly tasteful and excellently engineered, but he said it was middle-aged, so thought I might as well try and find a new swimming costume and by that time I was in full shopping mode so frittered away my last childfree day. Anyhow still not packed but the new, less middle-aged me doesn't stress about that kind of stuff.

From: Nell Fenton
To: Michael Fenton

Tried to phone but I think the phone might be off the hook, it's been engaged for hours. Either that or you're having an affair and feel awkward about speaking to me just now and have deliberately unplugged it. Journey ok for first bit, utterly hellish for the Paris–Bordeaux leg. Plane was delayed so we had a really long wait and they were all exhausted. Rob kicked Josie for some insult or other so she punched his arm which apparently broke it. Unfortunately my failure to treat the breakage with the gravity it merited tipped him into a state of near hysteria. All made me very, very happy to see Pa at the airport. Charlotte arriving tomorrow. Anyway it's lovely to be here and I'll speak to you later (if you're not too busy with your new girlfriend). xxxx

From: Nell Fenton
To: Michael Fenton

Don't forget the cat sitter is picking up the key this evening and don't forget to leave money for Cynthia tomorrow morning. Charlotte and children arrived today and I can confirm Dan wasn't exaggerating when he told you she looks like she's going to give birth to a full-grown adult. It's not fat which is the scary part. It's made me really want to see the baby (or adult) when it arrives. Ollie cried about you last night, v overtired, but had quite forgotten you by this morning. xxxx

From: Charlotte Bailey
To: Dan Bailey

AAAAAAAAAArgh, actually AAArgh. Journey not too bad, everybody leaping around to help me unable to believe I wasn't going to give birth there & then. One terribly helpful kind woman asked me in nicest possible way what possessed me to embark on journey with 3 small children in my condition & no one to help. Told her about Astrid & how she had been supposed to come & you trying to save holiday for when the foal I am carrying is born. She did lots of sympathetic nodding, clearly thought I was insane but was incredibly nice. Listened for hours while Hugh craply told her the plot of some of his favourite Thomas the Tank Engine stories. Nell came to collect us at the station, fantastic to see her. She tried to hide it but could see she was a bit shocked at how gigantic I am. Lovely to be here, children have all disappeared & I'm paying Isabel to help mind Hugh. Adrian is supposed to phone this evening with update on Susan – be nice to him. Speak later, love Cxxxx

From: Nell Fenton
To: Michael Fenton

Beautiful day today, v hot so children swimming all day only emerging to eat like wolves and then back in the pool. Anna and Geoffrey went off to Provence this morning, have left

Guy and Isabel to look after the others. Not too optimistic about how this will work, only been a few hours and the only evidence of 'looking after' I've seen is Guy punching his brothers and telling them to shut up. They're not much trouble but still it's 5 extra children to feed and Mum and I are trying to get Charlotte to rest more. Her own children are too much for her at the moment (esp Hugh whose daftness seems to have actually increased since we last saw them). Phone me later. xxxx

From: Nell Fenton
To: Michael Fenton

Wish you were coming sooner, I feel a bit worn out. Charlotte has finally agreed to stop lumbering around and lie down after she started getting regular contractions (settled down now) so Mum and I are now looking after the 11 children (Pa never to be seen as usual). Hugh and Ollie are totally untrustworthy, found them heading towards the river with a galvanised bucket (luckily the clanking as they dragged it along alerted me). Told me they were off to get minnows for pets. Having detained them also frisked them (curiously lumpy pockets). Hugh had an oyster knife (in case of a snake) and Ollie less dangerously but more disgustingly had a pocket full of pasta left over from lunch (to feed the minnows). Thought it was better to let them get the fishing trip out of their systems so found them a fishing net and bribed Guy to look after them. Didn't tell Charlotte about the spot of unsupervised fishing the boys had planned, or the oyster knife, no point in alarming her. Dan, thank God, has decided to come early and Tom and Maude coming soon. Can't wait to see you. xxxx

From: Charlotte Bailey
To: Louise Corrigan

How are you? We're all very well, children thrilled to be in France with their cousins, wish I could say the same. Anna & Geoffrey have buggered off to Provence for 5 days leaving Isabel & Guy 'in charge' of Rory, Theo & Greta. Hugely competent as Isabel is (Guy sweet but hopeless) she IS still only 13, & amazingly self-sufficient as progeny that sprang from Anna & Geoffrey have to be, they still require feeding, sending to bed, supervising at the pool, etc, etc . . . Theo & Rory fight all the time at the moment which is boring & exhausting, & Greta, despite much evidence to the contrary, is convinced she can swim & keeps taking her armbands off. As I am vast & sweaty & already struggling with my 3 (Hugh – thanks to Greta – also labouring under the misapprehension he can swim) adding Anna's lot into the equation not perfectly timed. Terrible for Nell & Mum who are trying to do everything esp as day before yesterday was running around so much (mainly after Greta) started getting quite regular contractions so then Nell was freaking out & made me lie down & Mum rang the Dr who advised a glass of wine to relax everything. Have to say after months of abstinence alcohol highly effective & had lovely snooze. Unfortunately Dan rang while I was asleep so Isabel aka Miss Too-Much-Information told Dan I was having 'major contractions' (untrue) so then he started really panicking & got Nell on the phone & was shouting 'Oh my God, she's not having a miscarriage, is she?' so Nell pointed out bearing in mind baby due in about a month prob wouldn't qualify as 'miscarriage' at this stage & anyway pichet de vin rouge had done the trick. Good thing is Dan so alarmed by it he's coming out early now. Meanwhile Anna rang to say she's having a lovely relaxing time doing lots of drawing & could they stay 1 extra day? Mum, who answered the phone, said maybe not such a good idea this time as it was a bit much for Nell & me with me being so pregnant so then Anna all contrite saying of course etc & promising to bring Provençal lavender bath oil back to help relax me so then Nell was muttering not having to look after 5 extra children would be more relaxing. Anyway Dan arriving tomorrow which I am so relieved about as can then hand over the mantle of keeping Hugh & Greta alive to him & Tom & Maude who are both terribly helpful and arriving at the w/e with Betsey & Lily. Love Cxx

From: Nell Fenton
To: Michael Fenton

Things are reasonably under control again, insofar as that's possible with 84,000 people under one roof. Tom, Maude and Dan all here now. I think Geoffrey and Anna had a v nice time, Geoffrey unusually relaxed and mellow, Anna obviously couldn't relax any more without slipping into a coma but v enthusiastic about their time away. Boys v excited about you coming, Ollie is going to show you he has learned to swim. Does such impressive swimming arm movements you'll hardly notice his feet walking along the bottom of the pool. xxxx

From: Charlotte Bailey
To: Louise Corrigan

I'm completely fine thanks, contractions a one-off but have continued with modest wine consumption for 'medicinal' purposes. Dan is here now which is fantastic & Geoffrey & Anna back from Provence, Anna vv brown & loaded down with purple chalky drawings of lavender fields. Anna said they had the most fantastic time like a 2nd honeymoon. Think we may leave a few days earlier than planned as unless I am bobbing round the pool find the heat pretty unbearable, also suddenly feel quite anxious to get back & sort everything out for the baby. Albert has done his usual thing of ringing me to tell me I won't like the colour I chose for the baby's room – apparently it's too green (was after celery, he says it's a vicious pea) – would just ignore him, but most unfortunately past experience has demonstrated he has an uncanny knack of correctly predicting my reaction to the many, many slightly wrong colours I have chosen over the years. Send my love to Walt. Love Cxx

AUGUST 01

From: Rachel Lockwood
To: Nell Fenton

Dear Nell

How is it going in France? We are installed in the cottage now and the house is sold. I thought I'd feel sad about it but in fact I feel quite liberated and like I'm ready to make a fresh start. All our furniture is in Jane's garage at the moment. I was even tempted to sell the lot and start again, but Jane talked me out of it and I expect she's right. Leaving my job was a great relief, I'd got to the point of being afraid to meet Ron's eye, he always looked so hopeful.

I've been trying to sort out Peter's office for him. He's so appreciative you'd think I was giving him one of my kidneys, but I quite like organising things and Peter seems perfectly happy to have Jonathan following him round the farm 'helping'. Jonathan wants nothing more so it's working out very well. He's earning 50p a day for his farm work (though not the most reliable employee as he runs off to play as soon as his friends turn up, which they do most days). Either way he's very active all day and came in yesterday evening, slumped down on the sofa and said 'What a day!' in a weary, adult tone. I almost offered him a stiff drink.

I think I might have found a flat. It's a bit grim but I can brighten it up and it's reasonably near to Jane and the local primary school is supposed to be quite good. I'm having a survey done this week so we'll see.

Fondest love to all, especially give my love to Charlotte, Rachel xx

From: Nell Fenton
To: Rachel Lockwood

Dear Rachel, so glad your summer's going well and v glad to hear Jonathan has found himself gainful employment. Lovely here but the usual zoo. Charlotte is going to go back to London a bit early – it's too hot for her here which is a real shame, but Michael has promised to take a couple of days off in Sept so I can make a brief trip to England to inspect the baby. Good luck with the flat survey. Love Nell

From: Charlotte Bailey
To: Nell Fenton

Journey fine apart from having to stop every 20 mins to pee (by the end even children saying 'Not again, Mum' & me all defensive saying 'YOU try having equivalent of bag of puppies wriggling on top of YOUR bladder & see how YOU manage.' V stupid thing to say as then had to spend rest of journey explaining to a v tearful whiny Hugh (who had spent 10 ecstatic minutes thinking I was going to give birth to a litter of puppies) that puppy reference merely FIGURE OF SPEECH & unfortunately was only going to provide boring old baby brother or sister. So after ages of me describing what FUN baby brother or sister was going to be he very grudgingly said 'Okaaay, I'll have a baby brother then' – too terrified of consequences to explain won't necessarily be a brother, could be another stinky sister, so just did lots of enthusiastic agreeing that it would definitely be a brother . . . Oh dear, shall now have to stick nadgers on it & dress it as a boy for rest of its life in now highly likely event of it being a girl.

From: Nell Fenton
To: Charlotte Bailey

OR if it's a girl, you could buy a puppy to go with it and pretend you had twins, one of which by great good luck wasn't human.

Mum up to her usual tricks. Martine phoned to say she and Jean-Claude are driving up from Italy and will be in the area the day after tomorrow. Of course Mum couldn't just say come and have lunch, in spite of the fact that none of us can stand them AND they can stun a whole room into silence by the boringness they give off. Instead she's asked them to stay for a couple of nights to break their journey. Mum fairly sheepish but says it would have been rude not to ask them to stay and they're not that bad. Reminded her that last time Martine came she made Mum look at several hundred photos she had on her laptop, INCLUDING some of damage to their house caused by a burst pipe taken for insurance purposes. Did not feel it necessary to labour the point any further but left Mum to think about what she had done.

PS. How was the bedroom colour?

From: Charlotte Bailey
To: Nell Fenton

Of course Albert was right, I had picked a most alarming & unrestful green. However, he is being an absolute trooper about repainting it & went off v cheerfully to the fancy paint shop with the colour-matching computer holding a stick of celery . . . has also finally fixed the front garden fence.

From: Nell Fenton
To: Charlotte Bailey

Tragic news here – the chicken population has been halved overnight. Fortunately M. Bonneau was the one to discover the carnage and cleared it away before any of the children saw it. Strongly suspect a fox or poss a dog from the village to be responsible but Josie, Isabel and Guy have much darker theories and are planning to investigate the matter and get to the bottom of it. Investigation has so far consisted of them sitting around animatedly discussing some very unlikely scenarios. We are awaiting a dramatic denouement, especially Theo and Rory, who vowed to guard the chicken coops day and night and actually did so for almost 20 mins.

From: Charlotte Bailey
To: Nell Fenton

So sorry the girls & esp Hugh aren't there to enjoy the drama. Feel really guilty about them, it's so boring for them here & I'm so immobile & grumpy. Toby & Keran are taking them all out for the day tomorrow which is fantastic as I have loads of cleaning & sorting out to do. Got the invitation to private view for Toby's exhibition this morning. Looks very swanky. 6 other people exhibiting alongside him. Told him to send invitation to Julian & Geraldine as they are rich & patronise the arts.

From: Nell Fenton
To: Charlotte Bailey

Martine and Jean-Claude are here. He has bought a very fancy telescope. NOT the Hubble Space Telescope, though might as well be for the reverence he treats it with. Fancy telescope with a neurotic owner and a large number of boisterous, inquisitive children is not a successful combination. Stupid telescope has to 'settle' apparently so Jean-Claude (with endless tweaking and adjusting) got it in position and then hopped around it yelping if any child came within 100 yards. Unfortunately the air of mystery telescope is now invested with has made it utterly irresistible and am not at all confident that the strict talking-to all the children have received about not touching it will be enough of a deterrent. Martine still as poker-arsed as ever. Boys were practising their armpit farts at the lunch table (how will they ever improve if they don't practise?), Martine looked as though she was going to spontaneously combust her face was so red with disapproval, which I naturally would have ignored but Mum (traitor) told the boys to stop.

From: Charlotte Bailey
To: Nell Fenton

Find I am now v glad girls & esp Hugh are no longer there. Presumably Martine has her camera with her so should any of the children damage telescope in any way she can take photos for insurance purposes & then show them to Mum next time she visits.

Adrian rang, Susan is well enough to come home (hurrah), with Catherine of course, but will need very careful monitoring & I will have to continue with syringe-feeding the cranberry juice as precautionary measure for next few weeks, also although her arse is nearly better still needs bum cream once a day. Hurrah.

From: Nell Fenton
To: Charlotte Bailey

Adrian is a miracle worker. Let's hope Susan is better by the time the baby comes, don't want a pesky baby distracting you from nursing Susan through her convalescence.

We all had a tremendous treat last night. Got to look through Jean-Claude's telescope. Stars look very different I can tell you. Instead of a small sparkly whitish-yellow circle in the sky you see a larger, clearer, whitish-yellow circle in the sky. Quite an experience.

From: Charlotte Bailey
To: Nell Fenton

That total wanker Brian Turner & the fat-arsed Hildegard have reported us to the council for not applying for planning permission for our new front-garden fence. I know they're the ones who reported us as 1) they have nothing better to do than snitch on neighbours, 2) they wheedled fact we hadn't applied for planning permission out of Albert, 3) they own a pug called

Hermann. As new garden fence is identical in every way to old one except not rotten & falling down, none of us (except Brian & Hildegard) had any idea it was necessary to alert the council. Now we've had this snotty letter saying we can apply for post-something planning permission but if we're refused it we'll have to take fence down. Don't think I've ever seen Albert so cross, says fence is coming down over his dead body. Dan rang Joe & he says it'll be fine as fence is identical & we'll definitely get planning permission. In the meantime will have to be physically restrained next time Brian & Hildegard speed-walk past me with their repulsive little dog as am planning to run after them & kick at least one of them to death.

From: Nell Fenton
To: Charlotte Bailey

Still experiencing that wonderful serenity then. Anna and co left today. Geoffrey had done his usual eccentric packing of the car, lots of stuff where Anna's feet should go though there was still room in the boot. Suggested to her she move the stuff to the back which she seemed to think was a really inspired idea. Packing the car and prospect of driving all day put Geoffrey in a v shouty mood, though Anna as ever didn't seem to mind or even really notice. Charlie, Julia and the boys arrive this evening, though only staying the weekend. Will be lovely to see them, haven't seen them since last summer.

From: Charlotte Bailey
To: Nell Fenton

Obviously the calming effect of their 2nd honeymoon has worn off Geoffrey. Had an antenatal this morning where midwife told me although the baby is big, still has quite a lot of space to move around, also head not engaged yet (so why am I walking round like supersized Frankie Dettori then?). Good news is am now a trifling 4 weeks too big for my dates. Had to take all the children with me to antenatal, Hugh in the waiting room with the girls bitterly disappointed when I emerged 20 mins later STILL with no baby. On drive back home Maddie asked me why our baby took so much longer than everybody else's to come as Hannah's baby only took 3 months. Carefully avoided any jokes as they only confuse Hugh, just said it only seems that way. Can no longer bend or twist at all which makes housework even more tremendous fun than it was before. Keep ringing au pair agency to bleat at them but to no avail. No new ones on list, just same old weirdos I've already turned down.

From: Nell Fenton
To: Charlotte Bailey

Sure something will turn up soon. Sympathise with the children by the way. V bored of your pregnancy now. Get on with it.

From: Charlotte Bailey
To: Nell Fenton

Spent the afternoon assembling the baby's room with the girls. It was really lovely except I was sitting on the floor sorting stuff out & kept getting stuck down there so then Ellie would be trying to pull me up while Maddie crouched behind me going Grrrrr & trying to push me up. Felt like the mother in Gilbert Grape. The girls laid out all babygros & teeny-tiny clothes saying 'ahhh'. Hugh was 'too busy' to help & instead went

358

off & built some huge edifice using all the Duplo which he brought back v proudly & said it was for the baby. Told Fran about it & she says I can't disassemble it but must keep it till the baby is born. Pointed out that nobody can play with the Duplo now so she said I must buy new Duplo. Too fat & exhausted to argue.

From: Rachel Lockwood
To: Nell Fenton

Dear Nell

Hope all is well in France, we're having a really lovely summer, the weather has been beautiful for the most part and Jonathan is outside all day and is a different child. He's spent the last 3 days (when not doing his farm labouring) damming the stream with his friends. It's a chore, but someone's got to do it. He's really going to miss being here, Gemma is his 'best friend which is a girl' and Douglas is his 'best friend which is a boy'. I've promised him we'll come back and visit often. He went for his first ever sleepover with them the other night so Peter and I had supper at the village pub. The landlady (quite a rough old bird) kept saying to him 'Got yerself a lady friend at last then' and winking at me. For some reason Peter felt he had to apologise for this though he was the one that was embarrassed, not me. Obviously I'm less horrified by the notion of us as a couple than he is, unfortunately I only seem to attract dysfunctional men or old, bald ones.

The survey on the flat I'm buying was OK, so we are going ahead. There's no way we can get everything done

359

before the start of school so we'll have to stay with Jane for a bit.

Fondest love to all
Rachel xx

From: Charlotte Bailey
To: Nell Fenton

Situation with Brian & Hildegard considerably worse. Brian stopped to ask me what my plans were for the front garden when I was standing out the front with Albert. As I can only lift my leg about 7" off the ground was unable to 'action' kicking plan, so instead meekly said hadn't yet decided. Meanwhile Albert in highly protective mode just exploded & shouted 'None of your bloody business & if it wasn't for YOU, madam' – pointing at Hildegard – '& THE WAR we'd still have our railings & would not be forced to install a wooden fence.' They both looked really shocked (so did Albert actually, think he only meant to think it, not say it) & did extra-fast speed-walking off carrying Hermann in his stupid little Adidas rucksack.

From: Nell Fenton
To: Charlotte Bailey

Touching that Albert is so protective but he does seem to be taking all this a bit too personally and though Hildegard looks like a tank and is a snitch, still not quite reasonable to hold her personally responsible for the melting down of railings.

From: Charlotte Bailey
To: Nell Fenton

Find supermarket shopping almost impossible now, barely able to walk let alone push a trolley so did my first internet shop last night. Can't believe it wouldn't be quicker to crawl on my hands & knees to & from the supermarket carrying each individual item in my teeth. Not helped by fact Dan stood behind me huffing & puffing. In the end got so irritated with him just said you do it so then he quickly sat down & did lots of v fast typing huffing all the while, wouldn't let me tell him what to buy so shall look forward to receiving shop today.

From: Charlotte Bailey
To: Nell Fenton

Internet grocery delivery is fantastic & delivery man even carried all shopping down to the kitchen when he saw my stomach was bigger than his. Was only after he had gone I noticed the 4 carrier bags filled with Granny Smith apples as genius Dan with all his fast fancy typing had ordered 10 kg of apples instead of 10 apples. Rang the supermarket who said just keep them, so now have box of apples by front door & everyone who visits gets apples as a going-away prize. Excellent news on the au pair front. Linda from the agency rang today to say they have several new girls on their books now & one in particular called Annette sounds really promising. Linda sending me details today. Feel quite tearful with relief.

From: Rachel Lockwood
To: Nell Fenton

Dear Nell

I've made a rather impulsive (not to say alcohol-fuelled)
decision. Peter brought round some of his home-made
cider yesterday and it was so pleasant out in the evening
sun we sat for ages talking and drinking. The cider is a bit
rough and incredibly strong but we were so busy talking I
just drank it anyway. Being quite drunk I started telling
Peter how miserable I felt about the prospect of living in
the depressing little flat I'm buying. He said why don't
we forget about the flat and stay in the cottage and I can
pay what I can afford in rent (he must have been quite
drunk too) or carry on giving him part-time help in the
office instead and get another part-time job if I need it.
He became quite animated and said Jonathan could go to
the village school which is really good. Peter knows the
headmistress and is going to introduce me. I am so happy
at the idea of us being able to live in the cottage (which I
love) instead of the flat (which I hate). It's a very friendly
village and Jonathan already knows children who go to
the school. I'm not sure how sensible this decision is, not
having done my usual cautious weighing up of all options,
but I've said yes anyhow and have told the estate agents
to their huge annoyance that I'm withdrawing my offer
on the flat.

Fondest love
Rachel xx

From: Nell Fenton
To: Rachel Lockwood

Dear Rachel, you must have taken leave of your senses. What an insane idea to decide to live somewhere you feel happy and to send Jonathan to a good school where he has friends. Am sure it's not too late to go back to plan A and buy the poky flat that makes you miserable. Next you're going to tell me you've found a job you like. Love Nell

From: Rachel Lockwood
To: Nell Fenton

Dear Nell

I've found a job I like.

Actually I haven't started yet so I can't tell, but I think I will like it. I met the headmistress of the village school, who is a very brisk, reassuring type of woman. Peter had obviously told her I need a job and that I am a genius of organisation (which I am compared to him) so I will now be school secretary in the mornings and will work for Peter in the afternoons. The old school secretary (who I also met) is retiring (unsurprising, as she looks about 94). Obviously the salary isn't fantastic but I don't have to pay a childminder any more. Everything seems to be working out at last and I feel happier than I have in a long time.

Fondest love to all
Rachel xx

From: Nell Fenton
To: Rachel Lockwood

Dear Rachel, so delighted to hear your news (and slightly smug at my own prescience). Love Nell

From: Charlotte Bailey
To: Nell Fenton

Extremely bad day for me, but worse for Hermann as I reversed over him this morning. HE IS OK but I am absolutely not. Heard yelping & then felt a sort of scrabbling under my car & he shot out the front to the sound of blood-curdling screaming from poor, poor Hildegard. All the children started screaming & crying too. It was SO awful. Anyway Albert drove H & H to the vet (I was in too much of a state) & when they got back saw Hildegard carrying him into the house with a bandaged paw. Went over to apologise (again), children in tow & find out how Hermann was & offer to pay the vet's bill, Hildegard answered the door looking as though she'd been sucking a lemon (don't blame her) & said Hermann was very lucky to be alive & I was not fit to drive a motor car & I have a very rude builder (although now he has apologised). Grovelled a bit more & then left. Dan very sympathetic & said Hildegard should never have let Hermann out of the rucksack but we did both agree perhaps best if I minimise driving & get Albert to park for me.

From: Nell Fenton
To: Charlotte Bailey

Dan is right, her own stupid fault for not watching her dog properly or better still keeping it in its little bag, but you

364

should cut down on the driving. Sure Hermann will be fine (at least his eyeballs stayed in). Leaving tomorrow which is sad, dread the marathon journey but children all v accomplished travellers now and as Michael is with us for the journey, the flight won't be too full and there won't be any delays etc as those only ever occur when I'm travelling alone with them.

From: Charlotte Bailey
To: Nell Fenton

Hildegard & Brian slightly mollified by elaborate Get Well Soon cards & tin of tuna (Hugh's idea) children took round this morning. Ellie came back to report Hermann had 'passed a comfortable night & is exerting slight pressure on his injured paw this morning' (terribly impressed she remembered all that). Feel even worse about Hermann if that's at all possible as Albert told me this morning that Hildegard told him it was the old lady next door to them who reported us to the council about our fence.

From: Nell Fenton
To: Charlotte Bailey

Perhaps you should find out if she has any pets you can reverse over. Journey home ok except for a terrifying few minutes at Charles de Gaulle when we lost Rob. For some reason he decided we'd gone out of the airport and took himself out through some revolving doors when I thought he was following me. The whole place was jammed with people so as soon as I noticed he was gone I went into full-blown panic and started screaming his name at the top of my lungs. Michael too dignified to do anything like that so searched silently (note to self: club husband to death for being unwilling to shout in public even to save own son from perverts who lurk in public places waiting to snatch unattended children). Thank God having not seen us outside Rob came wandering back in, heard my hysterical screams and wove his way through the crowds to come and find me. Took me about two hours to recover my composure.

Quite nice to be home – it always is after a long time away, though I feel more jet-lagged than usual.

From: Charlotte Bailey
To: Nell Fenton

How awful. Few things more traumatic than losing a child in a crowd, hope you had a stiff drink on the plane. The birth pool I hired came yesterday. Hospital can't guarantee you one so you have to bring your own. It's enormous. Hugh was terribly excited for a bit as Ellie told him it was a swimming pool. Now he's very cross with me & Dan, as Dan dropped it off at the hospital yesterday evening, so this morning Hugh raging about how 'the ill people have all the fun & swimming'. Find I am currently a source of great disappointment to all around me. Hugh because I'm not having puppies & I gave our swimming pool away, the girls because I am still pregnant & Dan because I've already lost the new mobile he bought me in case anything happens.

SEPTEMBER 01

From: Charlotte Bailey
To: Nell Fenton

House a total pit & I nearly choked Susan to death while syringing cranberry juice into her mouth today. Was so busy fantasising about arrival of new au pair was not paying attention to Susan & think I must have squirted a bit hard as she started really spluttering & I had to put her over my shoulder & pat her back. Anyway am very sanguine about everything now as Annette the Swedish uber au pair is arriving day after tomorrow.

From: Nell Fenton
To: Charlotte Bailey

Delighted to hear it.

Spent the morning trying school uniform on the children and found they'd all bloody well outgrown it over the summer, even Ollie (though can't reproach him for growing as am always trying to encourage him to do so). The boys' trousers all too short and I can't even shorten Rob's for Ollie because they're all manky at the knees and Josie's skirts don't close.

Will have to take them all downtown to get new stuff, tiresome at the best of times but especially a pain at the moment as I either ate something dodgy or have got a stomach bug. Threw up after supper last night and still feel queasy today.

From: Charlotte Bailey
To: Nell Fenton

I am in such HUGE trouble with the children. Have failed them terribly as although today is my due date (so baby MUST arrive today) AND they were out all day with Toby & Keran (so LOADS of time for me to do my business) AND they are back to school tomorrow & will really not be able to show their faces if they don't have a new sibling by then, I have still failed to produce anything. Ellie's precise words when she got home & saw me were 'Oh, for goodness sake!' Would have given her a clip round the ear except was stuck in an armchair at the time. Keran hustled her out of the room & have no idea what she said to her but 10 mins later Ellie came back & said 'I'm sorry, Mummy, poor you.' Would have slumped to the ground in amazement at heartfelt & genuine apology but was still struggling to get out of armchair. Are you feeling better by the way?

From: Nell Fenton
To: Charlotte Bailey

Bit queasy but nothing serious. Have you managed to get out of the armchair yet? Should have one of those ones old people have with a seat that lifts you up when you press a lever. I went to Meet the Teacher Day at school today with the children. I'm sure Josie's teacher is ADHD, kept bouncing out of his chair for no particular reason. Rob's teacher seems unremarkable but Ollie's teacher is a woman with the slopiest shoulders I've ever seen, must make carrying a shoulder bag almost impossible, but as being a good teacher in no way depends on the ability to carry a shoulder bag I do not intend to dwell on it.

From: Charlotte Bailey
To: Nell Fenton

Had a bit of a failure to cope today. Had terrible morning trying to get girls off to school in time, can literally barely walk any more, back bloody killing me & house a complete pigsty & ALL shoes awol though *definitely* set them out last night (I think). Bloody Hugh crying the whole morning as stupidly said I was not going to call new baby Mrs Kyndley or Hugh or even Toneeblair. Just as his tantrum was at its pinnacle, Linda from au pair agency rang all panicky & apologetic & said she was terribly, terribly sorry but Annette (new uber au pair) had changed her mind & wasn't coming. Have to say what very little sanguinicity I had left after hellish morning entirely deserted me & I burst into tears. Linda hearing me hiccuping down the phone became even more panicky & apologetic, said she'd see what she could do & rang off. Had just cleared up the kitchen, got myself under control & was in the playroom putting cream on Susan's bottom while Hugh nagged me to wrestle with him, when Albert came in & noticing even redder & puffier than usual face asked if I was ok. This set me off again so Albert took Susan (squeaking angrily by now) off me, led me into kitchen & made me v nasty cup of tea. Albert incredibly kind & soothing & offered to take Catherine & Susan to live in the countryside with his daughter & grandchildren as at least that will be one

369

less thing to worry about. Did not ask any questions & just said yes.

From: Nell Fenton
To: Charlotte Bailey

Really nice of Albert, why don't you ask if his daughter will take Hugh too? Don't much like Mrs Kyndley as a name and obviously calling new baby Hugh would cause all sorts of confusion (particularly if it's a girl) but don't think you should entirely close your mind to Toneeblair.

From: Charlotte Bailey
To: Nell Fenton

Everything is ok again. Linda rang this morning to say she has an unhappy au pair in north London who is looking to move to smaller family with less children. Momentarily thought Linda had gone barmy and gently reminded her of imminent arrival of 4th child (poss even crowning now if feeling in front bottom is anything to go by). Linda all airy & casual saying Ermentraud's family are Jewish Orthodox & have 11 children so 4 will be a piece of cake for her. V encouragingly, the Goldblatts are gutted she's leaving. Hurrah. Ermentraud coming for interview tonight, jokingly told her to bring all her stuff.

From: Nell Fenton
To: Charlotte Bailey

V pleased for you, though can't help feeling a pang for Mrs Goldblatt. Ermentraud a bit of a scary name though (and best

370

not let Albert talk to her about front fence). Sad to report that a very boring family have just moved into Suzette and Kane's house. So far all they've done is nod and smile in a polite and friendly way and are not remotely noteworthy (except the father has a terribly flat head). Still, no one could fill Suzette's shoes. I've emailed her with our news to try and encourage her to keep in touch but it won't be the same of course.

From: Charlotte Bailey
To: Nell Fenton

Thank you, Lord. Ermentraud doesn't get jokes & brought all her stuff over for interview. After I told her she'd got the job she celebrated by tidying up the kitchen & before she went to bed said she would get up with Dan to do children's breakfast as I must rest. When I came down to breakfast this morning children all lined up eating waffles & Ermentraud whistling German folk songs & washing up. Toby's private view tonight & Ermentraud says she will wash my trainers in honour of occasion. Am never letting her out of my sight ever again. Amen. PS Told me v proudly her name means 'total strength'. She is well named. PPS Suspect she will be good at wrestling.

From: Nell Fenton
To: Charlotte Bailey

She sounds fantastic, like the sort of person who knows what to put on stains to get them out. Get her to teach the children a few songs then you can be like the Von Trapps.

From: Suzette Lee-Saito
To: Nell Fenton

Ciao Nell!

Well, here we are in La Bella Italia. The last few weeks have been wild but things are finally settling down and we've already made some wonderful friends. The Italian men are quite something – you'd think they'd never seen a redhead!

The girls have made remarkable progress with their Italian – they both have such an amazing ear for languages. They've overtaken me though I've been studying hard. You know my views on self-improvement! They're both going to the American school here which they are very excited about and Kane has made quite an impact in his new job – I think his colleagues don't quite know what's hit them!

Anyway I must dash, I have a riding lesson in a few minutes, never an idle moment!

Saluti a tutti!

Suzette

From: Charlotte Bailey
To: Nell Fenton

It's really really late but HAD to mail to tell you about Toby's private view. Evening completely brilliant & very very edifying. Facts I have discovered as follows:

1. Toby no longer Toby but now Tobias P. Bailey – top photographer.
2. Keran looks fab in a sari.
3. Julian not a figment of Geraldine's imagination but real, living gay man in miniature form.
4. Keran's grandparents have greatest names ever.
5. Fran has a driving test tomorrow.
6. Albert CAN smell Gordon's armpits.
7. Other photographer in exhibition (Olly Olsen) does boring in-focus photos.
8. Baby never coming out – I will simply remain pregnant for ever.

Re 1. Toby thought Toby sounded too babyish so called himself Tobias, added initial as although does not actually have middle name felt it helped distinguish him from other Bailey photographer. (Dan said he felt his work did that already & P stands for pretentious.)

Re 2. Keran looks fab in a sari.

Re 3. Fran & I saw Julian from a distance across v crowded gallery & both thought Phwoar. He was looking through peephole at photo called 'Peep Show' (one from the 'Soho at Night' series by Tobias P. Bailey) & then turned round & flashed dazzling smile at us both & waved from far side of vast gallery. Was just thinking how TALL he looked too when he got off dais he had been standing on to look through peephole & started walking towards us. As Fran said later, 'As he came towards us he just didn't get any bigger.' Julian is TINY, incredibly handsome, perfectly groomed (smelt better than me or Fran), utterly charming & unbelievably camp.

Re 4. Keran's nan is Dora Clementine, her grandad was Edgar Arthur, love both names of both grandparents & now naming problem entirely solved (except Dan says absolutely not).

Re 5. Test tomorrow Fran has been keeping secret in very

unlikely event she fails it. However, this will not happen as Lucasta has done her a special pass-your-driving-test spell.

Re 6. One of photos from the flying bath series by Tobias P. Bailey shows Albert grimacing with face near Gordon's armpit. Albert (obv invited to private view) says couldn't smell a thing and it was the strain that made him grimace (do not believe him).

Re 7. Self-explanatory.

Re 8. Was planning to soak baby out in bath but left bath running & all hot water has gone down overflow pipe. F.F.F.

From: Dan Bailey
To: Nell Fenton

Dora Clementine born 5.26am this morning.

58 cm long, 11 lb 1oz (approximately 9 lb of it her face). She has lots of hair and looks like you.

Charlotte and Dora both very well and everybody, even Hugh, thrilled with her. Dan

AFTERWORD

DVLA

07.09.01
Francine W. J. Austerberry
Automatic Driving Test

FAIL

Time Out
Art Preview

'Contemporary Scream'
Black Sphere Gallery, East End

Benjamin Brandt has brought together the work of seven new, up-and-coming artists: Jay Abbot, Tobias P. Bailey, Marcus Klantz, Dita Ngu, Olly Olsen, Jayne Standing and Roma Whitbread. While styles and subject matter are immensely wide-ranging and disparate, the element that unites them all is the vibrant energy and freshness they all bring to their work. Notable among the seven is the work of the sculptor Dita Ngu whose moving piece 'sticks and stones will break my bones' powerfully evokes the fragility of the human condition and encourages the onlooker to engage with her palpable emotional and physical vulnerability. Another bright star in the making is Tobias P. Bailey. While often discarding the convention of focal clarity, he unnerves the onlooker with his oblique and visually challenging references to the world as a melting pot. In 'Fear of Flying' he uses a panorama of images to provoke a sensation of surreal dreamlike disquiet, beginning with an apparently airborne bath and finishing with the haunting, unfocused silhouette of an anguished crouching man. A sparkling debut for all seven artists and an absolute 'must see'.

Zane Cohen

Nell, Michael, Josie, Rob & Ollie
are delighted to announce the birth of
George Luke Edward
April 29th, 2002
9lb 2oz

Peter Bailey & Rachel Lockwood

request the pleasure of your company

at their wedding

Saturday 24 May 2003

11.30am Canterbury registry office

and afterwards at

Locket's Farm, Mill Lane,

Wittersham, Kent

RSVP

Thanks to Ginny Yule who unwittingly gave us the idea for this book, Ben Macintyre who introduced us to HarperCollins, Michael Fishwick for taking the idea up with such enthusiasm, Venetia Butterfield for her tremendous encouragement and our agent Gill Coleridge for her invaluable guidance and advice. We would also like to thank Arthur Fulljames, the real-life Albert who has always been so much more than a builder, and finally thank you most of all to our families, especially our husbands, for their wonderful support and for not minding us ignoring all domestic matters while we wrote this book.

Friends too busy to shop for books?
Then let us send one of them an *Au Pair* for just 99p!

That's right, just fill in the coupon below and send it back to us with 99p (plus p&p), and we'll send a copy of *And God Created the Au Pair* directly to your nominated friend. It's simply too good an offer to turn down. Don't have time? Then get the au pair to do it . . .

To Apply:
Complete the coupon below, attach a cheque or postal order for £1.98 (99p plus 99p p&p) payable to 'Au Pair Offer' and return it to **Au Pair Offer, PO Box 142, Horsham RH13 5FJ**.

Alternatively, you may place your order by telephone using a credit/debit card on 0845 1307778 (lo-call rate).

Closing date: 30th May 2005

— —

I enclose a cheque/postal order for £1.98 payable to 'Au Pair Offer'.

1. Your details:

Title: _____ Initial: _____ Surname: _____

Address: _____

_____ Post Code: _____

Telephone (in the event of a query): _____

Please tick this box if you do not wish to receive details of other family offers ☐

2. Please deliver a copy of *And God Created the Au Pair* to:

Title: _____ Initial: _____ Surname: _____

Address: _____

_____ Post Code: _____

— —

Terms and conditions: We aim to forward books upon receipt of payment though please allow up to 28 days for delivery. The closing date of the offer is 30th May 2005. The offer is only open to delivery addresses within the UK. The offer is subject to availability of stock.